OTHER BOOKS IN THE WHAT IF... SERIES

What If... Loki Was Worthy?
What If... Wanda Maximoff and Peter Parker Were Siblings?
What If... Marc Spector Was Host to Venom?

BY REBECCA PODOS

The Mystery of Hollow Places
Like Water
The Wise and the Wicked
From Dust, A Flame

WITH JAMIE PACTON

Furious
Homegrown Magic

WHAT IF...
KITTY PRYDE STOLE THE PHOENIX FORCE?

MARVEL

WHAT IF...

KITTY PRYDE STOLE THE PHOENIX FORCE?

AN X-MEN AND AMERICA CHAVEZ STORY

REBECCA PODOS

RANDOM HOUSE WORLDS
NEW YORK

Random House Worlds
An imprint of Random House
A division of Penguin Random House LLC
1745 Broadway, New York, NY 10019
randomhousebooks.com
penguinrandomhouse.com

© 2025 MARVEL

Penguin Random House values and supports copyright. Copyright fuels creativity, encourages diverse voices, promotes free speech, and creates a vibrant culture. Thank you for buying an authorized edition of this book and for complying with copyright laws by not reproducing, scanning, or distributing any part of it in any form without permission. You are supporting writers and allowing Penguin Random House to continue to publish books for every reader. Please note that no part of this book may be used or reproduced in any manner for the purpose of training artificial intelligence technologies or systems.

Random House is a registered trademark, and Random House Worlds and colophon are trademarks of Penguin Random House LLC.

Jeff Youngquist, VP, Production and Special Projects
Sarah Singer, Editor, Special Projects
Jeremy West, Manager, Licensed Publishing
Sven Larsen, VP, Licensed Publishing
David Gabriel, VP of Print & Digital Publishing
C. B. Cebulski, Editor in Chief

Hardcover ISBN 9780593598207
Ebook ISBN 9780593598214

Printed in the United States of America on acid-free paper

1st Printing

First Edition

BOOK TEAM:
Production editor: Kelly Chian
Managing editor: Susan Seeman
Production manager: Kevin Garcia
Copy editor: Laura Jorstad
Proofreaders: Emily Cutler, Lara Kennedy, Karina Jha, Megha Jain

Title page art by Terry Dodson (Kitty Pryde), CRACK!!! (texture) by Sanford Greene adapted by Edwin A. Vazquez
Book design by Edwin A. Vazquez

The authorized representative in the EU for product safety and compliance is Penguin Random House Ireland, Morrison Chambers, 32 Nassau Street, Dublin D02 YH68, Ireland.
https://eu-contact.penguin.ie

*To Books—
the person, the friend,
the legend, the fact-checker.
Thank you for everything.*

WHAT IF...
KITTY PRYDE STOLE THE PHOENIX FORCE?

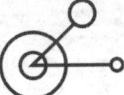

KITTY PRYDE IS ON FIRE.

It isn't the kind of flame that consumes flesh. Not yet. But she can feel it everywhere at once just the same. In fact, she can feel *everything*, from the birth of a star in some distant galaxy to the rapidly cooling dead body at her feet. She feels the sufferings and the secrets and the hopes of each soul that ever was, or is, or might someday be. All of it is contained within the fragile, inadequate shell of her.

This fire will devour her.

Probably, she will deserve it.

The Phoenix Force was surely meant for a champion like Jean Grey to wield. Who else could possibly withstand it? It is *power*, raw and infinite, terrible and glorious. The power to burn a world, a dozen worlds, one thousand. To destroy and create and unmake. To collapse matter and defy time itself. Abilities like these would be an unfathomable burden on even the greatest of heroes.

And Betsy Braddock was right: Kitty was never a hero.

CHAPTER 1

JEAN GREY

AUGUST 1, 1975

WELCOME TO THE LAST MOMENTS OF A YOUNG WOMAN'S LIFE. HER name is Jean Grey.

Breathless with fear on the flight deck of the Starcore One, she stares through the shuttle's windshield. The solar flare ahead of them—a massive arc of electromagnetic radiation bursting from the sun's atmosphere—makes for an impossible obstacle in their path back to Earth. Impossible for anyone but Jean . . . or so she promised her team. Promised that she alone could save them all and survive. Even in his steel-like Colossus form, Peter couldn't have withstood the onslaught of radiation for this long. Regardless, he couldn't have piloted the shuttle. And her teammates who know how to fly would've died quickly, horribly. *Scott* would have died. But not Jean. By sifting through the memories of Dr. Corbeau—the shuttle's creator—she made herself a capable enough pilot to take the yoke and steer the damaged shuttle through the flare without the help of their malfunctioning flight control computer. Blocking the worst of the rays with her telekinetic powers, she would be able to keep herself alive. She swore this to the X-Men before they locked themselves safely (*Lord, let them be safe*) in the Starcore One's shielded life-cell. She told them there was hope.

They saw through her, of course, none more than Scott. That man could have found his way to her in every world with his eyes closed. Certainly, he could see her terror in their last moments together.

He's just now waking up from her psychic blow, held back by Kurt and Peter, pleading to be let out of the cell to . . . what? To save Jean? It's too late for that. He'd only doom the rest of their friends, who have no pressure suits to protect them. Kurt and Peter understand this, and Professor X, Ororo, Sean, Logan, and Dr. Corbeau as well. Thankfully, Scott's giving in at last, falling apart. Jean can sense his pain from the flight deck and squeezes her own eyes shut against it, but she won't let herself follow him. She can't let herself fall apart so close to the end.

Someday he'll understand that it had to be this way. That it was Jean, or it was all of them. Someday he won't hate her for spending the last words they'll ever say to each other on a lie as obvious as: "I'll be all right."

The spasming shuttle threatens to rattle her bones from her body as it plunges toward home, but they're almost through, only twenty minutes from Earth's atmosphere. The radiation sensors are at the top of their scales, and her powers are at their limits, a scream trapped behind her gritted teeth. But she can last, she can last, she can—

As if it were the shuttle's battered windshield, her telekinetic shield cracks under the bombardment of the radiation. Then it shatters, and Jean Grey's body begins unraveling too quickly for her mind to comprehend. *SCOTT,* she screams without words as her pale skin withers, her green eyes cloud over with cataracts, her blood boils. After all this, she won't make it to reentry. None of them will. *Dear Lord, hear my prayer and help me!*

Jean Grey is dying.

She can tell because there's light everywhere, not in the stars beyond the glass but behind her, all around her, never mind that she's gone blind.

And then . . .

Be not afraid. A voice plays like music in her mind even as Jean is beyond hearing.

The pain ends.

Everything is ending.

But something is with her now; a force lifting and holding the diminished form that Scott—the love of her life—would no longer recognize. Perhaps someone has heard her desperate prayer.

Who . . . what are you? Jean thinks, because she can no longer speak.

The sum and substance of life and hope and dreams, the voice answers. **All that is, is known to me. I have known you, Jean Grey, from the moment of your conception, as I have known the universe.** Out of the infinite whiteness, a figure begins to materialize; not a body, but the idea of a shape of a body, with multicolored light like an aura around it. Holding both arms out to her, it says, **You cried out for aid. I heard. I came.**

This is crazy. I'm crazy.

No more than any finite being confronted with the infinite. Your form, child, is so fragile. How can you possibly endure?

"I must," she insists, words somehow finding their way out of her ruined throat.

To save the X-Men, the entity guesses. Its shape is clearer now, the idea crystallizing into execution. **And most especially . . . Scott.**

Then he's with her in the whiteness, too. Her heart could shatter at the sight of him, and at the thought of all that almost was and never will be. Though she knows he's only a memory dredged from her mind—the real Scott Summers would be beyond her reach even if her fingertips weren't whittled down to bones—it's good to see him one last time.

But she has to let him go now.

"What do you want?" Jean demands of the figure.

You called, child of man. And I, mother of stars, answered. It is for you to name your heart's desire.

She wishes she could see her friends one last time, too.

She wishes she could have kissed Scott goodbye.

No, she wishes . . .

Jean forces herself to look the entity in the face, almost fully realized now. The halo of bright light outlines a body she knows as well as her own, because it *is* her own (or was, before she became a wreckage of herself). "To save the X-Men, I'd dance with the devil himself," she grits out through crumbling teeth. "And . . . I want to live."

All things are possible, child. The entity offers its hands made of light.

After a moment's pause, Jean takes them, closing her eyes as the light flares and spreads to cocoon her desiccated body.

Something is beginning.

To anyone watching when the Starcore One slams down onto the runway at JFK, crashes through the barrier, and plunges into the waters of Jamaica Bay, it would seem impossible that anyone aboard could have survived. But the X-Men have always been notoriously hard to kill.

One by one they break the surface, gasping for air as they bob amid broken pieces of the shuttle like flotsam themselves.

"Cyclops! I was the last one out," cries Peter, vulnerable for the moment in his human form.

"Then we are all safe," says Ororo, the floating strands of her bone-white hair a stark contrast to the oil-slicked waters of the bay.

It isn't true, though. Jean is down there somewhere, and Scott won't be kept from her. "Get in my way this time, and I'll kill you!" he growls as Kurt fights to stop him from diving down.

Scott will drown himself searching for what precious little remains of Jean Grey before he lets her go.

But as he tries to thrash himself free, something kindles below them, like coals glowing at the bottom of the bay where the wreckage of the shuttle now rests. The choppy surface grows more agitated still, steam rising to merge with the lingering, yellow-tinged smoke from their crash. It's the only warning they get before great plumes of water shoot skyward, and Jean Grey explodes from the depths.

"HEAR ME, X-MEN," she roars. "No longer am I the woman you knew." Clothed in a green-and-gold suit they've never seen, fists raised and flame-red hair wild, it's a claim they cannot help but believe. "I am fire, and life incarnate. Now and forever, I am the Phoenix!"

—

KITTY PRYDE

1980

SUNRISE FINDS THEM ON CENTRAL AVENUE IN DEERFIELD, IN FRONT of Kitty Pryde's house. Though it certainly hasn't changed in the past twenty-four hours—the same white picket fence, same neat walkway, same egg-yolk-yellow front door—it looks strange to her now. That's because Kitty has changed. She's no longer the thirteen-and-a-half-year-old who trudged home from ballet class yesterday with a skull-splitting headache and her parents' impending divorce stuck like a splinter in her heart.

She's a mutant. Just like the X-Men. Just like that horrible woman, Emma Frost, who called herself the White Queen.

According to Professor X, Emma Frost and her minions only managed to find Kitty because he and the X-Men tracked her down first. Emma had been spying on the professor, planning to peel away the young mutants he sought to protect, and recruit them instead for the Hellfire Club: a shadowy group of bigwigs scrambling for wealth and power in the world, and more than willing to use their mutant powers to get it. She'd beaten the professor and his students to Kitty's house by mere moments, then laid a trap to wipe out the X-Men once and for all, thus eliminating the Hellfire Club's competition. It was beginner's luck that Kitty managed to sneak away and contact Jean Grey, who'd been on a mission elsewhere with the remainder of the team.

She supposes if the X-Men hadn't come, she'd be asleep in her bedroom right now.

But then she'd be alone. And that sounds scarier than the night's dangerous ordeal. Instead, she's surrounded by people who see her for who she is, and accept all of her. People who risked their lives to protect her, and in turn, Kitty risked her life to save them from the White Queen, discovering that she was brave and capable in the process. Kitty-of-yesterday couldn't have imagined a feeling like that, a friendship like that.

The lace curtains in the living room window twitch to the side, seconds before the front door bursts open and her parents come running across the lawn, still in yesterday's clothing.

"Kitty!" her father bellows.

"Oh, baby, we were so worried!" her mother cries. "You were gone all night . . . We didn't know what had happened. We called the police. Where were you?"

"Hi, Dad. Hi, Mom," she mutters. Inadequate, and she knows it. Her mother collapses as she reaches Kitty, kneeling in the dew-glazed grass to fling her arms around Kitty's waist. Her tears soak into the clean shirt Ororo lent Kitty so she wouldn't turn up on her doorstep in a soot-and-bloodstained top.

"Good morning, Mr. Pryde—" begins Professor X.

"Shove it, mister!" her father cuts in. "What have you been doing with my daughter? She goes off with your students and disappears—*you* disappear. The malt shop was burned to the ground! We thought she'd been killed till the police identified the bodies!"

Honestly, this is getting out of hand. But how can Kitty even begin to explain herself?

When her parents last saw her, she was headed out for an ice cream soda with student representatives from Xavier's School for Gifted Youngsters, leaving them to speak privately with the professor. They claimed they were considering boarding schools—Ms. Frost's Massachusetts Academy among them—for the sake of Kitty's education. It's true that she's top of her class at Deerfield Middle. But

Kitty guessed their true purpose weeks ago, and it isn't because of her bright future. Her parents only want to shuffle her out of the way while they and their lawyers unravel their life together without distraction, dividing up their furniture, their dishes, their daughter.

Then the White Queen had to go and blow up the malt shop. Did her parents hear the blast from eight blocks away? Did they spend the night on the living room couch together, closer than they'd been in years, eyes glued to the local news while calling anybody they could think of to try to find her?

This is hopeless.

They'll never let her leave now, no matter how badly they wanted her out of the way yesterday. She'll go back to Deerfield Middle, to ballet class, to synagogue, back to her same old life behind the egg-yolk-yellow door. Only she won't be the same. That moment yesterday afternoon when her powers first manifested—when she slipped right through her bed to find herself on the living room floor below, then lied to her parents to cover up what she couldn't make sense of—that was when everything changed forever, though she didn't know it yet. Maybe she hasn't got blue fur and a tail like Nightcrawler, an impossible mutation to hide. But she'll forever be terrified of being discovered. Kitty's heard of anti-mutant groups, just as she's heard of the X-Men. People who insist that the very existence of mutants means the downfall of humankind. Who go on television to shout about stopping mutants at any cost, squashing them out before they can overtake *Homo sapiens*. They held a march in Chicago last summer; Kitty saw it on the news.

Do her friends hate mutants? She never thought to ask. What about her teachers? What would those people who marched in black T-shirts with white crosses do to her if they found out, and would her parents protect her?

Kitty thinks so, but she can't be sure. Not sure enough to tell them who she really is.

"I don't know what your game is," her dad is bellowing, red-faced, jabbing a finger at the professor. "But . . . it's good to see you again!"

The professor blinks up in surprise while her father beams back down at him, clasping his hand to shake it.

What's going on?

Her mother climbs calmly to her feet, tears glittering and forgotten on her cheeks. "Let's get your suitcases out of the attic, hmm, Kitty? We'll pack you up together. I'll sure miss my little girl, but we just know you're going to shine at that school." She drapes an arm around Kitty's shoulders to lead her inside while Dad invites them all in for celebratory brunch.

Looking back over her shoulder, she scans the faces of her new friends: stunning Ororo, Cyclops, Wolverine, Colossus (he's so handsome, she can feel herself blushing to the tips of her ears), the professor. Among them all, only Jean Grey seems unfazed by her father's sudden change of heart.

A change of mind, more like.

Well, Kitty will take the win. All that matters is that in the very moment Kitty's life was falling apart, the X-Men have saved her again by offering her a new one. A new home, and a new family, even. It feels too good to be true, but with everything the X-Men are capable of—everything that *she's* now capable of—Kitty Pryde will choose to believe in the unbelievable.

—

KITTY

1990

"WELCOME TO THE RED KEEP." KITTY FLINGS HER ARMS WIDE AS SHE leads Rachel Summers and Betsy Braddock into the bedroom of her stronghold in Krakoa's Hellfire Bay. With flowering vines climbing its stone walls, twined around the posts of her canopy bed, and pressed against the glass ceiling, the sunlit chamber is unlike any place on Earth. That's because, like everything here, it was created by Krakoa. A gift from a sentient island. Funny, considering that she and the island got off to such a rough start.

When Professor X first remade Krakoa into a sovereign nation-state for mutantkind, the X-Men planted Gateways across the planet to act as portals, accessible by all mutants. Or *nearly* all; Kitty was left off the guest list. A quirk of her powers, as best she can guess. Her ability to phase through solid matter somehow kept her from passing through the Gateways like the rest of them. Left to make her own way to the island, she didn't take it well. She can admit that now. Between stealing a stranger's boat to sail to the island and drinking half of the Canadian Club whiskey Logan requested from the mainland along the way, her bottom was starting to look pretty rocky. It was Emma Frost of all people who finally snapped her out of it, and that's funny, too, since she and Kitty got off to a rough start of their own. But the White Queen offered Kitty a job, and a direction when she needed one most. Kitty would serve as the Red Queen of the Hellfire Club—their once-nemesis, now turned ally in the mutant cause—as well as captaining the Hellfire Trading Company's massive ship. Tasked with sailing the globe in search of mutants who never made it to Krakoa, whether because of kleptocratic rulers or militarized governments, gene cults or anti-mutant organizations, she's discovered her purpose again.

Just as the X-Men once did for her, she finds her people and brings them home.

Rachel crosses the bedroom to step out onto the balcony, nearly level with the pristine blue waters of the bay. "Love your view!" They both watch as, in the distance, the purple speck of Lockheed dives down to skim the surface of the waves, then rises again with a flash of silver, some fish clamped between his jaws. Rachel turns back to beam at Kitty, green eyes glittering in the reflected sunlight. She looks so much like her mother that Kitty has to catch her breath, though Rachel is a woman all her own, with a style all her own. She's chopped her red hair into a pixie cut and wears a tailored red jumpsuit and jacket far cooler than the uniforms of their childhood. She's a little older now than Jean Grey was when Kitty first met the X-Men. Kitty had no clue at the time that Jean would soon prove to be the most powerful mutant on the planet. On any planet, possibly. Or that someday, her almost equally powerful daughter would become Kitty's classmate at Xavier's School for Gifted Youngsters, then her roommate, and then her best friend in the world.

Betsy joins her girlfriend on the balcony, where the sea breeze ripples her violet hair and the cape of the white, red, and blue uniform she wears as Captain Britain. Their days together on the X-Women—back when Kitty still went by Shadowcat, Betsy by Psylocke, and Rachel by Marvel Girl—were long ago now, and seem even longer. Yet time and again and despite death itself, they always find a way back to one another.

It feels a little like a miracle.

Betsy presses a kiss to the nape of Rachel's neck above her jacket collar, and the softness of it would be unbearable if Kitty didn't love them both so much. Then Betsy steps back into the bedroom. "I adore your . . . barrel full of swords."

Kitty pats the full-sized cannon in the corner. "It's a pirate's life for me, all right." Combined with the ship's wheel mounted above the steamer trunk that holds her wardrobe and a framed Jolly Roger on the wall, it is a bit much. But no more than her own uniform: a red captain's frock coat with gold-tasseled epaulets, sailor's boots, and a cutlass strapped to her belt. She's come a long way since roller skates and kitchen gloves.

"What do you think, Rach?" Betsy asks. "Should we abandon Braddock Isle and move the whole family to Krakoa? Plant a flower and see if the island grows us a nice little bungalow?"

Rachel laughs, leaning over the railing. "I'd love to see Brian's face when you suggest that."

Kitty turns three rocks glasses upright atop the barrel that serves as a makeshift bar cart. "How are things at the family manor?"

"Well enough. We moved the manor off the mainland just in

time, I swear—anti-mutant sentiment in Britain is running high these days, as you're aware, no doubt."

"And everywhere else." Kitty frowns, pouring three generous servings of whiskey from her decanter. "You know it's slim pickings in Krakoa when one of your few diplomatic allies is Latveria."

"Speaking of Doom, his ex-lover's been quite the thorn in my side lately. It turns out she's behind the Furies who've been hunting down the Captain Britain Corpsmen. She meant to replace me with a corrupted captain who'd be more . . . amenable to her commands. Luckily, Morgan le Fay was no match for Rachel." Betsy watches her girlfriend approach them with full-moon eyes.

Kitty hands them each a glass. "You two have been up to a lot while I've been marauding."

"Oh, no more than the usual." Rachel shrugs. "Traveling the Multiverse by day, spooning by night."

"Enough about us, though. We're here to toast *you*." Betsy raises her glass. "To the Red Queen!"

Rachel leans an elbow on Betsy's shoulder. They're so casual in their closeness that Kitty can tell they'd never stop touching by choice. "To the Red Queen."

Kitty hoists her own glass, accepting this with a smile.

"Is this also a present from Krakoa?" Betsy asks after a sip. "I know it's not Wolverine's."

"From Emma, actually."

"You and Emma seem to have gotten close," Rachel observes, more diplomatically than Kitty would have thought her capable. There never was any love lost between Rachel Summers and the woman her father was dating in place of her then-dead mother when Rachel first came to this world. Or rather, the *variant* of Rachel's father and mother who exist in this world.

Complicated would be an understatement.

"We . . . understand each other," Kitty replies carefully, matching her tone.

"Well, this is spectacular. The White Queen has taste. Another of these"—Betsy waggles her glass in the air—"and Rach may finally get her wish. She's been wanting to replay the timeline where I was a princess and she, my companion."

"Betsy . . ." Rachel groans.

"Gross," Kitty says cheerfully.

Her own love life may be dead as disco, but it's impossible to feel bitter about it in her friends' presence. And it's impossible to feel alone on the island—even if it took what felt like a lifetime to get here—where she's surrounded by the people who love her, the family that raised her. The X-Men.

Where—and who—would she possibly be right now without them?

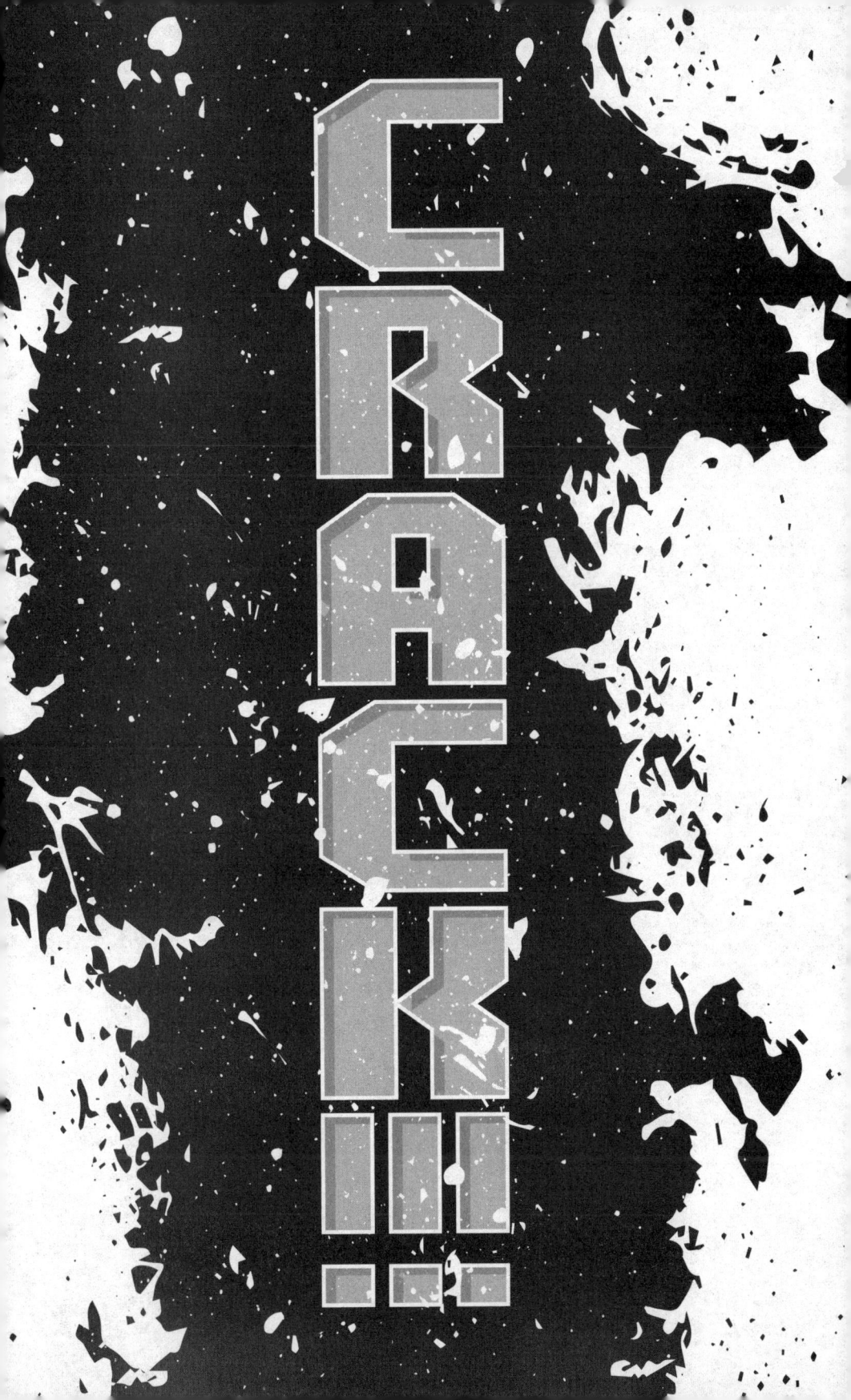

CHAPTER 2

DOOM

JULY 1, 1975

VICTOR VON DOOM HAS COME HOME, IN A MANNER OF SPEAKING.

This isn't the Latveria of his birth, which he left behind countless worlds ago. But some things remain constant across the Multiverse. The smell of the woods where he spent his childhood running wild: sharp and spicy pine, and damp earth after a welcome summertime rain, and the subtler traces of things both rotting and alive. The sounds of birdcalls and rustling boughs, all dampened by the thick layer of pine straw that carpets the forest floor. And the glorious sight, when he staggers past the tree line, of Castle Doom, a fortress perched upon a mountaintop. Once the seat of power for the Sabbat lineage in the capital city formerly known as Hassenstadt, it will have belonged to the Doom of this world since he overthrew its previous ruler, Baron Sabbat—the man responsible for the death and disassembly of Doom's family, who had remade himself as King of Latveria. But king or baron, it mattered little in the end.

He died with Doom's iron hands around his throat all the same.

Doom stops a moment to brace himself against a tree trunk at the forest's edge, taking inventory of himself while his ragged breath whistles out through his mask's mouth plate. The mask—forged to withstand fire and acid and all manner of attacks—has nevertheless been degraded, melted away around the eyes to reveal burned flesh beneath. Scraps of the prize he sought in the last world remain embedded like shrapnel in the titanium alloy of his armor. One of his gauntlets is crushed beyond use, and the combination of an adamantium crescent dart still piercing his chest through his breastplate, as well as the lingering poison in his system, has left him slowed and aching. Wrapping his intact gauntlet around the moon-shaped dart, he grits his teeth and rips it free with a spatter of dark blood. He throws it to the forest floor, sickened more by self-disgust than by the taint of poison. He failed to obtain the powers that would allow him to mold any reality into a shape of his choosing, powers he's finally determined constitute the essence for which he's been searching the Multiverse: nexus beings. And he's been weakened in the bargain.

Yet Victor von Doom learns from his mistakes.

Any common scientist knows that in the acknowledgment and examination of one's errors lies opportunity. And Doom is no common scientist. He is master of all—of the domains of both science and magic; the natural forces that drive the steady heartbeat of the world, and the supernatural forces capable of disrupting it. Hasn't he conquered space and time themselves? With his stolen shard of the M'Kraan Crystal, he can access the nebulous corridors between realities, a thing precious few have managed. Failure has always been beneath him, but concession?

Unthinkable.

It's his good fortune, then, that the Multiverse provides infinite chances to try again. To rise again.

Besides, those past worlds were nothing more than experiments. Each success or setback was merely a paving stone in the path that led him here, where he was always bound. Now he's had enough of trifling with substandard outcasts and curiosities, none of whom would merit so much as a glance from him otherwise. This time, he is coming for Jean Grey, the greatest of all nexus beings in his estimation (and there is no keener estimation in the Multiverse than Doom's). And this time, he will take the power he needs to seize reality by the throat until it, too, bows before Doom.

No one will deny him what's his by right, not even the Multiverse itself.

Engaging the twin jetpacks mounted to his suit, he lifts off from the needle-strewn ground, rising up along the cliffside. If anyone is capable of breaching these castle walls by force or secrecy, it's him, but that would be repeating past miscalculations. He has attempted in other worlds to manipulate his counterpart, to disastrous effect. What he requires now—besides the laboratories and resources to both repair and prepare himself—is an accomplice worthy of him.

Doom touches down on the cobbled footbridge in front of the gatehouse and steps forward, tilting his ruined mask up to face the startled sentries on the battlements above. "I come bearing knowledge for the current master of Castle Doom," he announces, his deep voice echoing off the roughly carved stones to be heard by all, "and great opportunity."

CHAPTER 3

AMERICA

JULY 1, 1975

AS THE STAR-SHAPED PORTAL CRACKLES CLOSED BEHIND HER AND the last world winks out, America Chavez stands on a street corner and contemplates this new world.

Coming out of a drugstore in front of her, an old white man in a white straw boater hat blinks at her sudden appearance, his mouth open wordlessly. He seems to be the only one who notices. A beautiful Persian woman with a cloud of brown curls practically floats by, grocery bags balanced on her shoulders, her marigold-orange kaftan streaming behind her. Sitting on milk crates outside of a place called Nick's Luncheonette, a circle of young Black boys continue to trade baseball cards with one another. Spray-painted peace signs and slogans like FREE THE PANTHER 21 fade away on the brick façade behind them. The sultry air smells of onions and garlic from somebody's kitchen, and cigar smoke, and everything that percolates in the dented metal trash can beside her. From the propped-open window of an apartment overhead, ranchera music drifts down.

She recognizes that voice, Juan Gabriel, crooning over the guitarrón and vihuela Mexicana, but not from the cosmic collection of Watcher's memories to which she has a key, or *is* a key. Se Me Olvidó Otra Vez. It's a memory that belongs to her. And this place—Washington Heights—she knows in her bones, if not this exact version. The date printed on the newspapers in the drugstore window stand reads: JULY 1, 1975.

America squeezes her eyelids shut against the glut of sensation to search this timeline for the Whisperer; for Doom, she now knows. But even with the Watcher's vision that extends well beyond the viewing portal she's left behind, she can't see him, can't pluck him out from the billions of people going about their lives, blissfully unaware of any reality beyond their own. Whatever mechanism Doom has used to cloak himself from the Watchers in previous worlds seems to be protecting him still.

Damn.

At least she knows how to find half of the equation that called her to this world. Jean Grey will be at Xavier's School for Gifted Youngsters, nearly due north in Westchester. A vision of bright-red hair, brilliant-green eyes, and phoenix-shaped fire has told her all she needs to know about Doom's next intended victim. In fact, America's portal should have spilled her out at the school, where she would find the entity whose kind Doom has been hunting across the Multiverse; beings whose life force anchors their reality, just as one particular Marc Spector anchored his own, and a Wanda Maximoff, and a Loki. It seems unbelievable that the fate of a world could hinge upon one person—one nexus being, as America has come to know them—even someone as powerful as Jean. But then again, as a Watcher, she's seen worlds turn upon less. A single battle, a single choice.

A small hand, ice-cream-sticky, tugs on her own, startling her. "Are you magic, miss?"

Opening her eyes, she looks down to see the littlest boy from outside the luncheonette, his face shining with wonder.

He tries again. "¿Mágica? Pienso que vi . . ." He drops her hand to spread his arms and wiggle his gummy fingers, imitating (she supposes) a star.

America musters a weak smile. "Something like that. Ve a jugar, niño."

After he trots back to his friends, she wipes her now-sticky palm against her striped and spangled jacket, the worn denim a comfort. She needs to think, to concentrate. But all around her, the heat and colors and sounds are . . . overwhelming. Children on stoops, street vendors selling sizzling meat and cold lemonade, laughter spilling from a dozen doorways bricked open to invite a breeze.

And that song . . .

Suddenly she remembers being as young as the boy, walking home from school. Stopping to wave at the elderly barber who kept a bowl of tamarind candy by his door and always played records—an ever-changing mix of ranchera, mariachi, salsa, and merengue songs. She remembers breaking through the hard sugar shell of the candies with her back teeth to get to the chewy center, both sweet and sour. And right next door to the barbershop—

Bodega Santana.

Has it been years or centuries since she last thought of the Santanas? The family who fished her out of the water at Jones Beach, carried her back to their apartment above the grocery store, and loved and raised her as best they could. They tried to keep her safe, though they couldn't stop her from becoming who she truly was, to their chagrin.

America's feet turn her toward the arched underbelly of the Washington Heights Bridge, stamped across the summer-blue sky in the near distance, and so toward the bodega. Javi and Ceci, her adoptive parents, ran the place together for years before they pulled her from the surf. She recalls that now. But they won't know her yet. In fact, the Santanas alive in this reality in 1975 will never know her.

Which begs the question: Why is she *here*?

If her portals always take her where and when she truly needs to go, what does it mean that they've brought her back to the place she once called home?

CHAPTER 4

SCOTT SUMMERS

AUGUST 1, 1975

WELCOME TO THE LAST MOMENTS IN THE LIVES OF THE X-MEN.

This isn't the ending Scott hoped for. He *wanted* to believe he could stop it. Without a functioning flight control computer, someone had to pilot their damaged shuttle, ensuring that the rest of the team would survive. And Scott is an expert pilot; it's in his blood, after all. Blood now boiling within his body as he grips the yoke with ruined hands, exhausting the last of his strength. Beside him, Kurt—the Amazing Nightcrawler—cries out as his blue skin sinks into withering bone and his yellow eyes cloud. His tail shudders in pain and drops from its grip around Scott's waist. He collapses, too weak to teleport them back to the life-cell with their friends.

No matter. In a few heartbeats, there'll be nothing left of either of them to save.

It had to be Scott, and it had to be Kurt, too. If he'd stayed on the flight deck alone, Scott would have died from the radiation within moments, leaving the Starcore One to hurtle toward Earth totally uncrewed. So Kurt memorized the flight deck just before launch. Teleported the two of them back and forth from the shielded room while their bodies unraveled bit by bit, placing Scott behind the controls in key moments to keep the shuttle roughly on course. That was the plan: stave off death long enough for Scott to fly their friends safely home. They hoped it would be enough.

But the plan has failed. Scott admits this to himself only when his hands slip nervelessly from the controls. He stares out the windshield at a planet tinged yellow by his ruby quartz visor. Continents surrounded by a golden ocean. On their current trajectory and traveling faster than the speed of sound upon reentry, they'll slam into the Atlantic instead of landing at Kennedy Airport, smashing to pieces in a collision that even Peter in his armored form can't possibly survive. If they even make it that far. The unpiloted shuttle may well break apart before then, its passengers set adrift in the airless, endless ocean of space. Either way, the X-Men as Scott knows them will be gone.

In the last, lingering seconds of his own life, he can feel himself becoming bones, and knows that those bones will be dust by the time they crash. The pain is incredible, indescribable.

But it isn't the worst pain he's ever felt.

Because the truth is this: The better part of Scott Summers died just two weeks ago with Jean Grey, at the iron hands of a madman. She was the home he'd dreamed of as an orphaned child, the teenage girl who glanced his way and changed him forever, the woman who owned his heart and owns it still. So if this is the end of the rest of him, then let it end.

Eventually, everything must.

—

KITTY

1980

SUNRISE FINDS KITTY PRYDE ALONE ON HER LIVING ROOM floor with no clue how she got down here from her upstairs bedroom.

Sitting up, she presses the heel of her palm into her forehead, even though no trace remains of yesterday's headache; the latest in a rotten string of them over the past few weeks. It took root dur-

WHAT IF . . . KITTY PRYDE STOLE THE PHOENIX FORCE?

ing ballet class. Walking home, she was half blinded by it, relying on her feet to pilot her. She made it to her bedroom at last, where she closed the blinds and collapsed onto her sheets to lie in the dark and the quiet. (Or the mostly quiet. She could still hear her parents bickering behind a closed door in their bedroom, where her dad hasn't slept for months.) Her skull felt like an egg cracked open against a pan, and every second, the pain grew and grew and grew until . . .

Suddenly she was on her living room floor, without ever having climbed out of bed.

Maybe not, though. Maybe she'd stumbled out of her room in search of a glass of water. Maybe she'd collapsed at the top of the stairs, dizzy with pain, and tumbled all the way down. But wouldn't her parents have heard her fall over the sounds of their imploding marriage? Besides, if she'd fallen, wouldn't she feel worse? In fact, she felt better than she had in weeks, the pressure in her head completely gone.

And now it's happened again, whatever *it* is.

Kitty test-drives her body. No stiff limbs, no bruised hip or twisted ankle. She may as well have dripped through the ceiling like water. Obviously, that's impossible.

"I thought I heard someone down here." Her mom stands in the stairwell, yawning as she ties the belt of her old fuzzy bathrobe. "What are you doing up so early, baby?"

"Just . . . couldn't sleep," Kitty lies.

"Keep me company, then?" Her mother shuffles over to the couch and pats the empty cushion. "There's something I want to talk about. A good something, I promise."

"Yeah. Sure." There's no reason not to. None that Kitty can come up with quickly enough to avoid hurting her mom's feelings, at least. Head spinning with questions but still pain-free, she drops down beside her mother with a *whumf* and tucks her feet up beneath her.

"Well. You know your father and I have been looking at schools that are a little more challenging, don't you?"

"Yeah, but why bother? It's only a couple months until summer," Kitty mumbles. As if she doesn't know, deep down.

Her mom fixes on a smile. "We just see how bright you are, baby, and we hate to watch you waste that, even for a few more months. Seems silly to wait until high school to find a better education for you, doesn't it? Especially now that we've found the perfect place. And, Kitty, you have to see the brochures. This school is *miles* beyond Deerfield Middle. Miss Hester's has a whole building just for dance workshops! *And* an equestrian team. You always loved horses."

Sure, when she was eight and deep into the Equestrian Friendship chapter book series. Kitty can't recall mentioning a passion for horses in the years since.

"There's a lap pool on the grounds, too," her mother goes on.

"We can afford that?" She's heard her parents lament the cost of her dance classes alone.

"That's the best part. They've offered you an academic scholarship! There are some expenses we'll need to cover, but we'll make it work. And the classes are top-notch."

"You already applied?" She feels herself stiffen in her seat.

"Oh, Kitty, you've just got to look at the brochures. I know Connecticut is a hike from Illinois, but it's one of the most prestigious private schools in the—"

"Connecticut?" Kitty screeches, too loud in the still-quiet house. "I thought you were looking at schools near Chicago, so I could come home on weekends!"

"But this way you can really be involved in campus life, go to the movie nights and the parties. Give it a chance—"

"Don't act like you care about movie nights!" she accuses, pressing her back into the couch arm as she scoots out of reach. "You don't care about anything but getting me away from *you*."

"What an awful thing to say, Katherine." Mom tugs on a lank strand of blond hair fading to gray, her nervous habit. "You know that your father and I . . . we love you. We only want the best for you."

But Kitty knows no such thing. Love her or not, she's heard the latest subject of her parents' bickering over these past weeks, seeping in between headaches. How anxious they both were to find a place to stick Kitty while their lawyers got to work dividing up the house, the bank accounts, their whole lives.

She jumps to her feet and snaps, "Just say you don't want to deal with me anymore. You don't have to lie to me like I'm a little kid." Then she storms upstairs (very much like a little kid, she guesses) and slams her bedroom door shut to lock it behind her, not caring whether she wakes her father in the den.

Connecticut.

Getting her out of the house wasn't enough for them, was it? Her parents had to send her halfway across the country so they could tear the family apart in peace.

She can't just stand here with this feeling, this rage building and building. She'll boil herself down to nothing but bones. Kitty has to put it somewhere, so for the first time, she does what she's only seen angry people do in movies: She punches a wall.

Maybe Miss Hester's won't want a new student with a busted knuckle.

She slams her fist through the wall beside a poster of Baryshnikov, anticipating pain and a shower of dust and drywall and blood. But neither happens. Instead it's like plunging through water, her arm sunk up to the wrist in the painted yellow plaster. It feels like nothing.

She feels nothing.

Kitty falls backward, only to sink up to the elbows in her bedroom carpet. With a strangled scream, she wrenches herself up again, retreating to huddle on her bed as though the floor will swallow her whole if she sets a foot down. Maybe it has already, and that's how she landed downstairs.

But that's impossible, isn't it?

She reaches for the teddy bear she's definitely too old for, clutching it to her chest . . .

Suddenly she's not in her bedroom at all, but standing out on the front lawn, surrounded by strangers. A woman with bone-white hair and deep-brown skin. A bald man in a wheelchair. A blue-skinned man with too few fingers, and . . . is that a *tail* poking out the back of his trousers? She doesn't have time to examine the rest before the front door flies open and her parents come sprinting across the lawn toward them.

"Kitty!" her father bellows as he runs.

"Dad, what's—"

"Oh, baby, we were so worried!" Her mother throws herself down to kneel in the grass at Kitty's feet, wrapping her arms around Kitty's waist. "You were gone all night . . . we didn't know what had happened. We called the police. Where were you?"

"What are you talking about?" Kitty can feel herself beginning to panic now. "I've been right here!"

Her mother sobs, tears soaking into a cherry-red jacket that definitely isn't Kitty's. She wears a crisp white blouse beneath it, tucked into a pleated skirt, neither of which Kitty's ever seen in her closet. And where have her pajamas gone?

The bald man moves his chair forward. "Good morning, Mr. Pryde—"

"Shove it, mister!" her father shouts, jabbing a finger into the man's face. "What have you been doing with my daughter?"

"Dad, stop! What's happening? Somebody tell me what's happening!" Kitty screams . . .

And finds herself on her mattress again, still clutching the bear she's outgrown.

Still screaming.

She jumps as a fist pounds against her bedroom door. "Kitty? What's happening in there?" her father demands, rattling the locked doorknob.

Her mother joins him the hallway, explaining in a low voice how badly Kitty's taken the news. Her father snaps at her mother, scolding her for botching their talk. Kitty claps her hands over her ears, wanting . . . what?

To be held.

To be left alone.

To be the same girl she was yesterday afternoon, with the future she'd planned. Start Deerfield High this fall, graduate early if she can manage it, and join a ballet company when she's seventeen, maybe in New York. Marry Mikhail Baryshnikov (even if he is a little old for her) and, once she's retired from the stage, have kids and never let them feel the way she feels right now. Like she's sliding right out of her life, and there's nobody anywhere who can catch her.

—

KITTY

1990

AH, THE WHITE KNIGHT HAS RETURNED.

As the White Queen's consciousness reaches icy tendrils toward hers to speak inside her mind, Kitty Pryde freezes in place. "Ms. Frost, I—" she says, too loud in the empty third-floor hallway of the apartment building. All else is silent except for the tortured electric buzz of a flickering sconce light several doors down. Her neighbors are at this hour either asleep or condemned to their night-shift jobs at the laundromat, the diner, wherever. She's never spoken to any of them to ask. Point is, nobody's around to see her phase into her door, passing through the steel as simply as if it's fog. On the other side, she checks the half dozen chains nailed permanently in place, and the locks glued shut for good measure (she'll never get her security deposit back, but the club pays her rent anyway, and good luck to the landlord hunting down the alias on her lease). Only after she's satisfied that nothing's been disturbed does she answer properly. "It's late, Ms. Frost. Didn't want to wake you. I planned to check in tomorrow."

Dear heart, how could I possibly rest till I knew you were safe?

It seems unlikely that Emma Frost has lost a moment's sleep over Kitty.

What an awful thing to think, she admonishes.

Feeling no older than sixteen, Kitty mumbles, "Sorry. I just meant... I was tired, and it was late, and... I'll come by headquarters tomorrow morning to make my report."

Not quite. I'm at the Academy right now. Be prompt, darling— I've a call with the D'Bari ambassador at ten. I'll be waiting with bated breath to hear how the best of my Hellions let a solitary, aging scientist slip away from them. Don't keep me waiting long. Her words fall as cold and hard as diamonds, slicing at Kitty from the inside. Then the tendrils of the White Queen's consciousness retreat.

Crap. *Crap.*

One of her teammates must've beaten her to their report, though the most powerful telepath on the planet often senses when an assignment goes sour without any snitches required.

Kitty toes off her boots and heads for her phone-booth-sized bathroom, grimacing as she peels off the sharply tailored, white military-style coat that marks her station within the Hellfire Club. Quite a change from the maroon bodysuits of her youth among the Hellions, though Kitty herself hasn't changed much. She was an angry sixteen-year-old desperate to prove herself to a dazzling stranger named Emma Frost, who fished her out of a juvenile detention center in Connecticut. Now she's an angry twenty-three-year-old desperate to prove herself to Emma Frost.

She certainly failed to do so tonight.

The mission was straightforward: lead a squad to apprehend the mutant once known as Beast, who had a history with the Avengers and had worked briefly alongside the mutant rebel Magneto. This was before the Hellfire Club captured Magneto some years ago, imprisoning him inside a plastic, purpose-built cell far underground, all to keep him from unraveling the fabric of a society that the club had stitched to their liking. These days, Beast runs on his own, but he's still strong, fast healing, and dangerously smart. Also, at present, dying. When the White Queen got ahold of intel that Beast had recently undergone a secondary mutation, the changes to his physiology threatening to rupture the heart in his massive, furred chest, she thought he might make for a willing asset. With the tempting scientific and financial resources Kitty was offering, and nobody else to turn to, how could he afford to turn them down?

But Kitty had failed spectacularly. And it wasn't because Sunspot and Empath (more like Sociopath) kept sniping at each other. Or because of Mirage, who helped nothing by telepathically siccing that passing stray cat on them both in her annoyance.

It was because *it* happened again.

One moment, Kitty was standing in an alleyway behind a Thai food restaurant with the Hellions, bracing as Beast galloped toward them on all fours. The next moment, she stood in a strange and sunlit room where vines embroidered themselves up the walls and across a ceiling made entirely of glass. Kitty tilted her head back to stare up at a perfect turquoise sky.

Another slip, but a pretty one, at least.

"Love your view!" called an unfamiliar voice.

Kitty looked toward the source. Across the room was a balcony, the doors flung wide to invite the smell of an ocean inside. A woman in a head-to-toe red jumpsuit stood at the railing, staring out over the sunlit water of what looked like a cove. Beyond her in the far distance, a strange purple bird (some kind of tropical raptor?) drove down toward the sunlit water. Kitty couldn't see the woman's face, only the back of her close-cropped hair, nearly as red as her suit.

But the woman walking toward her from the balcony, Kitty did recognize: Betsy Braddock. Member of the Hellfire Club (through blood only; her father once served as Black Bishop of the Inner Circle) and sister to Brian Braddock, otherwise known as Captain Britain. Another legacy member of the club and an uneasy sometimes-associate of their London office. Except this Betsy had flowing violet hair and wore a costume in Captain Britain's colors—one she'd never worn in real life, so far as Kitty knew.

The Betsy she'd met a handful of times was as mousy as someone with an obnoxiously symmetrical face could manage to be.

Not that it mattered. During these slips (as Kitty had thought of them since she was young), she'd see upside-down versions of people she knew, or people she didn't know at all, and places she'd never been. She'd long since stopped trying to make sense of any of it. All she could do once she found herself slipping was outlast it.

"I adore your . . . barrel full of swords," Betsy said.

Then the strange world spit her out again—this always happened, whether Kitty wanted it to or not—and suddenly she was back in the alley, with Beast right in front of her, swatting her aside to get by.

Of course, Kitty wasn't going to tell all that to the White Queen. Admit that ever since her powers first manifested, she's been plagued by occasional but totally-not-a-big-deal visions or hallucinations or psychotic breaks? She can't imagine it. She's been around mutants long enough to know this isn't normal, even among the abnormal. Nor can she imagine confessing that, lately, it's gotten worse. At first, there were months between slips. Now it's weeks.

Sometimes days.

Better to let Emma believe that she'd been sloppy than that her White Knight's mind could not be trusted, least of all by Kitty herself.

The claw marks haven't cut deep, at least. A defensive swipe without true intent to wound, though they should've slipped through her like she was mist. She flings open the medicine cabinet to find the antiseptic spray. Holding her arm at an awkward angle to reach her biceps, she hisses at the sting of the spray, then grabs a gauze pad from a box and tears it free from the wrapper with her teeth. Her torn coat, she leaves in a ruined puddle on the floor once she's done bandaging herself.

In the bedroom, she collapses onto her twin mattress with a moan of relief. She'd better sleep while she can. The drive to Snow

Valley from Manhattan is three hours without traffic, unlike the convenient dash from her apartment in Inwood down to Fifth Avenue and the Hellfire Club Building: a stately brick-and-stone mansion that provides cover for the many sublevels that serve as the hive of the Inner Circle, of which Kitty is a member.

The lullaby of Manhattan at two in the morning bleeds through her locked and barred bedroom window—the bleating of taxis, the whine of impatient engines, and the wail of the occasional ambulance on the street below. Across the street, the neon sign above Mama's Maple Bacon and Eggs Diner is so bright, it slices between her third-floor blinds, throwing bars of orange light over her walls. There's nothing on the plaster except for one much-creased poster of Baryshnikov. An artifact that hung in her childhood bedroom and, later, her dorm room at the Massachusetts Academy, then in a string of shabby apartments over the five years since graduation. Emma Frost finds her nomadic tendencies distasteful, unworthy of her rank. But Kitty prefers a place like this to a penthouse in some sleek, Upper East Side high-rise with twenty-four-hour security. There are no cameras in this building, nor a doorman to track her comings and goings, nor any HOA sticking its nose in her business. Nobody notices her here. If she had to, she could slip away on the shortest possible notice. Just grab her backpack and go. Everything else she owns is expendable, aside from the fragile poster, her attachment to which even she can't explain. Maybe it reminds her how far she's come, and why she can't ever go back. Her life may look as bare as her current one-bedroom, but unlike that thirteen-year-old Kitty in Deerfield whose whole world seemed to be ending, at least this life belongs to her. Yes, she has her orders, her allegiance to the club. But beyond that, Kitty controls where she goes, and why, and with whom (without anybody, if she can help it). And that's something, isn't it?

Exhausted, she lets her eyes slide shut at last.

Kitty Pryde!

She bolts upright at the posh voice echoing in her head. It's unlike the White Queen to return after a dramatic exit . . . But no, the accent isn't Emma's, and this presence doesn't feel like sparkling, diamond-bright frost creeping along the chambers of her mind. Instead, the image of a butterfly appears to her, of all things. Spectral and bright pink, patterns like large eyes on its luminous wings. Whoever's found her, their mind is unfamiliar, and unwelcome.

Unfamiliar? We're not close, I'll grant you, but we are clubmates. Doesn't that make us friends-by-association?

"Who is this?" she demands aloud.

Elizabeth Braddock. You may know me better as Betsy.

Kitty's blood crystallizes like ice in her veins.

It has to be a coincidence that one of the guest stars in her latest slip is reaching out to her for the first time, though they've hardly ever spoken before. It doesn't mean anything.

But she sounds less steady than she'd like when she asks, "You go around breaking and entering into people's brains as a habit, or am I just lucky?"

Forgive the intrusion. You're a very hard person to find in person, if you know what I mean. And I think this is something of an emergency.

"You *think* it's an emergency?"

It's really better explained face-to-face. I'm just around the corner from the club, as it happens, so no time like the present, hmm?

"It's two in the morning," Kitty mumbles into her pillow. "Do not disturb."

Please, Kitty. The bravado slips from Betsy's psychic voice, and something like desperation seeps in to replace it. **You see, there's something deeply wrong with the world, and all I know is that it has everything to do with you.**

CHAPTER 5

KITTY

1990

MAMA'S MAPLE BACON AND EGGS IS AN OVERLY LIT, 1950S-style place with scuffed checkerboard floors and violently orange booths. Even at half past two in the morning, it's stuffed with all kinds of people in all states of dress. Freshly off-work bartenders spangled with body glitter, smelling strongly of sweat and cigarettes. A pack of men in dirtied jeans and gray maintenance button-ups. College students, their table cluttered with nothing but textbooks and coffee cups. And then there's Betsy: perched at a high-top for two, her golden-blond (not purple) hair slicked back into a sleek low bun to match the sleek, double-breasted midnight-blue suit that would be unremarkable in the Financial District. In an all-night diner, it's pretty remarkable.

At least Kitty slipped on a crisp white trench—her only remaining coat—as befits her station. Of course, she's also got a boning knife strapped to her outer thigh, but the coat is both her favored weapon and her armor. Though her powers render her untouchable in a fight, she likes this tangible reminder to her enemies and allies alike of who she is, as well as the unspoken implication of everything she's done to get here. Kitty outranks and outmatches Betsy, who would do well to remember that.

Because if this is some kind of trap, the telepath will live (very briefly) to regret it.

"I've got a company car to catch to Massachusetts in three

hours," Kitty says in greeting as she slides onto the empty stool. "So you've got three minutes to convince me this is my problem, whatever *this* is."

Betsy considers her, then begins, "Have you ever lost someone very close to you?"

She hops back down from the stool. "Time's up. Funny how it flies when you're asking questions that are none of your business."

"If you have," the woman continues as though Kitty never spoke, "then maybe you know what it's like to wake up the morning after. Before you remember what's happened and to whom, you still *feel* it." She holds Kitty's gaze, her eyes as deep blue as her suit, shining under the diner's fluorescent lighting. "Have you ever experienced that?"

Kitty riffles instinctively through every past ache filed away in every cobwebbed corner of her heart. Every fallen teammate she hardly knew, and the few who might've mattered to her if they'd lived longer. Maybe, but maybe not. Each of them blurs into the next, back and back and back, all the way to . . .

Grandpa Prydeman.

A stoic but kind man, always cold in the heat of summer, dressed in sweater-vests with his shirtsleeves rolled down and a black velvet kippah pinned in his swan-white hair every Shabbos. Her grandfather's been gone for . . . God, has it been nine years? Nine long years since she was summoned to the headmistress's office at Miss Hester's. Since she heard her father's voice on the phone, rough with grief, offering her a plane ticket to Chicago for the funeral only if she swore to behave herself (she'd been at boarding school for less than a year, and was on her second warning of the semester already). She recalls walking to her dorm to pack, the new pit inside her growing deeper and darker with every step. And the next morning, waking up in her old bedroom in Deerfield that no longer felt like home, it had taken her a few ragged breaths to remember why she was there and why she hurt so badly.

"I'm asking," Betsy presses on in the face of Kitty's silence, "because I've had that feeling for three days now. I can't shake it. And

I can't explain it. I've had these moments before. As if I've misplaced something or lost someone very important, and maybe I could find them if only I could remember. It's never been this strong, though, or lasted so long. I can almost see it, like somebody's left a psychic trail through the woods. I've been following it with my powers, and I haven't caught a glimpse of them yet. But I can see you on the trail, of all people."

"*Me?*"

In the half hour since Betsy's unwelcome summons, Kitty's been racking her not-too-shabby brains to guess the woman's motive, and come up empty. Aside from the unsettling coincidence of having seen Betsy just this evening, it was the uncertainty that drove Kitty from her bed. The idea that somebody out there wanted something from her that she couldn't anticipate made her skin itch.

Whatever she'd suspected, it wasn't this.

"Please . . . just hear me out?" Betsy plucks a napkin from the tabletop dispenser, twisting it frantically between her fingers. "I know how it sounds."

Reluctantly, Kitty climbs back onto her stool, but she does her best to feign indifference. "It sounds like something that isn't my problem."

"I suppose it does. But it has to be somebody's. I tried talking to Brian and to RCX. The agency thinks I'm . . . well, they don't believe it's worth looking into. And my brother is preoccupied these days. Lots on your plate when you've got a baby in the house for the third time *and* you're champion of the British Isles."

Kitty has heard of RCX. A covert agency under the supervision of the British government, assembled for the purpose of handling superhuman matters and threats within its jurisdiction. RCX also holds Captain Britain's reins—and clearly his sister's. The organization is a matter of some concern for the London office, but known to look the other way from Hellfire Club affairs in exchange for the occasional generous donation. "Let me get this straight. You think somebody important to you is dead—"

"*Lost,*" Betsy insists.

"Sure. But you don't remember who, and your bosses don't believe you, and your brother doesn't believe you. Even if you did see me on this . . . psychic trail . . . what exactly am I supposed to do about it?"

Betsy's eyes blur like watercolor then, peering through Kitty as though she's nothing but smoke. Kitty waves a hand in front of her face: nothing. Maybe this is her chance to slip away from this strange woman, this strange night, and back into her own life. That's where she belongs.

"The thing is," Betsy says before she can, "my powers first manifested when I was sixteen, and ever since, I've had these moments. Only they were so jumbled together with the thoughts of thousands of people in my head all at once that it took me years to tease them out. And after . . . well, something happened to me, and it got worse. I have these bursts of certainty that things aren't as they should be. That I'm not where I should be, or with whom. Like a wound without an answer."

For the second time tonight, Kitty feels herself freezing from the inside out.

"But I've never had a lead before now." Betsy tosses the last remaining shreds of the napkin aside. "The trail doesn't stop with you. Now that we're together, I can see deeper into the woods, and up ahead it's bright. Sunlight or fire. I still can't see who it leads to, but I know where. Rather, I know when."

"Meaning . . . ?"

"The past. That's where the trail is leading me. Leading us."

"You want me to go to the past with you? Time travel—is that even possible?"

"Well, I've never done it personally. If you really want to talk about practical applications of travel through space and time, you'd need to talk to Captain Britain. I'm just his sister, and more of a lab assistant than a field assistant. But I've reviewed every file at RCX headquarters that isn't classified above my clearance level, or nearly every file, and it's certainly possible."

Before Kitty can sift through the tangle of her thoughts, a waitress in a plasticky bouffant wig appears between them. "Whatcha hungry for tonight, sweetheart?" she asks Kitty, prying her order pad from the pocket of a frilled apron. Her eyes skate right past Betsy, who doesn't even have a plastic cup of ice water in front of her; the waitress has long since written the woman off.

Which means Betsy's been here quite a while. Much longer than Kitty guessed, if she's missed that many chances to pad the waitress's meager paycheck.

Which means that Betsy had already guessed the meeting place Kitty would propose.

Which *means* that she knew where to find Kitty well before making telepathic contact. Betsy's been watching her, and who knows for how long? Tonight may not even be the first time she's rooted around in Kitty's thoughts. Perhaps she somehow found out about Kitty's slips, though Kitty's never shared them with anyone. All this talk of trails and gut feelings might be to tempt Kitty with the lie that she isn't just . . . broken.

"I'm not staying," she announces to the waitress. "Don't worry, though. My friend will tip you for the trouble."

Betsy's jaw tenses, but she says nothing.

Sensing the mood between them, the poor waitress tucks her pad away again. "I'll just give you another moment to look at the menu," she says, already retreating.

"Kitty," Betsy tries once she's retreated, "please—"

"No. I'm not walking away from everything I've got going on in my life to solve a problem you can't name, if it even exists. And now I have to move again, when I finally found a building with a working elevator. So thanks for that."

Betsy's stunning face sharpens, mesmerizing in her anger as she leans forward to hiss, "What exactly have you 'got going on'? I was in your head tonight. From what I saw in your surface thoughts alone, you're just like me, Kitty Pryde. Every choice you make, you make out of fear. You're terrified all the time."

"I'm *bored*," Kitty insists, aiming for White Queen iciness even as she feels the blood boiling in her cheeks.

Standing, Betsy flips a card across the tabletop, where it skates to a stop in front of Kitty. "Give us a ring when you're ready to admit the truth. To me and to yourself." She sniffs, tosses down a stack of US bills from the pocket of her unfashionable suit, and then heads for the door of Mama's Maple Bacon and Eggs.

The business card stamped with an RCX logo waits for Kitty either to pick it up or to walk away and leave it behind, along with every question—and answer—that might come with it.

CHAPTER 6

★

AMERICA

JULY 1, 1975

FOR A VERY LONG TIME, SHE STANDS ON THE SIDEWALK IN FRONT OF the grocery store, staring at its brick exterior, reading and rereading the blue lettering on a plexiglass sign over the red awning:

BODEGA SANTANA
COLD BEER & SODA—ICE—COLD CUTS—FRUIT

Her eyes drift up to the center window on the second floor that was her bedroom.

Or will be.

Or *would* be.

When the Santanas brought her here, they offered her everything they could. A spare bed, a nightstand, and a little shelf already piled with books. That, and safety. They could've turned her over to the police and the foster care system, but the country she was named for never did kindly treat people who exist in a place without proper paperwork, nor their kids. So Javi and Ceci kept her, claiming her as a relative from their previous home in San Juan. Then she had a home, and a big brother—Berto—and a little stuffed blue hippo she slept with every night.

Until she didn't.

After years of sneaking out, patrolling the neighborhood, trying to prove herself a hero, the gulf between who her adoptive family wanted her to be and who she knew she was had become too painful and exhausting to cross. She had run away, and then...

Then what?

When did America Chavez lose herself, or choose to bury herself inside the untouchable shell of a Watcher? And *why*? She can't remember. She's still sifting through and picking out the shards of herself, her memories, her life.

The shop door swings open with the chime of a bell, and a small Puerto Rican woman shoulders halfway through, her arms full of grocery bags. America shakes herself from stasis to step forward and open it all the way.

"Gracias," she says, propping the bags on either hip to march on down the sidewalk.

Awash in cool air—the Santanas had a window unit down here before they ever had one upstairs—America remains in the doorway. Bodega Santana looks much the same as the shop she once knew by heart. Plastic crates of fruit along the far wall; apples and bananas, yes, but also papayas and quenepas. Coolers of milk and juice and bottled beer. Neatly arranged shelves stacked with boxes and cans and bags of rice. Leaning halfway in to peer down the closest aisle, she can almost see the checkout counter at the front of the shop, where a younger Javi or Ceci must be staffing the register.

She plants one sneaker on the tiled floor.

"¡Aléjate! ¡Déjala en paz! I said leave her alone!"

America spins away in an instant to follow the sound of trouble. Down the block, the woman with the bags shouts at a pack of preteen boys. They're circling a young Dominican girl with long brown braids, weighed down by a backpack almost bigger than she is. One boy darts forward, grabbing for a textbook clutched tightly to her chest in an attempt to peel it away, while the rest laugh. The woman jabs one chancla-clad foot in their direction, her arms too full to swat them away, but they only sneer and shout back at her.

Well, enough of that.

America's no sooner thought it than she appears in the midst of them without needing to portal—her Watcher's powers require only a thought to teleport. Nor does she need to lift a finger to send the boys scattering like bowling pins across the sidewalk. She *could* have sent them all flying through shopfronts and car windshields, if she'd wished it, or simply tossed their molecules across the universe.

But she'd never . . .

She *could* never . . .

Except that she could. Any Watcher is capable of that much and more. She's defied their inviolate policy of non-intervention, but the truth is, a Watcher choosing to intervene could mean the undoing of any mortal in the universe. Or every mortal. America freezes in horror at the thought while the boys scramble up and away, sprinting off down the street. Only children. Nasty ones, but kids all the same.

The Puerto Rican woman backs a step away, then two. At some point, she's dropped her shopping bags, and her groceries tumble out over the sidewalk. A shattered jar of mole negro oozes dark-brown paste. The smell of smoked chili wafts off the hot concrete. "¿De dónde apareciste?" she demands. Where did you come from?

America knows what she means, but doesn't know how to answer.

Instead she strides away before the woman draws attention to them both, in the opposite direction from Bodega Santana. Javi and Ceci had hated the trouble she got into. Every time a policeman hauled her home from the worst parts of town after dark, she got the same lecture: that people who looked like America and the Santanas needed to keep their heads down, play by the rules, avoid the notice of the cops, who were bigger threats to many of their neighbors than gangs or looters. This went on until the night of her brother's baby shower, when she stumbled into the party late and smelling of the dumpster where she'd fought a Dominican Spirit Larva. Then it all blew up.

"If you want to be part of this family, you need to start acting more responsibly!" Ceci had screamed.

"If I have to choose between being one of you," America shouted back, "and being who I really am . . . being who my moms would want me to be . . . well then, that's easy."

Her moms.

She remembers now.

Elena and Amalia Chavez. Before the Santana family took her in, she belonged to her mothers. They belonged to her.

And then they didn't.

CHAPTER 7

KITTY

1990

SNOW VALLEY IN SPRINGTIME IS POSTCARD-PERFECT, FROM the cornflower sky and buttery sunshine to the green hills and the meadows strewn with wildflowers. As her driver speeds down the winding roads of the Berkshire Mountains in the black Cadillac—with Hellfire Club plates, of course—Kitty presses her forehead to the window glass to get a better look. She feels as she always does, turning onto the private, tree-lined lane approaching the Massachusetts Academy. Like it's been a lifetime since she first saw these grounds, and at the same time, like she's sixteen all over again.

THEN

KITTY'S REALLY DONE IT THIS TIME.

Miss Hester's didn't expel her when she disappeared from school for two days during her first semester. Kitty was having a rough time with the divorce, her parents pleaded, and deserved a little grace.

They didn't expel her when she punched Julia Bettencourt in her second semester. It was over Pesach, and Julia sniffed at Kitty in the cafeteria line when she asked the lunch lady for a tray of vegetables instead of the chicken Alfredo, sneered at the Star of David around her neck, and called her a freak. Luckily, the lunch lady spoke up for Kitty, so she was only suspended for a week, with all campus privileges revoked (Julia wasn't punished at all).

They didn't expel her for breaking into the headmistress's office last month, but only because they couldn't prove it. The office was locked, and neither the headmistress, the groundskeeper, nor the janitor had misplaced their keys. Nobody could explain how the files of every student currently under disciplinary warning ended up at the bottom of the lap pool, with the gymnasium doors still locked as well. Kitty may have been the prime suspect, having been called to the office just that morning for skipping class and her extracurriculars, but the school's hands were tied for lack of evidence.

There's no way Miss Hester's will keep her now, though.

If calling the cops to drag her off campus didn't make that clear, then the night she's just spent on a stiff bunk in a juvenile detention center with nobody coming to claim her sure does. So when the guard leads Kitty down the whitewashed cinder-block hallway toward the visiting area in the early morning, she can't imagine who's waiting for her. The headmistress won't want anything to do with her, and her parents couldn't have flown out from Chicago this quickly, could they?

The guard steers her to a chamber just big enough to hold a table, glassed in on two sides so that even before she enters, Kitty sees the woman perched on the edge of the tabletop with a briefcase beside her. She's the most arresting person Kitty's seen in real life, like a sculpture of a woman masterfully carved from marble. Glossy, pearl-colored hair cut in a sleek, sharp bob to match her sleek, sharp clothing. A broad-shouldered, ice-blue suit jacket buttoned up over a high-collared white shirt, with a matching skirt slit high on the side to show knee-high white boots and one long, perfect leg. "That'll be all," she commands the guard in a voice soaked through with wealth and privilege, much like Kitty's classmates at Miss Hester's.

They're left alone, though any passing guard could see them through the windows, and a security camera mounted in the corner of the room means that somebody is watching.

"Tell me, Katherine." The woman casts her cool blue eyes up and down Kitty, from her too-big slippers to her too-frizzy brown curls. "What are you doing here?"

Kitty glances toward the security camera. "I'm not supposed to say anything before the trial, right?" Maybe this woman's a lawyer, hired by her parents. The idea sends a spike of dread through her chest; Miss Hester's won't take her back, but she figured her parents would let her come to . . . well, one of their new houses. But if she needs a lawyer, maybe things are more dire than that.

The woman laughs, quick and elegant. "I'm not a lawyer, Katherine, and don't worry. Nobody can see or hear us. And you can skip the part of the story where you were caught by the security guard spray-painting your school's stables and tack shed. Even the saddles, Katherine? Tsk. As a former equestrian myself, I can't say I approve. But what I'd very much like to understand is why you're *here*, when we both know you could've slipped out of the shed, out of the police car, out of this whole facility if you wanted. No one can hold you if you wish otherwise, Katherine. So what's keeping you?"

The blood drains from Kitty's face in a rush, and her brain sparkles with panic. This woman knows, she knows, she *knows*—

"Have a seat, darling," the woman says, nudging a plastic chair toward Kitty with the toe of one pristine suede boot. "You're looking faint."

Obediently, Kitty drops down to sit.

"The truth please, Katherine," the woman prompts.

"I . . . I couldn't . . . the guard already saw me. He knew who I was. If I got away, he'd know . . ."

"That you're a mutant?"

Her ears roar and her chest aches as though she's sinking through dark water, down and down.

"It's all right. I understand better than you know." The woman lifts one manicured hand between them, and in the soft center of her palm, one perfect, ice-blue rose buds from nowhere, blooms, and dies in a matter of seconds. Then the woman closes her palm, and the brown skeleton of the flower vanishes. **Only an illusion. Much like the security guards watching the cameras are seeing right now. So far as they know, you and I are having a very uneventful conversation.**

Kitty startles backward, her chair squeaking across the linoleum at the cold tendrils of a thought that isn't hers. "You're a . . ."

"A mutant," the woman agrees, as mildly as she might announce her height or that she's left-handed. "I'm also the headmistress of a very special school, and I'm here to help you."

"How?"

"The warden is prepared to release you into my custody this very morning."

Kitty blinks up at her. "But I thought my parents had to pick me up. And my hearing is tomorrow, isn't it? How did you even know I was here?"

"With my line of work, I like to keep a watch on juvenile centers across the country for intriguing cases. For instance, a vandal caught inside a still-locked building following months of similar incidents around town, without a trace of a culprit until now. And it was a teenage girl all along?" The woman shrugs one elegant shoulder. "You caught my attention. But none of that matters now. There won't be a trial, or probation, or any punishment. Your parents need never get on a plane, since they've already happily accepted my offer from afar. All that's left is for you to accept."

"What offer?"

Unclasping the briefcase beside her, she fishes out a brochure.

"The Massachusetts Academy?" Kitty reads as she takes it, studying the glossy photos of students clustered in the grass around a marble fountain, and smiling over textbooks in a gilded library.

"Your parents were thrilled. An excellent education for their bright but troubled daughter, at one of the best private schools in the country, only a few hours north of here. Besides, it's a better scholarship than what Miss Hester's offered. That school wasn't serving you, Katherine. They didn't know what a gem they had in hand. But I know what you really are, and I know that you'll thrive in an environment like my school, alongside a selection of peers who are... talented, like you. Like us." Her crystalline eyes pin Kitty in place. "Don't you want to stop hiding?"

Is that what she wants?

It's been three years since Kitty's powers manifested. Three years of listening to her classmates talk about mutants as though they're bogeymen, hiding in closets and under beds to spring out at unsuspecting children. Of watching speeches by pastors and politicians about the dangers these genetic deviants presented to humanity, which her teachers played in class. And always, she thought of Grandpa Pryde, and his stories of growing up in Warsaw. Well before the war and the Germans, things were getting worse for Jews—Polish nationalism ever rising, and pogroms and prejudiced laws chipping away at their lives and rights. As a young man, he'd emigrated to America when there were fewer and fewer ways of getting out, hoping to send enough money home to bring his parents and little sister over after him. A typical immigrant story. But the war had come too quickly. And so he sat alone in his rented bedroom in a Chicago tenement, listening to radio broadcasts that quoted Nazi claims about his people as parasitic vermin, dangerous, the enemy of mankind.

Julia Bettencourt is about as fond of Jews as she is of mutants. It's almost funny. Kitty doesn't "look" or "sound" Jewish, whatever ignorant people think that means, and the surname her grandfather was born with—Prydeman—he chopped short to avoid prejudice in America. If not for the Star of David necklace Kitty's grandparents gave her as a bat mitzvah present, she could've passed as gentile at Miss Hester's just as easily as she passes for a non-mutant. But even if Julia had never once muttered "dirty Jew" right behind her in the cafeteria line, or asked Kitty where she kept her horns, Kitty would still have to listen to Julia spew her hatred about others. The same way she listens in silence to her classmates and teachers spew anti-mutant sentiments and slurs, so they don't figure out who she really is.

She really doesn't want to be that girl anymore.

At last, Kitty nods.

"Wonderful." A flawless smile curls across the woman's face. "Let's get you out of here and into something less polyester, hmm?" She reaches out again, this time for Kitty to take her hand.

Though Kitty wants nothing more than to be led out of here, she hesitates. The woman knows about her ability to melt through walls, clearly. But should Kitty mention her . . . slips? Those moments when she's found herself standing in some strange place with people she doesn't know? It's only happened a handful of times since the day her powers first emerged and ruined everything, and she's never been sure whether it's because she's a mutant or not. If it *is* because of her mutation, then what good is it? She can't predict the slips. She can't control them. All they've ever done is make her feel insane.

Better not to say anything, she decides. The woman may not want her if she does.

"Something wrong, Katherine?" she asks, her hand still outstretched.

"No, it's . . . It's Kitty, actually."

"Very well. Call me Ms. Frost." The woman leans in close. "Now then, all you have to do is walk with me out of this place and into a better life. No more hiding, Kitty Pryde."

NOW

THE WHITE QUEEN WAITS FOR KITTY BEHIND HER ENORMOUS white marble desk, as cool and elegant as her luxurious-yet-minimalist office. Gone are the padded shoulders and high collars Emma once used to disguise herself in public. A crisp, snow-white blazer over a white buckled corset top hides little, but as always, she looks utterly at home in her skin. It's a quality Kitty's always envied. The morning sun through the floor-to-ceiling windows alights upon her sleek high bun, like polished white gold. Kitty tugs self-consciously at her brown curls, frizzed and mussed from sleeping in the company car on the drive to Snow Valley. Emma's office overlooks the lawns, the fountain, the gazebo bordered by perfect blue roses, not a wilting petal among them. Everything as picture-perfect as the headmistress.

The vast majority of her students have no idea that beneath the manicured campus, an entire stone-and-steel complex exists to further the school's true purpose: recruiting young mutants, training them, sharpening them into superpowered weapons, and pointing them at the hearts of enemies of the Hellfire Club.

Emma drums her fingertips against her desk, recapturing Kitty's attention. "So glad to see you intact, dear heart. From Empath's account of the evening, I feared the worst."

Without meaning to, Kitty flexes her arm, the tape on the gauze below her white jacket tugging at her skin. "I'm fine. Like I said, it was nothing."

"Nothing? Hmm. Beast is in the wind now and knows we're hunting for him. I'd say that's something."

"If Empath and Sunspot weren't sniping at each other the whole time, we'd have—"

"Infighting among the Hellions? How terrible. If only there were someone, a squad leader perhaps, capable of controlling them." Emma's quiet words slice knife-like through her excuses.

Kitty shrinks back even as she hates herself for it. When she was sixteen and starry-eyed, trailing like an adopted puppy after the woman who'd saved her, the White Queen's approval was a prize she'd die to obtain (and almost had on more than one occasion). But even now, she just cannot stop reaching for the prize, no matter how many times it's been snatched away.

Then Emma twists the blade. "Granted, when I made you my White Knight, it wasn't because you'd shown leadership potential. Nor because you were beloved by your teammates. You keep to yourself, and you look out for yourself, and I don't begrudge that. In fact, I admire it. Self-preservation is a useful quality in a knight. Stops me from having to train a replacement too often, and I appreciate that the only person more important to you than you are, is me. You know that I gave you your freedom, your power, your position. And *I* know that you'd do anything to keep it all. So if you *want* to keep it, find a way to get your team in order."

Nervous sweat mists her upper lip, and she's fairly sure that Emma doesn't need telepathic powers to hear the speed of her heart right now. "I'll do better," she promises.

"I'm sure you will." Emma dismisses Kitty, already turning back to her work.

Kitty should leave now and collect her dignity on the long car ride back to Inwood.

But . . .

If there's a chance, however slim, that Betsy wasn't lying, then maybe Kitty *should* tell Emma. If she'd told Emma the whole truth about herself from the start, the most powerful telepath on the planet could have helped Kitty get to the bottom of it. Or she might have walked out the door and left Kitty in that detention center, having lost interest in acquiring an unreliable asset.

"Something else on your mind, dear?" the White Queen asks, noticing Kitty's continued presence.

"Just that . . . a club member reached out to me last night. Or more like this morning. Betsy Braddock."

"Who?"

"Captain Britain's little sister."

"Ah." Emma frowns with mild interest. "Whatever for?"

"She said . . . that someone who was supposed to be here is missing. And that she's always had a feeling the world is, um, wrong. It sounds insane, I know, but—"

"It certainly does. If I remember my history, Betsy Braddock carries quite a bit of baggage. She had a nasty brush with a creature called Mojo, and spent a long time trapped in his realm. He nearly took down Captain Britain as well, but eventually, RCX tracked him down, and he managed to fish her out of the Wildways and bring her home. She's never been the same. Traumatized, poor thing.

Pity, she could've been a real asset to the Inner Circle. I wouldn't worry yourself. But perhaps it's too late for that?"

"Not worrying. Maybe wondering." She shifts on her feet. "Do you ever think about . . . whether you would be different, in a different world?"

Emma arches one pale eyebrow, the only sign of impact. "I am the White Queen of a club that counts among its ranks the wealthiest and most influential members of society—senators, ambassadors, princes, movie stars. And here we are, at the very center of the Inner Circle. Who else would I want to be?"

Kitty knows all of this, knows that the Inner Circle's roots of influence run practically down to the planet's core. They've even convinced the world's governments to keep their Sentinels—giant, mechanical mutant hunters, incredibly sophisticated and adaptive, which countries employ to root out their mutant citizens—clear of the Hellfire Club's territories and interests.

And yet.

"But we're still hiding." Kitty sees it clearly now, maybe for the first time. Nearly seven years since Emma offered her a better life, a life in the light, and here she is still clinging to the shadows. She's *never* stopped hiding. "I'm just saying, we have control now. We have power. What if we—"

"What, Kitty? Do you propose that we become a public face for mutantkind?" Emma scoffs. "There was a man who played that part, once. Ran his own school while I was still buttering up the board of trustees, taking hold of this place to remake it for our purposes. He believed a world was possible where *Homo sapiens* coexisted with *Homo superior* as equals, and that this could be achieved by showing society that despite our vast genetic advantages, we're not a threat to humanity. Instead of training the next generation of mutants to use their abilities for the benefit of our own, he pointed them at his fellow mutants, fighting on behalf of the very people who hated them. Hated us all. Do you know his name?"

Kitty shakes her head.

"Of course you don't. Few do. He and his beloved students died some time ago, before your mutation ever manifested. And nobody remembers them. No one considers all his good deeds before spitting on mutants. We can't rely upon goodwill to protect us. It certainly didn't protect Charles Xavier or the X-Men."

Emma's right; neither name rings a bell. "So we just have to be scared forever?" Kitty challenges.

"Not scared," Emma snaps, wheeling her padded leather desk chair back and standing. "Smart. Kitty, haven't I always done my best to look after you like a daughter when your parents had no use for you, to protect you, to teach you?" She crosses the room to lay a careful hand on Kitty's injured arm, almost mother-like, and Kitty finds herself melting under her touch.

"Yes, Ms. Frost," she answers dutifully.

Without warning, Emma's skin hardens, crystallizing to her diamond form, prisming ribbons of multicolored light across the white floors and furniture. Her grip hardens along with it, shimmering fingers sawing into Kitty's bandaged upper arm. "Then learn this lesson: There's no point in ruminating on what might have been. You have enough to worry about in the present, like getting my Hellions in hand. It's that, or kindly take off that white coat, turn in the keys to your latest *quaint* little apartment, and pray that all the people my patronage has protected you from—outside the club and in—don't seize their chance to take a former knight off the board for good."

Frozen by the White Queen's diamond-eyed gaze, Kitty doesn't even think to phase out of her grasp.

Not before Emma releases her, crystal skin returning to pale flesh as she sways back to her desk, folding herself elegantly into the chair. "A different world." She laughs again as she considers it, crisp as ice tinkling in a glass. "Why would I want to change anything? *This* is the world we made."

Kitty's still shaking when she stumbles right through Emma's closed door into the hallway, then out of the administration building and into the spring sunshine.

It's all her fault, of course.

She'll try harder, she'll do better, she'll make this up to Emma. She has to—without the Hellfire Club, what does she have? Her heart spikes again at the thought of it.

You're just like me, Kitty Pryde. Every choice you make, you make out of fear.

If time travel were as possible as Betsy Braddock claims, Kitty would go back in time and talk herself out of ever walking into that diner. She was better off before the psychic barged into her life, into her business, into her brain. Now she's standing within shouting distance of the woman who forged her from a lonely freak into an agent of the Inner Circle, in the only place she's thought of as home for the past decade. But she just feels . . .

Lost.

And that's before her stomach gives a too-familiar swoop and the world slips out of place. When it sets itself right again, she stands in the same strange glass-ceilinged room with vines curling up the walls from last night's slip. Only this time, it isn't Betsy and the redhead here with her, but Emma Frost.

It takes a moment to clock the subtler difference between this Emma and her own. A particular pastel-gray shade of lipstick that Kitty's never seen the headmistress wear, and an ice-white tuxedo suit instead of a corset top (granted, with no shirt beneath the jacket that buttons just above Emma's waist). "Now, what's really bothering you?" she asks over the rim of a champagne flute.

When Kitty was younger and used to experience these slips, she'd panic every time. Demand to know what was happening to her, who these strangers were, where she was. All it ever earned her was concern and confusion, before she inevitably slipped back. She's long since trained herself to simply ride the episodes out. No point in engaging with people who are probably nothing more than hallucinations. That way lies *actual* madness.

But... just this once...

"Do you ever wonder whether you would be different in a different world?" she repeats.

This Emma quirks her head to the side, considering Kitty. "I've been a lot of versions of myself. Held different titles, worn different costumes. Worn a few different noses, too."

She can't help but laugh.

Emma's eyes sparkle as she takes a sip from her flute. "I've made my choices, Kitty. Most of them objectively correct in the moment but awful for the soul all the same. Yet I like to imagine that I was always headed here. I feel like I'm who I was meant to be. Don't you?"

"I don't know," Kitty admits, despising the break in her voice.

"Well. Lucky for you, I do." Then Emma steps forward, and Kitty barely has time to brace herself before Emma throws her arms around her, holding on tight. Every bone in Kitty's body locks up before she feels herself giving way, loosening into the first real hug she's had in years. When Emma pulls back to look at Kitty, it's the expression on her face that truly sets her apart from the White Queen whom Kitty knows so well. This Emma gazes at her with real warmth in her gemstone-blue eyes. With unabashed pride.

Then, in a blink, Emma is gone. The world has slipped back into place, back to the Massachusetts Academy she knows, the fountain back and burbling beside her, and Kitty is alone on the lawn again.

She doesn't pause to second-guess herself before pulling out Betsy's card, still stuffed in her pocket from early this morning. By the second ring of her Hellfire-Club-issued communicator, the psychic answers, greeting her before she can announce herself.

"Are you still in the city?" Kitty strides toward the car waiting for her in the lot.

"I am. I'd hoped to hear from you, but I really wasn't sure I would. Does this mean—"

"Listen. I'm not promising anything. Maybe my life doesn't look like much to you, but it's the only one I have, and I'm not gonna make it worse by messing with the past. All I'm saying is . . . this trail you talked about, leading back in time. You're sure there's a way to follow it, just to take a look?"

Betsy's silent for a long moment before answering, unable to suppress the hope in her voice when she does. "Of course there's a way. It's a bit complicated, as I said, but . . . Kitty, have you ever been to Latveria?"

CHAPTER 8

☆

AMERICA

JULY 1, 1975

ON THE OTHER SIDE OF THE PORTAL, JONES BEACH WAITS FOR HER like a memory.

She lands on the boardwalk beside the great sandstone-and-brick Center Mall. Decades from now, it'll be a ruin. Gutted by fire and degraded by floodwater and erosion. She knows this not because she's seen it herself but thanks to the great repository of cosmic knowledge to which every Watcher holds a key, or *is* a key. The mall will be torn down, leaving nothing behind but a cavity in the sand until it's raised anew. America can see its past, too. Some of this world's historians say the beach was conceived of as "whites only" by the nature of its design. Low bridges along the parkway—built by the same infamous urban planner who bulldozed Black and Latino homes to put in parks and routed highways through Black and Latino neighborhoods—keep public buses from passing beneath. Only those who own automobiles, vastly white and upper-class, can reach the beachfront with ease. The whiteness of beachgoers as far as America can see doesn't exactly disprove the theory.

But this, too, can change . . . *if* this reality survives Doom.

Pinned between the boardwalk and the glittering blue-green water, the beach is alive with people. Nearby, long-haired women and men lie in a pile atop one another, some fully clothed, one plucking at a guitar. A pack of knee-high children spring between striped beach umbrellas identical to the hundreds more along the shore. Four white, suntanned teenage girls stuffed together atop a lifeguard's chair laugh around their cigarettes. And that's to say nothing of the seabirds, and the tall grass and goldenrod growing in the shallow dunes. Even the beach seems to breathe as she steps tentatively off the boardwalk, and sand shifts beneath her sneakers.

She turns her gaze toward the ocean.

THEN

AMERICA WOKE TO NIGHTTIME. INFINITE STARS OVERHEAD AND dark water around her, rocking her. The sheet of debris she lay on washed in with the surf, and she sat up as it scraped across damp sand. She was soaked and shivering . . . but she wasn't alone.

A man and a woman and a boy stood on the otherwise empty beach. They fished her from the water and wrapped her in a big blue sheet they'd been using as a picnic blanket while they stargazed.

The woman with curly hair and kind eyes asked, "Mamita, where are your parents?"

"¿Les pasó algo?" asked a strong-shouldered man, who helped to towel her hair with gentle hands. Did something happen to them?

"Si," America answered.

Though by then, the memory of her mothers was already washing out with the tide, gone by the time they carried America to their car to bring her home.

NOW

HOW COULD SHE HAVE FORGOTTEN THEM AGAIN?

Tearing her gaze from the Atlantic and the island she knows is out there, she lifts a foot and brings it down to stomp a portal into the beach. Sand slips over its crackling edges, pouring through. The guitar player and her pile of friends cry out, toppling their umbrella as they throw themselves backward and away from her. But she doesn't spare them a glance before stepping one foot over the edge of the portal and letting herself fall.

When she lands, she stands on yet another beach, this one empty. The narrow strip of unspoiled sand quickly gives way to what could be mistaken for a lush jungle, bursting with palm trees and tropical plants that have no right to thrive this far north. No wonder kid-America once convinced herself this was some kind of utopia. Really, it's just a small landmass a few dozen nautical miles off the shore of Long Island, bought by a very rich man named Gales with a mission her mothers had believed in: finding a cure for a fatal genetic disease that both of their daughters were diagnosed with. This place was special, said the man. Suffused with an energy unlike any place on Earth.

A magic.

America closes her eyes and tries to feel it now, the way she felt it then. The magic that worked its way into her cells and remade her failing body and rewrote her future. It gave her gifts. Superhuman strength and durability, decelerated aging, the ability to portal between dimensions and to fly (how had she ever forgotten that she could fly?). But the magic took from her, too. It took her mothers, too, in a way. They sacrificed their lives to save America—and all the little girls of the so-called Utopian Parallel—from Gales. The man had become so obsessed with his work, with his mandate, that he was willing to burn through the girls he claimed all of it was for. Her mothers saw that in the end, and regretted having come. They regretted helping Gales to meddle with forces that none of them understood.

And then they died.

What would they think of America now if they hadn't?

What would they tell her to do if they were here?

She opens her eyes again, searching for some trace of her mothers on this island where they've never been and nobody will be for years yet. Brightly colored birds rustle in the thick green foliage, unbothered by her presence, unaware that these very trees might someday be knocked down to lay the foundations of one man's colossal mistake. Gales believed he was doing the right thing. So did her mothers. They would likely tell America to do what she believes is right . . .

Still, how can she be certain?

She's been so lost for so long, both omnipotent and bound by her Watcher's mandate, observing world upon world only as it spins by. Gazing down at life and death from an eternal perch behind her cosmic window. Somewhere beyond space and time, that chamber exists. She can sense it even now. Yet all of this—the world and the people in it—is *real*. Maybe not to the Watchers, who see every world as nothing more than a story shelved inside an infinite library, to be skimmed through over the course of an evening and then put back, perhaps never to be thought of afterward. They are not supposed to change the stories or let the stories change them.

The Watchers are wrong. Of that much, she *is* certain.

Likely, they're peering through their own cosmic windows right now, searching for her. They'll try to stop her.

But America knows herself now. And she cannot, *will* not, sit by while Doom destroys Jean Grey, and this reality and its people along with her.

Taking a steadying breath, she lifts one knee and, for the first time in a very long time, rises from the earth and toward the sky.

CHAPTER 9

KITTY

1990

"RCX DOESN'T BELIEVE YOU ABOUT YOUR MISSING PERSON, but they gave you the company jet anyway?" Kitty appraises the sleek little plane parked outside the private jet terminal at JFK.

Betsy shields her eyes from the glare of the afternoon sun overhead as she clips down the tarmac, leading the way in her neat navy suit and glossy heels.

Kitty hopes she has some combat boots stored in that oversized briefcase she carries.

"Actually, this is the family jet," Betsy informs her. "We're quite rich."

"How nice for you."

"It's nothing compared with the wealth you're used to in the Hellfire Club, I'm sure. That's the whole point, isn't it? Security through wealth and power? You must be well compensated regardless of your . . . lifestyle," she finishes delicately.

Kitty only snorts in reply as they climb the airstair to the jet's open clamshell door. She *is* paid, and well, though wealth was never the point. She attended boarding school with some of the richest kids in the country, both at Miss Hester's and at the Massachusetts Academy. And while it may have bought them the loyalty of their sycophantic peers and smoothed away the consequences of their actions (consequences Kitty's family couldn't afford to buy her way out of, hence her expulsion), she never craved the same.

Money or no, she would never be one of them. For her, the Hellfire Club meant being a part of something. People just like her, united by a shared purpose, even if that purpose still eludes or even repulses Kitty at times. She remembers zipping into her Hellions uniform for the first time, and later, when Emma Frost gave Kitty her first white coat, raising her up into the Inner Circle. How it felt to belong to someone, something. Almost like somebody finally saw her for who she was, and wanted her. Almost like a having family again.

Granted, it's the kind of family that spends as much time scheming against one another as it does against humankind, if not more. And right now Kitty's teetering on the edge of it, just one shove away from tumbling out the door and back into the cold.

Flying off to the Carpathian Mountains without permission probably won't help.

At least Kitty can think of less luxurious ways to self-sabotage. Aboard the Braddock jet, half a dozen padded seats as large as armchairs line the polished-wood aisle, and water bottles wait on matching wood tables before each chair. "Don't tell me this is a dry flight," she sighs, dropping into the nearest seat.

"Briefing first, cocktails later," Betsy says laconically. She buckles herself in across the aisle from Kitty as soon as she sits. "How much do you know about Victor von Doom?"

"Never met the guy, but I know the bullet points. Supreme ruler of a country he named after himself. Half evil sorcerer, half mad scientist. Has a wardrobe full of titanium. What else is there? Another megalomaniacal white man who wants to control the world, but unless he comes too close, he's not our problem."

Betsy pulls a thick portfolio folder out of her briefcase and slaps it down on her personal table. "He isn't white, actually."

"No?"

"Doom is Romani. Born in Latveria under the rule of a baron who, like much of Europe, discriminated terribly against his people. His mother was murdered by the baron's soldiers for crimes of witchcraft, and later a young Doom and his father were driven out of their camp and into the mountains by the same forces, where the father froze to death. Victor *is* a madman, but the roots of his quest for revenge and power were watered with the blood of his own."

"Hmm." Kitty picks up her water bottle, toys with the cap. "Guess we've all got a sad backstory."

"You suppose a childhood of birthday parties and ballet lessons in Illinois qualifies?"

Kitty flushes to her ears. "Screw you. I don't care if you've read one of your creepy little files on me, you don't *know* me."

The overhead speaker chimes to life just then as their contracted pilot announces their departure and runs down their route plan, forcing them to fume silently. As they begin taxiing down the runway, Kitty's traveling companion grips the leather armrests of her seat, her knuckles white, while the jet rumbles forward, gathering speed.

Kitty finds herself smirking. "Nervous flier?"

"No. Nervous passenger." Betsy clamps her jaw shut as they lift off, tilting skyward. Moments later, she admits above the whine of the engines, "It never feels right back here. I was a charter pilot once, in another life."

Another life.

It's only an expression.

But Kitty can't hide the hint of hope in her own voice when she asks, "You honestly believe there's something wrong with the world? Like, we're not who we're supposed to be?"

Betsy gives a tight nod. "The feeling's only gotten stronger now that we're under way. The trail's even clearer than before." Her blue eyes glaze over as though peering right through the paneled wooden doors between them and the cockpit, out the windshield, toward a path carved through the whitecapped ocean below them. "We're going the right way, I know it."

"If you say so. But if we do manage to hijack Doom's time machine—"

"Time platform," Betsy corrects, releasing her hold on the armrest to reach for the files again. She shuffles through pages of schematics and floor plans and aerial drone photos of an honest-to-God medieval castle on a cliffside darkened with towering trees. "The sub-basements of Castle Doom are vaster than the aboveground levels, and much of our mapping is guesswork, aided by accounts compiled from those who've been inside and managed to survive. Reed Richards's notes were particularly helpful. RCX managed to, er, acquire them from some of our occasional partners across the pond." She lays out a page with a gridded cross section for Kitty to study. "We believe we're headed for sub-basement level four. The defenses we'll encounter along the way are more than formidable. Minimal Latverian guards posted at the front gate and main entrance, loyal but human, so avoid their deaths if at all possible."

The Hellfire Club has no such compunction, but Kitty doesn't need to kill. And phasing their rifles into their own shoulders won't *kill* them, exactly.

"However, there are unknown numbers of Guardian Robots patrolling the surrounding woods, the towers, the parapets, and presumably every level and sublevel of the interior. They're programmed for combat and equipped with all manner of weapons, from pulse guns to missile launchers. Then there's the castle's weaponry systems and defensive traps. An energy shield capable of repelling most physical and energy-based attacks, stunners, shock fields, laser grids, electrified floors—"

"No sweat," Kitty brags, passing the sheet back. "I can walk us right through the front doors. Just make sure you keep up. I have to hold my breath to phase us, and I'm not passing out inside a wall because *you* slowed me down."

"We are trying to maintain some level of secrecy during our unsanctioned mission. RCX would loathe having to deal with an agent gone rogue, and I suspect the Hellfire Club won't be happy about it, either. So I suggest we aim for a more discreet point of entry. The pilot will land us in this clearing, here." She slides an aerial map of Doomstadt onto Kitty's table. "It's a decent hike to the castle from there, all while avoiding the notice of the guards in the woods. I can psychically block us from detection by the human soldiers, but robotic troops are obviously another matter. As we approach the castle, there's a little-used submersible entrance where the Klyne River flows beneath the castle; it'll feed us into the catacombs. Sparsely guarded compared with the rest of the grounds, only a handful of human guards and Doombots. If you can get us inside, I can navigate us to the platform."

"Won't be a problem. But then what? We pop back in time, figure out who your missing person is, hustle back to the castle, and book a return trip to a brave new world?"

"Just so."

Kitty studies Betsy from across the narrow aisle—the way she chews on the corner of her lip with one canine while she shuffles through her documents again and again with seeming intensity, but without stopping long enough to look at any of them. "It's that easy, huh?" she prods again.

"Well. We should be cautious in how we interact with the past."

"How cautious, exactly? Is this a 'Sound of Thunder' situation?"

"Hmm?"

"They didn't read Ray Bradbury at your boarding school?" Kitty sniffs. "A rich dude buys a trip back in time to hunt for a *T. rex*, but panics, steps off the path. Flash forward to the future, and everything is worse than it was, all because he squashed a butterfly under his boat shoes."

Betsy frowns. "No, I—I don't think so."

"You don't *think* so? Damn, I was kidding! Don't you know how this works? Doesn't RCX have a file on time travel?"

"The agency is . . . concerned with more material matters."

"So you *don't* know how time travel works!"

"Well, I've never done this before!" Betsy nearly shrieks, hands fluttering through her papers at a frantic pace.

"You have to be kidding me." Kitty presses the heels of her palms into her forehead, fighting the urge to phase right out of her seat and through the fuselage, dropping out of the belly of the jet into thin air; she'd find a way to survive, she's sure.

"It's . . . it's a risk, Kitty. I never said it wasn't. There's a chance that we'll upset things further. But plenty of heroes have messed about in time without breaking anything."

"Okay, but *we're* not heroes. We're lackeys at best. And what if somebody screwing around in time is what messed it up in the first place . . . if that's really what's happening?" Kitty demands.

"It *is*," Betsy shouts over the noise of their ascent, dropping her files at last to resume a death grip on her armrests. She squeezes her eyes shut. "I can feel it. I'm not wrong, *reality* is wrong, no matter what my brother thinks."

She's never been the same. Traumatized, poor thing. Pity, she could've been a real asset.

Emma had dismissed Betsy out of hand, dismissed her fears, deemed her too damaged to trust. Seems that the famous Captain Britain has as well.

But instead of stoking Kitty's panic, she feels herself settling, softening as the jet finally levels out. It's easier to be heard now as she mumbles, "I don't think you're wrong. Or maybe you are. I don't know you, either. But . . . I've seen things, too."

"You have?" Betsy sits forward to meet her gaze at last. "What did you see?"

"I—it doesn't matter what. People. Places. Took me years to meet another mutant, but when I did, none of them mentioned semi-regular hallucinations. I figured it was just me. But if it's not . . . if reality really is broken . . . then I don't know. Maybe I was just slipping through the cracks or something?" She feels foolish, admitting this new hope.

But Betsy exclaims, "How fascinating!" with no attempt to conceal her own excitement. "This is proof, don't you see, Kitty? It has to mean something, if it's both of us. It's as if I've been sensing the existence of these—cracks, let's keep calling them—but you've witnessed them directly. I wonder whether the difference has something to do with your powers. Some particular interaction, in the same way my psychic abilities have shown me the trail."

"What, like I'm phasing into some other dimension? Like the Wildways?" she asks, remembering Emma's history lesson.

Betsy's shoulders stiffen instantly, and Kitty regrets her words. She wasn't trying to be mean; not this time.

"Anything's possible," Betsy answers in a carefully neutral tone. "We're discovering new permutations and manifestations of mutant powers all the time. Something to explore and study when we've the time to do so properly."

What a nerd.

"I don't know about all that," Kitty protests. "I'm just saying I believe you. About some of it, anyway. But how are you so sure this will work? We're risking a lot to chase a mystery person who *might* be able to fix the world somehow. Or . . . to fix us. What if we can't find them? Or what if we find them and it changes nothing, and you have to live without them, except then you're more miserable than you were before?"

Betsy considers this, chewing the corner of her lip once more, and Kitty starts to think she's convinced her that this is a fool's errand.

Whether Kitty would be relieved or disappointed, she can't tell.

But at last, she shakes her head. "Even if we fail—and we *won't*—I'd rather remember them than forget, however painful."

Now it's Kitty's turn to consider. She guesses that she wouldn't give up her memories of Grandpa Pryde, no matter how painful the echo of his death, and that he would never give up his memories of the family he lost. And there must be people who'd feel that way about Kitty, if she slipped right out of the world. She thumbs through her mental files of allies, enemies, and family, finding that most of the folks in her life don't fit neatly into any one category.

Her parents . . . Well. Outside of trips home for the holidays, she hasn't spoken much to her parents since they sent her off to Miss Hester's. And after transferring to the Massachusetts Academy, she opted to stay on campus over winter breaks and, increasingly before graduation, summer breaks. They'd feel it if she disappeared from the timeline, she hopes. But she also admits to herself that it would take them a while to notice her absence.

And her squad of Hellions? They'd probably seize the chance to turn on one another, the survivors eager to snatch at her abandoned title in the Inner Circle.

Emma Frost would certainly be nagged by the loss of her. But as she made crystal-clear this morning, Kitty Pryde is entirely replaceable. Her mentor has never once looked at her the way other-Emma did.

Clearing her throat, she slams shut her window shade and reclines her chair, shoving her little pile of documents back at Betsy.

"Kitty, what are you—"

"I'm running on two hours' sleep over the last two days, so I'm taking a nap."

"But there's still so much to plan!"

"So plan, then. Read your files again, if you think it'll help. Just wake me when we get to the Balkans," Kitty instructs, closing her eyes before Betsy can see the shine in them.

CHAPTER 10

★

AMERICA

JULY 1, 1975

DESPITE THE URGENCY OF HER MISSION, AMERICA CAN'T HELP SMIL-ing into the wind as she streaks toward Westchester. How long has it been since her last flight? How long since she's felt the cool relief of clean air currents this far above the smog and boil of the city she's remembered to love; felt the sunshine baking her from overhead, its heat coiling pleasantly down her spine; felt anything but the unchanging, glass-cool neutrality of her chamber out of time? Beneath her winds the steel-colored Hudson River, and ahead, the green trees and quieter streets of Westchester County. Around her, the world. It might not be hers, but it is *good* to be in it again.

She's cradling this precious realization when the blast from above hits her square in the back, knocking her out of the sky. America tumbles toward the ground like a shot bird, every molecule in her body crackling with incredible cosmic energy. Seconds later, she plunges into the water below, convulsing as she sinks. She can't move, she can't breathe, she's—

She is six years old, so young, and so cold. Adrift in the ocean, clinging to some piece of a ship's flotsam. Waves lap at her small body, threatening to tug her off. She cannot remember who she is, how she got here, or where her home is. Under a night sky spackled with stars, she is all alone . . .

Until she isn't.

Damp sand clings to her skin as she scrambles out of the surf and onto the beach, toward the hands that reach for her, wait for her, help her, hold her—

When she hits river bottom, the blow jolts America back to the present. Not at Jones Beach. Not a child. Not helpless.

Planting her feet beneath her in the pebbled muck, she kicks off with just enough strength to break the water's choppy, sun-warmed surface, the sensation slowly returning to her body. Now she sees her attacker: a being tall enough to straddle the river with ease, feet broader than the foundations of skyscrapers planted on either bank. He peers down at her through eyes as large as city buses.

A Watcher.

Instinctively, America reaches for her own Watcher's abilities. Size is a matter of the mind, and she is capable of growing as vast as his current form.

Or she ought to be.

But as she aims to rearrange her molecules on a whim, that same energy sizzles again through her bones, her blood, every stitch in the fabric of her, and she slips back beneath the river's surface, momentarily unable to tell up from down. As though she's caught in a storm, and also, she is the storm itself.

It's all she can do to claw her way out of the river. "What . . ." she rasps, then coughs up brackish water onto the grassy, trash-strewn bank. "What did you do?"

"It is what *you* have done," he replies in a cavernous voice that could burst mortal eardrums if he wished it. "I am only the conduit by which your brethren deliver this message: You have abandoned your post, Watcher."

America spits out another mouthful of silt. "So you take my powers?"

"No, not taken. But not yours, unless and until you answer for the dereliction of your duties."

Some kind of Watcher shock collar, then; a weapon unfamiliar to her. It seems that, within the vast library of the Watchers' collective memories and observations, some remain restricted. Not *all* knowledge belongs to all Watchers.

Interesting.

"My duties are to protect the people of any world, and this one's in danger." Her voice is hoarse, her throat carved raw by the river, and though she only needs to think in order to be heard by a Watcher, she won't give him the satisfaction of her silence. "The Whisperer is Doom, and he's here right now. You can see what he's capable of. He's going for the nexus being. He's come close before. We can't let him win. But I'm done asking you all for help. Just stand down, and I can—"

"You cannot," the Watcher thunders. "You believe you have arrived in time to meddle in this world's fate, but you are wrong. What will happen has already happened, has always happened. The foundation of this reality is already slipping. In the future, two incompatible timelines have already begun to crack apart. To break. In time, it will fall."

"There's always a way," she insists. "There's always a choice."

"*We do not choose.*"

Now even America must clap her muddy hands over her ears.

When the ringing in her bones stops, she looks up to find that the Watcher has shrunk to a human's insignificant size and is standing in front of her. His blue cloak ripples in a wind not of this world, his broad face utterly expressionless as he repeats, "We do not choose. We do not intervene. Previous attempts have proved disastrous, engendering the destruction of worlds we only meant to protect."

"Yes, but—"

"We serve the cosmos by witnessing what must not be forgotten." He speaks over her protestations with ease. "That is our only purpose. You, Watcher, have betrayed this purpose, and after you were fairly warned. Thus, the abilities of your station have been suspended until you return with me to face the Council of Watchers and be judged for the abdication of your responsibilities."

Like hell she will.

She grinds her teeth, river grit still trapped between them, tasting this imperiled planet. Then she stands, spine still aching from the blow, lungs still tender. Whatever weapon he's used on her, if what he says is true—that her Watcher's abilities are beyond her access—well, so be it. She wasn't born a Watcher or raised in those unchanging crystalline cages from which they watch impassively as worlds are born and species die.

She was raised in New York City, and she has always known how to fight.

With a cry, she launches herself into flight and speeds toward the Watcher, fists raised. For the first time, there is something like an expression stamped across features that seem carved from the oldest stone in the cosmos.

If she didn't know better, she'd think he was surprised.

CHAPTER 11

—

KITTY

1990

APPROACHING LATVERIA, THE COUNTRY AND ITS CAPITAL CITY reveal themselves as a land displaced in time. Kitty presses her nose to the window—careful not to phase through the glass entirely—to stare down at the forest below. The densely packed pine trees slope down the hillside into a valley, where there sits a village ripped from a book of fairy tales. Clay-tiled rooftops blaze copper in the sunset, with an occasional pale steeple in the mix. Beyond the homes and churches of Doomstadt, all quaint looking from this distance, looms the castle on the cliffside. As the sun flares for the last time and winks out behind them in the west, Castle Doom is a sinister collection of cloud-piercing stone towers darker than the twilit sky behind it.

Kitty whistles, impressed despite herself. Even Emma Frost doesn't have a castle.

In the seat across from her, Betsy fidgets, distracting Kitty from the corner of her vision until she peels her face away from the window to turn on the woman. "Relax," she snaps. Which, admittedly, is not the most relaxing tactic. "You picked the girl who can walk through anything to break into an impenetrable fortress with," she tries again. "We've got it in the bag."

"The last thing we ought to be is complacent. Just when you start to feel invincible, someone's bound to show up to prove otherwise."

"Okay, Captain Buzzkill." Kitty slumps back against her seat, sighing. "If we survive this, we need to work on your joie de vivre, or whatever."

Betsy scowls, releasing her seatbelt to stand. "Oh please, teach me to live as carefree as you, behind a boarded-up apartment door." She extracts a garment bag from the overhead compartment, then strides off down the aisle before Kitty can punch back, leaving her to stew alone.

The lights in the cabin flicker out, and the jet descends, nearly scraping the treetops as it banks, avoiding the valley and circling to approach the cliffside from the north. Lights or no, Castle Doom likely has some kind of radar for aircraft detection.

They'll have to move quickly.

They dip even lower, approaching the promised clearing their pilot must see from the cockpit. Betsy emerges from the rear of the plane just in time to belt herself in, and Kitty clocks her change of clothes with eyes still adjusting to the dark. Having shed her godawful striped suit, she wears a sleek black full-coverage bodysuit with a matching utility belt and combat boots that make Kitty's signature white trench coat, worn black jeans, and thigh-high platform boots look amateurish. (Emma's been hounding her to visit the Hellfire Club's stylist for years, but then again, Emma used to fight in a fur-lined cape and bikini-cut underwear. So her old headmistress shouldn't judge.)

"Did you change in the bathroom?"

"No, the bedroom."

"*What?* This thing has a bedroom, and I had to sleep in my seat?" she hisses.

They touch down with a jolt, coasting across the grass to a stop before they crash into the trees on the far side of the clearing. Together they head for the jet's emergency hatch instead of the boarding door. But Betsy stops in her tracks, flicking the collar of Kitty's white coat. "Lose this, will you? You're as inconspicuous as a polar bear."

She's right, but it still feels wrong, peeling off the coat that

Emma Frost gave her, no matter that she threatened to tear it from Kitty's back just this morning.

"Ready?" Betsy whispers.

Kitty isn't. She nods anyway.

Breaking into a magical dictator's impossibly weaponized castle in the heart of his own sovereign nation: How hard can it be?

THE FIRST UNIT OF LATVERIAN SOLDIERS IS EASY TO DETECT and avoid, such that Betsy's powers aren't needed. As the two of them move through the trees, melting into deeper shadows where the old-growth pine and oak and elm trees shield them from moonlight or starlight, the forest teems with the sounds of nighttime—owls calling, insects chirping, and in the far distance, the unsettling scream of a bobcat. Even so, they hear the crunch of multiple boots across the carpet of dead needles and downed branches. The men make little attempt at stealth. Light glints subtly off their rifle barrels as they step into a patch of the forest floor exposed to the sky overhead. Kitty feels Betsy's hand at her elbow, and she backs them through a thick tree trunk. They both squat down to take cover in a knee-high patch of sedge until the unit passes.

Moments after the men stomp off, they continue on, winding toward the stone turrets and spires that rise above the treetops. Summer though it may be—a brief season in Latveria, according to Betsy—the damp air of the woods is cold and getting colder. Kitty begins to shiver in her tank top, missing the coat she left behind. Of course Betsy couldn't have packed *two* secret-agent bodysuits in her garment bag. Hopefully wherever her psychic path leads them to in the past, it's a timeline with a readily available sweater.

When the Guardian Robot finds them, it's even harder to miss than the Latverian unit—a hulking construct more than twice their height. The dome of its metal skull bashes through the lowest branches. It thunders straight toward them, lifting a massive arm mounted with a force blaster as it announces in its flat-pitched, mechanical voice: "*Intruders! If you resist, you will die.*"

Beside her, Betsy takes an uncertain step backward in the same moment Kitty sprints forward, drawing in one last deep breath before phasing.

A blast passes through her intangible shoulder to slam into a tree trunk behind her, the resulting shower of bark shrapnel just as harmless. Right before they reach a collision point, Kitty kicks off hard from the forest floor to swan-dive through the robot's midsection. Clearing the other side, she tucks and rolls, making sure she's not partially embedded in any branches or bracken before she lets herself breathe.

Yards away, the robot grinds to a stop. Its giant limbs seize in place before it tips over, taking down a sapling as it goes.

Betsy locks eyes with Kitty over its fallen body, one brow ticking up.

"I mess with electrical systems when I phase through them," she explains. If anybody on Doom's payroll was close enough to hear the robot crash, silence after the fact isn't going to help them. "Wasn't that in my file?"

Betsy sniffs. "You could have mentioned it during our briefing."

"A girl likes to keep *some* secrets. Any idea if these things can be fixed remotely or get some kind of fail-safe reboot?"

"Reed's notes didn't specify. We should get going, just in case."

They point themselves toward the distant spires once more, moving swiftly.

Another mile or so, and faint light begins to seep through the trees from directly ahead of them, rather than from above. As they approach the forest's end, Betsy pauses, shuts her eyes, and stretches her psychic powers to seek the presence of human minds between them and their point of entry. Kitty waits, hugging herself against the cold; hopefully a castle built by an evil scientist that's stuffed up to the parapets with cutting-edge weaponry and tech will have central heating, too.

Impatient, she edges forward, clinging to the deep shadows. A break in the trees just ahead reveals her first close-up view of Castle Doom. By cutting through the forest, they now stand opposite a near-vertical cliffside into which its stone foundation was built, rather than facing the bridge and gatehouse. And just a hundred feet down a sparsely vegetated slope between Kitty and the base of the cliff, the slow-flowing River Klyne runs into the arched submersible entrance. It's warded by a portcullis as well as the distant silhouettes of two more Guardian Robots; likely, the handful of human guards are waiting within, but as long as Betsy can block them from noticing their approach and summoning backup, this should be easy as pie.

That's when Kitty feels the tilt of a slip—not from the earth beneath her feet, but inside her.

Not now. Not *now*.

But sure enough, the castle has vanished. Instead, she's in a cavern carved not out of rock, but out of roots or maybe . . . vines? The sinewy green walls are studded with giant mushrooms and patches of alien-looking foliage, and glowing golden orbs hang from the ceiling like fruit.

Also, she's on horseback.

"Make way!" the familiar voice of Emma Frost announces behind her to the dozens of people who pack the strange chamber. "The Red Queen has returned!"

Red Queen? That's one of the titles of the Inner Circle, though Kitty certainly hasn't climbed high enough to hold it. But everybody's looking expectantly up at her.

A shorter man in full uniform—a black-and-yellow suit, with a black eye mask with wings like bat ears on the yellow hood—lifts a glass to her.

"Congrats on losin' yer resurrection cherry, kiddo."

"My wh—"

But before she can ask, the world tips right-side up. Kitty blinks, turning back toward the river just in time to see the massive metal arm whistling out of the dark before it cracks across her face.

CHAPTER 12

—

KITTY

1990

THERE'S BLOOD IN KITTY'S MOUTH.

It's her first thought after successfully clinging to consciousness (and it was touch-and-go for a minute there): the metallic taste as she presses her tongue against her teeth, testing for anything knocked loose—one molar *definitely* feels a little wobbly—and the sticky trail seeping from one nostril, which she instinctively lifts a hand to wipe away.

She wishes she hadn't. If the nose isn't broken, she'll be pleasantly surprised.

Which leads to her second thought: that a giant robot has likely broken her nose.

With a groan, Kitty rolls over from her back to climb to her knees. She spits blood into the dirt and dead pine needles and leaf litter, then staggers to her feet to see Betsy Braddock holding off three hulking Guardian Robots all at once.

It seems that Betsy's kept some secrets, too.

Boots braced in a fighting stance, Betsy clutches something bright in the dark woods, like pink flames forced to assume shape. Her gritted teeth and sweat-slick brow are visible in its cast-off light as she swings a massive, glowing morning star, its staff three times the length of her arms, its head as large as a beach ball—one covered with deadly sharp, six-inch spikes. Kitty can't tell whether she's having trouble holding the weapon, or holding it back. The morning star flares brighter as it crunches into the knee plate of a robot, piercing the armor as effectively as any metal weapon, and Betsy wrenches it free with a cry of her own. She spins in the same motion to lift what's now a round, glowing pink shield, and a shot from the second robot's arm-mounted force blaster glances off its shimmering surface. Then she hurls the shield away from herself like an oversized Frisbee, sending it spinning toward the third bot . . . only for it to flare and transform again in midair into, of all things, a cartoon-style bomb, its lit fuse sparkling pink.

Betsy turns toward Kitty, her face stamped with horror.

Ignoring the pain as her head pounds in time with her footsteps, Kitty sprints straight for her, right through the Guardian Robot with the bashed-in knee joint. She doesn't bother looking back as it topples to the forest floor behind her.

The bomb drops with a thud, rolling through the mulch to stop at the steel feet of the remaining bots. Just as the fuse burns down to its perfectly round shell, she collides with Betsy, toppling them both to the ground as she phases with Betsy tucked into her arms.

For a cartoon bomb, the explosion a mere second later is very real, and very loud. Bits of robot, sliced-through tree branches, and sparkling pink mortar rain down around them, through them, the shrapnel winking out of existence as it falls.

Kitty gapes into Betsy's face, inches from her own. "What the hell was that?" she asks once it's safe to take a breath. "You could've blown yourself up!"

Betsy's own breath heaves out of her, whole body shaking with exertion. "It's an . . . unreliable ability at best. One I don't like making use of. But you strolled right out of the woods into their view, Kitty! What the hell was *that*?"

Rolling away, Kitty sits up. She tests her still-throbbing nose gingerly, then probes at her stinging cheekbone with bloodstained fingertips. It's definitely sore, but it feels intact at least. "I saw— never mind. I'll explain later, and then you can explain . . ." She makes a fist, then mimics the bomb with splayed hands and puffed-out cheeks.

"Fine, let's just get moving. I'm sure we've been heard by someone in the castle. We may need to sacrifice stealth for speed, depending on what we find inside."

Kitty nods. "You keep a lookout for the human guards, I've got the bots. We go quiet where we can, but be ready to book it for the time platform. Agreed?"

"Agreed."

Despite Kitty's aching face, this is almost nice: a mission without either of them jockeying for power or trying to seize the glory for themselves. Maybe she can turn the Hellions around when she gets back to the present . . . if Emma will take her back.

Together they skid quickly down the hillside to the river, following the water where it flows through the lowered portcullis into the tunnel. With no robots left to stop them—they must have come running up the hill when Kitty appeared at the top—it's a moment's work for Kitty to take Betsy's hand and melt with her through the black water glazed with moonlight, then through the portcullis. Inside they find two human guards crumpled to the stone floor of the slender, human-made channel and submersible dock that replaces the weedy riverbank.

"Dead?" Kitty whispers.

"Just asleep. I was working on it when the bots found you."

The entrance to the lowest sublevel of Castle Doom is a vast, high-ceilinged cavern with smaller access points at the far end leading to a honeycomb of stonework tunnels that run deep beneath the foundation. Half are collapsed, according to Betsy's files, built long ago by one of the original ruling families to lead them to safe houses in the village and countryside, should the castle's defenses fail. Now the tunnels have become part of those defenses, their entrances warded by invisible laser grids. To be safe, Kitty phases them through each archway as Betsy leads them forward according to the sketchy floor plans she's memorized. The air down here is damp and clinging, colder than the woods, and Kitty clamps her teeth together to keep them from chattering.

Once, Betsy picks up the thoughts of a pair of approaching

human guards, shielding herself and Kitty from detection. "If Doom knows we're inside, word hasn't made its way this far down just yet," she whispers after the guards pass. "They won't have anticipated an intruder who can pass through walls and weaponry alike. Those guards weren't hunting for us, just patrolling as they would on any shift."

At the top of the steep stone staircase leading up to the fifth-level sub-basement, they find themselves face-to-leg with a Guardian Robot whose presence they more or less expected. Kitty leaps through its legs, planting a boot against the wall of the narrow corridor to kick off, spin around, and cling to the bot's back. She phases with it, sinking them both down through the rough-hewn floor to half embed the bot inside the stone. Let it come back from *that* to give chase.

Half dragging Betsy behind her, she dashes down the corridor, where the castle's original doors have been replaced with steel set in centuries-old stone, likely locked, possibly rigged with traps to prevent access to the cells and laboratories beyond. Not that any of that would stop Kitty, but their destination is still one level above. She spares a glance for the ceiling high overhead, and so misses it when her boot lands on a tile that drops out from beneath her. The floor around them follows suit, crumbling into the sub-basement below with a thunderous crash, and even as she falls, Kitty wonders how this castle can possibly be a functioning home base, peppered as it is with traps as reckless as this one.

This time, Betsy grabs on to her, lifting her free hand to summon that scintillating pink flame into a vine that hangs thick and twisting from the ceiling above. She grabs at it desperately to halt their fall, and Kitty jerks to a stop, shoulder aching in her socket as she hangs from Betsy's grip.

Then the rope hisses, coiling around Betsy's wrist—not a rope. A freaking snake, its glinting spectral teeth as capable of doing damage as that damn bomb.

Betsy jerks her hand away with a shriek, and they plummet for another heartbeat until Kitty phases them both, bringing them to a stop in midair.

Screw this. They're taking the shortcut.

Almost as easily as climbing a ladder, Kitty shifts her atoms between molecules of air to walk them both upward, an insubstantial Betsy clinging somewhat unnecessarily around her waist. Who knows where the ceiling will spit them out, but that's a risk they'll have to take—after that racket, every guard and bot in the castle will soon be on their tail. Time for speed. And if word makes it back to Emma Frost that her White Knight was meddling in Victor von Doom's business, well, she'll find a way to explain herself when they return from the past . . . depending upon the future she and Betsy return *to*.

But instead of a roomful of guards with guns and force blasters trained on them, they surface inside a cavernous laboratory containing an army in pieces. Dozens of steel worktables are strewn with gleaming arms and legs, half-assembled torsos, and skulls comprising wiring instead of bone.

As Kitty pauses to catch her breath, Betsy picks up a lifeless faceplate from the table next to them, holding it aloft so the overhead florescent lighting streams through its empty eye sockets. "A Doombot," she says, almost reverently.

"A what?"

"Victor von Doom's private army of highly advanced robots built to be exact replicas of Doom, physically and mentally. I'd heard of them but never encountered one."

"Not a lot of opportunity in the RCX file room?"

"I *have* been in the field, you know."

Before the Wildways, Kitty guesses, but she knows better than to voice it aloud this time.

Betsy sets down the faceplate. "We should move quickly. The castle must be on full alert, and with security cameras everywhere, they could be watching us right now."

"Yeah. Sure. Any idea which way?"

"Our knowledge of the sub-basements' layout is highly imperfect, but if this is the large chamber mapped in Reed's notes, it may be this way." She points them toward the far corner. "If we go through the walls rather than chance the maze of corridors this floor contains, we might buy ourselves enough time to get there."

They phase into a second chamber containing an elaborate computer console and something that looks like a beefed-up, sinister version of a salon dryer chair. "The necrophone!" Betsy cries, again straddling fear and fascination. "Doom invented this to contact his mother's soul in hell. He—"

"Talk less," Kitty insists, panting, before tugging her through the far wall.

Several chambers and hallway cross sections later, they find their target at last.

She'd expected an impossibly complex web of machinery or some kind of phone-booth-shaped spacecraft by which they'd hurtle through time and the cosmos toward the past, but the time platform is neither. It is, actually, a platform in the center of a small room. An unadorned rectangle of dull-blue light set in the stone floor. Betsy heads straight for the console beside it.

"Can you work that?" Kitty asks, stepping carefully around the platform's perimeter.

"Reed has made use of the platform before, and studied it intensively, lucky for us," she explains. "I should be able to operate it."

"And does your . . . psychic trail have, like, mile markers? Do you even know what year to send us back to?"

"Shh, let me work."

She'd have preferred confident reassurance, but a moment later, the platform comes to life, alighting pool blue with a core of perfectly white light as electricity arcs across its surface; at least Betsy knows where the power button is. The psychic squeezes her eyes shut in concentration, and in their silence, Kitty hears the distant thunder of footsteps from the corridor beyond the chamber door above the hum of the platform.

"Betsy..."

The sound draws closer.

"Betsy!"

Her eyes flutter open. "Get on. I've got it... I think."

"You *have* to stop saying that," Kitty hisses. But she steps into the rectangle of light.

Betsy hurries around the console, joining her just as the energy that snakes painlessly around Kitty's ankles begins to rise, and with it the fine hair on Kitty's arms and at the nape of her neck. Panic follows, swelling inside her chest as the crackling pool of light reaches it.

"This is stupid, this is stupid, this is stupid..." she mutters, grasping thoughtlessly for Betsy's hand to phase them out of here, likely as not breaking the machine—held together by whatever combo of science and magic—in the process. But she forces herself to hold, to stay solid.

As the energy rises to their shoulders, the door to the chamber slams open heedless of any locks or traps, and the flickering light cast by the platform illuminates the figure that crowds the whole doorway.

Titanium armor, head-to-boot.

A green, hooded cloak.

A gleaming faceplate just the same as the one Betsy held in the assembly lab, but with eyes behind the mask's sockets, fury radiating from them even at this distance.

Then the platform's energy field rises past Kitty's vision, surrounding her and Betsy, swallowing them. There is nothing but brilliant white light blotting out the world, and now, she does take Betsy's hand. Not to bolt but, once again, to make herself stay.

When the light recedes, the pool of comingled electricity and magic draining toward the stone floor once more, they stand inside a room unchanged except that the door is closed and the figure is gone.

"Where are we?" Kitty asks, her whole body abuzz, her voice trembling embarrassingly. "I mean, when?"

Betsy sounds just as unsteady when she answers. "It's June 30, 1975."

"Oh. Great. Super normal. And was... was that a Doom-bot?"

"No. I don't believe it was."

THEIR TREK THROUGH THE HALF-COLLAPSED ESCAPE TUNNELS OF Castle Doom's lowest sub-basement and into the village of Doomstadt feels painfully slow, but Betsy insists upon stealth once more. Bad enough that they were discovered in the present (the future?), but with no clear idea how their actions in the past (the present?) might ripple forward, they need to avoid detection at all costs. Best to stick to Betsy's psychic trail and disturb as little as possible, lest they crush a butterfly and return to a timeline where Victor von Doom rules the world, or some equally rotten consequence. The scarcity of guards and bots in the sub-basements seems a piece of luck, though it's almost worryingly easy after their fumbled, frantic break-in. Maybe Vintage-Doom isn't as paranoid as his future self. Or maybe the castle's troops and defenses are trained on some less lucky enemy at the moment.

When the third tunnel they attempt spits them out at last, it's bright midmorning, and Kitty blinks in the sunlight as she takes in the storybook village before them. She'd glimpsed its tiled rooftops briefly from Betsy's jet, its winding lanes and picturesque steeples aglow in the honeyed sunset light, not a smokestack or skyscraper in sight. If she hadn't, she'd worry that Betsy zapped them back to 1775 instead of 1975 (a year Kitty has yet to wrap her brain around, all the same). They stand outside one of Doom's inconspicuous safe houses as noted in Betsy's files, facing down a cobblestone street. To the left, a church, a bank, a boardinghouse. To the right, a stable and blacksmith's shop. Ahead, two mop-haired children in honest-to-God lederhosen chase each other around a large stone fountain in a village square, shouting happily. The clear air smells of... okay, horses, yeah, but also baked goods drifting from the propped-open windows of the boardinghouse, and somehow lavender.

Kitty wraps her arms around herself, conscious of the dirt and crushed rock and cobwebs clinging to her tank top, and her ponytail frizzed from the damp of the tunnels, probably still tangled with pine needles. "Seems kind of quaint for a dictatorship." Her voice sounds overly loud after their long silence as they traveled.

"Latveria *has* been ahead of much of the world in scientific and technological advances since Doom seized power. Its citizens are in overall good health and well fed, and the robust economy breeds almost no crime. But so does Doom's iron-fisted rule. According to RCX files, the borders are tightly secured, as is media exposure. Any whisper of uprising or dissent is crushed before word can spread. That's the purpose of the Doombots. So I suppose it depends whether you factor freedom of speech or movement or choice into your quality of life."

Despite the welcome morning sunlight, Kitty shudders. Sure, she lives her days according to her orders from the Hellfire Club. But at least she's able to come and go as she pleases.

Suddenly, the fresh Latverian air feels suffocating.

"Maybe in your different world, Doom wouldn't be that kind of ruler."

Betsy turns to her with a raised eyebrow, and Kitty's gratified that she looks mussed as well, her previously sleek blond hair sweaty at the temples and her catsuit showing the dust of the tunnels. "Why, Kitty, that almost sounded like optimism!"

"Gross," she grunts back. "If the border's that guarded, what's our plan? Unless your psychic trail conveniently ends in Doomstadt."

"Alas not." Betsy frowns. "We need to go west, and for some distance—that's all I can tell from here, but the trail is clearer already. I suggest we catch a few hours' sleep in Doom's safe house while we can, and round up what food there is, as we've not yet been detected. Then we get ahold of a car and head for the border."

Now it's Kitty's turn to raise an eyebrow. "Not that I care, but won't grand theft auto raise a red flag in a country without a crime rate?"

"It would, but we won't be stealing anything. A kindly citizen of the prosperous autocracy of Latveria is going to offer us their vehicle." She taps one finger against her temple, a devious smile that Kitty hasn't seen on Betsy before—and honestly doesn't hate—blooming across her face.

CHAPTER 13

KITTY

JULY 1, 1975

THEY'VE LEFT LATVERIA BEHIND WHEN TWILIGHT CATCHES UP WITH them, inking out the sunset in the rearview mirror of their stolen car. And it is stolen, whatever else Betsy tells herself; doubtful that the swarm of Latverian guards at the border crossing would've let them off on a telepathic technicality. Luckily, Betsy was able to psychically shield them from perception, while Kitty tightened her grip on the steering wheel and drove them straight through the barbed-wire-topped fences. Phasing the car wasn't quite as effortless as bringing Betsy along, but it was manageable, and they repeated the act at the Serbian border—which, Kitty was obnoxiously informed by Betsy, is *actually* the Socialist Federal Republic of Yugoslavia in 1975. The isolated road carves through the hills, darkening silhouettes of limestone ranges looming ahead of them in the distance.

As the stars come out, Betsy pipes up from the passenger seat. "Want to swap?"

"Huh?"

"I can take over driving if you want. And we ought to think about finding a place to stop for the night. Good Lord, could I use a shower and a stiff drink." She arches her back to stretch inside the cramped cabin of the car, some boxy little European model neither of them had heard of. A tiny silver crucifix dangles from the ignition key, handed over to them by a middle-aged man with a blissful smile and blank eyes.

"You planning to 'ask' for all that, too?" Kitty snorts.

"Why, are you having a crisis of conscience?"

"Hardly. I'm just surprised you're not. We have a Cap in the US, for all the good it does us, and he wouldn't steal so much as a parking space."

"My brother is above reproach, at least in the eyes of the public, as Captain Britain must be. But RCX operates in shadow and holds itself to no such standard. I very much doubt that the Hellfire Club's Inner Circle does, either."

"We don't steal," Kitty corrects her. "We acquire. We execute hostile takeovers. We absorb assets."

"Is that so?"

"Sure. Just ask the Antitrust Division of the Department of Justice, or the Federal Trade Commission, and they'll tell you we're totally aboveboard. No fraud, money laundering, kickbacks, bribery, or anticompetitive conduct here. Then again, most of the committee members and the attorney general are on Emma Frost and Sebastian Shaw's payrolls."

"As are you," Betsy points out.

"Yeah. Yeah, I am." Suddenly exhausted, Kitty scrubs a hand down her face, wincing when her palm comes in contact with her nose. It flares with fresh pain before coiling back to an ever-present dull throb. "Look, we haven't passed a town in half an hour, and I don't see any lights up ahead. We don't know where we are, except that we're driving west, and all the signs are in Serbian. I say we camp for tonight."

Betsy sighs. "I suppose that drink will have to wait."

"Should've let me take that hundred-year-old bottle of Latverian brandy we found at Doom's safe house," Kitty points out, turning the wheel so that they coast slowly onto the grassy bank that runs alongside the roadway.

"And you should've let me do more for that nose before we left. How's it feeling?"

Kitty flips down her mirror to look at her swollen nose. There's a thin strip of masking tape across the bridge—the best they could scrounge up—accompanied by deep-violet bruising beneath her eyes. "Barely broken."

"Hmm. I admit, I didn't think anything could touch you. What happened out there?"

"Don't worry about it," Kitty grumbles. She flips the mirror up again and cranks her seat back to recline within the limited space she's allowed.

"Nothing to be ashamed of, we all get caught out at times."

Maybe she's imagining the teasing edge to Betsy's consolation, but she can't stop herself from bristling. "It happened again. Another slip. I was in . . . a weird cave. I don't know. And there were people there whom I knew, but I don't really know *how*. Then I was back, and the bots were right in front of me. Anyway, you're one to talk about mistakes, when you could've blown us both up," Kitty reminds her. "Speaking of which, isn't it explanation o'clock now that we're not on the run?"

All falls quiet inside the car.

From her laid-back position, Kitty watches the psychic stare down at hands fidgeting in her lap, though her face is inscrutable from this angle and in the dark.

Finally, Betsy begins. "I know that you know about me and the—the Wildways, already. You mentioned it earlier."

"Emma told me some," she confesses. "But not much."

"Well. It isn't a place I like to think on. It's a . . . sort of gap between dimensions that gives Mojo and an accomplice called Spiral access to Earth. They took me to the Mojoverse, used me in the Wildways, turned me into a lure to gain worshippers on Earth. The chaos, the unpredictability . . . it gets inside you after a time. Inside your mind. Before I was taken, I had some limited ability to wield my telekinetic powers as a physical weapon. They're greater now than they were, but just as reality inside the Wildways was unstable, so are they. When I try to wield them outside my own mind, I can barely control them, especially under pressure, which makes them impossible to trust. So I can hardly expect my brother or RCX to trust me. And I've seen what they think of me, quite literally. They believe that place is still inside me, or that . . . that part of me never came back."

Both of them sit for a long, silent moment, Kitty staring up at the ceiling of the cabin as she considers this. She's known for ages that she can't rely upon other people in this world. Not the family who sent her away at the first convenience, nor the teammates who'd scrabble over her fallen body to seize knighthood for themselves. And apparently, not the mentor who sold her on a life in the open but prefers that she stay angry and secretive and fearful; more fuel for Kitty to burn before she someday burns out. And yet Kitty trusts herself to keep her safe. She has her powers and can depend upon them even when she can't depend on anybody or anything else. As much as she's wished that those powers never manifested over the past decade, often as not, they're all she has.

Betsy Braddock doesn't even have that.

"Isn't it weird," Kitty starts, "that there's a past-you in 1975, who none of that's happened to yet?"

Betsy ticks her head toward the driver's seat, stunning profile silhouetted in the moonlight streaming through the windshield, and Kitty clocks the quiver in her chin before she lets out a startling, humorless laugh. "It's true. Somewhere in New York City is a teenage-me, snubbing her parents' fortune to chase her dreams of modeling. Her powers haven't even manifested. Honestly, I hadn't thought of that until just now."

Neither had Kitty.

How hasn't she stopped to consider that in Deerfield, Illinois, there exists an eight-year-old Kitty Pryde? A Kitty who loves riding her bike to the public pool, still plays with dolls, and wants nothing so much as a pair of bell-bottom jeans like her five-years-older cousin. A Kitty whose life is a closed loop between elementary school, synagogue, ballet, and the local park. A Kitty whose mutant powers have yet to manifest, and so she still believes herself to be normal, imagining a future that she will never have. Kitty has spent the past decade grieving those dreams, though she'd never admit it to anyone, not even Emma Frost.

There's a younger her halfway around the world right now who's destined to do the same.

"Betsy."

"Hmm?"

"Do you ever wish..." But before she can confess the desire she's never shared with anyone (and has done her very best to forget since joining the Hellions), the car rocks on its wheels as though caught by a sudden, sustained gust of wind. Despite the night's calm, the crucifix keychain rattles madly against the steering column.

Betsy plants her palms on the rattling dashboard, leaning forward to stare up through the windshield. "What the devil is that?"

Bracing her boots on the seat, Kitty stands, phasing her upper body through the car's roof just in time to see the sky descending upon them, a starless expanse crushing down.

No, not the sky.

A plane, she realizes when her eyes adjust to catch the shape of it, or a jet, all black, bigger and much meaner looking than the Braddocks'. Clearly built for stealth, it moves more silently than she'd have thought an aircraft was capable of, just a high-pitched whine emanating from its engines and a hiss from the thrusters, rather than the expected roar. It swoops from directly over them to hover above the grass ahead, so close to them that she would've caught a face full of exhaust if she were solid.

Kitty phases back into the driver's seat. "Is it Latverian?" It must be, because nobody else around here would have that kind of tech. Their getaway from the castle *felt* clean, and there've been no signs of pursuit since. Still, maybe Doom's been biding his time? She turns on the ignition, preparing to floor it.

But Betsy puts a hand over hers on the steering wheel. "We can't outrun that thing, and you can't hold your breath forever. Besides, if they'd wanted to kill us, we'd have been a crater in the Serbian countryside before we knew they were there."

"We still might be," Kitty mutters, but she holds for the moment.

They watch through the windshield as the jet lowers its gear. It descends in a perfectly vertical landing, coming to rest not a dozen yards from them. The long, sharp, nearly flat nose points away so that they can see it in the car's headlights when the hatch opens on its belly and the staircase drops down.

"We can drive right through them," Kitty insists. "By the time they get back in the air, we'll be far enough ahead that we can ditch the car and make a run for it in the woods."

Again, Betsy stops her, tightening her grip on Kitty's wrist as her wide blue eyes drift out of focus. "Wait. There's something . . . Just wait."

A pair of boots appears on the staircase, and seconds later, their owner is revealed to be a leanly muscled woman, unusually tall, with dark skin and long, moon-white hair held back from her beautiful face by a black tiara. She wears a long black cape with gold trim, billowing around a black two-piece bodysuit barely connected by a ring at her midriff, paired with gold bangles at her wrists and thigh-high black boots.

And Kitty *knows* her.

Not from the world, once again, but from a slip. Her first ever slip. The woman is far too striking to forget, and would be even if the first time Kitty found herself inside a strange version of her life wasn't engraved in her memory.

Next down the staircase comes a thickly built man in a tiger-striped suit of yellow and black and blue, his arms bare and brawny. He's considerably shorter than his companion, though his distinctive, winged black eye mask—the same one she saw across that cavern only hours ago—makes up the difference, rising half a foot above his yellow hood.

"I don't think those are Doombots," Kitty whispers.

Out in the open between the jet and the car, the pair stop in their headlight beams, exposed, seemingly waiting on their move. Whether as a means of disarming or intimidating them, Kitty can't tell. If Emma could extend her psychic tendrils across the decades, she would remind her (and none too gently) that Kitty shouldn't stick around to find out. In fact, now would be the perfect time to stomp on the gas, swerve for the road, and drive as far and fast as they can before the jet ascends and they have to flee on foot. Crouched in the dark beneath the trees with a psychic to shield them from view, they stand a more-than-decent chance of disappearing—a particular skill of Kitty's.

Then Betsy says dreamily, "They're here for us," and gets out of the car.

Which is just . . . fantastic.

She *could* still run. Take the car, and halve her pursuers at the very least. If Betsy is so desperate to be caught, dragged back to Castle Doom, and thrown in a cell, then who could blame Kitty for leaving her to her fate? Nobody would even know.

No one but Kitty.

Damn it.

Cursing under her breath, she phases out the passenger side of the car after Betsy. "What are you doing?" Kitty hisses, clutching her by the arm to hold her back before she can take another step.

They're here for us, Betsy repeats without speaking, her words like the flutter of butterfly wings inside Kitty's mind, brushing against her thoughts. **This is where the trail is leading!**

Kitty appraises the mismatched pair. **Is this them? Whoever's missing from the future?**

The trail doesn't stop here. It moves beyond them, just as it did with you, and I still can't see its end. Whoever I'm meant to find, we haven't reached them yet. But . . . I've got a sort of déjà vu. Can you feel it? They're trail markers, like you.

More than Betsy knows. So far as Kitty can remember, this is the first time she's seen in real life somebody she'd only ever glimpsed during a slip, rather than the other way around. Now that she stops to think about it, that has to mean something, right? It's one thing for a mind to mix real and made-up people in a dream, and another to see dream people in real life.

If I'm wrong, Betsy continues when she doesn't answer back, **then at least you'll get to tell yourself that you were right.**

It's a poor consolation, but it's something.

Reluctantly, Kitty lets go.

When Betsy takes the next tentative step forward, it seems to encourage the woman in black and gold, now only a dozen feet opposite them. "Please, do not be afraid," she says across the distance at last, her deep voice pleasantly accented. "We apologize for our alarming entrance. We've been tracking your progress—rather, our friends have—but we dared not draw attention to you within Doom's borders, nor to ourselves. We are here to help, I assure you."

"Who's 'we'?" Kitty demands.

The woman's shorter and burlier companion grins, his canines flashing in the twin headlight beams. "You ever heard of the X-Men, kid?"

CHAPTER 14

AMERICA

JULY 1, 1975

AS AMERICA MEETS THE WATCHER IN MIDAIR, HER PUNCH DOESN'T land—of course, it was never going to.

Momentarily surprised though he may have been, the Watcher's powers are almost total. As an omnipotent being, he can see her every thought, predict her every move in nearly the same instant it's decided. He can manipulate space and time and energy and matter. Powers America *should* be able to wield. Without them, all she can do is move in the micro-second between her thoughts and his reactions.

It isn't enough.

As the Watcher teleports from her path as easily as blinking, she pivots to smash a portal into thin air, diving through to emerge down the bank beside his next location. But by the time she reaches him, he's moved again, up into the sky. Before she can change paths, America is shunted back to Earth by a wave of energy extending from the Watcher's vast hand, this time falling to land half in and half out of the river.

"Let this be done," the Watcher declares in a voice like stone. "You will return with me now and face trial by those who honor the duties you have spurned."

America climbs painfully to her feet, her boots still half submerged in the muck. "Okay," she grits out, tasting blood. She raises her dripping palms. "Okay."

"Do you concede, Watcher?"

"Sure. But I just wanna say . . ." America throws herself backward into the river in the same instant the idea occurs. Twisting in the water to dive toward the bottom, she pulls back a fist and punches downward with enough force that, even slowed, the shock wave hits, rocks and sand billowing upward. A star-shaped hole in the fabric of reality appears directly beneath her, impossibly bright in the depths below the sun's reach.

Kicking downward into the light, America Chavez makes the only choice that she can in the moment: She runs.

Portal after portal, world after world.

First, an Earth packed in ice, the sky above blocked from view by the pitch-black ash cloud of a nuclear winter. Next, an Earth where magma oozes upward through seams in the steaming pavement, and all around her, buildings and trees alike burn perpetually. There is an Earth where New York City nearly mirrors her own, except that when the shadow of Spider-Man crosses hers, she looks up to catch a quick glimpse, and finds him . . . different. Shorter, rounder. Unless her eyes are mistaken, his mask is distended by long ears that stream in the wind behind him. And is that a snout?

She sprints onward.

Always, she senses the Watcher at her heels. She can't slip between universes fast enough to outpace him, not while she's his sole focus. Maybe she can find a world to hide in? But America only knows of one man who's managed to shield himself from the Watchers, and she has no idea how Doom is accomplishing it.

Coming to land on a Cretaceous jungle Earth, America dodges a dinosaur's footfall. She plows through ferns taller than she is to duck behind a massive tree trunk. She's been moving scared, moving blind, with no goal except to stay one step ahead. But eventually, she'll have to stop running. What she needs is a plan. If she can't shake the Watcher, and she cannot hide from him, maybe there's some other way to redirect an omnipotent being beyond the laws of space and time.

Reaching for her Watcher's memories, she realizes that these, at least, still belong to her. Whatever cosmic weapon was wielded against her, it didn't strip her of *everything*. It seems there's a difference between her physical Watcher's abilities and her knowledge. Besides, she still has her own powers—the powers that she may not have been born with, but that came from her mothers' love for her nonetheless. They always take her where and when she needs to go.

Just as her relentless pursuer appears yards away to loom above the ancient trees, she closes her eyes and punches through to the next world, holding one image in mind: a being scraped from eons' worth of Watcher's observations. She throws herself through the portal to land on a cratered patch of earth. All around her there is rubble, with only a few towering, arrow-shaped buildings left standing, like the last leaves clinging to a dying tree. Though she sought out this world from among the unlimited offerings of the Multiverse, her bones still turn to water as she looks up into a strange sky crackling with beams of energy.

Beyond the violent tangle of light is a face, vast and dangerous as a moon crashing toward its planet. It's half shielded by a purple helm, two massive prongs seeming to pierce space and the stars above. Eyes as big as cities glow like fire, and the jaws open wide as those energy beams sweep the surface of the planet, drawing out its life force to feed an insatiable entity. The only one of his kind in the cosmos.

Galactus, Devourer of Worlds.

All at once, the Watcher stands beside her, shrunk down to her height. Too busy watching America to predict her ultimate destination—because, while a Watcher can observe almost any world, he can't see every world at once—he's unknowingly joined her on a doomed planet.

He peers up into the ruined sky. "What have you done?"

CHAPTER 15

DOOM

JULY 2, 1975

THE DETAINING CELLS OF SUB-BASEMENT 3 ARE NIGH IMPOSSIBLE TO escape, by Doom's own design (technically, by this other Doom's). A combination of magic, machinery, and localized force fields dampens the abilities of any superpowered prisoners within while rendering any tech upon their personages useless. Doom could shoot a force bolt from his gauntlet—the one that isn't ruined—or engage his ionic blade, and neither would so much as dent the cell bars before he was flattened by the concussive rebound. So there's little for him to do but wait for Other-Doom's curiosity to drive him down to speak with the suspected imposter he ordered imprisoned without any meeting between them.

Inevitably, it will.

He passes the time by counting and re-counting the gray stones of his cell walls and floor, when he isn't memorizing the timing of the guards who march past at precise, programmed intervals. That's in addition to those standing permanent sentry at the end of the corridor. Robots, all. No Latverian human soldiers have been trusted to monitor him thus far, which is the correct choice. Because even without access to his equipment, he has no doubt of his ability to turn them toward his cause. Neither does Other-Doom, it seems.

This far underground and with the only light provided by constantly burning torches in the corridor, it's impossible to tell night from day. But by his best accounting, and his growing hunger and thirst (annoyances, as any reminder of his mortality would be), more than a full day has passed since his imprisonment in this place where his enemies have been left to wither and decay.

At last, though, Other-Doom comes. He studies him silently from outside the cell's bars—far less effective than the retrofitted dampeners—for a long moment. Then: "Let us speak of facts, you and I."

Doom waits.

"Upon your capture, you made the claim to my gatehouse guards that *you* were Victor von Doom. Do you maintain this claim?"

"I do."

"An impossibility," Other-Doom says, dismissing him. "Likely, you're a rogue Doombot that my enemies have gotten hold of. Perhaps your dampener has been disabled, allowing you to maintain delusions of your own personhood even while in your master's presence."

Slowly, Doom approaches the bars, allowing the weak light from the corridor to glint off his ruined mask and reveal the puckered skin beneath. "Have you considered other explanations?"

Other-Doom pauses for only a moment before pondering aloud, "The second most likely scenario is some kind of magical conjuration, or an ill-intended clone. I once met a mutant who specialized in cloning. Either way, my best means of determining the truth is your immediate disassembly. Whether circuitry or spell work or stolen DNA is the culprit, I'll soon find out in my laboratory."

"That's one option. Consider, though, that I might be of more use to you intact."

"Doom needs no one."

"I didn't say *need*. I said *use*."

Other-Doom scoffs.

He grinds his molars together but resists the urge to leap for the bars, and for Other-Doom's throat. Because there is much that *he* needs from his other self. His laboratories, his resources, and—he's willing to admit this to himself—the sounding board of a fellow genius unmatched in his own reality. "Allow me to demonstrate my utility," he suggests. "As I said at the gates, I come with information and opportunity. You need only listen before you judge."

"Convince me, then."

"You're not yet aware of the Multiverse—isn't that so?"

Other-Doom wraps titanium-gloved hands around the bars of his cell. "I am master of space and time, of the sciences and the dark arts alike. There is none with an intellect to match mine, nor the will to wield it. There is nothing in this world that escapes me." His counterpart is close enough now that Doom can read his eyes in the torchlight. No one else would recognize the flicker of doubt in their cold depths.

But of course, Doom can. "In this world, no. But across infinite worlds?"

"You speak of realms."

"I don't, point of fact. I speak of a collection of alternate universes that number into infinity, diverging from one another in ways both minor and significant."

Other-Doom rears back. "If such a thing was true, then I would know."

"But you do, because I *am* you, only born to another universe. And another time, but I suppose that's less imperative at the moment."

"Other worlds," his counterpart murmurs. "Other Dooms. An incredible notion, but unprovable from where you stand. If you truly wish to demonstrate your use to me, I have more immediate questions. Yesterday in the early hours of the morning, castle sensors caught movement on the levels belowground. The fifth sub-basement and the tunnels. No traps were triggered, and my considerable forces have scoured the castle and grounds without discovering the cause. There's been no disturbance in Doomstadt or the surrounding villages that we can find. But whoever the trespasser was, their presence overlapped with your arrival. Which leads one to the inevitable conclusion that either your purpose was to provide a diversion, or your arrival *was* their purpose."

Doom strains to disguise his impatience. Of course Other-Doom would be forced to draw the conclusion that two such incidents occurring near simultaneously must be connected. Doom himself is none too comfortable with it, coincidence or no. But there's nothing he can do about it from inside this cage, and the unfortunate synchronicity serves as yet another obstacle to getting *out* of the cage.

Well, he expected resistance, didn't he? Presented himself at the castle gates knowing that it would lead him directly to the dungeon—that's what he would have done with himself—instead of scheming or forcing his way inside. He wanted this conversation with his younger counterpart, and so now he must move cautiously. Slowly, steadily, and with his hands tucked behind his back, he approaches the bars. "If your enemies managed to make their way inside, then they're enemies of mine as well. I would help you discover their identity, if you'll let me prove my own. Let me tell you about Victor von Doom, and together we—"

"If you have no knowledge of the intruders, then you are a waste of my time." Other-Doom turns, his cloak whipping behind him as he marches off down the corridor.

When next a robot guard passes by, it brings a flask of water with it. Doom waits until it passes out of sight again to ease his thirst, then prepares to bide his time and conserve his energy until opportunity presents itself again.

It will, if he knows himself at all.

CHAPTER 16

KITTY

JULY 2, 1975

AS TENSE AS THE FLIGHT FROM NEW YORK TO LATVERIA WAS, THE flight back to New York on the X-Men's jet—the Blackbird, as the white-haired woman who introduced herself as Storm referred to it—promises to be worse. Knowing their new companions' fate feels like flying with two ghosts.

But at least the Blackbird is much, much faster.

With Storm in the pilot's chair, her shorter teammate, code-named Wolverine, straps in alongside them in the passenger cabin to continue the explanation they cut short in favor of putting some distance between themselves and Latveria.

"Chuck don't usually get pinged by mutants old enough to order a beer, unless he's lookin' for someone specific."

"Professor Charles Xavier," Storm calls back from the cockpit, words peppered with disapproval.

"Sure. Anyway, when kids don't know what to do or where to go, Chuck gives 'em a place."

"A place to what?" Kitty asks.

"To learn, I guess. Ain't that what school is for?"

She weighs this against her memories of the Massachusetts Academy, where she can't recall classes or grades being of concern. Sure, there were non-mutant students to pad the Hellfire Club's coffers with their tuition and provide a screen of legitimacy, none of whom had a clue about the school's true purpose. But Kitty wasn't exactly in danger of expulsion if she failed home economics because she was infiltrating a government building during the final. The Hellions were in their own classes, supposedly the "Honors Track," and only occasionally mingled with fellow students to keep up appearances. They mostly spent their days training and fighting, while her parents got a glowing report card each semester. There *were* some courses Emma prioritized as relevant, at least for some of them. Certain languages, civics, poli sci, and chemistry, all the better to engage in espionage and homebrew explosives with. Otherwise, who cared if she never learned to bake an apple pie or do long division? Kitty mastered the most necessary skill for life after graduation: survival.

"Anyway, when you two both lit up Cerebro from inside Castle Doom at the same time, Chuck couldn't figure out why, but he said there was a good chance you were in big trouble. So here we are."

"Cerebro?" Betsy asks.

"Somethin' Chuck built. He's a telepath, you know, real powerful, but Cerebro gives him a boost. Helps him find mutants all over the world."

A mutant-detecting machine; Emma would've killed to get her hands on something like that, Kitty bets. **Another telepath,** she thinks deliberately in Betsy's direction. It's getting easier to communicate this way, though she still has to fight the instinct to phase out of psychic reach.

I can handle a telepath. At least, I should be able to shield our thoughts, as I shielded our presence from human detection, if this professor doesn't push too hard. And I'd suggest we reveal as little as possible for now. We stay on the path and leave the past undisturbed, insofar as we're able, until we've a better grasp of the situation. Agreed?

So, no telling the X-Men that they're all going to die?

This thought catches Betsy by surprise, her beautiful, dust-streaked face blanching. Finally, Kitty knows something that Betsy with all her files does not. Though it's hard to feel even a little bit smug about it, given the circumstances.

By what means? And when?

She shrugs as subtly as possible. **Emma didn't go into detail. But if it's soon, I hope we're not standing too close.**

Sounding as rattled by the thought as Kitty feels, Betsy says too loudly, "We appreciate you coming to our aid. Goodness knows, we've nowhere else to go."

This, at least, is perfectly honest.

―

DAWN CHASES THEM ACROSS THE FINAL MILES OF THEIR JOURNEY, the Atlantic glowing bright and vast beneath them under a clementine sky. Soon the coast unfolds in front of them, and the skyline of New York City as it was in 1975. Then, at last, their destination: sprawling lawns tinged golden under the morning light. Centuries-old oaks. A glittering pond, and in the center of it all, a stately mansion not so unlike the headquarters of the Hellfire Club, but rooted in the countryside instead of Manhattan's Upper East Side. The jet sinks vertically from above, and as it does, Kitty glimpses the manor—a stone-and-brick façade, twined with climbing ivy—before a paved courtyard beneath them yawns open, split neatly down the middle. She can just see it with her forehead squashed to the window, before the Blackbird lowers into an underground hangar bay. It closes after them before the jet is powered down, shutting out the daylight above.

In the seat behind hers, Wolverine snorts awake.

If only Kitty could've slept. Instead, she spent hours staring out the window at the pitch dark, and then the dawn, wondering what the X-Men could possibly mean to her . . . or might have meant, in Betsy's different world. Now she gets to meet some powerful mind reader while her nerves are as frazzled as her half-collapsed ponytail.

Storm unharnesses herself from the pilot's chair after releasing the exit hatch. "You must be exhausted and hungry. I will introduce you to the professor, as I'm sure you must have questions, and then we'll see you both settled in."

Once they leave the hangar bay, they find themselves at the mouth of a long, steel-paneled corridor, its walls lined with riveted steel doors, all shut. Not so different from the Massachusetts Academy, then, with its honeycomb of secret facilities and detaining cells beneath the campus's immaculate lawns. Kitty takes a breath, and a moment to remind herself that nothing down here—nothing *anywhere*—can hold her against her will.

"How many students do you have here?" Betsy asks.

"At the moment, none. Only former pupils of Professor Xavier's who've grown up together and remained, like Cyclops and Marvel Girl. Then there are those of us who joined the cause later on. Colossus, Banshee, Nightcrawler, Th—I mean . . ."

She frowns. "Who?"

"Just myself. I believe the rest of the team are off grounds at the moment, but you'll meet them soon."

Kitty doesn't press. She can guess the reason behind the stumble: Teams lose members all the time, don't they? The Hellions have. Nothing to do about it but forget and move on, or stew in the inevitability of it happening to you someday, whether at the hands of an anti-mutant mob, or those of another mutant. Either option is just as likely.

Up an elevator they go, warded by a keypad lock rather than a laser grid. At last, Wolverine tugs back his cowl to reveal an abundance of gravity-defying black hair, accompanied by the thick muttonchops growing down to his bristled chin. When the doors open on the ground floor, he doesn't follow. "I'm beat. Besides, you got a mansion full of babysitters to look after you," he grunts.

Once the doors slide shut again, she turns to appraise their surroundings. They stand just beyond the entryway to a high-ceilinged atrium, where morning light streams through frosted-glass panels to either side of a pair of front doors (good to know the exits, even if she doesn't need them). To the left, a wide, burgundy-carpeted staircase spirals up toward the second floor, which can be glimpsed through the rails of a grand balcony. Storm steers them down a long hall to the right into an antechamber, where Kitty wouldn't describe the décor as timeless, exactly—never mind the crystal chandelier overhead and the polished dark-wood paneling, the pea-green velvet settees look like fancier versions of the old sofa in Grandma Pryde's sitting room.

Storm knocks on the next door, waits, and—though Kitty hears no response—opens it to usher them through. She pauses on the threshold to look back at Betsy, whose blue eyes hold the same unfocused glaze they did in Serbia, when the Blackbird first landed. Still following her psychic trail, Kitty guesses. Even so, she answers Kitty's raised eyebrow with a nod, and then Kitty senses the shimmering pink wings of her psionic abilities, like a cocoon around her own thoughts. She's become so used to Emma's presence in her mind over the past decade that her particular telepathic flavor is instantly recognizable, like icy fingers on the back of her neck. Betsy's presence is becoming familiar, too, she realizes. How she feels about that, she's not sure.

The office is formal, its walls nearly taken up by shelves packed from the polished-wood floor to the high, wood-paneled ceiling with clothbound books. By nature of the décor, it's darker in here than the atrium despite the tall windows and open velvet drapes bracketing a man who sits at a solid mahogany desk.

And Kitty knows him, too.

He was there on her front lawn in the first slip, along with Storm. She'd grown up thinking it wasn't real, but here he is, as real as she is: the man who must be Charles Xavier. Despite a perfectly bald head, he appears no older than his forties, with a sharply carved face and dark, steeply angled brows. His smile is inviting, though, and his lined eyes seem curious rather than suspicious. None of which lessens Kitty's suspicion, which she reaches for as habitually as her white coat. If only she had the coat now, she'd feel safer, no matter that it's only cloth. The professor, meanwhile, wears a green herringbone suit jacket and orange turtleneck; she'd wondered whether all the mutants-in-residence stayed in costume constantly, but apparently not.

He moves out from behind the heavy desk to greet them in the expected wheelchair, with a blanket tucked neatly over his lap and down to the tips of his shoes. "Katherine Pryde," he declares in a deep—and deeply moneyed—voice. "Elizabeth Braddock. Welcome to you both."

With Betsy silent and concentrating beside her, Kitty begrudgingly takes the lead. "Uh . . . yeah. Thanks for the ride. Nice . . ." She scans the office, searching for some compliment to offer. "Nice books," she finishes weakly.

Charles's eyes crinkle at the corners. "Most, I can recommend. Some were inherited along with the estate."

"By you, right?"

"Indeed. An old family estate, converted into a home for a different kind of family."

"Isn't this a school?"

"Xavier's School for Gifted Youngsters, yes. I consider myself a teacher foremost, and began this place with the mission of teaching young people. Young *mutants*."

Kitty can't help flinching at that word out of a stranger's mouth after all these years. "I think we've aged out of the education system, don't you?"

"It is never too late to learn about ourselves, our powers, and our responsibility in this world. However, this estate is also home to friends and former students, and a safe place for those afield as they come and go. It can be one for you as well, if you're in need of it."

Does he mean a safe place? Or a home?

"Just like that, you'll let random mutants into your . . . estate?"

"That depends." The professor moves closer while throwing a reassuring nod to Storm, who slips back into the antechamber, shutting the door behind her. "I suspect that whatever led you into Doom's territory is quite a story. When Cerebro detected you in the castle, we dared not make direct contact in Doomstadt; violation of foreign laws aside, the possibility existed that you were there of your own free will. But as we tracked you across the border, it seemed less likely. Would you like to tell me what happened?"

Kitty licks her dry lips, still tasting the dust of the tunnels under Castle Doom. How to lie to a psychic? And how much truth should she tell? "We wanted . . . we were looking for somebody."

"Someone in trouble?"

"It seemed like it," she says carefully. "We followed a trail to Latveria, but they weren't there."

"Perhaps I can help. As Storm and Wolverine may have mentioned, I've a knack for finding people. Mutants, particularly." He touches two fingers to his temple in a kind of question.

Before Kitty can answer, Betsy speaks up at last. "Our search led us to Latveria initially, but now I believe that it's led us to you."

He frowns. "You believe your missing friend may be among us?"

"Not yet, but they may be headed in this direction. We'd like to be here if they make their way. If you'll have us."

"So long as you can promise that you'll do no harm to any who live here, and I can be assured of your honesty."

"We're no danger to you or to your students," Betsy promises. "And we have no reason to believe our friend is, either."

However much she must let her psychic guard down, it seems enough to convince the professor, who appears reassured. "Very well. Storm will show you upstairs to the guest quarters, and provide you with any amenities you might need. Or perhaps you'd rather head to the kitchen for breakfast?"

Though Kitty's stomach grumbles, emptied of their last meal scavenged from the safe house's stock of pickled and preserved food, Betsy is quick to say, "Sleep would be best. We're dead on our feet. It's been quite a long couple of days."

Twelve years long, point of fact.

"Of course. We'll speak again when you're rested. And you'll meet the rest of my X-Men."

Kitty scrapes together a thin smile, even as Emma's scathing words replay in her mind: *He and his beloved students died some time ago, before your mutation ever manifested. And nobody remembers them. No one considers all his good deeds before spitting on mutants. We can't rely upon goodwill to protect us. It certainly didn't protect Charles Xavier or the X-Men.*

As promised, a waiting Storm escorts them back to the entry staircase and up to the second floor, where the hallway splits left and right. She leads them to the right, and to a pair of closed bedroom doors beside each other at the end of the corridor, explaining, "This wing of the living quarters is largely unoccupied at the moment, as it would have been the student dormitories. We've had some friends depart of late. There are changes of clothing in the drawers, which ought to fit you—the advantages of predicting your arrival, or hoping for it, in any case. You will also find such toiletries as you might need in all the common bathrooms." Her crystal eyes linger on Kitty's nose, reigniting the pain she'd mostly pushed out of mind. "And we can reset that in the medical bay, once the swelling goes down."

"I believe I can handle it," Betsy says.

Kitty fails to suppress a shudder as she imagines an oversized cartoon mallet made of sparkling pink energy, swinging straight toward herself.

"Very well. If there's anything else—"

"No, this is plenty," the telepath answers for them both. "Thank you, Storm."

"You may call me Ororo outside of combat. The others' true names, I will leave for them to share, but all else under our roof is available to you. Please, make yourselves at home. Should you need anything, the team sleeps in the west wing, and my room is just above you in the attic. Please don't hesitate to find us, day or night . . . though I can't in good conscience recommend waking Wolverine," she advises with a wry little smile.

Then she leaves them to themselves.

Inside Kitty's spacious assigned room, she finds a vanity table, something that looks like an oversized computer console—or maybe just a very complicated television—and a large bed with a bookshelf built into the headboard, and drawers beneath. Skeptically, she toes one open by the bar pull to see a neatly folded striped pajama set, the button-up collared kind that she's never owned nor wanted, alongside an assortment of clothing. Raising her boot again, she kicks a pair of jeans off the top of the pile and onto the burgundy shag carpet.

Bell-bottoms, of course, and in her size.

The next drawer holds a confusing stack of black-and-yellow spandex, which she has to pull out and hold aloft to make sense of: a full-body black leotard with yellow boot cuffs, yellow briefs, and a triangular yellow chest piece that flares into capped and pointed shoulders, not unlike Wolverine's. Also in the drawer, a pair of yellow boots, yellow wide-cuffed gloves, a thick red belt with a fist-sized black-and-yellow X buckle, and a black cowl that would in no world fit over her curls.

Oh, to hell with this.

Tossing the suit across the room, she turns and marches through the wall into Betsy's guest room next door just in time to see the woman slipping on her own pair of pin-striped pajamas.

"Kitty!" she shouts, wrapping the unbuttoned top across her stomach to cover herself. "You don't knock?"

"You didn't see me coming? These people did. They have *uniforms* for us, Betsy! Ugly ones, too." Charging toward the bed, she drags open the right-hand drawer to yank out an identical leotard. She holds the costume up by its strange, stiff shoulders to thrust the horror of it in Betsy's face. "It has *hot pants*."

Betsy frowns, batting the costume aside with her free hand. "Storm . . . Ororo said that our arrival was anticipated."

"Well, they anticipated my pant size. A little invasive, don't you think?"

As she spins away to button her top, Betsy says over her shoulder, "It seems they're used to mutants showing up with next to nothing to their name, and I'll remind you that we qualify."

"This isn't socks and a spare toothbrush. This is an X-Men uniform, and I'll remind *you*, we're not X-Men. Not in this life."

Betsy quirks an eyebrow. "Have you got something to share with the class, Kitty?"

She claps her hands over her ears, as though that would help. "If you're poking around in my brain—"

"I'm not," she soothes. "I wouldn't, no more than Charles would without cause."

"But he *has* cause. These people don't even know us! We could be anyone. We could be agents of the Hellfire Club. We *are* agents of the Hellfire Club, kind of, and he just gave us their guest bedrooms. No wonder he's gonna get them all killed."

"We don't know what will happen to them, or why," Betsy protests, "and anyway, we won't be around long enough to find out. We're here because this is where the trail led, and we've just got to hold out while changing as little as possible until we reach the end of it."

"So we lie until then? Put on our hot pants and pretend we're happy to be included?"

"Why, Kitty, have you suddenly come down with a conscience?" Betsy snaps.

She winces. "I . . . no, I just . . . I want to know the plan."

With a deep breath, Betsy sinks down onto her bed. "Of course. I didn't mean to . . . I'm just exhausted." She plunges both hands through her blond hair, still streaked with dust. "The plan is to reveal nothing for now. But maybe when all is said and done, we can put things right for the X-Men as well as us. In a different world, perhaps they survive whatever's coming for them."

"You think so?"

"Why not? Perhaps this school becomes a refuge for countless future children in need of one. It's a noble idea, anyhow. Goodness knows, I could've used a place like this when my powers were first manifesting."

Kitty eases down onto the bed beside her. "The thing is, I think they *were* there the day my powers manifested." She describes it then: How one moment she was in her bedroom, putting her fist through a wall without impact or pain. And the next, she stood outside her house with a crew of strangers, and her parents were sprinting across the yard, screaming. "What do you think that means?"

Betsy shakes her head. "I'm not sure yet, beyond that we both had a rough introduction to mutanthood."

"Didn't it help to be unfathomably rich? Maybe not Julia Bettencourt rich, but—"

"Who is Julia Bettencourt?"

"The other richest person I know, unfortunately." Kitty scowls, remembering. "Her family actually owns an island. A little one, but still."

Betsy squirms uncomfortably on the mattress.

"Shut up!" she gasps. "Don't tell me you own an island?"

"My *family* does. But I was in New York when I got my powers. I spent weeks alone in my ratty apartment, crawling toward the door to pay for takeout I couldn't afford, then locking it again until the next day, all the while wondering whether I was losing my mind. I didn't know any other mutants until S.T.R.I.K.E.'s Psi Division came to recruit me. Perhaps you were lucky the Hellfire Club found you."

"Not soon enough," Kitty mutters.

A twist of guilt accompanies the admission, but isn't it true? The three years Kitty spent burrowed deep inside herself, terrified to be seen by people who were guaranteed to despise the view, felt like decades while they passed. She couldn't even sleep for the first weeks at boarding school except when sheer exhaustion kicked in. What if she phased into the bedroom below hers while sleeping, or into the soil below the school's foundation? What if she just kept sinking, and nobody would ever know where to find her, if they thought to look? And when, finally, she *was* recruited by Emma and the Academy . . .

Well. A safe place and a home. They're pretty promises. But Kitty's heard variations before, back when she was young and silly enough to believe them.

CHAPTER 17

KITTY

JULY 2, 1975

"THIS WON'T HURT AT ALL IF YOU DON'T MOVE," BETSY INSTRUCTS.

Yet another promise Kitty's too old to believe. But she stiffens on the bathroom countertop and grips the overhang until her knuckles turn white, willing herself to keep still. This isn't her first broken-nosed rodeo, and she vividly remembers the aftermath years later. The almost minty blast of discomfort. She scrunches her eyes shut and grinds her molars together, preparing herself.

But though she hears the haunting crunch of the cartilage straightening beneath Betsy's careful fingers, the pain never comes.

"What did you do?"

Betsy smooths fresh tape taken from the bathroom's first-aid kit over the bridge of her nose. "Just a little psychic block, useful for tending to agents when they've stumbled in out of the field. Bit like a local anesthetic, only the thing that stops your brain from receiving signals from your nerves is . . . well, me. As I said, I could've done it in Latveria, if you'd trusted me."

Kitty opens her mouth to point out the way Betsy's powers glitched disastrously under pressure, but then lets this one go; the telepath probably doesn't need another person's doubts piled on top of her own. Instead, she sniffs tentatively. Still stuffy and swollen, clearly, but it's easier to breathe already. "Thanks."

"It'll wear off, as with any anesthetic. Might want some ibuprofen on hand when it does. If I recall my history, it's just come on the market here in the States."

"I can handle it." Kitty hops down, smoothing out her borrowed bell-bottoms and red collared blouse. She's pretty sure that one just like it hung in her mom's half of the closet, its fabric oddly shiny, with the same oversized mother-of-pearl buttons. And this was the best shirt on offer. God, she needs to find the washing machines on these premises. Though her tank top might be beyond repair, stained with nose-blood as it is.

It's not much of a comfort that Betsy's dressed in a ridiculous pink, halter-necked jumpsuit, cinched at the waist with a gold belt as thick as her arm. Even in dated clothing and with her blond hair pinned at the nape of her neck with a tortoiseshell clip, she looks like a professional dancer on her day off.

Kitty looks as if she tripped in a thrift store and broke a clothing rack with her face.

Her red-rimmed eyes aren't helping anything. She could've used a few more hours' sleep, or days, honestly. After yanking the curtain rod down from above her bedroom window to embed it strategically through the doorframe as a makeshift dead bolt, she'd finally managed a nap. But Betsy, anxious to continue down the telepathic trail, was soon rapping on her door, jarring her awake.

Together and unattended, they wander the rooms on the ground floor, none of which are particularly unusual. There's the kitchen, where they quickly forage for snacks to hold them over until the dinner hour, and the attached dining room. A TV room with leather couches positioned in front of a TV set that's nearly as deep as it is wide. There's a formal reception room with a grand stone fireplace, and a library with long tables for students and former students. Out the window of something Betsy speculates is called a dayroom, they see a glittering, teal Olympic-sized swimming pool.

"Big deal," Kitty assesses. "The Academy had one, too."

"We never had one at home."

"Seriously? A private jet but no backyard pool?"

"Too cold to be practical in our part of the country. One year, I missed summer entirely while trapped in the bathroom after eating an undercooked Scotch egg."

"Was that, like, a joke?" Kitty presses a hand to her chest, feigning shock. "Indecorous!"

But Betsy's attention has already wandered. "What do you think, the grounds next, or belowground?"

The only folks allowed in the sublevels of the Massachusetts Academy were Emma Frost's Hellions, and occasionally her prisoners. If there are secrets to be dug up, Kitty bets they'll be locked behind the riveted steel doors she and Betsy passed upon arrival . . . As if that could keep them safe. "Definitely down," Kitty decides. Reaching for Betsy, she sinks them both through the floor as easily as a knife through butter.

The basement level is normal enough for a school, wine cellar notwithstanding. There's the laundry room—that's useful information, anyway. But the furniture storage and utility room hold nothing of interest, nor the space Betsy identifies as a mainframe, full of humming electronics, processing units the size of clothes dryers, and one hulking computer in its center. At least, not to Kitty. She fidgets in the refrigerated air, the static charge in the room setting her nerves on end. "Think there's anything useful in here?" she asks.

"I'm not sure." Betsy bends close to examine the setup but doesn't touch anything. "Probably not for our purposes, but something to keep in mind, if we could figure out how to use it. For now, let's keep moving—not sure how long we'll be left to our own devices before someone comes looking for us, and cyber-espionage would be a bit harder to explain away than miscellaneous snooping."

"Dunno if struggling to turn on an antique computer counts as espionage," Kitty points out, but down they go again, ignoring the elevator bank with its keypad once more to phase through the ceiling.

The level containing the hangar bay is as empty as the last, and slightly more interesting. There's a cluster of labs, distinguished from the neighboring medical bay with its multiple beds by equipment that seems better designed to dissect than to heal. There's a gymnasium, squeaky flooring and all, with a weights room attached.

"Any more trail markers?" Kitty asks, dubious.

"Not so much."

"How can you tell? I mean . . . You said you could see it, but if you don't see places and people the way I do, then what's it like?"

Betsy chews her lip, considering. "It's hard to explain if you've never experienced psionic phenomena. Like describing color to a blind man, I'd expect. But aside from that feeling I mentioned, that sort of certainty detached from explanation—"

"A wound without an answer," Kitty says, recalling her earlier description.

"Yes, exactly. Aside from that, I suppose you *could* use another sense to describe it. Like the smell of lemon in another room, and as you follow your nose and move closer to its source, you can just about taste it. That's how it goes. As I follow the trail, I can very nearly see it. It's—" Then Betsy stops, cocking her head to the side as though hearing a sound at a frequency above Kitty's ability to register. "Wait. There's something coming. Someone."

Then she's gone, drifting down the corridor toward the hangar bay entrance.

"Betsy," Kitty hisses after her. "We're not supposed to be down here, remember?"

Granted, the professor never told them *not* to wander, and Storm invited them to make themselves at home. A passcode-guarded sub-basement still feels like a stretch. But whatever signal Betsy's picked up on, she's not hearing Kitty, or at least she's not listening. As the floor vibrates beneath them and the sound of the jet's descent rumbles beyond the hangar doors, Kitty rushes forward to pull Betsy away; they've still got time to climb up through the ceiling, or duck back into one of the labs. But when she grabs for Betsy's wrist, the woman flicks her off, grabbing Kitty's wrist instead.

"Trust me, will you?" she begs. "Just trust me, and stay?"

Well.

Against Kitty's better (or maybe worst) judgment, she hadn't ditched the woman in Serbia when she had the chance. So she guesses she's along for the ride. The bay doors slide open, and the previously absent members of the X-Men file through.

First, a man at least six and a half feet tall, with biceps the size of Kitty's head that bulge beneath the sharply winged shoulders of his red-and-gold costume. His boots hug equally impressive and equally bare thighs. He blocks the hallway and then blots the rest of the team from view as he stops in his tracks. "What's this?" he rumbles, the words colored with a Russian accent.

She has to crane her neck to meet his blue eyes. With all that muscle, he might be her type. But Kitty's always tended toward older flings, and something in his face tells her he's too young for her. "Hey there. We're . . . new."

"New recruits?" another voice, heavily accented—German, maybe—asks behind the tall man. Yellow eyes flash around the man's arm before there's a poof of blue-black smoke, accompanied by a distinctly acrid smell. Then another mutant materializes right in front of his teammate, and she should be able to say he's unlike anyone she's ever seen . . . except she can't. Indigo fur and golden eyes that glow like smoldering coals. Pointed ears and an arrow-tipped tail that snakes hypnotically through the air behind him. Beneath the gloves and boots of a full bodysuit, fewer fingers and toes than there ought to be. "Guten abend," he says softly, almost shyly, fanged canines peeking out.

Familiar or not, Kitty feels the urge to take a defensive step back. But it only lasts a moment; one of her old teammates was a full, yellow-eyed werecat after all, even if she smelled pleasantly musky instead of sulfurous. If Catseye had lived long enough, Kitty thinks she could've been fond of her.

Since Betsy remains useless and silent, Kitty sighs and answers his question. "Yeah. New recruits, I guess."

"New recruits? Shift yourself, will you, Peter?" Yet another accent, Irish this time. As the beefy Russian shuffles to the side, a middle-aged man with flowing strawberry-blond hair steps past him. He props his fists on his hips to observe them both, displaying striped fabric like the membrane on some kind of flying squirrel attached to his green-and-yellow suit from wrist to back. Something to augment his powers, whatever they are?

The unnecessarily high popped collar, she can't see a mechanical purpose in.

Anything yet? Kitty thinks pointedly in Betsy's direction.

Still transfixed by the hangar doors, Betsy really doesn't need to answer.

Next to enter behind the human blockade is a man in a relatively simple blue bodysuit (aside from the standard yellow hot pants and enormous X-belt) covering him from his boots to the crown of his head. In fact, all that's visible is a square, clenched jaw and nose, thanks to a bulky yellow visor with one narrow red slit running horizontally across its center. It seems he can see well enough, because he studies them both in turn. "You must be the ones Storm and Wolverine went out to retrieve. I'm Scott, also called Cyclops."

Once again, the task of answering is left to her. "Kitty . . . Just Kitty." Then she kicks Betsy's ankle as subtly as possible, because dammit, Kitty *cannot* be solely responsible for making a first impression after she's spent the past few years being noticed by as few people as possible.

It's hopeless, though. Betsy is staring at the woman who's just joined her team, the hangar bay doors sliding closed behind her. With long, gently curling ruby-red hair and an emerald-green minidress, her lovely face slightly obscured by a winged yellow eye mask not unlike Wolverine's, she's definitely what Emma Frost would call "striking," if wildly and impractically outfitted for a field mission. But the way Betsy's watching her, goggle-eyed and deathly pale all of a sudden, can't be explained by appearance alone.

Is it her? Kitty thinks.

The woman trains eyes the same vibrant green as her costume on Kitty. **Am I who?**

Oh, fantastic: yet another telepath.

And that's the moment Betsy picks to clutch at her head and collapse in a heap upon the corridor floor.

CHAPTER 18

KITTY

JULY 2, 1975

ONCE BETSY COMES TO AFTER HER BRIEF AND DRAMATIC COLLAPSE, the visored man named Scott helps her to sitting. Still pale and shaking, she assures them all that she simply hadn't eaten much since arriving at the mansion. Meanwhile, Kitty stands there as awkward as a fish at a black-tie ball, trying to keep her head empty just in case the wrong telepath catches another stray thought, until she's given permission to help Betsy back upstairs.

Once they can speak privately behind Betsy's closed bedroom door, Kitty rounds on her. "So? Is the redhead our girl?"

"I don't know," she says, dragging her hands through her uncharacteristically disheveled blond hair. "It's hard to explain. It feels . . . not that Jean is so important to *me,* but that she's important. But if I've read about her in the RCX files, I never retained it. They're less focused on the past than on present threats and potential allies and assets, which I suppose is why the X-Men aren't mentioned. And I don't suppose Ms. Frost imparted any further wisdom?"

Kitty shakes her head. "Just that Charles Xavier once led a group called the X-Men, and now they're all ex-X-Men."

"That's not funny."

"Am I laughing? Look, if I had any idea what to do here, I'd share it. You think I don't want to get this over with and get back to . . ." She flails momentarily for some compelling reason to return to the present. She's *sure* one exists, or maybe it will, if they can accomplish . . . whatever it is they're meant to do here. "Back to my life?" Kitty finishes after a long pause that isn't fooling anyone.

"Well, there's something here that we're still missing," Betsy concludes. "Or maybe the answer hasn't presented itself yet. We don't have enough information to form a plan. But the trail has led us this far, and we'll just have to wait for it to reveal what's next. Meanwhile, we stay here, stay close to Jean, and keep our purpose to ourselves for the moment until we know how to move without crushing the proverbial butterfly. Agreed?"

Kitty shrugs. She sure doesn't have a better idea.

BY THE TIME THEY GATHER IN THE FORMAL DINING ROOM THAT EVEning, Betsy's looking more like her typical, tightly clenched self, though she only picks at their meal: bowls of cream of tomato soup, plates of salad, and platters of beef sirloin and roasted turnips. The X-Men are out of uniform, dressed in a spectrum of khaki and denim, floor-length skirts and pistachio-colored blouses, turtlenecks and tartan dinner jackets. Kitty fidgets with the enormous buttons on her shirt cuffs while, one by one, they tell their stories between bites.

"When the professor first came to me," Ororo begins, "he was met by a goddess of the storm. Or so I was known to the locals, who had been my mother's tribe when she was among the living. They would come to me with their complaints of drought or flood, and I would summon the elements according to my whims, and receive their prayers and praise. But they did not know who I truly was—a mortal, an orphaned thief, and a mutant. Professor Xavier knew, and he came to me with a proposal. Do you remember, Professor?"

Seated at the head of the table, he tips his head. "Of course. I asked you to trade the worship of people who saw in you only what they wanted for the likely enmity of a world which needed you, but might only ever see you as a mutant." His usually serious mouth quirks up at the corner. "A wonder you didn't summon a tornado to blow me back to Westchester, with an offer like that."

"It was a difficult bargain, certainly. But fairly spoken. I *have* known hatred since then. But I have also known friendship, and the bittersweet sureness of fulfilling a hard purpose."

"Well, I was no goddess," Peter—the beefy one—says, busy digging trenches through his vegetables with a fork that's dwarfed within his giant paw, "so I suppose my own bargain was easier to accept."

"A farmer, were you not?" asks the mutant named Kurt. His furred, midnight-blue skin and glowing yellow eyes are only slightly less startling when clothed in a striped knit polo and pants.

"Da. My family worked a communal farm in Siberia. One day I was in the wheat fields and saw that the neighbor's tractor had run away and veered toward my little sister, Illyana, half hidden in the stalks. I did not think. I simply ran, and as I did, the beat of my heart . . . it seemed somehow to send energy not just throughout my blood, but through and across my skin, turning it to steel. Then I was between my sister and the tractor, and as it hit us, it burst to pieces. I stood in the smoking wreckage with Illyana in my arms."

"You were unharmed?" Betsy asks.

"As though I were wearing armor."

"Ain't we all taken a tractor or two to the face?" Wolverine asks around a mouthful.

"Oh please, boyo!" The older Irishman chuckles. "Your face would've been lying in the wheat till you healed."

"That is when the professor approached me," Peter cuts in diplomatically. "He had found me, as he found all of us, through Cerebro. He asked me to come to America with him, to train, and use my powers for the good of the world. I did not want to go at first—my heart remained with my mama and papa. But my conscience told me that it was right to do so."

"It's the conscience that gets you," says the Irishman—Sean, Kitty remembers. "Me, I wasn't a goddess or a hero when I met the X-Men. In fact, I was part of a mission to kidnap the professor. Weren't my choice—a villain had me under his thumb. The professor freed me, and it wasn't the last time he did so. When he caught up with me down the road, he asked me to join up. Gave me a chance to stick to the straight and narrow. I took it. For now." His eyes crinkle at the corners.

"He is only teasing," Storm assures them earnestly.

Kitty squirms in her chair. For the first time, the loss of her white coat doesn't leave her feeling exposed, but like its absence is another kind of disguise, shielding her from being seen as she truly is.

"I had never hurt anybody," Kurt says quietly, and even the scraping of forks and spoons stops around him. "But if you asked the people of Winzeldorf, they would say I was a monster. They chased me with pitchforks, torches, crosses. Cornered me. The fools half burned down their village to get their hands on me, and would have staked me in the street, when I had only ever wanted peace."

Peter claps him on the back—a gesture of support that nearly sends Kurt face-first into his cream of tomato soup.

"Professor Xavier saved me," he continues once he's regained his balance, gazing adoringly at Charles. "He did not promise to make me normal. He could not. But he promised to teach me to live fully as myself."

"A fine thing to be," Charles says, deep voice running deeper with emotion.

Kurt looks to Wolverine beside him, whose flowing muttonchops ruffle as he chews.

At last, he swallows. "Wasn't an X-Men. Then I was. For now."

Across the table, Scott sighs.

Then it's Jean's turn to tell her story while a riveted Betsy watches, the hunger in her blue eyes enough to give Kitty second-hand embarrassment. "I only lived an hour-and-a-half's drive north from here when I was a kid. My father taught at Bard. One day, I saw . . . well, I saw a close friend die." As she stumbles over the words, Scott reaches for her hand on the tablecloth, rubbing circles across her knuckles with his thumb. She looks at him with adoration in her jewel-green eyes, then continues. "It was awful enough to watch, but suddenly, I was inside of my friend's mind, and I felt . . . everything. After that, I was a very different child, buried deep inside of myself. My parents brought me to therapy, cycled through loads of therapists they hoped would help, but none of them understood. Because it wasn't only my thoughts I struggled with, but everyone's. I could hear everybody around me, all the time, and it was killing me. I shut myself away from the world to survive, but I think it *would* have killed me, eventually."

"I—" Betsy starts, and Kitty's shocked she's able to speak to Jean, with her jaw metaphorically on the floor since the moment of their meeting. Her cheeks color, but she continues, "I felt the same, when my telepathy first started, and the thoughts of the entire population of New York City swarmed me all at once. I locked myself inside my apartment for a month. By the time I came out, I was down to so little money and food, I practically had to crawl to the door."

Kitty manages to keep her face from registering surprise—she has a decade of practice dissembling—but wonders why Betsy left out that detail during their car confessional. Did she think Kitty wouldn't get it? Granted, her own powers manifested less violently, but clearly, she understands what it is to be alone.

Jean is smiling warmly back at Betsy. "Awful, wasn't it? But I was lucky. After some time, a psychiatrist I was seeing recommended his colleague, Professor Charles Xavier."

"He had no idea that I was a mutant, of course," Charles fills in, dark eyes twinkling.

"But the professor knew what *I* was right away. He helped me. Saved me. And when I was old enough, he recommended that my parents send me here, where I met the X-Men. Where I met Scott."

He lifts her hand to press a kiss to her knuckles.

It's a bit much, really. Maybe it's Kitty's innate saltiness spoiling something sweet. Though judging by the violent scrape of Wolverine's fork tines against his plate as he stabs through his sirloin, it's not just her.

"I was the first student, though there were others by the time Jean came. I'm not sure I could tell my whole story before my dinner goes cold." Scott reaches to fidget with the red-lensed glasses he's now wearing in place of the strange visor. "There was an accident when I was young. It left me unable to control my powers. I spent years mistrusting myself, terrified of hurting people. Convinced that I would always be on my own, and what's more, that I should be. Then the professor found me. And he explained his plan—to form a group of mutants known as the X-Men, who would live together, train together, and share his dream of ending the distrust between mutants and *Homo sapiens*. He convinced me that we could build a world where none of us needed to fear one another. It was a beautiful dream, when I needed one badly. And I'm still here, because despite everything, I still believe."

You're not swallowing all this, are you? Kitty tries to probe Betsy.

But Betsy's thoughts are closed off to her for the moment.

She's busy processing that when she realizes that the table has fallen silent aside from the scrape and slice of forks and knives, and worse yet, they're all looking at her expectantly. Her cheeks redden as she chews what now feels like an absolutely enormous bite of sirloin, before she swallows at last. "What . . . What am I supposed to say here? I don't think my tragic backstory can compete with any of yours."

It's supposed to be a joke, but she feels the truth in it. Yes, she *felt* as though she'd lost her family and her dreams and any tentative grip a thirteen-year-old could have on her life, all at once. Yes, she felt alone. And angry. And afraid. But that wasn't the same as experiencing your best friend's death, or being chased by an angry, pitchfork-wielding mob (her teenage nightmares about this exact scenario notwithstanding). So why are they all here among trusted friends when Kitty can barely stop herself from sniping at her only ally?

What's wrong with her?

"You needn't share more than you're comfortable with," Ororo says kindly. "We only wish to explain how it is we've come here from all the scattered corners of this world, united under a shared identity and a common cause."

"Protecting the people who hate mutants?" The echo of Emma's words slips out of Kitty's mouth before she can stop herself, and not even Betsy's sidelong glare can stuff them back in.

At the head of the table, Charles tips his head. "I do believe that humankind is worth defending, even from the danger it presents to itself, and the calamities of its own creation that threaten us all. As much as some would like to believe otherwise, we mutants share this world with non-mutants, and thus we share a fate and a future. As evidence, look to a man named Boliver Trask—an anthropologist turned scientist for the military—who first revealed our existence to the public, some ten years ago. He coined the now-popular term *mutant menace,* which you may be familiar with."

Kitty is plenty familiar with that phrase, as it happens. She's seen it spray-painted on the corpses of mutants in newspaper headlines, and heard it hissed by the teachers at Miss Hester's during social studies lessons.

"Trask declared mutantkind to be a greater threat to humankind than the atom bomb," Charles continues his history lesson, "and warned that we were each of us bent toward the ultimate goal of conquering, enslaving, and destroying the human race. I encountered him in a debate soon after, where I pled with the public to understand that mutants are not monsters but rather people born with a particular gene, perhaps their own children. To succumb to fear and suspicion, I argued, was to engender their *own* destruction. Trask proved as much when he demonstrated his creation, a prototype of what he named the Sentinels—artificially intelligent robots designed to hunt down mutantkind with their incredible processing power as well as defensive and offensive capabilities. Their programmed purpose was to save humanity, but Trask underestimated the weapon he had created. According to the Sentinels' calculations, the only way to save humanity was to rule it. After the machines kidnapped their maker, Trask saw sense, and helped us destroy their headquarters along with Master Mold from which further Sentinels might be created. There are those among mutantkind who would call us fools for rescuing Trask, or leaving him alive."

Wolverine—dressed down in a plaid button-up—snorts around a mouthful of beef. "Lucky for him I wasn't there."

Scott sighs heavily. "Those were the days."

"Before you had competition, huh, bub?" Wolverine growls.

As he starts to respond, Jean lays a hand on Scott's shoulder, and he lets his square jaw click shut.

"However," Charles says, interrupting their bickering (tame compared with Kitty's memory of Hellion mealtimes, which were not infrequently interrupted by murder attempts rather than mild death threats), "I have to believe that both humans and mutants are capable of change. That a world is possible where we coexist, neither in fear of the other, each free. *Everyone* free, regardless of race, religion, sexuality, or, yes, genetics. We are all so much more alike than not, and given the chance, perhaps even the smallest men among us may see it."

This time, Kitty doesn't need Betsy's unnecessary glare; she knows better than to inform him that Sentinels are part of nearly every government's anti-mutant defense program in the future. Their patent was first purchased and adapted by the United States, then bartered to its allies or sold at extravagant cost to its enemies. Of course, the Hellfire Club, as an early investor, was able to place members strategically enough to write certain vulnerabilities and exceptions into the Sentinel coding. But the fact remains that Charles's mercy appears to have solved nothing in the long term. As Emma taught her from a young age, mercy seldom does.

"What if someone *isn't* capable of change?" Kitty asks.

"An excellent subject for debate, Miss Pryde. Any thoughts, class?" he asks the table.

It's Jean Grey who answers. "Everything changes because everything must. Whether for the better or not is only revealed by time."

"And if someday Trask changes for the worst?" Kitty challenges, knowing she's treading dangerously close to stepping off the path.

The redhead frowns thoughtfully. "If so, well, none of us can go back and make a different choice. But by that same token, we couldn't go back if we'd wrongly decided that Trask needed to die in order to tip the odds toward our own survival. So we act in hope instead of fear."

Charles nods his approval. "Well said, Miss Grey. We act in hope of a better world."

A better world.

She and Betsy are here chasing just that, though Kitty hasn't really paused long enough to consider what kind of world it would be. If Jean Grey turns out to be the reason they're here, and they manage to fix the future, will teenage Betsy Braddock somehow avoid being lost in the Wildways, instantly transforming *her* Betsy into a confident, competent version of herself? Will the kid-Kitty who's probably being tucked into bed by her parents right now come into her powers among the X-Men, as it happened in the slip, instead of all alone? Will she end up here, instead of being found and heat-forged into a weapon by the woman who's recently threatened to toss her out into the cold? If so . . . well, it isn't *so* bad here, dated fashion and doomed optimism notwithstanding. The X-Men don't seem to pose an immediate danger to anyone but themselves. Some of them seem kind. She'll probably sleep easier here than she ever did at Miss Hester's or the Massachusetts Academy.

But she still leaves the curtain-rod dead bolt stuck in her bedroom door that night, just in case.

CHAPTER 19

DOOM

JULY 5, 1975

BY THE TIME HIS COUNTERPART VISITS THE CELL AGAIN, DOOM MUST admit that he's somewhat diminished. The guards have not brought water in two days, and food has yet to be offered. Besides which, the injuries he sustained in battle before arriving to this world remain untended. Flesh wounds though they may be, the fever of infection licks at the edges of his consciousness. Fortunately, even a dulled Doom is a sharper weapon than any man on his best day. Sitting on the cell floor, he does not attempt to rise as Other-Doom approaches, standing grimly beyond the bars and blotting out the light of the corridor. He merely lifts his chin in acknowledgment and waits.

"Information and opportunity," Other-Doom says at last. "You promised me both. You have yet to deliver."

Doom recalls *informing* him of the very existence of the Multiverse, but it would not help his case to say so. "Then allow me a second attempt." His voice rattles like a stone dropped down a dry well.

"Very well. You were about to tell me about myself in a bid to prove your own identity. Yet even my Doombots are programmed with my memories, all the better to impersonate me flawlessly in diplomatic situations, as well you know," Other-Doom scolds. "And if you are some living clone or mystically conjured imposter, my enemies would have fed you whatever information you believe sustains your claim. My greatness is well known in this world and beyond. So you see, there is no proof you can offer."

Here is his opening, even if Other-Doom doesn't recognize it yet. "Fair enough. Well then, I will not speak of our greatness. It is known by our allies and enemies alike, and proves nothing. Instead, I will speak of our weakness, which we have confessed to no other and kept from the minds of even our robotic replicas. We alone know that every life we have claimed in service of our purpose of remaking this monstrous world began with the first: the Latverian soldier who came to claim the baron's reward upon our head. We were little more than a child when we strangled him in the woods of a homeland that had never loved us. We felt his pulse flicker and fade and die beneath our trembling hands. That night, we wept with shame, fearing ourselves damned from birth, heir to our mother's demons. Until we remembered our destiny. We remembered that we are above guilt, above fear, above pain, above dreams. Above the curses of humanity, miserable and many. And above all who would oppose us and our great works."

"Above even the devil himself," Other-Doom agrees, his voice now ragged, his fists clenched so tightly around the cell bars that they begin to bow outward.

Doom inclines his head, waiting.

"Your words may ring true, but your intentions remain unknown." Other-Doom steps back from the cell. "Would you trust yourself upon meeting if you were in my position?"

"Oh, but I have been. I have met myself, and aimed to manipulate rather than collaborate. I attempted to puppet the Doom of yet another world into doing my bidding, all to facilitate the destruction of his world's nexus being."

Other-Doom's curiosity is revealed by his silence. He won't deign to take Doom's bait, but he won't cut it free and risk losing it, either. His hesitation is itself an invitation.

Doom presses on. "In each universe of the infinite universes, there exists a nexus being—not superior, simply born with functional importance to their reality. Only a component like any other, but mechanically powerful, like the escapement in a clock. Remove the piece, and the machine ceases to function. But the power . . . *that* may be seized by a being with greater vision, who sees and understands the clock as a whole rather than concerning himself with the mundanities of cogs and gears. I have been moving through the Multiverse, studying these individuals so that I might learn more about them and harness the power that's nothing more than an accident of fate."

"And the results of these studies?" Other-Doom prompts, tilting toward the bars as though drawn to Doom unknowingly.

Excellent.

"In the first world where I chose to advance my experiments rather than observe, I hypothesized that removing a constant in a given universe might force the variable—the nexus—to reveal itself. I removed a constant that was Thor Odinson, which caused the variable, Loki Laufeyson, to show himself. My hypothesis was sound, and the experiment a success."

"By what means did you determine this constant?" Spoken like a skeptical scientist questioning his peer's methodology.

Still, Doom can sense the curiosity behind the challenge. "The more powerfully chaotic a nexus being is, the more an aberration among their variants, the easier they are to identify. In the beginning, my attempts were scattershot. Eliminating heroes whose existence seemed foundational in the majority of universes to study the effects, waiting and hoping for some pattern to emerge. But after Loki, I had an isolated variable to study. I determined, too, that the shard of the M'Kraan Crystal, which had been facilitating my Multiversal travel, had the ability to act as a kind of homing beacon to the nexus beings, albeit an imperfect one, as the shard is imperfect. Further research is always required. Still, I was ready to move forward.

"In the next world, I set out to determine the full capabilities of the nexus powers and whether they might be destroyed. I engineered the separation of the Maximoff twins of that reality, manipulating their paths in such a way to force Wanda to manifest her nexus powers. Another success. But the Doom of that world hampered my experiment with his own failure, and so the nexus being survived."

"Is the failure of a puppet not the failure of its puppeteer?" Other-Doom sneers.

Doom lowers his head, appearing to concede. It is a fair assessment. "As you say. In the last world, I set myself to the task of determining whether the nexus powers might be transferred from one being to another."

"To you?" Other-Doom surmises.

"Naturally. I sent the wretched creature Venom to retrieve a device for me, then converted its capabilities to funnel the powers away from that reality's nexus being, Moon Knight. But again I erred. I did not account for my pawns to conspire and convert the device into a bomb." Here he prods at the punctured surface of his chest plate, where shards of the device, the blasted psi-phon, are still lodged. "But this time, my failure was sweetened with victory. Moon Knight confirmed in his overly confident blathering that the powers given to the nexus being *can* be seized by another."

"And for what purpose? Where is this opportunity you claim to offer me?"

Doom forces himself to standing, locking the trembling muscles of his legs. "He who wields the power of a nexus being is capable of shaping reality through his will. Though few are aware of this ability, since few beings are aware of their mechanical importance to their own realities. My experiments are at an end now, and I am ready to proceed. I can take the power, but . . . I cannot take it alone. With use of your laboratories and the resources of your castle and kingdom, I can secure us a victory such as you've yet to imagine. Alone, we are easily capable of mastering our own worlds. But together, we are capable of mastering *every* world."

As he steps forward, Other-Doom steps back, releasing the bars; misshapen, but with no ill effect on the force field that keeps

Doom contained. "I'll consider your proposal," Other-Doom says, "and the value in keeping you alive, if it indeed exists." He strides off again without a backward glance, cloak billowing behind him.

But Doom has done what he came to do. He hasn't spoken a lie, even if he's omitted some truths. As he sinks back to the cold cell floor, legs giving out beneath him, he is satisfied.

And when next a robot guard approaches, it brings both a flask of water and a tray of food. Slices of roast pig prepared in Latverian fashion, and piles of native root vegetables that remind him of his childhood. Of home.

And Doom knows then that he has won.

CHAPTER 20

KITTY

JULY 5, 1975

AS THEIR DAYS PASS WITH THE X-MEN, THE CONSTANT PRESENCE OF people who seem overly concerned with Kitty's well-being begins to feel . . . not welcome, definitely. But ordinary, maybe.

While their family-style dinner doesn't repeat itself come breakfast, Scott and Jean are already in the kitchen when Kitty pops down to scavenge. Scrambling eggs at the stovetop, Scott offers her a helping, while Jean pours Kitty a cup of coffee from the pot. This pattern repeats itself anytime she drifts into the kitchen throughout the day, with someone inevitably foisting a bowl or plate upon her. At dinnertime, Peter hands her a serving of some kind of mayonnaise-based salad, which she holds awkwardly until he strolls from the room, then rinses down the drain and grabs a to-go banana instead. There doesn't seem to be a cafeteria in this school beyond the formal dining room, nor do there seem to be any classes. Which is a relief; she's not in the mood to sit through Latin lessons as a twenty-three-year-old when she skipped that class the first time around. But the X-Men don't appear to leave the mansion much, either, when they aren't being sent out to fetch a pair of lost mutants from a hostile nation in Eastern Europe, or to retrieve a stolen weapons cache from a megalomaniacal wizard; the mission that Jean, Scott, and the rest of the team were deployed on when they first arrived, Kitty learns.

So Kitty can't account for the large swath of daylight when

they all disappear together. She roams the grounds freely (though Xavier reminds them that some rooms and wings are restricted for their own safety, by which she guesses that their sniffing around hasn't slipped completely beneath his notice). But there's nobody in the library or classrooms, or on the outdoor basketball court, or by the pond. Not until late afternoon, when the mansion fills with X-Men again, all of whom (well, all but Wolverine) want to know whether she needs anything, and how she's settling in.

If you ask her, Betsy's *settling in* a little too comfortably. She catches Betsy leaving the professor's office, where Betsy claims they were discussing the works of T. H. White rather than anything that might compromise the mission. Then later, coming down the stairs from Ororo's attic apartment, which Betsy encourages her to visit. "It's extraordinary up there, like a greenhouse!" And that night, sitting with some of the crew in the TV room, watching *Happy Days*. Or rather, not watching. Jean and Scott lie on opposite ends of one of the sofas, their legs entangled, her slippers propped on his lap, and a bowl of popcorn in hers. Betsy watches Jean float individual kernels toward Scott's open mouth, and Kitty watches Betsy, whose eyes have yet to lose the shine of hunger whenever she looks at the redhead—something Jean must notice, unless she's so used to being ogled adoringly that it no longer rates her attention.

Fine, then. Apparently it's up to Kitty to stay objective, to keep a cool and distant eye on Jean Grey . . . and on Betsy, too.

It isn't until their third morning at the mansion that Kitty finds out what the team gets up to during daylight hours. While Betsy's in yet another conference with Professor Xavier, Kitty wanders through the classrooms of the first floor, then back down to the basement, then down to the sublevel where the gymnasium and labs and hangar bay are all currently unoccupied. Nothing new to see here. Returning to the elevator, she jams her thumb into the downward arrow, where it seems a lower level awaits. The keypad flashes red, refusing to admit her.

She punches in the elevator code she's been given, but the lock flashes once more.

Probably this means it's one of the professor's restricted areas. Still, if it's really for her own safety, rather than to protect some nefarious secret . . . well, how can a look hurt?

Holding her breath, she sinks down to a second sublevel: a long corridor with only one door, set halfway down. Whatever room occupies this level, it must be fairly massive. Approaching, Kitty tests the steel-paneled doors with her fingertips. The material feels thicker than expected, and . . . is that soundproofing? When she takes another breath and slides her upper body through, she expects to see cells like the ones Emma's built beneath the Academy to imprison her enemies. Instead she emerges up to her shoulders to see Kurt hurtling toward her, as though flung through the air by some giant's fist. Just before he slams through her intangible body and into the door, he vanishes in a burst of blue smoke that smells of brimstone. He reappears on the floor just in front of her, planted firmly on his two-toed feet. Blinking yellow eyes at Kitty, he smiles, milk-white fangs flashing. "Katzchen, have you come to train with the X-Men?"

Before she can answer, a massive silver claw descends to ensnare Kurt, yanking him up toward the ceiling of the vast chamber. He whizzes past Wolverine, who perches on the shoulder of a giant silver robot with an enormous laser gun barrel in place of its face; growling, Wolverine slices raggedly through its mechanical throat with long claws that seem to spring from his knuckles. As the robot's head flies free of its body, a last rope of electricity spits from its barrel, shooting clean across the room to scorch the wall beside her.

She flings herself backward and out of the chamber, landing on her butt on the corridor floor. The chamber door slides opens a moment later, and Ororo stands over Kitty in full costume, still panting for breath.

"What was that?" Kitty asks, still gazing up at her from the floor.

Ororo holds out a hand to help her stand. "That was the Danger Room, Kitty. It is how we train. Perhaps you'd like to see what it can do? And we will see what *you* can do."

LATER THAT DAY, SHE AND BETSY STAND IN THE SAME CORRIDOR IN their matching issued uniforms: the black-and-yellow spandex, the fist-sized belt buckles, the hooded masks and cuffed yellow boots.

"We look like clowns," Kitty mumbles.

"We look of the time period," Betsy half-heartedly corrects. "I suppose we have to earn the right to individualized costumes. I've only worn an RCX standard getup since joining the agency. Lots of black. All black, really." She tilts her head, considering. "Perhaps I'll choose something pink. What about you?"

"I'll choose nothing, because we're not going to be here long enough for custom costumes," she reminds Betsy.

"Well, yes, but if you *could* choose?"

Kitty sighs. "I don't know. Maybe . . . roller skates?"

"Roller skates."

"Yeah." She crosses her arms. "I'm good on roller skates. Great, even. Had my twelfth birthday party at the Skate Palace in Deerfield. I can go backward, forward, in circles. I'd be fast *and* untouchable."

Betsy holds her palms up in defeat.

That's when the door opens to admit them, and after sharing a last wary glance, they step inside together.

Ororo, Peter, Kurt, Wolverine, Sean, Scott, and Jean wait for them in full gear inside—should she think of them by their code names if this is a training situation? She guesses so, even if they aren't engaged at the moment, the presently empty chamber as long as a city block and several stories high. Gone are the obstacles, leaving smooth, strangely patterned steel paneling across almost every inch of floor, wall, and ceiling, broken only by a viewing window set high up in the far wall. Beyond the glass sits Professor Xavier. He leans forward over what might be a control panel—hard to say from this distance—and a moment later, his deep voice floods the room. "Welcome, Kitty and Betsy, to our training field. Non-lethal, rest assured."

"Non-lethal, but not non-dangerous?"

Wolverine grins at her. "We ain't training for the ballet."

"Ballet is actually incredibly dan—"

"So, then." Betsy cuts her off mid-protest. "How do the X-Men train, then?"

"The professor designed and built this for us to sharpen our skills, and to learn one another's strengths and how to work together as a team." Cyclops lifts a hand to wave at the professor behind the glass. The ground beneath her boots hums to life, and suddenly, things begin to shift. On opposite ends of the room, two of the steel floor panels slide out of place and flagpoles rise from the floor, pennants dangling from each. "So, two teams," he announces. "Kitty, Nightcrawler, Wolverine, Betsy, you're on blue." Cyclops gestures to the blue pennant on the pole nearest to the viewing window. "Marvel Girl, Storm, Colossus, and Banshee, you're on gold. And I'll be refereeing from the control booth with the professor."

"This isn't . . ." Kitty swivels to look between the flagpoles. "We're not playing . . ."

"Capture the Flag?" Betsy sounds delighted. Probably because she never had to play Capture the Flag with a gym class full of girls who despised her (girls whom Kitty could've driven into the ground, literally, only she had to take every *accidental* elbow to the face and sneaker to the shin for fear of being found out).

Hidden gears whir again, and the panels running down the center of the Danger Room flip themselves over, leaving a thick red line midway across the field. "You know the rules, then. Each team tries to take the other's flag, then make it back across the center line without losing your own flag. Lose your flag while on your opponent's side, you're in the holding zone." A section of the wall behind each flagpole slides outward to create two platforms, which click to a stop a dozen or so feet up. "Make it to the holding zone without being tagged yourself, and free a teammate. You both get safe passage back. Well, safe from your opponents, anyway," Cyclops concedes.

Remembering the room she glimpsed earlier, she doesn't feel comforted.

Colossus laughs at the worry that must be stamped across her brow. "No cause to fret. We are X-Men, yes?" he smirks, shifting into silver form.

"Not all of us," she mutters beneath her breath.

With a flick of her fingers, a duffel bag at Marvel Girl's feet unzips itself, and a pile of blue and gold pennants rise as if on strings, then float to each player according to their assigned team.

"Hang on." Kitty lifts an eyebrow. "How are we supposed to play with telepaths on the field?"

"That's why Scott split us up, isn't it?" Marvel Girl shares a private little smile with Betsy as she tucks her gold flag through her belt, and Betsy glows under her attention. "Plus you've got the teleporter."

Nightcrawler salutes, then poofs himself away with a crack of flame and the stink of sulfur, reappearing next to Marvel Girl to blow a sly kiss.

"Don't worry, Kitty. No mind reading of opponents allowed. And Nightcrawler, you know the rules—no bamfing between zones. Besides, the field has a way of evening the odds," Cyclops assures her. "And the most important rule of all: No powers may be used within six feet of the team flags. That *includes* a captured flag. Make it back to your side without powers . . . if you can. Everybody got it?"

Reluctantly, Kitty grabs her blue flag, still hovering in the air in front of her face, then nearly drops it as Wolverine claps her on the back. "Like Tin Man said, no reason to worry, kid. You're with us." He guides her into their team's zone with his furry arm slung around her shoulders.

"Ready, X-Men?" the professor asks through the speakers as Cyclops appears behind the glass beside him. "On your mark, get set . . ."

Kitty scrambles to thread her flag through her belt a second before an oblong panel beside her left boot moves downward, and from the geometric gap left behind, a striated metal pole as thick as a ship's mast shoots toward the ceiling. She skips back a step, only for the panel beneath her feet to sink again. Another pole rockets upward, and she jumps away as it pierces the air where she stood a moment ago. Everywhere, floor panels are sliding, sinking, soon replaced by a forest of silver poles so thick around her, she can no longer see Betsy or any members of the blue team. She wonders at the point of them until the top of each pole splits open with a ticking of hidden gears, dividing into three prongs that curve to shape themselves into massive claws.

Not trees, then. Arms.

They begin to sway around her, to seek. The nearest doubles in on itself, its clawed hand crashing down to stamp Kitty out, like some life-sized game of Whac-A-Mole. She phases before it smashes her into the floor, then darts straight ahead as the twisting arms and grasping claws pass harmlessly through her body. As she runs through each, the poles grind to a standstill, some crashing like trees felled by her natural interference with electronics.

Come to think of it, *every* obstacle will be powered by electronics. Or nearly. It won't be like it was in gym class, because here, she has nothing to hide and nobody to hide from.

Kitty can run this field.

Still, she can't hold her breath forever, and she'd best get clear of this murder forest before she needs to breathe again. That's the flip side of Kitty's powers: eternally battling her body's own instincts in order to keep it safe.

Once she's wrung the last drop of air from her lungs, she crouches, timing her jump so that the huge metal claw whizzing past just misses her. She collides with the pole instead, clinging to it as the claw rises again. Then she's airborne along with it, high enough to catch a view of the whole field and the X-Men scattered across it. The murder grove thins out the farther it gets from Kitty, which feels slightly personal. But then everyone is engaged by obstacles cooked up by the Danger Room (or by the professor in the control booth). Over by the far wall beside the gold flagpole, Marvel Girl hovers halfway to the ceiling, easily visible with her vibrant red hair and bright-green dress. One palm extended, she lifts a laser-faced robot nearly identical to the one Wolverine was dismantling earlier, only this one's got spinning buzz saws attached to its arms. Flicking her wrist, she sends it flying toward the ceiling and away from Colossus, who's currently battling his own robot. With a battle cry, he rips the chest plate from his opponent with his bare (sort of) silver hands. Overhead, Banshee sails through the air between jets of flame that shoot from nozzles in the wall, occasionally emitting a bone-rattling scream that seems to somehow keep him aloft—the code name makes more sense now, though Kitty suspects he's tamping down on his own powers for everyone's sake.

Meanwhile, on the blue side, Wolverine is slicing his way out of one of those giant nets descended from the ceiling, while Betsy hacks at it from the outside with something pink and scintillating, shaped from her psionic powers.

Is that a machete?

"The flag awaits, Katzchen!" Nightcrawler cheers as he swings between poles, clinging briefly with his hands, feet, and prehensile tail.

Then Kitty's own pole plunges downward again, whipping through the air to shake her off. She lets go and rolls free, climbing to her feet—with a few new bruises, she bets—before running onward, sending poles slumping and crashing in her wake.

When at last she breaks through to open space, she has a line of sight on the gold team's pole. But the second her boot crosses the centerline, Banshee comes swooping past, his striped fabric wings fanned out. She claps her hands over her ears as he lets out a scream that rings through her whole body, and so fails to notice Storm fly past on her other side, riding a wind of her own making. Trapped in the swirl of disorienting sound and wind, it takes Kitty a moment to realize that the flag that hung from her belt is now missing. When she does, she looks up to find Storm hovering over her, eyes white and crackling with lightning. She fries a flailing claw with a bolt conjured from one hand, holding Kitty's flag in the other.

A second later, the floor panel beneath Kitty propels upward as if on a spring, sailing her toward the yellow team's holding platform.

Storm nods as she flies past. "It's going to be quite a game, isn't it, Kitty?"

BY THE TIME SHE'S FREED, KITTY'S WATCHED THE FIELD ERUPT IN OB-stacles from every angle. Flame jets, laser beams, panels turned to flying razors, and a pile driver that ejects from the wall to slam Wolverine across the field. She might be imagining the crunch of his bones from where she stands, but she cringes in sympathy; her nose is still swollen and striped with tape. Danger Room, indeed. And that's not even factoring in the team-on-team combat that lands Colossus in the blue holding zone, then Storm, who's trying to free him as Betsy telepathically bends the arc of a flame jet toward her, driving her into Nightcrawler's path.

"Gehen wir!" Nightcrawler cries as he materializes on the platform beside her, stretching a gloved hand for hers to tag her free. "No teleporting from here, we'll have to hoof it."

She hesitates for only a moment before clasping his arm.

Once they've made their way back to the blue zone, they find Betsy and Wolverine back-to-back, making a stand in a crop circle of fallen robots.

"Let's take 'em out and hit the showers already," Wolverine growls. "Rush 'em all at once. Can't tag all of us with two of theirs in the clink."

"What do you think, Betsy?" Nightcrawler asks.

But Betsy laughs. "Don't look at me. Kitty's the one with leadership experience. Isn't that right?"

Kitty wonders whether Betsy overheard Emma Frost's eviscerating words while fluttering around in her brain.

When I made you my White Knight, it wasn't because you'd shown leadership potential. Nor because you were beloved by your teammates.

She can't pretend that Emma was wrong. None of the Hellions followed Kitty out of devotion. But then, how could they? The White Queen's favored training method at the Academy was pitting the Hellions against one another in life and in one-on-one matches. The supposed purpose was to sharpen their skills, while the true purpose was to expose their teammates' weaknesses. Kitty realized early that every moment of ridicule aimed at a fellow Hellion was a moment she'd spared herself. Every extra lap the loser was made to run around campus was a brief respite for Kitty. That was the first and most important lesson learned at the Massachusetts Academy: Someone must fail, and if it isn't the person next to you, then it will be you.

Still, she was the squad leader, wasn't she? And the White Knight of the Hellfire Club. She knows how to call a play based on imperfect information, even if she can't do it without worrying about what the White Queen will have to say about it during their debriefing.

And standing alongside the X-Men . . . it feels like what a team *should* feel like but never once has. Across the huddle from her, sweat beads Betsy's forehead and she's panting to catch her breath, but she's clearly having fun in her own British way. Maybe Kitty should, too.

"Okay . . . okay. How about this . . ."

With their plan hatched, they split up, dodging and teleporting around stun rays that shoot from the wall, machete-slashing through spinning fan blades that rise from the floor to cut them down. Kurt sticks with Betsy while Wolverine runs ahead of them both, and Kitty picks her way back into the flailing forest of claws, losing sight of them all. Which means that everyone loses sight of her. Even Banshee, screaming past to free a teammate, doesn't look down. That leaves Marvel Girl alone to defend the blue team's flag, not that it seems much of a disadvantage; Kitty watched her dismantle a cluster of robots with her mind during her own time in the holding zone. So it makes the most tactical sense to send their telepath in with Wolverine to block for Nightcrawler, whose agility will serve him in evading Banshee and a now-freed Storm even if (when) he has the flag in hand.

But that isn't the plan.

She waits long enough to watch Wolverine lose his flag to Storm, and watch Nightcrawler and Betsy make their charge regardless. Then Kitty fills her lungs with air and sinks down through the floor of the Danger Room.

Below the ever-shifting panels is a nightmarish maze of turning gears and traps waiting for the professor's signal to spring. If the Danger Room is non-lethal, the chamber beneath probably isn't. And she's got a long way to go.

Kitty begins her own charge, running straight ahead as best she can figure until her lungs seem to claw at the insides of her rib cage, begging for breath. Then she climbs the air around her to rise tentatively through the floor and finds herself standing beneath the gold team's holding platform; she nearly ran out of the room altogether. The flagpole stands behind her, but close enough.

From beneath the relative shelter of the platform, she sees Betsy locked in silent combat with Marvel Girl as each diverts the room's obstacles into the other's path, aiming to break the other's concentration. Nightcrawler, meanwhile, is pinned down by Storm and Banshee, who circle overhead as he leaps back and forth to avoid a pinpointed sonic blast here, a minor tornado there. There's little chance of him successfully breaking free without use of his teleportation, so it's only a matter of time before one of them gets ahold of the flag on Nightcrawler's belt.

And nobody's watching Kitty, which *was* the plan.

It takes her longer than it would take her teammates to scramble up the pole. The Hellfire Club has an impressive gymnasium for its members, and the Inner Circle, a better one. But she can't claim to visit the gym as regularly as she did at the Massachusetts Academy, when she was under Emma's thumb daily and workouts were mandated. She makes her way, one hand overhead, one forearm braced against the metal, knees locked around the pole. Standing in place, she pulls, lifts her knees, stands again. Again and again, until she's nearly at the top.

Then the Danger Room seems to erupt.

Obstacles are uprooted and spew toward the ceiling like lava made from scrap metal. Around them all, a spiderlike web, shimmering and pink: Betsy's telekinetic weapon. It's gone awry again, judging by how frantically she and the others flee as the web sparkles out and the obstacles crash down again. The X-Men scatter regardless of their blue or gold pennants, dodging clawed arms, spinning buzz saws, human-sized mousetraps as they fall.

As he sails back into the blue zone, powered by short bursts of a scream, Banshee spots Kitty clinging to the pole. "The lass has the flag!" he cries to his teammates.

Time to move.

Shimmying the last foot up the pole, she rips the gold flag free, then spins and jumps for the holding platform some dozen feet down, squeezing her eyes shut until she lands safely in Wolverine's strong arms. Tagged free, he leaps from the platform, absorbing the impact before setting Kitty down. And now they're running in reverse, with Wolverine blocking for Kitty while Nightcrawler and Betsy do their best to detain the rest, heedless of their own capture. They're only the decoys, after all. Wolverine is peeled off by a floor panel that rises and folds to entomb him, and then it's only Kitty, panting and sprinting for safety, flag clutched in her sweaty fist.

She falls across the centerline just as Storm descends, and by then, it's too late.

"Blue team wins!" Cyclops exclaims over the loudspeaker.

Immediately, every trap and obstacle conjured by the Danger Room recedes back into the floor and walls and ceiling, panels sliding into place, the room returning to form as Kitty bends to brace her hands on her knees and gasp for air. Maybe she should be spending time in the mansion's gym after all.

But she dismisses all that from mind for the moment, because she's won.

They've won.

Wolverine lifts her off her feet into a bear hug—impressive, considering that they're of a height—as Nightcrawler teleports over to offer her a three-fingered high five. Though now, she finds herself thinking of them as Wolverine and Kurt once more. Then the gold team is rushing in. Laughing, Peter grabs Kurt in a good-natured headlock until he bamfs free in a burst of foul smoke to lock an arm around Peter's massive silver neck. Ororo floats down on a gentle wind to land alongside Sean.

"Cheers, friends," he says, nodding. "We'll have you next time!"

Behind the viewing glass, Scott and the professor watch them all with obvious affection.

And now Betsy is running toward her, horrified. "I'm so sorry, Kitty. I only wanted to . . . it was my powers. I couldn't . . . I nearly cost us the game!"

But Kitty throws her arms around her in triumph, too elated to feign apathy or anger. "Damn, Betsy. You didn't tell me you were *that* powerful!"

After a moment frozen stiff in Kitty's embrace, Betsy relaxes at last, and even laughs. "I don't think I knew, either." Then she hugs Kitty back, as though they really are teammates.

As if they always have been.

CHAPTER 21

DOOM

JULY 7, 1975

SOME MIGHT CONSIDER IT HUMILIATING, BEING MARCHED THROUGH one's own castle in electronic shackles of one's own invention, surrounded by Doombots that reflect one's own visage. The bots' weaponry is not equal to Doom's, yet would admittedly prove an obstacle should he choose to attack Other-Doom, as would the shackles—thickly banded handcuffs wormed through with circuitry. They're designed to release an electric impulse that, whenever a superpowered prisoner attempts to access their powers, racks the body with intense pain. This, too, Doom could withstand and overcome if he had any intention of assaulting his counterpart.

But Doom has no such goal. Not while things are going exactly according to plan.

He's escorted through the halls and up many a staircase to the private laboratory on the eighth level, where Other-Doom waits. Not alone, though. He's brought with him one of the castle's resources, which Doom requested: a man whose wild hair and long tangle of a beard are as white as his belted robes. Even in 1975, Seer appears as old as the hills of Latveria. A stone cauldron sits on a pedestal amid the three of them, with amaranth-colored smoke roiling gently inside the bowl.

"You may obey this creature as though he were your true master," Other-Doom instructs the castle mystic, "until and unless I order otherwise."

Seer looks questioningly toward Doom.

"I require a vision," he commands. "Show us Jean Grey. Show us who she is. Show us what matters to her most."

The man looks uncertainly toward Other-Doom, but only for a moment; he has his orders already. Seer nods his unsteady head, tucks a wizened hand into the pocket of his robe, and withdraws a clawful of sand. He tosses it into the cauldron, and the colored smoke writhes toward the high ceiling in a shower of sparks. He mutters a language that isn't Latverian but that Doom is familiar with, though he does not speak it himself—a particular language of witchcraft and divination. His eyes roll back into his skull, suffusing with the same reddish-rose light. Seer raises his hands, and an image blooms from the smoke.

First, there is space: stars upon stars, and then the sun.

Next there is a ship. Just an insignificant speck representing the mechanical limitations of humankind.

Finally, there is a young woman in a tattered black dress, with red hair and green eyes. She clutches the yoke of the ship, staring out the windshield toward the vast and roiling surface of the sun.

The images vanish, replaced by smoke.

"More," Doom urges. "Show us more."

Seer looks to Other-Doom. "Your Excellency, my visions . . . they are but glimpses. Of the past, or in this case, I must assume the future. They are not always revealed in the manner of my—"

Doom moves like lightning, sidestepping the bots while evading one bot's grasp to tower over Seer. He reaches out to wrap an iron fist around the collar of the man's robes, but stops himself just short. He feels his counterpart's cool gaze upon him, waiting, measuring. Doom detects a test therein. Other-Doom may have instructed his servant to treat Doom as his master, but Doom will be expected to remember who the true master is.

He must show restraint, show deference, or prove himself a threat.

Instead, he smooths out the front of Seer's robe, sensing the flutter of the man's frail heartbeat, even through his gauntlet. "You are not the only one privileged with knowledge of the future. I know what you're capable of, with proper motivation. Consider me your motivation," he says reasonably, "and try again."

"Y-Yes, Excellency," he stammers.

Doom steps away, ceding ground to his counterpart, who nods appreciatively.

Another test passed.

Tossing a second palmful of sand into the cauldron, Seer murmurs furiously. The specter of Jean Grey twists from the smoke once more, only now the column of smoke billows outward, surrounding them all. It's as though he, Seer, and Other-Doom are standing inside the shuttle itself, though it appears through a veil of shifting red mist.

Other-Doom paces forward, the mist parting and reshaping around him. His footfalls are soundless as he stalks across the shuttle's bridge toward Jean. He leans close, scrutinizing her desperate expression, her clenched teeth and white-knuckled grip on the yoke. She doesn't flinch as he waves a hand before her face.

"Only an image," Seer tells him, the tremble in his old voice betraying his efforts. "She is but a projection to us. Nothing we do here affects the future."

Doom knows this already. He turns to move off through the shuttle, passing through the cabin door as though the ship's fuselage is fog. He stands in what ought to be the passenger cabin, but it remains empty.

At the back of the cabin is another door, and they pass through it to a small, sealed chamber where the rest of the team known as the X-Men are in chaos. The ones called Nightcrawler and Colossus attempt to grapple the one called Cyclops, who bucks and struggles frantically against their hold.

"Scott, no! If you open the life-cell, you'll kill us all!" Nightcrawler pleads.

"Let me go, blast you!" Cyclops roars back. "Let me go before it's too late!"

Tears track through Nightcrawler's dark-blue fur, tracing even darker paths down his cheeks. "It is already too late, my friend."

Doom's counterpart enters behind him. "What good is any of this to me? What good is the future to the past?"

"Is knowledge not the greatest power in the Multiverse? There's much to be gained here. You'll see."

Back on the flight deck, they watch passively as disaster strikes. Doom knew it would; long has he researched and prepared for this particular world, though Seer's talents were needed to witness the event that would change the course of history, as he now attempts.

The violence of the solar flare shatters Jean's considerable telepathic shield. As radiation pummels her mortal form, the meat withers on her bones, and hair drops from her scalp like cut wheat while her skin recedes.

Seer cries beside them, "My liege, I cannot . . . cannot hold this . . ."

"You will," Other-Doom rebukes him simply, "or you will prove yourself useless."

Jean tilts her skull back and unhinges her jaw to scream, but no sound comes out.

That's when the flight deck floods with the purest white light, cutting through the red-tinged mist as though they stand inside a star.

Be not afraid comes the answer to her prayer, spoken by a present but unseen being.

Then they're back in Other-Doom's laboratory, spit out by the smoke, which sputters and twists like a dying flame. Seer drops to his bony knees. The last thing they see before the fire in the cauldron hisses out and the smoke dissipates is the living skeleton of Jean Grey, who makes a vow to the shape of a woman haloed by colored light: "To save the X-Men, I'd dance with the devil himself."

Then she's gone.

"Leave us now," Other-Doom says, dismissing Seer.

When he raises his head, the light in his eyes is extinguished along with the smoke, leaving only the cloudy vision of an aged creature. Painfully, he climbs to his feet and gives a feeble bow.

Other-Doom has turned his back to Seer even before he's hobbled from the laboratory. "Well then? How is this useful in securing the nexus powers?"

Doom spreads his hands, his wrists still encircled by the electronic shackles, snug against his gauntlets. "We know now what matters most to Jean Grey—the X-Men and the boy. We know that they're more precious to her than her own life. Does it not stand to reason that she'd submit to us to save them? Whether this bargaining chip will become necessary, I cannot say, but it's advantageous to have nonetheless, as any contingency would be."

Other-Doom turns to the bots still flanking Doom. "Leave us as well," he commands them. "But keep near." Then he paces the length of the chamber, considering this.

Meanwhile Doom waits, head lowered just slightly. A portrait of humble deference.

At last, his counterpart declares, "You have no assets to command in this world, no freedom unless I grant it, and you have thus far failed in your attempts. You've said you cannot take the nexus powers without me. Your proposition intrigues me, but how, precisely, does a partnership benefit me?"

Doom holds his position; he is close now. "He who holds the nexus powers in any given universe commands that reality. How would you remake yours, if given the choice?"

The speed of Other-Doom's answer is as promising as it is predictable. "I have grown weary of exchanging blows with foes who hardly warrant my attention, and had enough of men whose inferior minds are celebrated while my own unparalleled genius is derided as madness."

"The Fantastic Four," Doom correctly guesses. Who else? "Men like Reed Richards can never understand us. They've never had to make the choices we've been faced with. Never sacrificed all that might have been good in the pursuit of greatness. They've never come from, nor become responsible for, a people who would have fallen beneath the cruel and careless knife of the world without them. And so they will never recognize that the only cure for such a world is a crueler master."

Other-Doom watches him for a moment that stretches to eternity, searching for the lie in Doom's words. He won't find one.

"They will never appreciate you," Doom presses, "because they do not possess the capacity to comprehend your vision. And so your rivalry has become a distraction from the work that is your true purpose in this world. You are like a god besieged by horseflies."

"It is as you say," his counterpart concedes at last. "Given the chance, I would rid myself of their meddling once and for all."

"It will be done," Doom promises. "I will see it done."

So close.

"And what guarantee do I have that you would keep your word?"

"We are the same," he reminds Other-Doom, "and so our goals are one. We strive toward them together. I can give you tech that you've yet to conceive of, create a next generation of Doombots that puts the last to shame—advances that you yourself would have discovered over time, but why delay what's rightfully yours? Everything I accomplish with the use of your labs will be yours when all is said and done, including the device I need to remove the nexus powers from Jean Grey. The means of its construction exist only inside my own mind. And there is a Multiverse of nexus beings waiting beyond the bounds of your reality. With the psi-phon in hand, their powers will be forfeit. We need only reach out and take them."

"It seems a great deal of work awaits you."

"Only half as much if we work together." Doom extends one gauntleted hand, the suppressing cuff glinting under the laboratory lights.

His counterpart reaches back, clasping hands as Doom knew he would.

Nobody will ever understand Victor von Doom better than himself.

CHAPTER 22

DOOM

JULY 10, 1975

THE RESEARCH AND DEVELOPMENT LABORATORIES OF THE CASTLE'S subbasements are woefully inadequate. They're filled with outdated equipment as well as experiments that Doom has either completed, discarded, or improved upon many times over in the future. His counterpart's private lab aboveground would have been marginally better, with access to his latest devices and inventions. But despite the gains Doom has made—freedom, food, and an intact faceplate—he has been denied use of Other-Doom's closely guarded domain. So, these labs will have to suffice for his current purpose: reconstructing what he needs to claim the nexus powers for his own.

The psi-phon.

An invention of a long-lost interdimensional being, the psi-phon was conceived of as a means to absorb and exchange life essences—powers unique to each living creature. One rogue Marc Spector once used it to absorb the essences of other Moon Knights, claiming their abilities and becoming Moon Shade. Of course, Doom cares nothing for the many unimportant Marcs strewn between realities, no more than he does for any variants of Jean Grey. But the psi-phon was proven capable of transferring the nexus powers—that was all he needed to know.

Doom has precious little to go on as he begins the work of recreating the device. Only the shards plucked from his ruined breastplate, now collected in a tray on the worktable, and his understanding of its properties.

He has certainly done more with less.

Now, as he spreads his schematics out on the table for his counterpart to see, Other-Doom sniffs at the design.

"It may not look like much," Doom concedes. On the paper, a simple arched band is connected on either end to two rectangular pads, with a small, round transmitter positioned over the wearer's forehead. "But it will deliver us the nexus powers. We'll need to improve upon its design, now that I have access to equipment. I never should have relied on the inferior designs of another. We must create an easily transportable power source, and an internal conduit to transfer energy between the wielder and the subject. The solution may be mystical in nature, rather than technological." He contemplates the possibilities.

When at last he looks up from the drawing, Other-Doom's eyes are narrowed behind the slits of his mask. "So many worlds, so many experiments, so many miscalculations. How can you be so certain that Jean Grey, among all nexi, is the one you've been searching for?"

Doom is already used to tempering his indignation. He knows it's all a part of Other-Doom's tests; prodding at Doom's humility as though seeking weak points in a suit of armor. He considers slamming his gauntlet on the worktable, letting Other-Doom claim a petty little victory to feed his confidence in his own superiority.

But the question is too close to the one Other-Doom *should* be asking. So, Doom restrains himself. "There have been miscalculations, as you say. But as my understanding advanced, and my findings increased, it became clear that, by whatever quirk of the cosmos, this world was an inevitable destination. Still, I waited until my experiments had proved out."

"And to what purpose? You've not yet said."

"Knowledge is purpose enough, isn't it?"

"At times, yes. But you spoke of sacrifice. 'All that might have been good in the pursuit of greatness.' The devil himself knows we have made such bargains, though not for the sake of science. You expect me to believe that you have no application in mind for the knowledge you seek?" His counterpart's frankness is surprising.

Doom had not thought he could surprise himself.

But Other-Doom is still predictable. As he speaks of the devil, Doom knows which sacrifice comes to his mind.

Valeria.

They were children together in the Romani camp, then sweethearts. He thinks of her and remembers autumn in Hungary. Their people preparing for winter. Dried leaves tumbling through the air, borne on a cold breeze that smelled of campfires. Her dark hair spilling through his hands, and the taste of their first kiss, warm and clean. Valeria, who stood by him after his father met his frozen fate, and when Doom turned to his long-dead mother's legacy of the dark arts, desperate for revenge. While Doom unlocked the secrets of science and sorcery both, she remained by his side. But when he had the chance to leave Latveria to pursue his studies in America, she would not follow. Too beholden to her family and their homeland, she begged him to stay. She could not comprehend his quest for knowledge, and the power it promised. So, he left her behind.

Then came Reed Richards, that fraud masquerading as his peer. Then came the necrophone, Doom's most fateful invention yet. Then came disfigurement, and the disgrace of failure. Then, at last, came Valeria to console him, and to tempt him back to the life they'd had, the man he'd been. But when she finally saw Doom for who he was and what he had become, she had fled into hiding.

In 1975, this will have happened recently enough to haunt Other-Doom as much as it drives him onward.

"All right, then. There is . . . someone. Not in your world, but another among many. One where I might have been content. At peace." He pauses to let the implication dawn on his doppelgänger. "I would find them again. But not until I possess the nexus powers. Until reality knits itself to my will, they cannot truly be mine."

Other-Doom's eyes are trained upon him like laser sights, and though Doom wears a full mask once more, he feels the same discomfort of being perceived against his will as he did during its absence.

Then Other-Doom looks down to hungrily consider the schematics. "And this device is the key?" he asks at last.

"It is," says Doom, and explains his plans for its reconstruction thus far.

He doesn't tell his counterpart that, after many years of searching, Other-Doom will find Valeria again, though it would have been much better for her if he had not. Doom does not explain that, someday, Other-Doom will make a pact with a clan of netherdemons, offering them something irreplaceable in exchange for control of the dark arts such as he has yet to dream of. He does not tell Other-Doom that this choice will redefine the concept of sacrifice for him in the future.

For now, let Other-Doom imagine that Valeria—or a woman like her—might be the *someone* who has driven Doom across the Multiverse. Let him imagine a hillside in Latveria, a distant campsite, and a young girl whose soft, dark hair once poured between his fingers like water.

Just as long as he does not question Doom further.

CHAPTER 23

KITTY

JULY 18, 1975

THE GIRLS' NIGHT OUT IS JEAN'S IDEA; A CHANCE TO UNWIND AFTER two long weeks each with five full training days, and a chance for Kitty and Betsy to see the city at night. Of course, Kitty's no stranger to New York City, though the club scene isn't exactly compatible with her lifestyle. Or her personality. She keeps out of the thick of it, clinging to the shadows, phasing through back alleys and picking up takeout when she must. The less people see of her, the less chance they'll remember her, and the less she'll be forced to change apartments and subway routes, dentists and aliases.

But since they're supposed to be strangers here, Kitty has little choice but to accept the tourist treatment. So on Friday evening, she, Betsy, Jean, and Ororo take the train from Westchester's city center into Penn Station. They walk together down to the brightly glowing Broadway, where the collected heat of the day still burns up from the concrete, and the air is ripe with the comingled scents of spicy cologne and cigarette smoke, spilled beer and street food. Outside the doors of LaBelle, a line stretches around the block. It's a sea of polyester and denim, pointed collars and metallic minidresses, Afros and feathered bobs. Most of these people will be waiting for hours, and Kitty's palms tingle at the thought of it.

But Jean has no intention of spending Girls' Night Out in the queue. Instead she marches them straight to the front to stand before the doorman—a burly guy whose black button-down shirt gapes open down to his navel, showcasing chest hair nearly as thick as his shoulder-length shag and soul patch (though he's got nothing on Wolverine). As he chews away on a toothpick, the bouncer's gaze flicks across Jean in a green sequined bandeau top to match her sparkling eyes, her red hair waving gently down to her elbows. Ororo stuns as well in a patchwork leather vest that bares her midriff, her dark skin dewy in the July heat, her bone-white hair glowing in the light cast off from the neon LABELLE sign. Even Betsy looks as though she was designed to stand onstage at a disco, uncomfortable though she must be in the blue spandex bodysuit borrowed from Jean's closet.

And then there's Kitty.

She wraps her arms around her waist, drops them, then tugs her borrowed, fringed suede purse across her body, scowling as the doorman eyeballs her. Though, honestly, her slightly cropped orange-and-white-striped halter top, flowing white palazzo pants, and white platform boots show less of her figure than those awful, skintight maroon Hellion suits of her youth. Still, this isn't her shtick. Kitty's not the flirt-with-the-facility-guard-to-distract-him guy. She's the phase-through-the-ceiling-and-steal-the-secret-alien-tech-before-melting-back-into-the-air-ducts guy.

Lucky for her that the doorman forgets all about her when Jean steps forward, pops her hip, points her chin toward the entrance, and asks, "Think you can find room in there for a few more?"

He grins around the toothpick, teeth big and pearl white.

Then they're walking through the velvet rope and into the club, no telepathic powers or shifting of atoms required.

Inside, every surface is brightly colored or glittering or neon. Three giant disco balls hang from a domed ceiling three stories high, casting stars across the DJ booth and the vast dance floor. The floor itself is bordered by waist-high mirrors, tilted in such a way to reflect the dancers back and back and back upon themselves to infinity. On either side of the bar, neon rings encircle floor-to-ceiling columns, each as wide as a hula hoop, glowing toxic orange and flamingo pink and slime green.

"So this is a disco?" Betsy bends down slightly to shout into her ear over "The Hustle" blasting through the speakers. "It's . . . a lot!"

Kitty tilts her head to shout back, "I preferred the Danger Room!"

"To the bar?"

She could damn sure use a drink, but the crowd around the bar is just as thick as the dance floor, which Jean and Ororo are winding their way toward now. "Go ahead, I'm just gonna . . . breathe!" With that, she splits off and heads toward the far wall of the club, where there seems to be a pocket of space and air behind an iron stairwell leading up to an equally crowded balcony. But it's like battling upstream, impossible to move through the crowd without the friction and jostle of other sweating bodies against her own. Finally, she phases until she can't hold her breath any longer, letting the world pour through her. It's a risk, sure, but she bets it's too crowded and confusing here for anybody to notice.

When at last she reaches the staircase, Kitty tucks herself in behind it. She needs to get a grip. And she needs to figure out what the hell she's even doing here. Sure, Betsy pitched tonight as protecting Jean. And it's possible that somewhere out on the dance floor, a stalker in a purple leisure suit is hunting her at this very moment. But putting Kitty's investment in her own future aside, why does she suddenly care so much? It can't *only* be for the sake of the world that will be, when it's all she's ever known. Because if she could go back (or forward) and tell herself she'll soon be zipping herself into disco boots and loitering awkwardly in a nightclub to protect a woman she barely knows, yet hates to remember a world without?

She'd never have believed it.

Why are you hiding?

Surfacing from the churning ocean of her own thoughts, Kitty startles to see Jean standing in front of her. "I'm not—" she attempts to shout, then gives up and answers in her mind. **I'm *not*. Just not big on crowds.**

Nodding as though this is reasonable, Jean slides in beside Kitty. She holds up a palm, and in an instant all the noise of the club cuts out. Like some soundproof bubble has surrounded them. "Psionic barrier," Jean explains. "We can't hear them, they can't hear us. And we can stand here all night if you like, though they might be playing a pretty great song out there." She tilts her head curiously before her plum-painted lips quirk up at the corner. "Never mind, it's 'Jungle Fever.'"

"I don't get it," Kitty mutters. "You're a telepath. How can you stand to be around so many people when you know exactly what they think about you—about *mutants*—all the time? They hate us."

"I know I slipped up when we first met, but you were a stranger in the mansion, and I don't usually barge into people's brains without knocking unless it seems necessary. You're right, though—some do. But some are just scared. And that doesn't have to be a permanent condition, you know?"

Kitty sniffs.

"You don't think people can change?"

"I think even when people are scared, they always pick the devil they know. And for non-mutants, that's hating mutants."

"Hmm." Jean considers this, relaxing back against the wall. "If that's true, then what's the devil *you* know?"

Running away. Being alone. It comes to mind so quickly, Kitty doesn't have time to censor herself before thinking directly at Jean. Perhaps if she melts through the floor right now, she'll never have to finish this conversation.

But instead of pressing her further, Jean kicks off the wall, spins, and holds out one hand. "Well, maybe it's time to change, Kitty Pryde," she says, then flashes her white smile in the neon dark.

A challenge.

Kitty makes a show of rolling her eyes, but she gives Jean her hand all the same and allows herself to be led onto the dance floor.

CHAPTER 24

★

AMERICA

EVEN OVER THE IMPOSSIBLE ROAR OF THIS PLANET'S DEATH THROES, America explains, "I figured of all the infinite Earths, there had to be *one* that Galactus had gotten his teeth around," knowing the Watcher can hear her. "I am not going back. In fact, I'm not going anywhere. You can call it a day, go back to the room where nothing happens, and tell the Watchers' Council I'm giving my notice. Or we can stay on this rock together until the end."

Beneath their feet, the tectonic plates shift. This world is breaking apart. The spear-shaped tower that stands fifty or so meters away from them across a pitted stretch of ground begins to collapse, steel and stone and glass crumpling like sheaves of paper. As it falls, two things happen at once:

The Watcher grabs for America, intending to think them both off this planet and drag her back with him across the galaxy.

In the same moment, the colossal shock wave reaches them, accompanied by billowing dust and flying debris. Rather than hunker down with her superhuman strength, America lets it catch her, tossing her back through the air and out of reach. A heavy beam whistles straight for her, colliding with her shoulder. It doesn't pierce deeply—America Chavez is stronger than steel, after all—but the breath is knocked from her body when she's sent smashing to the ground, pinned beneath it. She gasps in dust and God-knows-what as she wrestles an arm free. By then, the Watcher is there, reaching for her once more, and she shoves the beam off her chest to send it flying toward his stoic face. It doesn't strike him, of course. He blasts it from midair with the same energy that landed her in the Hudson River. Still, it buys her a moment to stomp a portal into the churned-up dirt and land safely (well, safe-ish) atop the newly collapsed tower's rubble.

The Watcher joins her in another blink. But he pauses in his interminable pursuit to try to reason. "This will not kill you. It will not kill me. A Watcher cannot die."

"Oh, but you can," she points out while massaging her aching ribs as subtly as possible. "In fact, that dude up there's one of the only beings who *can* kill you. And you know it, because I know it. He's killed your kind before. Ate you up for an energy boost. And me, I'm only nearly indestructible. You're welcome to try to stop him, if you're in a mood to intervene. You still got another blast in that chamber, I'm sure?"

"We do not—"

"Yeah, yeah," she interrupts, shoving her hands into her denim jacket pockets to hide their shaking. All around them, energy swirls across the ravaged landscape. Anything that was alive in this place has already been consumed, converted into the raw stuff of creation to be digested by a giant whose food source is life itself ... if it wasn't set adrift when the veil of atmosphere between this planet and the void collapsed entirely. "Well then, I guess it's you and me."

She sees it then: the first twitch of fear on the Watcher's ageless face.

"We Watchers summon ourselves back into existence by our will alone," he protests, just before teleporting himself to safety as a deep chasm splits the ground beneath them, the rubble tumbling down into the crevasse, toward the weakening core of the world.

America flies up to hover in the air, which feels little different from the vacuum of space by now. "Maybe you won't stay gone," she concedes. "But can you put yourself back together fast enough to take me with you? Kinda pointless if not. Me, I suggest you live to fight another day. But it's your choice, right?"

An agonizing moment passes, and she fights to keep her eyes on the Watcher rather than the unfathomable maw of Galactus above.

"Nothing will end here," he declares after what feels like eternity. "Not you. Not I. You will be held accountable for your actions, Watcher."

"That's not my name," she cries as the world comes apart beneath them, splitting from its center with a burst of sound that's beyond deafening.

But even as he vanishes, she knows he's heard her.

Thrown through the air once more, she twists to punch a star-shaped portal through the dust cloud. Then she, too, is gone.

When America spills out of the portal, she lands on grass so neatly trimmed, it bristles beneath her palms. Still coughing dust up from the depths of her lungs, it takes her a moment to get her bearings. This world is not where she left it, or rather, she is not where she was when she left this world. The sky overhead is midnight purple, crickets chirping the song of summertime in the countryside. A light drizzle of rain patters down. She suspects that days have passed, not hours, and for a heartbeat she panics—is she too late? Has Doom already gotten to Jean Grey, and she's only found her way back to watch this reality collapse like that tower?

Getting her feet beneath her, America takes in her new surroundings. She stands on the front lawn beside a driveway, just outside the open gates to an entrance courtyard. Beyond is a place she knows; from her time as a Watcher, yes, but before that. Ivy threads up the brick face of a familiar mansion with a bronzed plaque mounted beside the columned entrance that proclaims: XAVIER'S SCHOOL FOR GIFTED YOUNGSTERS.

Before she can brush the soot from her palms, the doors up ahead open, and Charles Xavier (a much younger version than she met before she lost herself) rolls out onto the marble front steps. Of course, he'll have sensed her sudden arrival. He's flanked in the doorway by this world's Cyclops.

"Well, it seems we're to be inundated with unexpected guests. How wonderful," Xavier exclaims, despite her singed and soaked clothing, and her lip bloodied from smashing into the riverbank. "Will you come inside?"

Here on the X-Men's doorstep at last, she hesitates for just a moment.

There is no going back. No retreating to the safety of her cosmic window. She knows this. She's chosen humanity, with all its pain and love and loss and greed and bravery and beautiful mess. A world with warfare and selfishness beyond fathoming. But also a world with sour gummies and cola, and the Highbridge Park Pool, where she once held hands with her adoptive brother Berto as they sank below the surface together with their eyes wide open. When she first came to this timeline, America had wondered why she landed in the neighborhood she used to call home, instead of conveniently landing at the estate on Graymalkin Lane, if her portals always spit her out where she was meant to go.

Now she's beginning to understand.

Ignoring the lingering ache in her ribs, she walks through the open gate. "You don't know me," she calls out as she approaches, "but I'm America Chavez, and I'm here to help."

CHAPTER 25

KITTY

JULY 18, 1975

HOW LONG HAS IT BEEN SINCE KITTY PRYDE LAST DANCED? SINCE she left Miss Hester's and its ballet classes, at least; no time for extracurriculars while training at the Massachusetts Academy.

Granted, she's not dancing now so much as standing hesitantly on the floor while Jean and Ororo join the crowd, swiveling to hip bump in time with the driving beat of "Get Down Tonight."

Betsy joins her from the bar, and pink butterfly wings unfurl inside her mind. Once again, Betsy's perfectly happy to barge in without knocking; Kitty might have to change the psychic locks when all this is done. **I've been scanning for thoughts and have yet to pick up on any interest in Jean. Not violent interest, anyway. Whatever the threat to her existence, if it's present tonight, I can't find it.**

Kitty replies in kind—because it's more convenient than shouting over the music—Great. So what are we supposed to do with our free time?

Perhaps we should . . . blend? Betsy frowns at the crowd. I've never been a fan of disco, you know.

Shocking. I'm shocked! I took one look at that woman who wore a suit to an all-night diner and thought, I bet that woman enjoys a funky chicken.

Don't tell me *you're* a fan.

Kitty watches a man in shiny gold polyester squat down to the floor and pop back up, swinging his arms all the while. **I mean, I'm not a fan of *that*.**

Hmm.

At Betsy's distracted hum, she turns and follows her companion's eyeline to find two women in color-coordinated jumpsuits a little way across the dance floor, hips bumping vigorously. They don't seem any different from Jean and Ororo, until the blonde threads her arm around the brunette's waist to keep her close, and the brunette lightly skims her fingertips down the blonde's hip. They break apart as soon as the song changes, but the secret in their lingering glance—and in Betsy's—speaks for itself.

Did you leave someone behind in the future? Kitty guesses. **Someone like that?**

Betsy shakes her head, then clarifies, **If I had, I think it would have been . . . like that. But there's no one.** She looks sideways at Kitty. **You?**

Now it's Kitty's turn to shake her head, grateful for the colorful strobing lights that hide her flush. **Not . . . Not that it would never be like that. Not that I haven't thought about it being like that. And I've, uh, gone on dates. With men, and women. I've had a few fun nights. Nothing stuck, though.** But that's not the truth, is it? At least, not all of it. Some of those dates tried to become more. Not many, but some. She's the one who slips determinedly out of reach every time, terrified to be tied in place by obligation or—God forbid—emotion. That way lies the cycle of rejection and pain and cynicism. **Maybe I'm hard to hold on to,** she concludes, though she knows it's more like refusing to be held.

Well, maybe we should try. Dancing, I mean, Betsy amends so quickly, it's a bit insulting. **We can't just stand here all evening as though we're guarding Buckingham Palace.**

For the second time tonight, somebody holds their hand out to Kitty.

For the second time tonight, Kitty surprises herself by taking it. And just until the song ends, she lets herself imagine a life like this.

Maybe she *could* be different, in a different world.

ONLY ON THE MIDNIGHT TRAIN RIDE BACK TO WESTCHESTER, AND after Jean and Ororo have fallen asleep on each other's shoulders, does Kitty dare to speak aloud.

"To recap," she starts, little more than a whisper. "Neither of us has a boyfriend, or a girlfriend, or a hot person of any gender waiting to dance with us in the future. We probably don't have jobs. Dunno about RCX, but Emma Frost isn't super forgiving when her henchmen go on sabbatical without permission. Okay, sure, you've got a brother, and maybe you do Sunday-night happy hours and reminisce about your childhood puppy—"

"We do not," Betsy whispers back. "I love my brother, of course. But he's quite preoccupied by being a father and husband and champion of Britain, and all that. Between his obligations and my work with the agency, there isn't much time left for family dinners."

"Well, I haven't been back to Deerfield for a whole bunch of Hanukkahs now, and I doubt my parents hold their breaths until I return their twice-yearly phone calls, where they mostly complain about the other one, ten years after their divorce." Kitty fiddles with the fringe on her borrowed purse. "Betsy . . . Whatever we're here to do with Jean, you really think we can fix our lives? Fix the whole world?"

Betsy considers this for a long moment. "I think that we can't predict the impact one life would have upon the world, but it might be greater even than we imagine. Maybe a future with Jean in it is a future where the X-Men still exist, and Charles Xavier's dreams have borne fruit."

"Mutants sharing the world with *Homo sapiens*, living together in peace. Yeah. Maybe." She tries to imagine it . . . or rather, to remember the wish she used to whisper into the dark as a teenager but has long since left behind. A world without instructive pamphlets like *Know the Signs: How to Spot the Mutant Menace in Your School, City, or Household*. Without news segments dedicated to reporting each day's successful captures or killings of mutants, tallied by a wild-eyed anchorman with a marker on a massive whiteboard. Without a thirteen-year-old Kitty Pryde waking from nightmares of Sentinels storming across the lawn at Miss Hester's to smash a massive metal fist through her dorm room window and drag her from her bed, too frozen with fear to phase away. Maybe in that world, she would've told her parents the truth of who she was. Maybe she'd have more people in her life to tell the truth to. Favorite teachers, or partners, or best friends.

"Kitty, I've been wondering. Have you had any of your episodes—your slips, I mean—since we've come back in time? You haven't mentioned any."

"No," she realizes as she says it. She turns to stare out the window but of course can't see anything beyond her own stark reflection in the rain-pattered glass. It's strange. She used to be afraid of the slips and what they said about her—that she was even more of a freak than mutant-haters would have guessed. Only it wasn't just that. She was scared of how she felt afterward. How sometimes, she wished she could have stayed in the world that she'd figured was a by-product of slowly losing her mind. Sometimes she felt she would've given anything, everything, if she could forever be the version of herself that she was in that other, better world. "Don't you think that means something?" Kitty asks.

Without looking, she can't tell what Betsy thinks of her confession. And for a long moment, Betsy doesn't answer.

Finally she begins, "I do. Kitty, if we—"

Jean bolts upright across from them, startling Ororo awake as she and Betsy jump in their seats. "The professor," Jean says, voice still blurry with sleep. "He says there's company back at the mansion. Not a mutant. She's looking for me. She says she's a friend."

Kitty feels Betsy's body tense beside her, along with her own. Could this be the threat they've been braced for? **Do you think we should tell her now? Just go ahead and step on the damn butterfly?** She can't keep her leg from bouncing against her seat with nerves. This could be it: the whole reason for their being here.

And their only reason for staying.

Betsy shakes her head subtly. **We can't stop these two from returning to the mansion. And maybe these are the best circumstances we could hope for. An early warning and the mansion on alert. We'll just have to be ready for what comes.**

The four of them catch a yellow taxi at the train station, and even though Jean maintains regular contact with Xavier to keep a telepathic eye on things, Kitty's still relieved to find the mansion peaceful upon arrival. Only the light in Xavier's office window so late at night suggests that anything is out of the ordinary. There's no storm of activity within the mansion when they enter, no sound of running feet from above as the four of them climb the grand staircase, no shouts from the office as they approach. The professor seems perfectly unharmed in his chair at the desk. Behind him, Scott leans against a bookshelf in giant, red-lensed aviators, a T-shirt, sweatpants, and plaid slippers. Not exactly poised for battle.

"Welcome back, you four," Xavier says pleasantly. "Our guest has said she's here to speak with you specifically, Jean, and we thought it best to wait until you all arrived."

The guest turns out to be a young woman about her same age with dark, dust-covered curls, wearing black jeans torn violently at both knees, and a rain-dampened denim jacket with red-and-white-striped shoulders and starred patches down both sleeves. She must be powerful to tackle a telepath like Jean Grey.

But as the woman turns her large brown eyes on Jean, she looks nothing but relieved. "America Chavez," she introduces herself. "I've been looking for—" Then her gaze skips over to the pair of them and snags, the slightest surprise registering before she tilts her head and tightens her jaw. "Didn't expect to find you two here."

Storm frowns. "You know each other?"

"Oh, for ages."

Xavier turns to them. "Ms. Chavez is the friend you've been waiting for?" he guesses.

Who is this girl? Kitty thinks directly at Betsy.

Betsy lifts one shoulder just slightly. "No," she answers aloud, and it must be true, if she isn't pinging Betsy's telepathic trail. "This is a surprise."

"To all of us," the girl replies.

"We'll find the others," Jean says. "Gather them in the dining room."

The professor nods his agreement, and she and Ororo head off while Scott bends over his desk to confer.

"You two." America nods at her and Betsy. "You look around my size. Got a change of clothes I could borrow for the night?"

This doesn't seem quite true. America's several inches shorter than oh-didn't-you-know-I-was-once-a-fashion-model Betsy, and has muscles Kitty can only dream of; no way they wear the same size jeans, with enviable thighs like that.

But Betsy says stiffly, "Yes. Just follow us up."

Of course, the moment the three of them spill into the antechamber and the office door swings shut behind them, the woman drops all pretense of pleasantry. Crossing her arms across her chest, she accuses, "Betsy Braddock and Kitty Pryde. You two don't belong here."

Another telepath or something? Wonderful.

Betsy tilts her head, concentrating, and Kitty can imagine the sparkling psychic tendrils of her powers reaching out like a butterfly's antennae. "Neither do you, America Chavez," she replies. "Perhaps we ought to have that chat, hmm?"

Before Kitty can interrupt their standoff to ask any of one million reasonable questions, the woman—America—holds up one finger and ushers them down the hallway toward the staircase leading to the dorms, as though this was *her* secret superhero mansion (not that it's Kitty's). "Figured we'd take a beat to clear this up between us and answer each other's questions," she says, "before one of us makes a move or a mess."

Kitty gestures grandly as they walk. "Please. Interlopers first."

"Interloper? That's a little hypocritical, don't you think? You two are in the wrong time. I've seen plenty of variants of you both, and none of them are running around in 1975. Not without training bras and braces, anyway. So how did you get here, and what are you up to?"

"What do you mean, 'variants'?" Betsy asks the question on both their minds as they reach the second floor.

"You know. The many, many Betsys and Kittys across the Multiverse. Betsy, you're a champion of Otherworld, you've met your— Oh," she says quietly, realization seeming to dawn. "Unless you're not. Look, let's start from the beginning. I'll make a guess at what's going on here, and you can tell me if I'm right. Judging by the fact that you're both old—"

"Excuse me?" Kitty sniffs. "*I'm* twenty-three. *Betsy's* the old one."

"I'm not even thirty," Betsy mutters, leading them down the hallway to the eastern wing.

"I mean older than you should be. Point is, you're from the future of this timeline, right? And somehow you've found your way back?"

"We are," Betsy concedes. "We did."

"Broke into a spooky castle in Latveria," Kitty begrudgingly fills in, eager to skip to the part where it's America's turn to answer. "Hopped a ride in a time machine."

Betsy corrects, "Time platform."

"Latveria, huh?" America chuckles darkly, as if there's some joke here that's flown over Kitty's head completely. "If that's true, then why are you here?"

"We're . . . following a path." The conversation pauses as Kitty phases through her bedroom door, and, begrudgingly, removes her makeshift deadbolt to admit the others. While she digs through the drawers beneath her bed for something that might fit America—and undoubtedly look better on her—Betsy launches into the explanation she gave Kitty upon first meeting, about the psychic trail carved by the loss of someone important. Her theory, which once seemed so insubstantial as to be made of nothing, that the absence of this missing person was echoing across the decades. "I followed the path to Kitty, and we turned out to have quite a bit in common. We followed it together into the past. It led us here, and seems to stop with Jean. But I still don't know what we're meant to change. I can't remember anything about Jean, or the X-Men, for that matter, beyond what little we'd been told."

America's eyebrows knit together. "What does that mean, you can't remember them? Aren't they . . . Aren't you . . ." She presses the heel of her palm to her furrowed brow, clearly trying to collect her thoughts. Then she expels a deep breath before asking, "You're telling me that in your future, you don't know any of the X-Men at all?"

"Should we?" Kitty demands, pausing with a simple red-and-white ringer tee in hand. It's already getting tiresome, being judged by this woman for who Kitty isn't and what she doesn't know, and they've literally just met.

"We can't suss out what we're meant to change. We've been waiting for a sign of what to do next and, well, perhaps it's you," Betsy offers, infinitely more generous than Kitty.

"Yeah. Maybe." But America doesn't seem convinced.

"Your turn," Kitty reminds her as she tosses America the T-shirt. "What were you saying about a Multiverse?"

CHAPTER 26

★

AMERICA

JULY 19, 1975

IT'S NEARLY TWO IN THE MORNING BY THE TIME THE FULL TEAM AS-sembles in the formal dining room. Professor Xavier sits at one end of the long table while America stands at the other, trying to compose her thoughts. How best to warn them about an existential threat to their lives—and to their reality—that she barely has a handle on? And now there's the further complication of an anachronistic Kitty Pryde and Betsy Braddock, still waiting on her explanation. On the one hand, she could certainly use some extra help. On the other, if Kitty and Betsy come from a future without Jean Grey or the X-Men . . .

That can only mean there's a future where Doom wins, and Jean dies.

Where America fails.

Damn it.

She takes a last deep breath before plunging right in; she can't afford another approach. Who knows how much time they've got until Doom turns up? "Okay, so . . . the Multiverse. The existence of infinite, alternate Earths across realities, most of which are home to infinite, alternate versions of this Earth's populace, living their best lives as we speak. Or their lives, at least. Ring any bells?"

Predictably, she's met with blank stares around the table as the X-Men struggle to process this.

All except for Betsy. "Well . . . I did once encounter another version of my brother, years ago. A variant, if that's what you'd call him. He was unpleasant." This seems like a deeply British understatement, as her whole body shudders with the memory. "You're saying he was one of many?"

"*Many* many. I've only been to a fraction of them, but I've looked into plenty in my, uh, line of work."

"I take it that you are not the America of our reality?" Xavier asks, steepling his fingers in contemplation.

"No. I'm . . . something else. A singularity. There's only one of me anywhere, in any reality." She holds up a hand as Cyclops opens his mouth to ask a question she probably doesn't have the time or the insight to answer. "Since that skews the complicated math of the Multiverse, let's ignore it for now, okay? What matters is I was following somebody else who's figured out how to move between realities—Victor von Doom. Not yours, but a variant from another world. I don't know which. Just that he's here now or will be soon. And that he's coming after—"

"Me," Jean finishes for her. Still in her green sequined top and clutching a mug patterned with orange and yellow wildflowers, the once-and-future Phoenix hardly looks prepared to take on an armored tank like Doom, though Jean Grey has immense powers all her own.

This fact doesn't stop Wolverine from bristling visibly across the table, nor Cyclops from scraping his chair as close to Jean's as possible, looping a protective arm around her shoulders. "We've tangled with our Doom before, but what does this one want with Jean that's worth crossing this . . . Multiverse?"

"Not her so much as the nexus powers." And here, of course, she loses everyone again. Even Professor X shakes his head as his team looks to him. "Okay then, let's break this down." She spreads her arms wide, making a starfish of her fingers. "Multiverse." Then she swings her arms closer together, holding her palms half a foot apart. "Universe. Each one its own reality." She drops one arm, holding the other at a right angle, pointed straight up. "For each reality, a timeline. Let's be basic and say that time is a river.

Upstream." She points to her fingers, then points to her elbow. "Downstream. Future and past. Most folks are just bobbing along in the timeline like twigs and pebbles in a river that flows powerfully forward. Incapable of changing its course."

"So if I step on a butterfly upstream"—Kitty speaks from where she leans against the dining room wall behind Betsy's chair, having eschewed the empty one meant for her—"that won't change the future, or the river, or . . . whatever word works for this metaphor?"

"Depends on the butterfly. Not usually, though. The timeline smooths right over most disruptions. Still, some people, some events, cause bigger disruptions by their nature. A log instead of a twig. A glacial boulder instead of a pebble. Big enough to shift a river's course, which is to say, to change a timeline." America angles her arm to the side. "But beyond that, there are the nexus beings. We don't know much about them—"

"Who is 'we'?" Storm asks.

Oh boy. "'We' is . . . beings like me, who observe the Multiverse and move through it."

"Is this Doom like you?" asks Nightcrawler.

"Definitely not." America grimaces, dropping her arm to stuff her hands in her jacket pockets, seeking the comfort. "Look, these beings aren't like anyone else. The nexus powers are . . . the gravity that pulls a river downhill. The current that moves it forward. The landscape that determines its course. Take them away, and . . . well, that I don't know yet. I've never seen a timeline without its anchor. But maybe you two have?" She turns to Betsy and Kitty, who freeze under the X-Men's collective attention.

Then Betsy's shoulders drop. "Professor, you were too kind to force our stories out of us—and I'm well aware that you or Jean could have, despite my own psychic barriers—but I know you've been waiting for them, and to learn why Cerebro only just broadcasted our existence. It's because Kitty and I aren't from here."

"Another reality?" Professor X guesses.

Betsy shakes her head. "This is our world, but it isn't our time.

Not these versions of ourselves. We're from the future. And in our future, there are . . ."

"Cracks," Kitty finishes.

"We've both experienced phenomena that I posit suggest an unstable reality," Betsy picks back up.

"Our world is messed up," Kitty translates.

"How so?"

Kitty's shoulders hike up nearly to her ears with discomfort, but after a moment, she answers. "I . . . see things, sometimes. I'll be standing in a place I know, and then suddenly I'm somewhere I've never been or with people I've never met. I've actually seen *you* all before. Not America, I mean, but the X-Men. We were together, like . . . like I was one of you. But then I was back in my life, and uh . . . I wasn't."

The professor furrows his sharp brow. "America, you said that a timeline could be changed by a meaningful enough disturbance. Can a timeline be bifurcated?"

"Two timelines, existing within the same reality?" She considers this. "Or do you mean a disturbance that cracks one timeline down the center to create a forked timeline? It isn't impossible. Not much is, in the Multiverse."

"This is starting to make sense," says Betsy.

"Is it?" Kitty asks wryly. "The more you all say, the less sense it makes to me."

Betsy sighs. "You said you haven't experienced a slip since we returned to the past. If you *were* somehow phasing between timelines, as I once theorized, that suggests that we now predate whichever occurrence may split the timeline, as the professor proposes. *That's* why the trail led us to this precise moment. Here we stand a chance of saving Jean—and the timeline along with her."

"But why *me*?" Jean asks, still clutching her mug with white knuckles. "It doesn't . . . I'm just a person!"

"You ain't just a person, Jeannie," Wolverine grumbles even before Cyclops can protest.

"He's right." America shrugs. "Though there's no link I can see between the nexus beings. It could be to do with the Phoenix, in Jean's case, but that doesn't explain the others." Seeing the return of their blank looks, she whistles. "Okay, well, buckle up. The Phoenix Force is . . . creation and destruction at the most primal level. In the future—not far from now at all, actually—Jean becomes its host. She'll be practically unkillable once it bonds with her. That must be why Doom shot back to the past. He has to take Jean off the board before it becomes impossible."

"And in the future we came from, he's succeeded," Betsy realizes aloud.

"Seems like it," America admits.

Again the room falls silent as they all contemplate this.

"But you know how to stop this from happening, yes?" Colossus asks at last. "Is that not why you came?"

The truth is, she'd like her chances better if she still had command of her Watcher powers. And that's her fault, isn't it? America should never have let her guard down, not for a moment. She knew when she left her post that the Watchers wouldn't look the other way this time, even if they're perfectly content to turn their all-seeing eyes away from Victor von Doom. "He's formidable, sure, but he's fallible. I know that we can stop him together," she insists, and that, too, is the truth.

"Well, hell. I'll wipe this Doom outta this so-called Multiverse myself," Wolverine growls.

"That must have worked out beautifully the first time around," Cyclops snaps at him, lifting his head from his palms. "Didn't you hear a word America said? If Doom's managed to kill Jean once already, then we should get her out. Now." He levels his gaze upon her, unreadable behind ruby glasses, but the tension in every line of his body comes through clearly. "You came here through a portal. You can take her someplace safe, can't you? Another country, another year, another reality, if that's what it takes."

"Scott! I'm not leaving you all to face Doom without me," Jean protests.

"Didn't *you* hear a word America said? Reality depends upon you, and there's a future where we couldn't save you. Even if the timeline could survive that, I . . ."

Jean tips her forehead against his, bringing a hand up to cup the back of his neck, and rests like that for a moment. "It's okay, Slim," she murmurs soothingly.

The tension goes out of him all at once, and he flows like water against her.

America has to look away. She's had girlfriends before—she remembers that now. She's been penciling girls' names inside hearts in her notebooks since middle school. Some of them she's loved, she's sure of it, even if she's not sure when she gave that feeling up for an airless, lifeless chamber beyond the cosmos. But she's not sure she's ever loved someone like *that;* enough to be still with them in the midst of calamity, or to be alone with them while surrounded by people.

Banshee breaks the moment by clapping a hand on Scott's shoulder from the chair on his other side. "Steady now, lad. It's eleven to one, isn't it? I'd say we've more than a fighting chance."

At the other end of the table, the professor motions for calm. "Sean is right. Our circumstances have changed thanks to our new allies. We may not know when Doom is coming, but this time, we're forewarned, and that will make all the difference."

"Exactly." America drops a fist onto the tabletop, wincing as the heavy wood creaks and splinters. "He'll have prepared, studied you all, gotten to know your vulnerabilities. He'll be ready for you. But he won't expect Betsy and Kitty. And he doesn't know about me, so he won't expect us to be ready for *him*. There've been . . . there were people I couldn't save in past realities." Couldn't, or didn't? The thought nags, the guilt stings. She pushes past it. "But I won't let him get Jean."

"Neither will we," Betsy vows for the pair of them, even as Kitty keeps silent, and America feels lighter for it. Maybe it's because every time she looks at Betsy Braddock, she can't help but recall the Multiverse of variants, of champions who make up the Captain Britain Corps, or who someday will. Some are less human than others, some more damaged. None are broken, though. Neither is this one.

"Let us compare notes on Victor von Doom," Professor Xavier suggests. "We've encountered our world's Doom, as Scott says, but anything you can tell us will be most appreciated, America. Then I recommend we sleep while we can. We know Doom's mind cannot be read, nor tracked telepathically or with Cerebro. So we'll post watches and rest in shifts. We *will* weather this threat together, my X-Men."

America Chavez isn't an X-Men, but she finds herself bolstered anyhow.

BY THE TIME THEY EMERGE FROM THEIR WAR COUNCIL, THE SKY IS beginning to brighten from midnight dark to the faintest flush of blue. Wolverine stalks off to take the first watch alongside Storm, muttering, "Couldn't sleep anyhow."

America doubts she'll be able to, either, but having been offered a spare dormitory, she at least looks forward to a deeply satisfying shower. She hasn't had a chance to wash up since her pit stop in the apocalypse.

She has one foot on the stairwell when Cyclops stops her. "A word?" he asks.

Nodding, she follows him as he leads her into the empty atrium, his teammates having reluctantly scattered to their own bedrooms. He scrubs a hand down his face as he turns to her, scraping across early-morning stubble. "I need you to understand something."

"All right . . ."

"The thing is, I'm not at all surprised that Jean's going to matter this much to the universe. Because she's the nexus, or the Phoenix, or whatever. But here's my problem, America: I don't care."

She blinks up at him, taken aback. "You don't care?"

"Jean matters to me because of who she already is. She's right—

she *is* a person, even if that person doesn't particularly matter to you."

Well, that stings. America crosses her arms—whether in defiance or defense, she's not sure. Maybe when she was a Watcher on active duty rather than on the run, someone like Jean Grey would've inspired distant curiosity, at best. But things are different now. She's different now. "Of course Jean matters to me, Scott."

He shakes his head. "No, it's fine. It's fine that you don't know her or care about her the way I do, because we're still in agreement. You want to save the nexus being, and I want to save Jean, right? Which means that, if things start to go bad, I know I can trust you to get her out."

"You're asking me to portal Jean against her will?"

"Yes. Farther than Kurt can. If all else fails, then you can save her."

"First off," America begins, "Jean's too powerful for me to keep her away, if she doesn't want that, and she'll be furious with us for trying. Second, we can't just run through the Multiverse forever. A reality without its nexus being around to anchor it won't hold. We know that, even if we don't know Doom's endgame. One way or the other, your reality needs her *here*."

"It's true, she's powerful. But she's also the best person I know. Just . . . just take her out of here long enough to convince her that surviving is the right thing to do. Tell her whatever you need to tell her. Buy yourself some time to find another way. She'll see that we're right. She's the love of my life, you know?" Though his eyes are hidden from her, the frantic way he runs both hands through his short, mahogany hair paints a picture of a man peering over the edge of a cliff, contemplating the terrible distance of the fall. "She's welcome to hate me for the rest of hers, as long as she's safe."

"Okay," America says at last.

"Okay." He sighs, and she doesn't need to see his eyes to hear the utter relief in his voice as his shoulders lower about three inches away from his ears, his fists unclenching.

"You should try to rest now. Or at least keep Jean company. We've got her back."

Cyclops nods in agreement and heads for the staircase up to the living quarters, all the fight seeped out of him. Maybe now he'll be able to sleep.

And she'll be able to shower.

But Betsy and Kitty are waiting for her in the guest wing of the dormitory, blocking the way. It's Betsy who rushes to speak, predictably. "America. I thought it best to ask this privately, given that there were graver matters to discuss, but something's been nagging at me. Are there realities within the Multiverse where Jean and I are particularly close? Because, you see, when I first started on this trail, I was following an absence that didn't only feel like the universe's loss. It felt like my own. Like I was missing somebody terribly, but I couldn't call their name to mind no matter how hard I tried. I suppose that must have been Jean, because the trail has stopped, even though . . . well, it doesn't feel like I've reached the end quite yet. But maybe she was some kind of mentor to me in the timeline Kitty's been glimpsing?"

America turns to Kitty. "This is what you two were talking about in the dining room, right?" Slips, Betsy had called them, but the conversation had barreled forward before America could press.

Kitty looks back and forth between them—at Betsy with concern, and at America with an ingrained suspicion that must have been stamped into her by her timeline. Finally, she says begrudgingly, "In the future, there were, uh, moments, when I'd see the other timeline. The right one. Except I didn't know what it was. I just thought . . . it's a long story."

She raises an eyebrow. "I guess it must be."

"Yeah, I'll buy you a drink in a disco club and tell you about it sometime. Just answer Betsy's question, okay?"

Seems like washing off the apocalypse will have to wait.

America closes her eyes, feeling her lids flicker as she rifles through the vast catalog of universes to which she still holds the key. "You knew each other," she says as she searches. "Were X-Men together, though often not at the same time. You and Rachel, though . . ." She opens her eyes, horrible realization dawning as she blinks back at Betsy and whispers, "Without this reality's Jean Grey, there is no Rachel Summers."

Betsy frowns at her. "Who is Rachel Summers?"

"I—I don't know how to . . ." America flounders. "It's hard to explain."

"'Cause it's all been so easy till now?" Kitty snipes.

There must be another version of Kitty Pryde out there in the Multiverse who's this much of a jerk, but America can't spare the time to fact-check that. So she takes a breath and treads carefully into the simplest explanation she can. "In another reality, on another Earth, Jean Grey and Scott Summers have a daughter, Rachel Summers. It's not a *good* world." America can see it as she describes it, in that set of memories that isn't her own. "Nations ruled by Sentinels, a planet perched on the brink of nuclear war, and mutants killed or sent to camps. But there was a mutant resistance. They believed that to change their own reality, they needed to change yours. Like I said: complicated. They succeeded in making contact with the X-Men, or they will, not so long from now. But it didn't work. Their own future stayed rotten, even as they managed to nudge your reality off the path of disaster. So Rachel was sent packing from her own reality off to this one, where there wasn't another of her already, since there *is* no other Rachel. Not anywhere in the Multiverse."

"Another singularity?" Betsy guesses, brow furrowed.

America nods. "Glad you're with me so far, but stay with me—it's about to get pretty timey wimey. Rachel was sent here from her world by . . . well, by *you*, Kitty. Or by her world's Kitty, who wanted to give her a chance at a better life. That's how Rachel came to live in your reality, to grow up here, and find . . ."

"Me," Betsy whispers. "But if Jean dies now . . ."

"Then there are no X-Men, and there's certainly no X-Kitty. With the timeline of this reality warped, there's nobody to pick up when that reality comes calling," America finishes filling in the blanks. "And there's no place to send Rachel Summers to save her. Especially if she was already in *this* reality's future when it cracked. She's basically caught in existential limbo."

"Then Jean and Scott will never get to meet their daughter. And neither will I."

Betsy's face has gone concerningly pale, even for a blond British woman.

America could explain how rocky Rachel's relationship with this world's version of her parents was upon meeting them, and how long it took them to make peace. But there's only so much of the future that's hers to share. If they can fix this world, then the three of them will find their way toward one another in time, just as surely as Rachel and Betsy find each other.

"I can show her to you, if you want to see. They're not my memories, but . . . you know those cabrones I mentioned downstairs? The ones with their giant omniscient skulls stuck up their butts? I can see other universes through *their* memories. And I can see a timeline where Jean lives, Rachel exists. I can show it to you. But you need to remember that we can get her back. We *will* get her back."

She doesn't look eager or certain of her decision. And behind her, Kitty's gone from skepticism to a kind of blank horror. But, shoulders set, Betsy raises a hand to her temple. "Show me," she commands at last.

CHAPTER 27

BETSY

1982

"SEE, MY SWEET AND SILKEN PSYLOCKE, HOW GENEROUS IS YOUR lord and master, Mojo. New eyes, wondrous eyes, I have made for you, whose substance blends your soul with mine. Now we'll never be apart!"

Betsy Braddock has been blind since the fight that ended her very short and luckless career as Captain Britain (her fault for putting on a suit too big to fit her properly, and borrowing her twin brother's heroic title, equally ill fitting), but in an instant, she can see again. The remnant of her wishes dearly that she could not, but it's buried too deep beneath Mojo's influence to matter.

She sees Mojo: her captor and master, torturer and creator. He is a massive, spineless yellow creature, welded to his spider-like mechanical carriage by thick cables that run from the back of his bulbous head. Clutching her by the throat with one clawed, four-fingered hand, he grins wickedly, a canyon of razor-sharp teeth into which she might tumble to her death at any moment. Her own smile mirrors his, the corners of her lips stretched achingly wide by the same mechanism that pins her new eyes open. And that is good.

Next, she sees his workshop, the cold steel tables upon which she was made new, and the soundstage where Mojo oversees and manipulates the matter of the Wildways—the transdimensional pocket where her scrambled pieces have been reassembled to her master's liking. And that is good, too.

Finally, she sees the children. Lined up onstage in their neat clothing, they smile mindlessly as Mojo's six-armed servant, Spiral, presents them for inspection. "Most are connected with Xavier's school, whose X-Men I have come to dearly hate," Spiral sneers.

Betsy Braddock has never heard much of the X-Men, but that's meaningless, because she isn't *just* Betsy. In reassembling her, Mojo has mixed himself in like two separate puzzles combined, the pieces jammed violently into place to make them fit. She's both a puppet—old, broken, boring—and her puppet master, currently delighted with his shiny new toys.

"Now, sweet Psylocke." Mojo uses the name he's given her; no other name has ever mattered. "Let your powers work through the twins to steal my pets' souls as I did yours, and set them happily riding the carousel within your mind."

She does as commanded, utilizing the powers of the twins known collectively as Template to sculpt these children into new creatures, as Mojo has sculpted her. She scoops them out and fills them with their only true purpose—to entertain their master—before transporting them inside her mindscape, where the Wildways pour through her. The children love it here on this endlessly churning golden carousel upon the otherwise barren plane of her consciousness, where they're both horse and rider. They have such fun. They adore their lord, as she adores him, for Betsy is inside them and all around them. Even when Brian, her twin, arrives, somehow rescued from his own imprisonment by the young X-Men who accompanies him now, he's quickly subsumed into her carousel. And it is good.

Until it all begins to . . .

crack

. . . as Spiral appears inside Betsy's mindscape to begin her chaos waltz. A betrayal of their master. She will tear Betsy out of herself, every last bit that remains, scorching and salting her consciousness along with the children held captive within. Betsy's mindscape quakes and splits, rent by the cataclysm of Spiral's vortex, and the carousel churns toward destruction. She can feel it but do nothing to prevent it. With her body and being consumed by Mojo, Betsy can't even care.

But the children care.

She watches with mild interest as they break themselves and her brother free, then set to work prying the pieces of her scattered psyche away from the corrupting circuitry of the Wildways, which runs through her. Shard by shard, they bring Betsy back to herself until her mind is her own again, even as Spiral continues to scheme and spin inside it.

In a desperate bid to tempt Betsy back into obedience, Spiral cries out, "The Wildways offers wonders beyond comprehension, adventures beyond imagining, eternal youth and beauty. The fulfillment of every heart's desire. Yours for the asking. All you need to do is say the word."

Betsy believed herself to be happy when her only want was Mojo's happiness. Now as reality seeps back in, so do the pain and the fear. She's seen terrible things, had terrible thoughts, and done terrible deeds while infected by the grotesquery of the Wildways.

"I have been hungry, Spiral"—she reckons with the truth of it even as she speaks the words—"and homeless. Hunted. Hurt. In body and spirit. All those things, I swore I would never be again. You offer salvation."

She stops to regard her brother, then the children, their faces strained with hope; they've fought so hard to save her, even after having to be saved *from* her.

"I prefer to make my own," she concludes, and with that, she blasts the villain from her mindscape. She burns out Spiral, burns out every scrap of Mojo and the Wildways.

Freedom is more dully colored than the Wildways, but it's a sweet sight, nonetheless.

When they bring the children back home to Graymalkin Lane,

Professor Xavier offers her a room of her own at the mansion, and Betsy gladly accepts.

"You're determined to stay here?" her twin asks as they stroll through the peaceful grounds together.

"I've been a victim too often, Brian. Too many have suffered because of my shortcomings," she explains, knowing in her heart that it's true. "Here at Xavier's School, I can learn how to better use my psi-talent to protect myself and others."

"I understand. If you ever need me, even if it's to simply talk—"

She throws her arms around her brother, the best friend she's ever had. Her hero. "You'll hear from me, I promise."

The process of learning to master herself isn't without pain and fear. But here, surrounded and supported by mutants just like her, she realizes that she's been hiding from herself and everything she's capable of. No more.

Betsy's new life is about to begin.

—

1987

AFTER BEING DEAD MORE THAN A YEAR, PSYLOCKE HAS FINALLY RE-turned home.

The school is so different from when she left it, completely rebuilt and rearranged, and that's only the beginning. Storm now heads the X-Men, whose members have since revealed their identities to the entire world. Cyclops runs the Xavier Institute alongside Emma Frost, a particularly unexpected and rancid development. Everyone's tried to make Betsy comfortable, of course, Henry especially. An interesting situation, considering that Psylocke died in his arms, the spreading pool of her blood staining his blue fur. But her resurrected body has been primed for impending disaster since arrival. And the visions she's been having aren't helping matters. Visions of Jamie—her and Brian's once-beloved older brother, the heir to Braddock Industries, who descended into criminality and madness, made infinitely more dangerous by his reality-warping powers. Now he's dead by circumstances in which Betsy's hands aren't entirely clean. Her family certainly is . . . complicated. Fingers crossed that these hallucinations are some combination of trauma and nerves, and nothing more.

All of this to say that, when her teammate Kitty Pryde asks her to speak with Rachel Summers (sorry, Rachel *Grey* now, out of apparent distaste for her father's new partner in the headmaster's office and beyond, which Betsy can't argue with), she hesitates. Doesn't she have enough on her plate without borrowing a spoonful of trouble from somebody else's?

But she can't deny that Rachel's going through it as well. To begin with, the girl's recently been a dinosaur. And that honestly seems like the least of her problems. The greatest of them being that her mother—or rather, the only mother this reality had to offer Rachel—is dead, lingering on school grounds as a memorial statue. A devastating loss for Rachel and all the X-Men (Betsy's trying her best not to compare the magnificent stone phoenix in the school's new courtyard with her own handful of memorial plants in the back garden). On top of that, Colossus is back together with Kitty, which apparently inspired an ugly incident between Kitty and Rachel a few weeks ago. An interrupted date that ended with the girls shouting at each other before Kitty phased herself and Peter out of her and Rachel's shared bedroom and into his, where she's slept ever since.

A tangled web, but maybe it would do Betsy good to get out of her own head.

One day, she sets her problems aside to hunt Rachel down in the school cafeteria and talk some sense into her. "She's your best friend, Rachel," Betsy says. "You can't hold a grudge forever."

Rachel scowls up at her from her seat. She's been moody ever since she was rescued from the Savage Land, and dressing to match. Gone are the tattered animal-hide bandeau and skirt she turned up in, replaced with a cropped red bustier of equal skimpiness, if more reliable fabric. She's kept the necklace of strung-together teeth, and her cropped, choppy red hair looks as though it hasn't seen a comb in her time back at the mansion. But her pretty features have fully returned to human form, and so her large green eyes are filled with deeply human disdain as she snaps, "I've been to the end of time and back, Betsy. What would you know about forever?"

"Well, aren't we in a mood?" Betsy sniffs, pulling out a chair to sit at the table across from her.

"I have a right."

"They did what they thought best," she reasons.

Rachel pounds a fist on the tabletop, drawing the attention of every student eating lunch—or she would have, if they weren't already eavesdropping on this strange conversation between two recently returned X-Men. "Maybe they should've thought better," she snarls.

"Oh stop. Either get over it or get out, girl," Betsy snarls back, at her wits' end. Honestly, if Rachel and Kitty are so close, why can't they *both* get over themselves and speak to each other to save their crumbling friendship, instead of forcing Betsy to act as a bulwark?

But when she leans back and looks at Rachel, truly sees her through the fog of her own struggles, she can sense the pain she's trying to mask beneath her rage, and beyond that, Rachel's fear of yet another devastating loss piled atop the last.

Maybe Rachel and Kitty's relationship is complicated, too.

Betsy tries for a lighter touch and a softer delivery. "Life is too short. And whining is totally unattractive."

It takes a moment for both of them to burst out laughing, and it's the kind of prolonged, chest-heaving, tear-inducing laughter that can't erase the grief that either of them carries but can lessen the weight for a moment as they share in the load.

Green eyes still glittering, Rachel hiccups and sighs, leaning across the table to speak beneath anyone else's hearing. "But Betsy, seriously. If my mom really is dead, as in never coming back . . . if her spirit really is severed from the Phoenix? Where does that leave me?"

"Alive, for starters," Betsy insists, and realizes the same is true for her. She died in her friend's arms, yes, but she's alive again, and given enough time, anything can be made right. "You have friends," she gently reminds Rachel, and herself as well. "You have Jean's folks, your grandparents, who love you all the more now that she's gone. Things could be . . ."

Some prickling of her psychic senses draws her gaze away from Rachel, toward the wall of sunlit windows across the cafeteria, through which the wild-eyed specter of Jamie Braddock, her eldest brother, peers in at her. He smiles, his gaunt face void of any tether to reality, and waves one skeletal hand.

". . . worse," Betsy finishes.

It isn't real. He isn't here.

"Betsy, what's wrong?" Rachel asks, barely audible above the heartbeat in her ears. "You just went all pale."

"Lost track of the time. I'm late," she blusters, leaping up from her seat, nearly overturning her chair as she rushes toward the cafeteria door. "Kurt's expecting me for a training session, gotta run!" she calls over her shoulder.

It *is* only a vision, the meaning of which will become apparent in time.

---

3 MONTHS LATER

THE X-MEN ARE IN EAST AFRICA—STORM, BISHOP, NIGHTCRAWLER, Rachel, and Betsy—fighting to stop a band of modern-day pirates from violently seizing the nation of Zanzibar. They're mid-battle and winning when the world around them appears to end. With a great blast of heat and light, the fabric of existence tears apart at the seams.

"My God, has the sun exploded?" Betsy cries.

Hovering in the air beside her, Rachel screams, "Everything's fading away!"

"Rachel, take my hand!" She reaches out to grasp for her teammate. "I'm still solid!"

"Betsy, I've lost their thoughts, I can't sense anyone—"

Then the world vanishes.

The light grows blinding, and Betsy squeezes her eyes shut. When she opens them again, she and Rachel float in nothingness. An infinite, unbroken field of white light, absent of life except for the two of them.

"What on Earth was that?" Betsy asks, her voice echoing through the empty space. "And what is this? I swear, if I'm dead again—"

"Wait, I know this place! At least . . . I think I do."

"Don't keep us in suspense, darling." Betsy flirts to disguise her own fear.

"It . . . It could be the White Hot Room."

"Which is?"

"The very core of creation itself," Rachel says reverently. "The heart of the Phoenix."

"Oh, for goodness' sake!" she shouts into the nothingness. "Does everything have to revolve around that bloody bird?"

"Considering the circumstances, do you really want to complain?"

"I *so* want to hit something," Betsy groans. "So . . . what happens next?"

Rachel's mouth quirks up at the corner as the light of the Phoenix, her inheritance, shines through her eyes. "Haven't a clue." The girl seems awfully calm, given the apparent apocalypse they've left behind on Earth.

Betsy spins around to explore, somehow able to move despite the absence of ground, and stops at the sight before her: version upon version of herself, stacked one after the other. A seemingly infinite trail of Betsys, with infinite variations. One in a scholar's robes, one a crowned princess, one heavily pregnant. All of them collected for inspection within the White Hot Room. "Just look at me," she whispers. "I never dreamed there could be so many possibilities. For every alternate Earth, an alternate Betsy Braddock. How utterly delicious. But . . . what about you?"

Rachel frowns, surveying the mere handful of selves behind her. "I've heard of some cross-time 'Rachels' that are the offspring of Scott and Jean. But none of them are me. In my case, what you see here is all there is. Not alternate versions of my present, just aspects of my past. Apparently, I'm unique." The scant handful of other-Rachels vanish, leaving her to sit by herself in the nothing.

"I don't get it," Betsy confesses, sitting down beside her.

"You think I do?" Rachel scoffs. "It seems like nothing in my life makes sense. And it's all so . . . difficult!" She flings her arms wide.

"You're alive," Betsy reminds her, reminds them both with a tentative smile. "That's a start."

The handful of Rachels scream back into being with a starburst of flame, shouting at her as one, "Don't you dare make fun!"

It's a terrifying sight, Betsy admits to herself, but she holds her ground. "When things seem this serious, kiddo, sometimes a little humor helps."

The few past versions of Rachel vanish, and alone and young and scared once more, Rachel mutters, "It isn't fair."

"Life's like that."

"I want my mom."

Betsy's heart breaks for the girl. "I know. But maybe—like Logan told you—this is your chance to live a normal life. To be all the things you missed out on originally. Or at least, considering our present predicament, what passes for normal when you're an X-Men."

"How can you be so calm?" Rachel whimpers. "Just thinking about my mom and the being-dead thing . . ."

"I was dead," Betsy reminds her. "Got better. Changes your perspective. All three of us have that in common. My brother, too.

Brian was killed and resurrected." Now the White Hot Room manifests her brothers: first Brian, flying proudly in the uniform of Captain Britain, then her usual hallucination of Jamie, her raw wound. "Both brothers, I think."

"Betsy, that's Jamie!" Rachel cries.

Freezing, she feels the blood drain away from her face. "You see him?"

"I've been seeing him for months now!"

Well, damn.

Her older brother smiles down on them, plucking at the strings of reality even from within the void. "That's enough downtime, sweeties. No more revelations. Back to the salt mines. World needs saving, you're just the gals to do it! I've gone through a lot of trouble to bind your lives and fates together, broken every rule there is. Don't make me regret it!"

The string becomes a cyclone becomes a vortex, hurling Betsy out of the White Hot Room and back into the world alongside Rachel, with questions as infinite as the many versions of herself . . . beginning with what he means by "bound them together"?

1989

"IT'S HER! IT'S CAPTAIN BRITAIN!" PARTYGOERS EXCLAIM AS BETSY AR-rives at the Hellfire Gala.

A media commentator—no doubt handpicked by Emma Frost—drones into their mic, "Along with Excalibur, the captain is making her first public appearance in months. Betsy Braddock is wearing a selection from the house of Jumbo Carnation . . ."

Cameras click and flash, capturing her entrance.

To be fair, she's worth capturing.

Her violet hair is pinned back into a structured updo, red roses pinned across her hairline, red makeup painted on her forehead and around her eyes in a high-fashion imitation of a domino mask. The bodice of her dress is a crossed red-and-blue nod toward the uniform she wears as Captain Britain, with her white skirt indecently short for any venue but the Hellfire Club.

Doing her best to ignore the media and the gossip, Betsy picks her way through the party with the intent of gathering information on her team's enemies. And so she does. As valuable as the intel is—Great Britain's alliance with Krakoa has unraveled, and Betsy's been rejected by her country of birth—there's little joy in it.

Duties be damned, she retreats to a balcony overlooking the glittering sea to wallow in solitude.

Her peace is soon interrupted by Rachel.

"I have a question," she says, joining Betsy at the balcony's railing. She's resplendent tonight in a red bodysuit with sharply horned shoulders, her short red hair slicked back and her face painted with an abstract black pattern that invokes the Phoenix.

Caught up in her feelings, Betsy can barely look at her friend. "Oh, go on," she sniffs. "Everyone else does."

"Has anyone asked you to dance tonight who wasn't trying to ply you for information?"

Betsy sighs. "No, not yet," she admits. "How sweet of you to remind me, Rachel."

Reaching across the space between them, Rachel clasps her gloved hand around Betsy's. "Let me be the first?"

Her heart flutters as though it's sprouted wings. Probably, it's gratitude; just the relief of being seen and understood. "You may."

Together they waltz across the balcony with no unwelcome eyes to observe them.

Halfway through a song, Rachel leans even closer and whispers into her ear, "I owe you an apology." She slides her other hand up the small of Betsy's back, drawing her body closer. "I made a bad call. Back when Malice had you taken over, I didn't pry. And I told others not to pry. All I could think about was if it was you in there . . ." She leans her chin on Betsy's shoulder, hand sliding farther up to cup the nape of Betsy's neck. ". . . how much the real Betsy would hate them prying."

To Betsy, this is all water under the bridge. But she seizes the chance to rest her cheek against her dear friend's, to simply be held by her, even as she shivers in the heat of her grip. "Come around the lighthouse more, Rachel," she says softly. "It . . . misses you."

1990

"I WON'T FORCE ANYONE TO COME ALONG," BETSY TELLS HER TEAM, her knights.

They gather around Mad Jim Jaspers's swirling red portal, poised to leap through and leave behind the Crooked Market for the Siege Perilous: the mystical gateway to the Multiverse that waits within the Starlight Citadel in the realms of Otherworld. At least, Mad Jim claims that's where it will take them. He could be betraying them, but hopefully his spite over Merlyn's betrayal—not to mention the knights rescuing him from imminent execution—is reason enough to play fair. Even if it isn't, what other choice do they have? The path back to Krakoa must be reopened so that their mutant brethren on the island can join them, overthrow Merlyn and his cruel regime, and reclaim the throne for Lady Saturnyne. The key to saving Otherworld is inside the Starlight Citadel.

She hopes so, anyhow.

"I can't promise this leads to the Siege Perilous," Betsy continues, "but I truly believe in this quest now. Gambit didn't die for *nothing*. I have to go on."

There's a rumbling louder than the chaos and clamor of the market, where King Arthur and his men storm forward on horseback to stop them, and Rictor cries, "The portal sounds like it's going to collapse!" His hands glow green with energy as he holds them aloft, struggling to stabilize it. "It's not anything I can hold—"

"But our fight with Arthur—" Kylun starts to protest.

"I *have* to go," Betsy cries. "It's why Roma brought us here . . . even if I go alone." This quest is Betsy's, after all: to save Otherworld and all the mutants within. But no more of her knights need to die for it.

Shaking her head, Rachel steps forward to clasp Betsy's hand between hers and draw her close enough that Betsy can't mistake the resolve on Rachel's face. Not when it's mere inches from her own. "Hey, I'm going with you, Captain. We all are," she insists. "I'm not leaving you again."

Before Betsy can swallow past the boulder in her throat to tell Rachel what it means to her, the portal groans and flares behind them, threatening to rend apart. "Then let's go!" she screams, diving through the energy field and tugging Rachel in after her while the team follows.

But when Betsy emerges, her knights—her friends—are gone.

She finds herself hip-deep in the rotting muck and mud of a dead swamp. The sky overhead gleams red through the choking smoke, the stars barely visible beyond it. All around her are bare, burned trees standing sentinel, and the crumbled stone foundation of a former castle, now just a shell of itself. Betsy is alone.

And then she isn't.

As Betsy plants her hands in the mud to try to claw her way free, a faint shadow darker than the darkness crosses her own. She looks up to see . . . herself. Well, *not* herself. One of an infinite number of Betsy Braddocks from across the Multiverse, many of whom she's met since reclaiming the mantle of Captain Britain and assembling the Captain Britain Corps. This particular variant, with her purple hair cut short behind the red-and-white-striped mask and a pierced lip, Betsy doesn't recognize.

She reaches a hand down to help tug Betsy out of the muck, but just as Betsy reaches tentatively back, she sneers. "What a mess you've gotten us into." Then she draws her sword to swing it down on Betsy's head.

In an instant, Betsy throws up a brilliant pink psi-shield in time to block the blade. She thrusts the shield backward with all her might—not inconsiderable, even when half buried—and sends the variant sprawling. As she climbs to her feet to regroup for the next attack, the psychic knife Betsy's flung with precision sinks between her shoulder blades, knocking the variant unconscious with its telekinetic impact.

Fine then. Betsy will just have to free herself.

Summoning her energy into a longsword, she stabs it down into the mess around her, grasping the hilt. She strains against the sucking, stinking mud, clenching her teeth. By the time she pulls herself out and staggers onto firmer ground, the sky above is filled with a swarm of variants, some of whom she's met, some of whom she once glimpsed inside the White Hot Room. A Betsy who's twelve feet tall at least. A Betsy with a glowing pink prosthetic leg. A gorilla Betsy in a mask and cape, and behind her just a straight-up goose, no clothes to be found.

"I don't need a hand up, so don't make the mistake of offering it again," she grits out. "I don't need that—not from any of you—and I'm not new to this kind of thing. I am quite used to fighting myself."

Raising her psychic sword and shield, she braces for attack as their psychic admonitions rain down on her:

You lost Gambit.

And gave up Shogo.

Is this your search for the Siege?

Pathetic.

A variant dives for her, and Betsy slams her aside with her shield. "Enough!" she screams. "I accepted the quest for my people, not just for me or any of *you*!"

We aren't here, one corps member thinks as she strikes down yet another.

You are all alone.

And then, once again, she is.

Chest heaving, Betsy scans the now-empty night sky and sees what she missed upon arrival: radiant red lines that slice across the heavens, blurring out the stars beyond.

The Siege Perilous. She's found it at last.

Now she just has to find her knights.

Taking to the sky, she streaks forward, searching, until a pillar of bright-orange flame in the distance shoots up toward the clouds. Though she's much too far away to feel its heat, her face warms as she recognizes it for a signal.

Rachel Summers has sent up a flare.

At last, she reaches the source of the flare and sinks toward Rachel, who waits on a swampy stretch of ground with the rest of the team—all but Gambit. His body is nowhere to be found, perhaps returned to the bloodstained cobblestones of the Crooked Market. Her heart aches with the loss of him now that there's no battle to distract her from the wound. Even so, she can't keep from smiling when Rachel stretches a hand toward the sky, as if to help her down.

"There you are!" Betsy sighs happily.

"Didn't I say I wasn't leaving you alone again?"

She flushes, still hovering just above Rachel, who stares up at her. Though the pillar of flame has served its purpose and vanished, Betsy's whole body is aflame now, an invisible wildfire that seems to spread from their clasped hands. "Rachel . . . Why are you looking at me like that?"

But she doesn't really need to ask, and she needn't use telepathy to understand.

What some might see as a constellation of complicated emotions shining in Rachel's bright-green eyes—fear, relief, joy, protectiveness, near-regret that was thankfully thwarted—Betsy recognizes as different facets of one single crystalline feeling. She knows this because she feels it, too.

It's simply love.

Rising to meet Betsy, Rachel cups her face with one hand,

thumb stroking tenderly along Betsy's cheekbone, and slides the other around to cradle the nape of her neck. Betsy's own hands drift up along Rachel's silver breastplate, one coming to rest over her ribs, the other behind her back, clutching the red fabric of her battle dress. Warm unnatural wind swirls around them, lifting Betsy's hair and whipping it about as Rachel's turns to flame. From somewhere in this scorched hellscape, a kaleidoscope of honest-to-God, shimmering rainbow butterflies manifests to surround them. And then at last—at *long* last, much longer than Betsy would have admitted to herself only moments ago—Rachel presses pleasantly burning lips to hers.

Their first kiss is cosmic.

It rearranges the stars, and Betsy along with them.

She's lost so much in her lifetime, and has been lost so many times. Hungry, homeless, hunted, hurt, as she once described it to Spiral. But all Betsy can think about now is how lucky she is. Because she's alive, for starters. And because, of all the infinite Betsy Braddocks in the Multiverse, there is only one Rachel Summers. How impossibly wondrous is it that *she* is the Betsy who gets to love her?

If Betsy Braddock has things her way, they will never leave each other's sides again.

CHAPTER 28

KITTY

JULY 19, 1975

BETSY SINKS TO THE CARPET, ARMS WRAPPED TIGHT AROUND HER own rib cage. "I remember her," she wails, kneeling down in the middle of the hallway. "She was *real*. She was *mine*."

If Kitty were the kind of friend who knew how to hold someone together while they fell apart, then this would be her moment. If she were stronger, better, she would know what to do for Betsy right now.

Unfortunately, she's just not that person.

Instead she stands frozen as America moves, crouching down to enfold the sobbing Betsy. "We'll save her," America promises again, "we will."

Minutes pass like this before Betsy's tears begin to abate. At last, she wipes her wrist across her streaming nose and looks back at Kitty, not yet bothering to climb to her feet. "You should see, too," she says, still sniffling. "I can show you everything America showed me. She was your best friend."

Still kneeling beside Betsy with one hand on her back, America raises the other to Kitty: an offering.

When Kitty finally moves, it's only to stagger backward down the hallway. Maybe she didn't mean what she said on that jet, when she and Betsy spoke of loved ones lost, or didn't really understand what she was saying. Maybe it's better to forget after all, if this kind of pain is the prize for remembering. "How about you just tell me?"

"There's so much to tell." Betsy shudders. "I saw her."

"Who?"

"Rachel." Her hoarse voice fractures on the name. "It was her trail I was following all along. It only led us to Jean because Rachel is her daughter, and Scott's."

"Oh." Won't Wolverine be thrilled to hear that. "Okay. And in the future—in the timeline that was before ours split off—you two . . ."

"We were teammates at first. Then we were friends. And then we were something else. Everything else. And you were there the whole time, Kitty. You were an X-Men, too."

"You're an X-Men in almost every world," America confirms.

She should be happy to hear it, shouldn't she? She should be thrilled. It's what she's always suspected but hasn't dared to believe, because it might have driven her mad. That the slips *aren't* just symptoms of a fractured mind, or some kind of curse other mutants had managed to avoid, but glimpses of a world where she really belongs. Where she lives life as an X-Men instead of a Hellion, with a teacher like Charles Xavier instead of Emma Frost, and true teammates like Jean instead of a shoal of fellow piranhas swimming in water that's starved of prey, and true friends. Like Betsy.

So why is Kitty more afraid than ever?

To cover for the pit in her stomach, the ache in her throat, she scoffs at them both. "But you're talking about variants. None of them are actually me."

There's kindness in America's deep-brown eyes that hurts to look at. "Maybe. Or maybe it's all you. Same basic ingredients, just baked by different circumstances across the Multiverse. I've seen universes beyond counting, and all of them are unique. But I believe some things are true in every reality."

Kitty's not at all sure about that.

Once, in home economics at Miss Hester's, they were assigned to bake puff pastries from a recipe—everyone else in pairs, but Kitty working alone. The class was odd-numbered, and even in even classes, an unlucky classmate usually had to be forced into partnership with the school pariah. When she pulled her tray out of the oven, whatever part of her had felt vaguely hopeful fell as flat as her pastries, which were nothing but dense blocks of dough. She'd forgotten to add baking powder, her teacher sneered, as Kitty wished desperately that she could phase through the floor and into the planet's core. Point being, it wouldn't be the first time that mistakes had been made, would it? Say there's a Great Baker presiding over the Multiverse. (A god for every world? A god *of* every world? Some cosmic salmon swimming in the great ocean of existence, laying alternate universes by the tens of thousands? If ever she joins a synagogue again, she'll have a lot of questions stored up to ask the rabbi.) Whatever the case, it seems entirely possible that something key got skipped over when it was Kitty's turn in the mixing bowl. Maybe that's why she's so scared all the time, even now, and there's nothing to be done about it when she's already baked.

Unless they can save Jean and change everything, Kitty included.

"If we fix things," Betsy pleads with America, echoing Kitty's desperation, "if we stop Doom from killing Jean, then what?"

"Theoretically, the future plays out as it should have. As it did in the original timeline, before the cracks."

"And I get Rachel back?"

"That's right."

"And then we fix everything, right?" Kitty all but pleads. "All Xavier's dreams come true—we get the good timeline and a good world? No more Sentinels, no more mutant bounty hunters, no more ultra-rich secret societies weaponizing every kid with an X-Gene they can get their hands on? Are we free?"

She ought to have known the answer before America begrudgingly delivers it. "No."

There it is: the drop.

"If there's a world out there like that in the Multiverse, I've never seen it, and neither have the Watchers," she says. "When I was a kid, I thought . . . I thought maybe it did. A Utopian Parallel. A perfect world, a perfect home." She smiles joylessly. "But it wasn't real. Bad things happen everywhere. To mutants and to humans. Dictators rise, movements and revolutions end, people suffer. Bad things will happen in the future, to both of you. Jean Grey becoming the Phoenix isn't a cure-all, and Charles Xavier isn't magic. He's a good man with great intentions, who sometimes makes terrible choices and worse mistakes. But you'll be with the X-Men, and you'll fight with them, because you believe in this world so deeply that you're willing to die for it."

Kitty takes another step back down the hallway. "I don't want to die for it," she whimpers. "I *want* to go home." Not to Xavier's mansion, or to her barely lived-in apartment in Inwood, and not to the Massachusetts Academy. To Deerfield, Illinois. To her childhood bedroom, and her childhood dreams for the future that she was silly enough to think might come true, though they never will.

"America," Betsy says, seeming the calmer of them now. "Can you give us a moment?"

The woman hesitates only briefly before nodding. "Just make sure you two get some rest, okay? And, uh, point me to the guest bathroom?"

Before Kitty can object that she doesn't want to be left alone with Betsy, Betsy sends America off, then turns back to her with tears still tracking down her cheeks. "This is a good thing, don't you see?" she insists.

"Is it?"

Betsy looks aghast, as though she's just invoked a curse instead of asking the logical question. "Of course! Now we finally know what we've come here to do, and why. It was all because of Rachel."

"She's why *you* came." Another step backward down the hallway. "*You* came here because you thought someone was missing, and the world was wrong, and things were bad because of it. *I* came because I didn't have much to lose. You already said it: I was Emma Frost's minion, living in a one-bedroom apartment with the front door welded shut, watching scenes from a life that wasn't mine, and . . . sometimes I really wanted it to be. I thought maybe we'd find this missing person, and I'd somehow become someone different." The confession stings coming out.

So does Betsy's certainty when she insists, "You can be, Kitty! You heard America. We save Jean, we save the timeline, we get back everything we grew up missing."

Kitty wishes she could be that sure. The trouble is, she *did* hear America. "The X-Men couldn't protect her before," she reminds Betsy. "Maybe America couldn't, either, and just doesn't know it." Every thought she's kept clamped behind her teeth since their war council began comes bursting out. "How do we even know the two of us haven't stood here before, having this same fight, only to drop the ball when it really counted?"

"That's not how time travel works," Betsy says, but she shifts uncomfortably on her feet.

"You can't know that. 'If you really want to talk about practical applications of travel through space and time, you'd need to talk to Captain Britain. I'm just his sister,'" Kitty says, quoting Betsy back to herself. "All we know is that Doom has tried this before, and Jean died, and the X-Men died, and here we are."

Now the look of fanatical determination in Betsy's blue eyes flickers into doubt. But she clenches her fists at her sides as she insists, "America says you and I can make a difference."

"Yeah, well, America doesn't really know us, does she?"

"What do you mean by that?"

"You can barely control your powers, and I . . . however many heroic Kitties there are bopping around in the Multiverse, I'm not one of them. Who's to say the two of us won't mess the timeline up worse than it already is? Besides all that, the professor is wrong. There is no reality where mutants are free. Even in the best-case scenario, we're still running and hiding and fighting. And that's if we survive past '75. We might die here with Jean and the X-Men.

Maybe we're all trapped in a cycle of trying and failing and dying, and we just don't know it yet."

Betsy throws up her hands in frustration. "I—I can't tell you the future, Kitty. I don't know exactly what will happen next, whether we win or we lose. It's apparent that nobody does. But if we don't even try, then I will always have spent those years trapped in the Wildways, and you will always have grown up as a mutant without family around you, without adults to protect you, without people to love you as you deserved."

"Well, I can live with that," Kitty snarls. "I have since I was thirteen and a half. So stop talking to me like you're the wise, bald professor and I'm your naïve little student, just because you want your ex back."

Betsy rears away as though struck, and Kitty feels it, too, like a pain in her knuckles after an ill-landed punch.

It is a terrible thing to have said.

"Betsy, I didn't—"

"Rachel Summers isn't my ex," Betsy says, so low that Kitty barely hears her over the crickets in the trees and the beat of her own pulse in her ears. "Rachel Summers and I belonged to each other, and we were heroes together. I saw it all. I saw you, Kitty, and you were a hero in the timeline that was meant to be, too." Then her lip twitches into a sneer. "But not in this one, I suppose." It's no worse than Kitty's told herself, but coming from Betsy, it *feels* worse. "If you're so ready to give up on the world, then why don't you hand in your hot pants and go find yourself another white coat, because you don't belong with the X-Men."

"Guess not. Good thing you've got them, right?" she manages to say around the boulder newly lodged in her throat. It sounds sarcastic to her own ears, and she can't bring herself to tell Betsy that she means every word.

Instead Kitty Pryde shoves past her in the hallway to head for the staircase, then keeps on walking.

This isn't her picking the devil she knows. She swears it's not.

She reminds herself of it over and over again on the train ride back to the city, where she phases down into the baggage compartment to avoid the ticket price she can't pay. Betsy—who somehow knows her better than anybody has in a decade, perhaps longer—has correctly estimated how little Kitty is worth without her white coat on. But she's given Kitty an idea. Because there's somebody in 1975 with the power to stop Doom. And it isn't RCX or the X-Men.

Whatever America may claim, Betsy is right: Kitty doesn't belong with the good guys.

It's time to try her luck with the villains.

CHAPTER 29

KITTY

JULY 19, 1975

SHE PEERS BETWEEN THE BARS OF THE HIGH WROUGHT-IRON GATES that separate the Manhattan headquarters of the Hellfire Club from Fifth Avenue. Its stately brick façade is pearled by early-morning light, while the many-paned windows glow from within. Judging by the luxury cars and limousines that line the private driveway beyond the gates—at least two are affixed with the car flags of ambassadors, and dozens of chauffeurs doze at the wheel—nobody inside has been to bed, even as a new day begins. A party, then. Kitty's no stranger to the club galas that run through the night and well into the next day, attended by the economic, political, and social elite. Bad luck for her . . . Or maybe not. Maybe she stands a better chance of slipping through a mansion full of drunk diplomats and hedonistic titans of industry than she would through near-empty halls.

But she doesn't like her chances in the cropped halter top and palazzo pants she wears, still smelling of smoke and patchouli from the disco, now streaked with grease and dirt from her trip to the baggage compartment. And her hair? A hopeless case.

So then. Plan B.

She steps off the sidewalk to phase through the gates, then makes for the towering hedge that lines the circular drive. Melting through dense shrubbery, sticking to blue morning shadows, she makes her way toward the mansion. Not to the main entrance, of course. Up a flight of steps and beneath a columned stone archway engraved with the club crest—an H with a three-pronged pitchfork slicing through it—the grand doors will be closely guarded. Instead she skirts around the corner to the side of the mansion, where a second staircase leads down to a locked door just offset from ground level. It was built as an entrance to the servants' quarters during construction of what once was a Gilded Age mansion, before the club bought and converted it. It basically still functions as one.

Only instead of footmen and scullery maids, this is where the girls come in.

Taking a chance, she sticks her body up to the shoulders through the plain wood door, prepared to bolt. But as expected, she finds the hallway empty, all the girls otherwise occupied finishing out their shifts. She may be a card-carrying club member, but she's used this entrance plenty to avoid unnecessary attention, even when there were no parties happening; Emma encourages it, especially since Kitty refuses to dress to code. She follows the passage to the windowless dressing room that, truly, won't change much within the next fifteen years. It's the same sort-of-Parisian pastel palette: lavender brocade walls, pistachio-green rugs, and oversized settees striped powder pink and cream. An empty martini glass sits on one of the cream-and-gold mirrored vanity tables beside a pile of hairpins and a discarded black corset top, with a pair of black boots slumped on the rug below.

Suddenly the door swings open, and an exhausted young woman with pinned-up black curls frizzing out at the nape of her neck slumps into the room. Her dark eyes light on Kitty, but there's no suspicion in them; only relief. "Are you the shift change?" Without waiting for an answer, she drips bonelessly onto one of the settees and peels off her above-the-elbow black gloves. "Thank the Lord you're early, because I'm beat. Just watch out for Mr. Shaw. Seems like he's in a foul one. He was giving me the hairy eyeball all night."

Kitty's never talked to the girls who carry drinks and hors d'oeuvres through the club, never paid much attention to them at all, except to pity them. Also to reassure herself that she's nothing like *them,* in their tiny corsets and bikini-cut panties and boots, serving powerful men who want them or hate them or both. Sure, they're just doing what they have to do. But Kitty only serves Emma Frost, and she's no bargirl. She's a *knight*.

At least, she was.

Now she guesses she's not much of anything.

"I'll watch out," she promises. "Is Miss Frost here tonight?"

"Who?"

Is this bargirl new or something? "Emma Frost," Kitty explains slowly. "The White Queen."

The girl unzips one of her heeled, thigh-high black boots to massage a swollen ankle. "Oh, you mean the Ice Princess?"

". . . Let's say I do."

God help this bargirl if Emma ever catches wind of the nickname.

"Still by the stage, I bet. There's one more show before the party ends. You know they've got a girl who dances with a boa constrictor while covered in honey? Couldn't pay *me* to get up there, not even if I could go to college after." Groaning, she stands in bare feet and crosses to a powder-blue privacy screen, grabbing a frayed bag out from behind it. She pulls out a pair of slip-ons and a worn, patchwork leather trench coat that's clearly been nursed through a few years in the city, and buttons it to the throat.

"Hey, are you gonna be okay walking home?" Kitty can't stop herself from asking.

"Aren't you sweet." The girl smiles, barely. "Nobody outside's as bad as who's up there. Take care of yourself, huh?"

Alone in the dressing room again, Kitty turns back to the abandoned uniform by the vanity table and grimaces into the mirror.

If only the men of the Hellfire Club had a kink for palazzo pants.

WHAT IF... KITTY PRYDE STOLE THE PHOENIX FORCE?

BY THE TIME KITTY WEAVES HER WAY INTO THE PARTY, CARRYING A silver tray with glasses of cordial she grabbed from a grateful bargirl headed in the opposite direction, she already regrets this whole damn plan. Her stolen boots are too big, the heels wobbling with each step forward. She can feel a headache coming on from the bobby pins shoved through her best attempt at the bargirls' signature bouffant. The hastily fastened corset digs into her ribs, and *how*, in this stuffy old mansion, is there a draft that raises goosebumps . . . pretty much everywhere?

Maybe it's the existential chill of being leered at by men as she passes, all perfectly if ridiculously modest in their white wigs and tailcoats, faux-Regency knee britches, and buckled shoes.

This is *exactly* why Kitty doesn't come to Hellfire Club galas. That, and the general fact of people.

But even as she's being ogled, the disguise is working. Nobody so much as looks at her face or bothers to wonder about her the moment she's beyond their eyeline, she'd bet. She's both impossible to miss and completely invisible among the throngs of rich men cosplaying as British aristocrats (though she's pretty sure that was a future duke she passed crawling across the floor toward his beckoning mistress back there). As the enormous grandfather clock in the grand ballroom chimes at five o'clock, she winds steadily through the mansion, keeping her eyes peeled for the young Emma Frost.

Emma may have scoffed at Kitty before. But if anybody in 1975 has a vested interest in keeping the party going, it's the queen of the Hellfire Club. If Kitty remembers her club history, then it's around this time that Emma and Sebastian Shaw overthrew their superiors in the club's Council of Chosen—the former iteration of the Inner Circle—remaking themselves as the White Queen and the Black King. From this sprang the idea for the Massachusetts Academy, Emma's brainchild, built for the secret purpose of securing and training young mutants for the club's future. Of course, Kitty didn't know any of that when she was recruited, though it wouldn't have changed much if she had. There was no Xavier's School for Gifted Youngsters when she was a teenager. She didn't have anywhere else to go.

In any case, whether she's queen yet or not, Emma Frost has always been exactly who she is. If Kitty can catch her ear, convince her that it's in her and the Hellfire Club's interest to stop Doom from destroying a world she's dead set on ruling, and the White Queen brings the full might of the club to bear . . . well, how can they lose?

Kitty pushes through another set of heavy wooden doors and finds herself in a room set apart from the rest of the party. In her limited experience at club events, she's never seen one like this. Dressed up like some kind of centuries-old English tavern, the room features round tables clustered before a raised wooden stage, currently empty except for a signboard that reads: HELLFIRE CABARET.

In a deep stone hearth, a crackling fire provides the only real lighting in the room aside from a few dim wall sconces, yet the room still feels cold in mid-July. Men in antiquated clothing and tricornered hats sit at the tables, hoisting their tankards as they call for the show to begin. Though the bargirl mentioned finding Emma by a stage, she's nowhere among their number; maybe she's grown exhausted from playing nice with them all, as she so often does, and retreated in peace to the office where she holds court whenever she's in the city.

A man seated at the piano, who also seems to be the cabaret's master of ceremonies, calls out, "We have a special dancer in the house tonight, my devils and dandies," as he plays the opening chords. "And she's guaranteed to wake you up quicker than a cold shower!"

That's Kitty's cue to leave. Just as she's setting her tray of drinks down on the polished bar top to abandon it, the thick, red velvet stage curtains part and a young woman steps through. A spotlight flickers on to trap her in its beam. Kitty pities her instinctively, but turns to make her own retreat.

"Making her Hellfire debut, I give you . . . the Ice Princess!"

At that, Kitty stops, turning back.

Emma Frost—a year or two younger than Kitty is now—stands unmistakably on the stage. She isn't costumed much differently from the White Queen whom Kitty knows, though her bustier is more frilled than her preferred severe corsets. Sure, she wears massive snowflake earrings entirely impractical for battle (not that Emma's fashion choices have ever been burdened by practicality), and her teased, ice-blond hair curls nearly to her elbows. But none of that would have thrown Kitty off. It's the look of panic stamped across her perfect features in the firelight that made her unrecognizable for just a moment.

In the seven years since Emma first fished Kitty from her life and gave her a new one, she has never seen the White Queen look scared.

She sees it now as Emma steps forward, then stumbles, the toe of her white stiletto catching on the stage.

"What is this crap?" a man from the audience calls.

"S-Sorry," Emma mutters, her voice amplified across the makeshift tavern, and steadies herself. "I'm trying . . ."

But it's too late, and the crowd is turning. They've scented blood and seem just as happy to attack as they would have been to watch.

"You suck!"

"Bring back the last girl!"

Now Emma's beautiful face twists into a furious snarl, and though none of these men know enough to fear her, Kitty certainly does. Ducking behind the barback, to the confusion of the hired bartender, she phases as Emma screams, "I'm trying the best I can!"

If the White Queen had Banshee's powers, glassware and eardrums both would pop like fireworks all across this so-called cabaret. But Emma's powers are more than formidable on their own.

Chaos descends, and Kitty peeks around the bar to watch it happen. Men clutch at their heads, vomit into their own laps, and collapse, toppling tables and shattering tankards as they fall. The master of ceremonies lurches face-first into the piano on his way down, leaving his blood streaked across the ivory keys. Beside her, the bartender crumples. Only Emma Frost is left standing at the center of it all.

Chest heaving, a drop of blood trickling from her nose, Emma's crystalline eyes fill with tears (of regret? Rage? Satisfaction?) as she scans the destruction.

Then she bolts from the stage, and the scene of her crime.

Kitty pushes through the party after her, trying to keep up. She squeezes past men who brush deliberately against her, men who place themselves in her path, who reach out as if to trail their thick fingers along her shoulders as she passes. They wouldn't have *dared* to touch the White Knight of the Hellfire Club, but to these people—her people, supposedly—she's nobody. The White Knight doesn't exist, and neither does Kitty Pryde. It takes every scrap of willpower not to make herself untouchable, drawing *actual* attention to herself.

All that matters is catching up with Emma.

It's easy enough, once Kitty figures out where she's headed. When she reaches the passage to the former servants' quarters, she breaks into a run and then bursts through the door to the dressing room. There Emma sits slumped at one of the vanity tables, clutching a bloodied handkerchief. She's examining herself in the mirror with the same diamond-eyed judgment she's so often turned on Kitty, leaving no room to mistake that Kitty doesn't measure up.

Maybe this should feel good. Like getting her own back. Maybe she should take this chance to twist the knife—an opportunity the White Queen never missed, while claiming it was for Kitty's own good. Every new scar, a memory of a mistake that Kitty would never make again.

But Kitty isn't the White Queen. "Are you okay?" she asks, shuffling forward in her stupid boots.

Emma gives one grave-dark chuckle. "Would I be here if I were?"

She has nothing to say to that.

Emma stands, unfastening her floor-length cloak to let it slide from her shoulders, then reaches for a shabby white robe hanging on a hooked stand beside the vanity. She cinches the belt tight before dropping back into her chair, still clutching the handkerchief. Then she meets Kitty's eyes in the mirror.

I saw you in the cabaret. You're like me, aren't you?

The tendrils of Emma's thoughts take her by surprise, even after only a week or two without them. They're familiar, but less, like cold water instead of burning ice. "How did you know?"

You wouldn't be conscious right now if you weren't. Emma sighs, then speaks aloud. "They'll come looking for me in just a moment. I can hear them. Hear *him*. You should get out of here, if you've got anywhere to go."

"Maybe . . . you should come with me?"

"Oh?" Emma sniffs. "Where to? Are you asking me to share your mattress in a closet in a hole-in-the-wall where you live with four other girls and an unknown quantity of rodents? Your cot in a shelter? Your childhood bedroom in the estate owned by your father, who's simply dying to say, *I told you so*?" Breaking eye contact in the mirror, she stares down at the handkerchief in her limply curled fingers, resting atop the vanity. "Been there, done all of that, darling. It all leads back to this place, or another just like it."

Emma might be more right than she knows.

There is no help coming from the White Queen—she doesn't even exist yet—and the club such as it is would never follow either of them into battle. Without Emma, maybe there's nothing Kitty can do to stop Doom, and all of this will just happen again. He'll succeed in murdering Jean Grey, splitting the timeline between what might have been and what will be. Jean will never have a daughter, and that daughter will never be the apparent love of Betsy Braddock's life. Without Jean in the mix, the rest of the X-Men will meet their yet-unknown but seemingly inevitable deaths. When Kitty's powers manifest five years from now, there will be no Charles Xavier waiting to teach her how to act in hope instead of fear. Emma Frost—who will rise impossibly from hired dancer in the Hellfire Club to the pinnacle of its Inner Circle, and headmistress of the Massachusetts Academy—will claim her instead, bent on accumulating young mutants like assets, rather than protecting them. And Emma will never admit to her students that once upon a time, she was alone, and afraid, and would have risked her own safety to protect a girl like Kitty. The version of Emma Frost who would have thrown her arms around her and held her close in a strange, sunlit chamber will never exist at all.

This Emma stares back up at her own reflection in the mirror, then says simply, "I really should've gotten that teaching certificate."

The door to the dressing room slams open, cracking the plaster beneath the beautiful, meaningless wallpaper, and Kitty whips around to find a man who won't age a day in the next decade and a half, looming thunderously in the doorway.

Sebastian Shaw, Black King of the Hellfire Club.

Someday soon, he will be Emma's counterpart, ally, and nemesis all in one; a man who's always managed to make Kitty feel like a little girl just by leveling his cold, careless gaze upon her. Now he charges toward her at the vanity. "Think I wouldn't notice you scampering about my brain? Well, I'm not one of your helpless Hellfire buffoons—" Then Kitty catches his eye, and he barely manages to stop himself from barreling forward. "Remove yourself from my presence, you brainless trollop," he snarls at her.

Kitty doesn't move.

But Emma does, standing to slip into the path between them. "Bargirl, go on and get a drink for Mr. Shaw, will you?" she says coolly, though Kitty sees the handkerchief slip from her nerveless fingers to fall to the rug.

Come with me, she thinks urgently, allowing a desperation she knows future-Emma would scold her for to pour into the thought. **We can help each other.**

It's a wild idea, a reckless request. And yet . . .

Kitty grew up believing that Emma Frost had made the Hellfire Club everything it was. And certainly, her vicious hand helped to shape it, just as she'd shaped Kitty. But Kitty sees it now; how the Hellfire Club made the White Queen what *she* was. Perhaps if the Ice Princess had any other choice, she'd never have picked this path, this life. Just as Kitty sees now that every choice she thought she was making—leaving that detention center with Emma to attend the Massachusetts Academy, joining the Hellions, and later, the Inner Circle—was nothing she would've picked if she'd believed a different life was possible. One where she might like herself, and feel safer than she would have all alone. A better life, if not easier.

Well, she knows now. And if she can change, then can't the Ice Princess?

But Emma only looks over her shoulder to offer one faint, sad curl of a smile. **Maybe in another world.** Then she barks, "Go on now, fetch that drink," managing to carry herself with the same poise and rich-girl authority as Kitty's peers at Miss Hester's, even as she must be trembling in her boots.

Still, Kitty hesitates. Because Shaw looks murderous, and she knows as well as anyone that it's more than just appearances. He can hurt Emma, he will hurt her, he'll kill her . . .

Except he won't. Because all this has happened before, would have happened without her here, and now Kitty knows exactly where it leads.

In the habit of obeying her superior, she goes. Not back to the party, but toward the servants' entrance as Emma intended her to, phasing back through the door to see bright, midmorning light she wasn't expecting. It's later than she thought it was, and the towering brick mansion glows peach. Kitty stands on the lawn, shivering in her stolen lingerie. Now what?

Kitty might not be the White Knight she was, nor the hero she should have been. Maybe she'll never be enough.

But her friends need help, and she's all she has to offer.

CHAPTER 30

DOOM

JULY 19, 1975

THE GYROSCOPIC AIRCRAFT IS A LESS SUBTLE MEANS OF TRANSPORT than Doom would typically prefer, but this time, it suits his purpose. An enormous cross between a spinning top and a flying saucer, it waits in the hangar bay of the second sub-basement. The exit—a set of hidden hydraulic doors built into the castle's courtyard above—opens to show a cloudless black sky sewn with beads of starlight, and a moon full and stark.

"The invisibility shield will keep us well hidden, regardless of clear skies," Other-Doom declares as he joins him.

Doom could remind the man that he knows the machine's design inside and out, and has learned enough since conceiving it to improve its design twice over. But a show of deference costs him little and continues to feed his accomplice's ego. "As you say. I've successfully kept the prying eyes of the Multiverse from falling upon me thus far. It's unlikely that the nexus being and her fellow X-Men will see us coming. Regardless, they certainly won't see *us* coming."

The pine-smelling wind of his homeland, cold even on summer nights, sweeps down through the hangar, where it tussles the green cloaks of an assembled army of Doombots. Only twenty-four in total—as many as Other-Doom was willing to spare from his castle's defense—but each outfitted with body armor identical to his own, equipped with weaponry comparable to his own: electric shock capabilities, jetpacks, force bolts and force fields that greatly dampen physical and telekinetic impacts, and more.

Not his equal, of course; nobody could be, and the Doombots are also equipped with dampeners that mildly deplete their power levels and silence them in his presence, as they always have been. They're plenty formidable nonetheless, as well as his exact duplicate by all outward appearances. They've even been programmed with the majority of his memories—or the memories of this world's Doom—and psionic-disguising circuitry capable of passing a mental scan by any menial telepath while remaining immune to telepathy.

Jean Grey is no menial telepath, of course. She alone among the X-Men may be able to tell the true Doom at a glance. This is no flaw in his plan, but a feature.

It's taken longer than he'd like to finish repairing his own armor and augmenting the Doombots with the tech that Other-Doom had yet to invent. And even that was minor labor compared with the uninterrupted days and sleepless nights they've spent in the workshops, re-creating the psi-phon. But the results were well worth his time.

He lifts and flexes the arm with his repaired gauntlet, testing its functionality, and feels magic at his fingertips once more. The electronic shackles are long gone, discarded during their work together in the laboratory.

Also worth his time and efforts: his careful management of Other-Doom. Striking such a precise chord of obsequiousness that his counterpart has clocked his attempts at manipulation yet underestimated the full scope of his plans. Nothing Doom could have done would have secured the trust of any version of Victor von Doom, the greatest strategist in any world. Other-Doom harbors doubts still, and will have made contingency plans in case of betrayal. And that serves Doom's interests, too. Other-Doom's misplaced faith in his own contingencies was necessary for his cooperation.

But none of that will matter once Doom has everything he needs from Jean Grey.

CHAPTER 31

KITTY

JULY 19, 1975

PERCHED ON THE ROOFTOP OF XAVIER'S MANSION, KITTY HUGS HER knees to her chest and taps one boot against the tiles. Though the heat of the city in July has yielded to a mild night with a cool breeze out in the countryside, she's warm enough in her awful, standard-issue yellow-and-black X-Men uniform (minus the cowl, which she still refuses to wrestle down over her ponytail). She simply can't sit still.

Not until Betsy climbs out through Storm's skylight to join her on the roof. Then every muscle in her body locks tight.

They haven't spoken since Kitty's walk of shame—or rather, her ride of shame in the backseat of the cab that was waiting for her at the Westchester City Center train station, thoughtfully sent by Professor X. The professor welcomed her back with a carefully magnanimous expression as she stood on his doorstep in knee-high black leather boots and a stolen green vinyl raincoat zipped up to cover for her lack of pants. Betsy, too, must have sensed Kitty's return, perhaps even heard her racing thoughts through the wall between their bedrooms. When she woke after a deep and needed nap in the late afternoon, Kitty lay in bed waiting to feel the butterfly brush of a telepathic presence in her mind, so she could begin to explain herself. But it never came, and eventually, Kitty gave up and reported for sentry duty, accepting that Betsy had nothing to say to her.

Even now, for an eternal moment, neither of them speaks.

Then at last: "I heard you turned up in knickers and a raincoat this morning."

"The professor told you that?" Betrayal.

"No. But Peter saw you from down the hallway, and his memory is quite vivid."

Kitty grimaces in the dark, choosing to ignore her mention of the younger man. "It was a wild night."

"Hmm." After a pause, Betsy sits gracefully down on the shingles beside her. She's wearing her X-Men uniform to match, also minus the cowl, which would've mussed up her carefully pinned golden chignon. "I'm not sure whether to ask why you left or why you came back."

"Why not both?"

"All right, then. Why did you leave?"

Kitty tucks her chin into her knees. "I went to the Hellfire Club. I thought . . . I don't know what I thought." But that's not true. "I thought if I could convince Emma and the club that it was worth their while to fight, we'd have a chance."

"I see. Well, did it work?"

She shakes her head. "I'm sorry."

"You trusted Emma more than you trusted me," Betsy says, but without judgment that Kitty can detect. "It's understandable. What are a few weeks of acquaintanceship compared with your formative years?"

"No, that's not it," she insists, and means it. "I can't say if I trust anybody *but* you. Not more than, definitely. I just . . . it all got so big, and I wanted it so bad, and I got scared. I didn't really come here to change the world, you know? I wanted to change myself. That's selfish, but I did. I wanted to become some different Kitty. I *want* to be the X-Man America thinks I am. But we haven't fixed things yet, so how can I be?"

Betsy sighs. "I don't know if people just up and become anything, Kitty. Or maybe we just make the choices we can, and that's how we become: choice by choice."

She swallows what feels like a throat full of glass. "Maybe."

"I'm sorry, too, you know. I've no right to judge you for a moment of doubt, when I've spent a lifetime doubting myself. So then, why did you come back?"

"Couple reasons. One being that . . . Emma wasn't always the White Queen, you know? The Emma I met, the Ice Princess, she wasn't a monster. She deserves the chance to make a different choice. I've seen who she could be in a world with Jean and the X-Men. And, I don't know, if Emma Frost of all mutants deserves that . . ."

"Then surely you do, too."

"Yeah. Maybe."

Leaning to the side, she nudges Kitty's shoulder with her own. "All right, why else?"

"I guess because you're kind of my only friend, which technically makes you my best friend. Temporarily, I mean, until we get Rachel back." It's the first time Kitty's spoken the name aloud. She thinks all at once about her slip the night Betsy first reached out; she and Betsy in the sunlit room, and the redhead out on the balcony whose face she never saw.

Softly, sweetly, Betsy says, "Rachel would like that, I think."

Not for the first time since last night's revelation, Kitty wonders what it's like to love like that, and to be so sure that you're loved right back.

"Kitty . . ." Betsy begins. "Do you want me to show—"

I'm picking up something airborne approaching quickly from the east on the Blackbird's radar. Storm's voice rings in their minds through Professor Xavier's telepathic link, connecting them all. **Wait. Now it's gone again. Whatever it was, it didn't seem to be a stealth vehicle. Too large. Equipped with some sort of radar absorption device, possibly? No visual confirmation yet, but Banshee is standing by to engage.**

The professor's measured thoughts replace Storm's. **All X-Men, take your positions. We must assume that Doom's arrival is imminent.**

They scramble to their feet as Nightcrawler materializes on the roof beside them in his signature billow of acrid smoke. Together the three of them look up to where Storm and Banshee have been circling the jet over the grounds and surrounding area. The Blackbird is invisible except for the moving arrow of starlessness in the clear night sky, like a streak of ink as it passes. But no such signs betray the presence of a second plane, as far as she can see.

I'm not picking up any nearby minds through Cerebro, the professor continues.

No thoughts on my end, either, Jean chimes in.

Nor mine, Betsy says.

Between the magically fortified armor and his essential Doomness, his mental shields may be too hefty, America reminds them all. **Almost impenetrable, unless he *wants* to let you in. We might have better luck at closer range.**

Why by air? Wolverine asks, a feral edge even to his thoughts. **Thought you said this chump could teleport. I don't like it.**

I don't like any of it, Cyclops says, a rare moment of agreement.

Kitty doesn't like it, either. She treads carefully down the slope of the attic roof to the eaves, as though ten feet of distance will reveal Doom's unseen presence.

Luckily, Storm has a better plan. The previously clear night sky begins to froth over, clouds forming to blot out the moon and stars above. Atmospheric wisps turn quickly to thick, dark clouds, whipped into a brewing tempest. Rain pelts the lawns and rooftop, bathing Kitty's upturned face. Then it lifts and twists sideways, swirling as if driven by a current. The river of rainwater snakes across the sky, seeking.

Before it can find its target, a comet of violently red light slices through the gale from somewhere above the towering oak trees across campus, blasting into the front of the mansion below them. Then it's chaos, bricks tumbling, shingles rippling as a section of the roof begins to collapse, sending Kitty tumbling over the edge.

The lawn four stories below seems to rush too quickly toward her, and she hasn't even pulled it together to phase when a pair of strong arms catches her around the middle, knocking the breath from her lungs. A poof of smoke surrounds her, and then, disoriented, she's planted down on the grass. Kitty staggers, still wheezing, and Nightcrawler grabs her arm to steady her. "All right, Katzchen?"

"Fine," she answers shakily. "I'm fine. Thank you. But where's—"

He's gone again before she can finish the question, returning a second later with Betsy on his arm just as America, Colossus, Wolverine, Cyclops, and Jean converge on the lawn from their stations across the campus. Together they survey the damage. Where the grand front doors once stood to welcome mutants, the entryway is now a gaping crater into the atrium, and a section of the exterior wall that hasn't yet collapsed seems in danger of falling at any moment.

"Jean, the connection is gone!" Cyclops shouts, then looks toward Xavier's office on the eastern corner of the ground floor. It seems to have escaped the worst of the blast, except that the tall windows have blown out of their frames, only scraps of glass left to reflect the cracks of Storm's lightning overhead.

But he's right: Kitty is alone in her head.

"I've got it," Jean says, booting up her own psychic link among the teammates. **"Professor, are you there?"**

No answer.

Cyclops whips his head to the side. "Nightcrawler?"

"I will go." He vanishes to check on the professor without having to be told.

Got eyes on Doom yet, Storm? America asks.

Not y— Look out!

Another blast from the sky crashes through the mansion's west wing on the second floor. America kicks a portal into the courtyard to pull Jean a safe distance away just before a third shot right into their midst sends the rest of them scattering. The comet-like blast carves a deep trench into the courtyard, soil and rocks and rubble flying in every direction. Kitty grabs ahold of Betsy to phase them both, and dirt and stone rain down right through them. Cyclops slices a flying hunk of pavement in half with his optic blast before it can flatten him, while a steel-skinned Colossus crouches over Wolverine to block the worst of the blast.

All right, pals? Banshee asks from above as the dust settles.

They each check in—all but one.

Nightcrawler, are you with the professor? Cyclops asks, then swears beneath his breath when no answer follows. **Nightcrawler, can you hear us?**

Again, no response.

Saw where the last shot came from, and I'm after it. Might want to cover your ears, Banshee warns before he drops screaming out of the jet's exit hatch, sailing through a sky brightened by Storm's controlled lightning by the power of his own sonic waves. He swoops through the air toward the grove of trees, chased by the snake-like current of driving rain.

"Cloaked or not, that aircraft is up there, and Banshee's powerful enough to take it down," Cyclops tells America, who hasn't been training with the X-Men for weeks.

Kitty appreciates his reassurance all the same.

Rushing just ahead of Banshee, Storm's rope of rainwater seems to lash against an invisible obstacle in its path, outlining the shape of a hull as it flows against it. Whatever it is, it's much larger than Kitty could have guessed. But it's only a moment's contact before the rain pulses outward in something very like a shock wave. As Banshee reaches it and the ring of water blasts back over him, his scream dies in his throat. Banshee drops like a stone from the sky into the dark treetops below.

Storm, get out of there! Cyclops commands just as Wolverine starts pelting straight toward the oak grove. "Wolverine, be careful!" he shouts after the man. "We don't know what else that thing can do."

Wolverine snarls without breaking stride, "Don't care. I'm the best at what *I* do."

Throwing up his hands, Cyclops turns back to the rest of the team. "Jean, can you bring that thing down?"

"I think so, but it'll be hard to concentrate. I can't support the link alone. Betsy, help me?"

With a deep breath, Betsy steps up beside her. She looks *right* with the X-Men, Kitty thinks of her friend, even as her stomach churns with nerves. She looks . . . home. Together the telepaths raise their palms together toward the amorphous obstacle in the sky, which now seems to be repelling the rain from its massive hull, making its size and shape even harder to anticipate. After a moment, Jean shouts, "Its shield is too powerful! Pushes us out just when I think we've got ahold of it." She raises both arms now, their muscles visibly trembling. "We can contain it within a psionic parameter for now, like a reverse force field. But the moment we slip and it gets another shot out . . ."

"America, can you fly through that force field?" asks Cyclops.

"I don't know," America admits reluctantly. "I'm pretty indestructible, but if it's Doom, we're talking magic, too."

Well . . . crap.

"If these two can keep the ship pinned down, and you can portal me up there, I can get inside," Kitty tells her. "Maybe I can find the source of the force field, mess with it, or . . . I think I can do *something*." That has to be true.

But America shakes her head. "I trust my powers and all, but as long as the cloaking device is up and I can't see where the ship is, I could miss by a millimeter, slam right into the force field, and fry us both. Bet it'd be the same for Nightcrawler."

Nightcrawler, come in? Cyclops prompts again, without success. **Professor?**

Kitty's heart sinks.

Until Colossus places an impossibly heavy steel hand on her shoulder. "I can get you up there, I believe. But tell me first, are you afraid of heights?"

CHAPTER 32

KITTY

JULY 19, 1975

IT'S A TERRIBLE PLAN. PROBABLY THE WORST SHE'S EVER COME UP with, and Kitty's hatched some rotten eggs in her time.

She stands just under the towering oaks, peering up through their branches at the chaotic, rain-streaked sky beyond. Colossus and America are beside her, while the rest of the X-Men take up their assignments. Storm, having hurriedly landed the Blackbird, wields her tempest from the partial cover of the mansion's caved-in rooftop to give them as close a target in the sky as she can. After crashing out of the grove with Banshee's arm slung over his shoulder, Wolverine deposited the man—roused but badly limping—on the lawn for Cyclops to patch up as best he could. Then he dashed off into the mansion to track down Professor Xavier and Nightcrawler, despite Cyclops's protests that none of them should go off alone. Meanwhile, Betsy and Jean concentrate on keeping their tenuous cage up around the unseen aircraft.

From here, it's up to Kitty, though not alone.

"Ready, little one?" Colossus asks.

No, she almost says, and *I'm older than you, remember, muscles?* But her mouth is dry with fear, her heart thundering under the pressure. Besides, there is no better plan. So she nods instead.

With that, America lifts one foot from the ground and flies up into the treetops to hover in wait.

Stepping out beneath the open sky, Colossus holds his massive palm steady for Kitty to step into, and she puts a boot in it while bracing her hand on his organic steel shoulder, cool and smooth beneath her sweaty fingertips. When he grips her boot and lifts her effortlessly to chest height, Kitty finds her voice.

"Has this ever gone bad before?"

"Well . . . I have never before tried it," he admits.

Then he crouches, cranes his neck far back to spot his dubious target in the sky, and thrusts her upward into the air, hurtling her away from him as though she were no heavier than a baseball. Kitty flies upward, so fast that tears stream from the corners of her eyes and down her cheeks before she pierces Storm's swirling current of rain; so fast that she suspects she couldn't breathe even if she *could* breathe while phased to avoid the invisible force field. She only knows she's broken through it when the rain stops writhing around her. Colossus gauged his throw well, and now she's beginning to slow. Any moment now, she might pierce the ship's hull from beneath and finally get a look at the airborne behemoth they're dealing with.

Except she sees nothing but night, even as she begins to fall again. Back out of the force field and through the rain, she tumbles over in midair as she plunges downward.

"Stop phasing, Kitty!" America screams from somewhere just below, then alongside her, then above. "I can't catch you if you don't phase back!"

It's another moment's falling before Kitty can let herself trust, because what if what if what if . . .

She solidifies, and America swoops in to snatch her out of midair, strategically enough not to break her ribs upon impact. Then she delivers them both safely back to the ground—a much shorter distance now than Kitty's comfortable thinking about. That was too close. But she guesses it beats plunging deep into the earth before she can slow herself, unable to scrabble back up before the lack of air in her lungs buries her alive.

"Strike one," she tells them both, her voice trembling as badly as her legs.

It takes two more pitches before they hit.

On the third try, Kitty soars through the rain, through the force field, and then finally through the ship's cloaking device. She sees, at last, a bizarre, hulking metal monstrosity that looks more like the flying saucers on the covers of her dad's old sci-fi pulp novels than any stealth craft. Then, almost before she can blink, she's through the hull, decelerating at the apex of Colossus's well-timed throw, and she digs her fist into the bones of the fuselage to stop herself. She steals a moment to breathe inside a crawl-space-like pocket at the very bottom of the aircraft.

Now what?

There wasn't a ton to her plan beyond "get into the ship, mess stuff up, get out again before Doom notices." Again, it wasn't a *good* plan. She wishes she had anybody's voice in her head to guide her, but Betsy and Jean need all of their focus to keep the fortress-sized spacecraft at bay, and the professor is . . .

No. One crisis at a time.

Well, she's smart, isn't she? Kitty was always placed in the highest classes at Deerfield Middle and at Miss Hester's. At least she was before she started skipping in a half-hearted effort to lose her scholarship, all while knowing she couldn't really go home again if she succeeded. She can totally figure out how to tank a spaceship before it blows up the school, the nexus being, and her entire reality.

Bracing herself, she phases to tilt forward out of the hull, trying to ignore the darkened ground far below as she leans out for a better look at the mechanism that seems to keep this thing in the air. A propeller . . . no, not that. A rotor, each of its blades as long as the school's basketball court. She learned about these, once; a field trip to the New England Air Museum with her science class in Connecticut. Found it interesting, actually, though she'd have taken that secret to the grave. That was so many years ago, but she remembers the very basics. If the pole feeding through the undercarriage of the ship is the mast, it must be attached to some kind of gearbox and, through that, the engine.

Ducking gratefully back inside the fuselage, Kitty moves farther into the ship and up alongside the mast to find herself inside a carousel-sized cage surrounding a stack of massive, churning gears. Nothing about them looks particularly electrical, and—phased or no—she's not eager to stick a limb into their midst. Onward, then. She passes into an even larger chamber attached to this one. The engine room, with its huge cooling fans. Once again, she'd rather not wedge her body into its pulverizing shafts and fast-moving belts and whatever else. But there, those thick steel pipes snaking off the engine and up through the ceiling—fuel lines?

That, she can work with.

She follows them up through the ceiling to a cluster of what can only be fuel tanks. Four of them, each twice her height. And at the bottom of each, where the fuel lines snake inside them: a shut-off valve.

Can it be this easy? Doom's plan thwarted thanks to a long-ago field trip?

Only one way to find out.

Crouching all the way down, Kitty grabs the first metal lever with both hands. She puts her whole back into it, muscling the lever from left to right. She'd better move quickly, because there's no way Doom won't be alerted. One by one, she scoots down the line, sweating as she shoves the levers over, shoulders aching by the time she reaches the last. Now it's time to move, especially when she hears the vibrations of thundering footsteps through the hull, hopefully far enough away to make a difference. She sinks into the engine room, where the machine is already sputtering audibly. The ship begins to shake, the last of the fuel running through the lines, running out. She races back to the gearbox and phases right through the undercarriage of the ship, wrapping her arms and legs around the mast to keep from falling through the rotor blades. Solid again, she's buffeted by their wind.

When the blades begin to slow, the aircraft tipping dizzily, that's her cue to jump.

Kitty hesitates just long enough to send a last wish out into the night that America is watching closely. Then she holds her breath, lets go...

And lands in a pair of waiting arms, thank God.

America grins as she speeds them out from beneath the ship, her black curls soaked nearly straight and plastered to her brown skin. "Badass, Kitty Pryde."

Kitty somehow blushes despite the cold and beating rain.

She watches over America's shoulder as the still-invisible aircraft crashes down through the treetops, snapping the trunks like matchsticks beneath its bulk. Just as she and America touch down on the lawn, a huge plume of turf announces the ship's final, thunderous crash. Its cloaking device flickers once, twice, then fails, and the ship reveals itself to all.

"Blimey!" Betsy says, skidding to a stop beside them, followed by Jean, then Cyclops, propping up a limping Banshee.

Colossus grins at them victoriously as he jogs to meet them. "Should I crack it open and see what's inside?"

But there's no need. With a mechanical hiss, a hatch levers open on the bank of the small pond in which the ship partially rests, and the hulking figure that Kitty first glimpsed in future-Latveria steps onto the ramp. Victor von Doom, illuminated by the ship's artificial lighting. Another step, and the light glints off his expressionless faceplate. The blank metal mask sends a shiver through her, though she tries to tell herself it's only her rain-soaked costume or the cooling night breeze. She alone just brought his spaceship down with the power of tenth-grade-level engineering. How can he possibly defeat the X-Men all together?

Then a second figure, just as broad and expressionless, steps into view. His plated armor clanks against the ramp, and his forest-green cloak stirs in the night air.

Then a third.

Another, and another, and another.

"Doombots," America whispers, a grim look on her face. "Don't know where he got ahold of those. He was traveling solo in the last world."

"**Storm, Wolverine, meet us on the lawn,**" Cyclops instructs through their restored telepathic link. "**Can anyone get eyes on the real Doom?**"

Betsy grimaces with concentration. "It's like they're all thinking the same thing, on endless repeat." Through the link, she shows them all:

Give us Jean Grey. Give us Jean Grey. Give us Jean Grey. Give us—

"Enough," Cyclops snaps, and the feed cuts off. "America, anything you can tell us?"

"The bots have programming to pass them off as the real deal, like . . . a hologram of thoughts, instead of organic. It's all for show."

Now the formation of Doombots shifts as they're joined by yet another and another. Kitty struggles to tally them all before the phalanx begins to advance, but there must be two dozen of them now, marching forward. None speak, but she suspects that the replay of their thoughts remains the same.

"Okay," Kitty says to stifle her dread and fill the silence. "Odds are shifting a little, but I'm pretty good with bots. I can take them out if I can get to them, and I'd like to see them stop me. Besides, the bots aren't as bad as the real thing, right?"

"No. But they're bad enough. Hold for now, Kitty—we don't know what kind of weaponry they're working with yet."

Just then, Storm descends from a sky that's starry once more. "Where is Wolverine?" She's right; he ought to have been back, with or without Kurt and the professor by now. "**Wolverine, do you copy?**"

Once again, no answer.

"That one!" Jean announces suddenly. "Third one in the back, on the left. Can't get a read on him at all. It's like it was in the ship, some kind of barricade keeping me out."

"I'm on it," Storm says grimly, rising goddess-like into the sky. With a hand stretched to the stars, she summons a bright streak of lightning, wraps her fist around raw plasma, and thrusts the bolt toward the true Doom.

He hardly misses a step, lifting one gauntlet as though to catch the bolt.

Well, crap.

Storm lifts both arms now, head tipped back, eyes cloud white, gathering bolt upon bolt of lightning to her body, throwing great arcs of it at the phalanx advancing steadily across the grounds as Cyclops steps forward to unleash his optic blast at Doom, distracting him while Colossus thunders toward the enemy at full speed. For a moment, it seems it might work: Doom's head rocks back as an optic blast catches him across the face, and when he lowers it again, a singed, scarlike streak across one cheek plate shows in the flash of Storm's lightning. But it's a surface mark only. Not harmed in the slightest, he rams into Colossus, and they meet at a dead sprint, crashing to the ground together.

Kitty isn't worried. Colossus is strong. She's seen how strong he is, felt it in the wind that buffeted her as she rocketed upward with nearly unbearable speed. A tractor couldn't dent him.

Indeed, he gains the upper hand, wrestling Doom to the ground as the bots march around them both. They seem as unbothered by Storm's attacks as their master. Kitty starts forward, prepared to phase through them all to get to Colossus, and short-circuit as many of them as she can touch along the way.

Then Doom presses a gauntlet crackling with purple light to his silvered skin, and Colossus flies backward. Before he even lands, a bot lifts a rifle-like weapon with a strangely forked barrel to fire, striking Colossus square in the chest with a golden bolt of energy. It doesn't dissipate as he falls, but spreads, snaking across his torso and down his legs. By the time Colossus hits the ground and rolls to a stop in the path of the advancing Doombots, he's encased head to boot in a translucent golden shell, frozen in position.

Kitty waits to see him blink, or breathe.

She's still waiting when Cyclops cries, "Fall back!"

"This is wrong," Kitty insists through chattering teeth. "This is all wrong."

"I said, fall back! They'll flatten us all out in the open before we can help anybody, and we *need* to keep him away from Jean."

In the face of twenty-something charging Doombots, she finds herself shamefully glad to join the rest as they sprint for the mansion. Just as they tumble together through the gaping wound in the school's front, a blast from one among the swarm's weapons sends a barely standing section of the wall crashing down in a cloud of plaster and pulverized clay. Cyclops shoots down flying bricks even as he doubles over coughing.

Professor? Jean cries desperately through the link. **Wolverine? Nightcrawler? Can anyone hear me?**

"America . . ." Cyclops grits out through another coughing fit. "Do it. Do it now, and we'll hold them off as long as we can. Betsy!"

Jean turns to look at him, mouth opening in protest as she seems to read his thoughts. But by then, it's a beat too late. As America raises a knee to slam her foot through the half-collapsed wall, her boot never touches brick. Instead the air splinters into a star-shaped portal as tall as she is, sizzling with blue-white light. The moment it stabilizes, Betsy comes sprinting in from the side like a defensive tackle to collide with Jean in a burst of brilliant pink psychic light of her own making. Jean grunts with the impact as Betsy sends them both crashing through the portal.

"What the hell!" Kitty screams, then without stopping to think, dives headfirst through the portal after them.

She phases as she lands to avoid tumbling into a desk—they're in the upstairs study hall at the end of the east wing of the dorms, its ceiling still miraculously intact—and sinks halfway through the floor instead.

Scrambling out, Kitty looks back just in time to watch America jump through after them . . .

But she never lands.

Poised halfway between the atrium and the study hall, she's

framed perfectly by her portal when a beam of cold white light entombs her from above. It's brighter by far than the jagged edges of the portal or Betsy's psionic force field. So bright, Kitty has to squeeze her eyes shut against it, the afterimage dazzling in the dark behind her eyelids.

When she can look again, still blinking away its scintillating imprint, America Chavez is gone.

CHAPTER 33

⭐

AMERICA

IN A VAST ROOM BEYOND THE PURVIEW OF EVERY UNIVERSE, AMERica finds herself on a circular platform. The Watcher who shot her from the sky peers down at her from a construct like a judge's bench, his broad face emotionless, his pupil-less eyes glowing bright as the high walls of the chamber, which appear carved from solid, quartzlike white light. Behind his bench, the stands of the Temple of Justice are filled with Watchers by the hundreds, maybe the thousands—she's never bothered to count their number. They are simply *they*, a compilation of cosmic beings beyond godhood, all-seeing, all-knowing, and completely united in their purpose.

Except for America, who stands before them alone.

"Send me back!" she cries, attempting to lift her combat boot and stomp it down upon the platform; to shatter a portal into its surface, or even just to destroy some part of this pristine place that smells of nothing. But she can't so much as raise her foot, trapped in place by the properties of the platform. "You have to send me back," she tries again. "Doom . . . the Whisperer . . . the X-Men don't know that he's—"

"You have been summoned to answer for your crimes against the code of the Watchers," her judge announces as though she never spoke. "You were warned, Watcher. After you placed those phone calls to Peter Parker and Doctor Strange, you were warned that intervention is neither allowed nor justified. You were warned not to transgress again. When you consorted with the entity known as Venom, abandoned your post, and continued to interfere in the affairs of mortals, you were given the chance to come with me of your own free will and face judgment."

"Sure, after you shot me," America mutters through gritted teeth.

"Instead," he continues, "you schemed to evade us." Here the slightest twitch of his lips suggests an uncharacteristic sneer as they both remember their brush with Galactus, but his expression smooths over again before she can be sure. "Since then, you have revealed your existence again and again, shared forbidden knowledge that should belong solely to the Watchers, and engaged in combat to serve your own allies and suit your own ends. So you have been brought here, whether you will it or not, and you will face us now."

CHAPTER 34

KITTY

JULY 19, 1975

THE LAST SPARKS OF THE PORTAL FLARE OUT AS KITTY AND BETSY finish picking themselves up from the floor. But Jean doesn't stand.

She simply rises to hover above them, the air in the hall around them seeming to waver like a heat mirage with her rage. *What are you doing?* she screams inside their skulls, and Kitty sinks back to her knees to clap her hands uselessly over her ears. Stacks of books left out on the long tables shudder, then rise, floating toward the ceiling along with sheaves of paper and shards of plaster fallen from the ceiling—still miraculously intact. But perhaps not for long. The lights flicker, the walls shake, and the bookshelves that run the length of the study hall threaten to splinter apart.

Suddenly, Kitty is keenly aware that, Phoenix or no, Jean Grey could telekinetically pry the bones from their bodies as easily as plucking matchsticks from a box if she wanted.

Judging by the tremor in Betsy's words, so is she. "It was Cyclops's plan. I promised. So did America."

What about him? But Jean doesn't give her the chance to explain aloud. Instead, she lifts her fingers to her temples, reading Betsy's thoughts.

Betsy trembles in place but manages to stand her ground.

Then Jean gasps. "*Damn it, Scott!*"

"Um." Kitty raises a tentative hand but stays in her defensive crouch. "For the telepathically ungifted among us, what's happening?"

"He made them promise to get me out if Doom got too close," Jean explains through gritted teeth. "He spoke to them both without my knowing. He thought she and America could somehow convince me to abandon my team along with my solar system."

"He loves you," Betsy insists, "*and* he wanted to save the world."

"Do you think I want to live in a world where I left my friends and the love of my life to die in my place?" Jean snaps. "How can I save anyone, if I can't save the people I care about most?"

"We care about the same people, believe me," Betsy says, holding her palms aloft. "The trail I spoke of this morning, the one we followed to the X-Men? It wasn't leading to you . . . or not only to you. It was leading to the woman I was meant to fall in love with." Betsy's chin crumples for the briefest instant before she collects herself and continues. "She's your daughter, Jean. Yours and Scott's. I never saw her before America showed me her memories, but it feels as if I've spent my whole life dreaming of her. And without you, she'll never exist."

"Our daughter?" Jean sinks back to the carpet, arms wrapped around herself as she touches down. "You're telling me that we . . . that you and she . . . Scott and I should have had a daughter?"

"You *will*," Betsy corrects. "I can show you, the way America showed me."

Kitty turns away, allowing them their moment; the one she wasn't brave enough for.

By the time she turns back, tears stream down Jean's face to collect at the corners of her wavering smile. "Our daughter," Jean whispers. "Beautiful. She's beautiful. Scott has to see."

"He will," says Betsy. "Doom isn't trying to take out the X-Men. Just let us get you out of here, and then you can—"

"Wait," Kitty interrupts. "How exactly do we get Jean out, with America gone?"

Now they both turn on her. "Beg pardon?" Betsy asks.

"Neither of you saw?"

"I was busy peeling my face off the carpet," Jean grumbles, swiping the last of the tears from her cheek. "I didn't expect to be clotheslined by my friends mid-battle." Then she closes her eyes, and when she speaks again, her annoyance has given way to alarm. "I can't find her."

Betsy frowns, conducting her own telepathic search. "Neither can I."

"Like, in the mansion?" Kitty asks. "Or—"

"Not for miles," says Betsy.

"Not on the *planet*," says Jean.

"What?" Panic flutters in her chest. "Can Doom do that?"

Before any of them can guess, the door to the study hall bursts inward off its hinges, and Kitty phases instinctively so as not to be speared by flying splinters of wood. "Give us Jean Grey," intones the Doombot, taking up the entirety of the empty doorframe.

Kitty sniffs. No bubbled-metal scar across its faceplate. A lone bot, which she's plenty capable of handling; she brought down a whole silly spaceship, didn't she? "Come and get her, you jerk."

Kitty, wait! Jean warns.

But she's already sprinted the short distance between them to punch her intangible fist through the bot's faceplate and out the back of its skull, carving a path through the circuitry that makes it such a threat; nothing she can't handle, with the disruptive side effect of her powers that she's never truly understood. And she doesn't need to. Kitty draws her fist back, solidifying to kick the fried bot's knees out from under it and let it topple to the floor with a satisfying *clang*.

Before she can, the bot barely twitches a palm, and with only the sizzle of some kind of electric weapon for warning, she's on the floor. Fiery pain crackles down her spine, stars bursting before her eyes. She can very dimly hear Betsy calling out to her, and then the crash of breaking glass and a scream. All of it sounds like the muffled murmurings of a TV set in a far room. But the bitterly sharp scent in the air around her, she can smell perfectly.

Now the bot is standing over her, staring down, brown eyes burning with triumph.

Not a bot, she thinks distantly as her limbs twitch beyond her control.

Then he disappears from her field of vision, thrown backward by a telekinetic blast from Jean that ripples Kitty's hair even on the floor. She closes her eyes against it . . . and when she opens them, she's not sure how long it's been. It feels longer than the time it ought to take to blink, but she still can't move.

Somewhere, glass shatters. Then comes that electric *szkkkt* once more.

Another long blink later, and Doom hovers over her again. Holding a limp Jean Grey aloft like a rag doll by the back of her neck, he considers Kitty from above as she twitches on the carpet. "I don't know who you are. But I know you're not supposed to be here. You aren't a part of this story." Then he lifts one armor-plated boot and brings it down.

CHAPTER 35

JEAN

JULY 19, 1975

SO THIS IS WHERE EVERYONE WENT.

It's Jean's first clear thought upon regaining consciousness. They're in the Danger Room, of all places, in its blank-slate form. Slumped against the far wall beyond her reach are the rest of the X-Men. Each wears a pair of thick metal cuffs around their wrists, the surface striped with circuitry. There are no such cuffs on Jean's wrists; she's held fast between two Doombots. A whole squadron of bots stands guard over the senseless bodies of Professor Xavier, Kurt, Ororo, Peter, Logan, Sean, and Scott . . .

"Scott," she calls hoarsely through cracked lips, tasting sour metal in her mouth, but he doesn't stir. And when she reaches for her telepathy, she can't sense Doom's thoughts, or her friends'.

For the first time in a decade, she's alone in her mind, and she doesn't want to be.

Maybe it's the aftereffects of the shock weapon Doom used on her; no wonder she feels as though she's been rammed by a speeding train. Or maybe it's the ball of crackling purple light one of the bots—no, *not* a bot, she can sense that—cradles in his raised palm, so bright at the center that it's almost pure white.

Magic.

America Chavez had warned them that Doom was a capable sorcerer, as well as an inventor and megalomaniac. But she hadn't expected this much firepower or so many of them. And not just the bots: Victor von Doom himself. There are two of them, she knows now, and doesn't need this Doom's unblemished faceplate to tell the difference. She can't read his thoughts, couldn't upstairs in the study hall, either. But he isn't the same man she rooted out from among robots by the downed ship, who led the charge on the mansion's front lawn. Even as her telepathy rammed up against a barricade in both encounters, she can sense that this one is different, and like nothing she's felt yet. It's like running her hand along a wall in the dark, relying on texture and temperature as clues.

Impossibly, this mind feels even colder than the first.

As the hulking figure armored from boot to faceplate steps toward her, Jean strains feebly against the Doombots' iron grips on her arms; it's all that's keeping her upright. A bead of blood drips from one nostril, but she can't reach to wipe it away. She can't even feel her fingers and toes, brushing uselessly against the Danger Room floor.

What the hell did he hit her with?

"You'll only harm yourself by struggling," Doom says matter-of-factly.

She doesn't need her telepathy to see the truth in that. She can't fight them all in her present condition. Not against the inorganic intelligence of the bots and the heavily fortified mind of Doom, with his magic to boot. But she'll have to keep him talking, because any moment now, somebody will come. America, Kitty, Betsy . . .

Someone, somewhere, is surely coming for her.

"You traveled all the way to my world to get to me before the Phoenix Force does, right? Well, here I am. Why do you need anyone else?"

Doom regards her for a long moment. "What do you know about the Phoenix Force?" he asks at last. The sphere of magic between his fingertips is mesmerizing in its brilliance, bathing her in its otherworldly light.

She's not sure she could look away if she tried.

"A little." Jean sees no point in lying, and perhaps she has to give a little bit to keep him going. "Creation and destruction. Life and death itself. My destiny."

"Who told you? The superfluous mutants upstairs, I suppose." Doom pauses, puffing out his chest slightly, as if he was proud. "Or perhaps the one who followed me here, thinking to stop me. As though America could."

Jean's pulse sputters. He knows about America, which can't be good, but at least wherever she is, she's beyond his reach. The others, though . . . "What did you do with Betsy and Kitty?"

"They were redundant to the scene."

Then there's nothing they can do for her right now, and nothing she can do for them.

"And the nexus powers? What do you know about them?" Doom continues.

It feels like treading on her own grave to answer, and she presses her cracked lips together.

Turning back to the line of bots, Doom raises two fingertips. One of the bots lifts the same bulky, pistol-looking contraption that she watched pour volt upon volt of electricity into Kitty, then into her own body, and levels it at Scott. His face is peaceful now as it never is awake; not for anybody but Jean, who's had the privilege of watching Scott Summers smile after a kiss, and sulk in bed with a cold, and eat cereal in his boxers on a Sunday morning.

She swallows her panic, and it tastes of her own blood. "I don't know. I don't know any more than I was told, and that isn't much. Nexus beings anchor realities, right? But I don't know how, or why it's me, or what you want with the power bad enough to ruin worlds for it. Can't you tell me that much before I die?"

Time. She just needs time.

To her surprise, Doom decides to answer. "Very well. As to the why, I've been trying across these past few worlds to work out what it is that makes any nexus being special. Why any of you were chosen to matter to your worlds so greatly." He bends closer now, so close that she can hear his breath whistling faintly through the mouth plate of his mask as he inspects her, and see the delicate veins in the whites of his brown eyes. "As far as I can tell, the answer is: There's no reason at all. Perhaps it's a question of chance, improbable and unreliable. Perhaps it is... simply your bad luck." Shrugging one shoulder as though the mystery means little to him, he retreats. "As to the what, with your powers, I can find what I seek among the infinite realities in the Multiverse. Home to a nexus being who is, for me, the ends. Your death, Jean Grey, is just a means to them."

CHAPTER 36

KITTY

JULY 19, 1975

"WAKE UP! I SAID WAKE UP!"

She hears Betsy's voice as if through thick layers of cotton, seconds before she feels a palm-shaped sting across one cheek, and a sharp, bright pain. "Damn it!" Kitty stumbles over the words, her tongue dry and heavy, her mouth tasting of iron. "I think my nose is broken again . . ."

"Oh, thank God." Betsy sighs. "I thought . . . Can I help you sit up?"

"Am I not?" Kitty groans and pries her eyes open, seeing that she is, in fact, lying on the study hall floor. As Betsy gently peels her off the carpet, the world tilts around her, and she closes her eyes again until it resettles. Once it does, she lifts one wrist to find it cuffed to the other by a pair of thick, ugly shackles, their surface striated with thin wires and tiny dials.

"I recognize them from Reed Richards's notes in RCX's files. The ones I pinched for my, er, personal use," Betsy explains.

Well, screw that.

"Just whatever you do, don't—"

Kitty phases free of them.

Or she tries to. But in the instant Kitty begins to disassemble and shift her molecules—a process as simple as holding her breath—pain like blue-hot fire licks up her skin from wrist to shoulder, scorching a path across her collarbone and up her throat.

It begins to recede in the next moment, but the process leaves her heaving for air, back flat against the carpet again. "What . . . the . . ."

Betsy's face hovers over her own, wincing in sympathy. "Don't use your powers," she finishes. "The electronic shackles fire impulses into the nerves whenever a superpowered person attempts to access their abilities."

"That is so . . . stupid," Kitty grits out.

"Nevertheless, we've got to get them off you, and we've got to do it now. Doom could be back at any moment."

"Which one?" She sits back up to scan the room despite the dizzying swoop that follows, and the protestations of every muscle in her body. Her spine feels like an accordion that's been run over by a semi-truck, but that's a problem for later. "There's two of them, Betsy."

"I know. Likely America's Doom and the one who currently resides in this reality in 1975. They're working together, it seems. It was this world's Doom who we encountered on the lawn, while I suspect America's Doom was busy inside of the mansion. Abducting the professor, picking the X-Men off one by one when they separated from the team. And after he shot you—"

"He *shot* me?"

"With some kind of shock weapon. I didn't last much longer. Got tossed out the window." She reaches tentatively for the back of her head, where her hair's unraveled from her careful bun to hang wild around her shoulders, tiny bits of glass still sparkling in the strands from the shattered picture window across the room. "My powers caught me before I hit the ground, if you can believe it. Like a telekinetic net. It took me a moment to get back. I had to avoid *this* world's Doom, and just barely did. Jean was gone once I got here, and you were . . . Kitty, I've been trying to find her, but I can't." To demonstrate, Betsy squeezes her eyes shut, and Kitty pictures pink butterflies winging through every corridor and room in the mansion, searching. But she shakes her head a moment later. "I don't hear her. I can't hear any of them, like I can't hear America."

Kitty's stomach seems to phase out through her rib cage. "Maybe Doom's blocking them out somehow."

"I can't lose her," Betsy whimpers.

Kitty knows just who she means by *her*. "So look again," she urges. "You found Jean from decades in the future, right? What's a little magic compared with that? You followed a trail before, so you can do it now."

Practically hiccuping with nerves, Betsy closes her eyes again.

While she waits, Kitty forces herself to breathe. *Please let this work, please.*

"Down," Betsy whispers, her eyes flickering beneath still-closed lids. "I sense something, but it's weak, it's . . . We need to go down."

"So whip out a psionic lockpick or whatever. Get these off me"—she lifts her wrists—"and lead the way."

Betsy does, wielding her shimmering pink psi-powers with a precision Kitty didn't know she had, and then down they go.

CHAPTER 37

JEAN

JULY 19, 1975

AS THE FEELING BEGINS TO RETURN PAINFULLY TO JEAN'S FINGERtips, she resolves to keep Doom talking just a little longer. She can outlast him as long as he's talking. "So what next? How exactly do you plan to steal something I was born with?"

From his cloak, he produces something shaped vaguely like the headset Scott wears while flying the Blackbird. It's surprisingly crude, though, as if cobbled together from shards of disparate metal, with a boxy earpiece at each end. "Between the fragments available to me for study, my other self's access to material components, and the combined mastery of magic and mental resources of the greatest scientists of their respective worlds, I was able to re-create a device that allows me to strip you of your powers from continents away. Worlds, perhaps. My improvement on a flawed design. Of course, my associate is unaware of this."

She laughs to cover for the fear roiling through her. "You lied to yourself?"

"I appealed to this Doom's desires and ego. He shares my hunger for knowledge, so I offered him technology he won't have developed for years, as well as access to the nexus powers. That was enough for him. He gave me use of his workshops, his equipment, and his mystic. A seer at Castle Doom—useless in my homeworld, but surprisingly skilled in this one. He showed me a vision of your fate. Of the selfless Jean Grey, sacrificing herself for love. My associate simply needed to believe that proximity was required, as was your death. It was nothing personal. And this may not be much comfort, but your death is nothing personal, either."

"Nothing personal? How can you say that? I *am* a person!" she screams into Doom's mask. "I . . . I'm supposed to have a daughter." Jean cradles the images of her—a gift from America's memories—as she wishes she could hold Rachel, just once. A baby girl with her mother's bright-red hair and gem-green eyes, and her father's smile—a little rare, but soft as warm rain when it happens. Then a teenage girl in a red-and-yellow uniform, tentatively wielding fire as she fights alongside the X-Men for the first time. Then a grown woman, in love and aflame, sure of what she wants and who she is. "I'm supposed to have a life!"

"Yes. A life of loss, and dashed hopes, and heartbreak," he says dispassionately, as though reading the ingredients list on the back of a cereal box. "And in that, you're no different from most souls in most worlds."

"Then why come all the way to mine? To my home? Why kill me, if I'm nothing to you?"

"Because it is one thing to reshape reality to my liking, and yet another to control life and death itself, so that none may threaten it again. The nexus powers can get me what I want, but there remains the question of keeping it. And you—though you may not be unique in the Multiverse, you present me with a unique opportunity. That, Jean Grey, is why I'm here, and why your friends are necessary. Their deaths prelude your summoning of the Phoenix Force."

"My summoning . . . You're not trying to evade it at all, are you?" Jean realizes aloud.

"No." Doom lays his palm against her cheek, almost gentle despite the freezing cold of his gauntlet. "I am not. What I want, Jean Grey, is what everyone wants. What I *need* is a means of keeping it. And that's why I need the Phoenix Force. As I said: It's nothing personal." Then he straightens and aims the hand still cradling magic at the X-Men—her friends, her family, her mentor, the love of her life—and lets loose a blast of otherworldly fire that engulfs them all.

CHAPTER 38

KITTY

JULY 19, 1975

PHASING THROUGH THE STUDY HALL FLOOR, THEY LAND IN XAVIER'S office on the ground level, where great holes blasted through the walls still smolder. The professor's fancy desk lies on its side, smashed to pieces, his belongings scattered in the debris. Half the windows have blown out, the glass sparkling on the carpet.

Wherever he is—wherever the rest of the X-Men are—they'll get them back.

She has to believe that they can.

Betsy tugs her toward the corridor, and they pass through the anteroom, even more of a smoking ruin. It pours through a massive hole in the floor from the room below, which looks like the mainframe, suggesting fire. Not that way, then.

There is no hallway when they reach it, no more than there can be said to be an atrium. It's all one big empty battlefield now, scattered with a few fallen enemies, but no allies. They run past what used to be the school's kitchen, its door and half the walls now blasted to nothing. In the reception room, a shredded Doombot lies in a pile of twitching titanium limbs.

She phases them into the basement, then down again to the first sublevel, then the next, where she pauses for breath in what seems to be an unscathed corridor. "Which way now?" Kitty asks, panting.

But Betsy's already running down a long, familiar corridor,

with only one steel-paneled door set halfway down. The Danger Room. Before she can follow, Kitty hears behind her the clank of metal on metal, and she phases just in time for a lightning-like bolt of energy to pass through her chest. It strikes the wall down the corridor, crumpling the paneling like it's aluminum foil. When she turns, the advancing line of half a dozen Doombots—probably stationed to guard the elevator they'd bypassed—are already lining up their gauntlets for the next shot.

CHAPTER 39

★

AMERICA

"WHAT DO YOU WANT ME TO SAY, THAT I'M SORRY?" SHE SCANS THE impassive faces in the stands of the Temple of Justice. "Fine. Then I'm sorry I spent so long thinking it was me the Whisperer was after. I'm sorry I didn't do something to stop him sooner. I'm sorry that I waited, and I watched, and . . . and people died." She meant to stay furious, to shout them all down, but her voice turns ragged as she wrings the confession from her heart. Because it's true, isn't it? If she'd put her ego aside sooner, if she only had stopped watching and *seen,* then maybe Doom wouldn't have gotten this far. "I thought being a Watcher meant I was more important than the people I was watching. Because I forgot who I really was."

"Who are you, then, Watcher?" her judge demands.

America looks down at her boots for a moment, then up to meet the inscrutable gaze of her assembled jury. "When I first landed on the Earth you've stolen me from, I wondered why my portal didn't bring me straight to the X-Men, or to Doom. Because my powers take me where I need to be, you know? I think . . . I was supposed to land where I came from. Not in some Utopian Parallel, but in New York City. I was supposed to remember that. Before I was anything else, I was America Chavez. I'm the daughter of Amalia and Elena Chavez, and after they died protecting me, I was raised by the Santanas of Washington Heights. I forgot that for a long time, but I won't forget it again."

The Watcher at the bench tilts his head. "Then you have judged yourself already, and ruled that you are not one of us."

America laughs and shoves her hands into her jacket pockets, because what else can she do? "Not if it means kicking back in a cosmic closet, sitting on knowledge that could save countless lives, could save countless *worlds,* but refusing to act because of some code I never wrote. If that's all a Watcher is, then what good are you?"

The gathered Watchers murmur among themselves in the stands, and the lightlike walls of the temple seem to pulse along with their consternation, as if participating.

"You believe yourself superior to us," guesses her judge, his booming voice a monotone. "But we Watchers have sworn off action because our greatest transgression led to disaster and destruction, as well you are aware. I may have suspended your physical abilities on that world, but I left you with access to our memories, our sacred records, so that you, too, would remember. When we attempted to enlighten the Prosilicans, we advanced their technology. We sought to better their lives, but we did not advance their ability to use our gifts ethically. The result was mass destruction across the cosmos, including that of our own home planet. Are you more cunning now than we were then? And are you wiser than this Doom whom you have declared a villain? Has he not claimed, in reality upon reality, to seek the salvation of humanity by forging himself as a god among them, then setting his knowledge to the purpose of conquering them? Weigh his deeds against his designs."

America treads carefully; there's danger here, but there's an opening as well. "How can I judge anything against his deeds when I don't know what's gonna happen because of them? I know that people have died. I know that if Doom kills Jean and takes the nexus powers, the timeline of her reality splits in two, and good people get lost. But what then? What will happen to worlds without a nexus being?"

The Watcher . . . well, he watches her, measuring the value of answering, she supposes. At last, he muses, "A divided timeline. Such a thing cannot sustain."

"Yeah, we figured." Then she bites her lip—best not to derail a monologue in progress.

"This has happened before. It will happen again. Picture a knife plunged into the surface of a frozen lake. The ice does not collapse all at once, but the crack spreads, seeks imperfections, points of weakness. Once the integrity of the ice has been sufficiently compromised, it shatters. So, too, will the timeline-that-was. Without a nexus, it will forever be beyond reach or repair."

America swallows back the taste of panic. "And the second timeline?"

"Without a nexus, the timeline-that-remains is unmoored, randomly reshaped, and lost among the chaos of the Multiverse. The reality remains defenseless, susceptible to corruption."

"Corruption. By Doom, you mean?"

The Watcher gives the slightest of nods.

"But . . . why? I thought the powers were the point, not the reality. What does he want with a corrupted reality? What *can* he want?"

"This, we have not seen. We must continue to observe, to study, until his intentions are known. Return to us. Resume your post. As one, we will discover the full truth. And as one, we will choose to act, when we know all there is to be known."

"The Watchers would act," she repeats, hardly daring to hope she's heard him correctly. "If you knew for sure that it was right, then you would choose."

Again, the Watcher nods.

This is what she wanted, isn't it? For the greatest collective power in the cosmos to *do* something, to make a single damn decision that wasn't refusing to decide. No plan or weapon that Doom could muster could ever stand against them. And once she knows the full scope of Doom's plans—once she has the answers to every question—she'll no longer have to wonder which choice to make.

She'll simply know.

Yet a question remains, and she can't ignore it. "But what about *this* world? If we abandon their reality, let it be corrupted while we sit back and take notes, what will happen to *this* Jean, and this Kitty, and this Betsy? Can a corrupted reality be repaired?"

"No." The word is stone, as immovable as its speaker.

"Then . . . no."

"You refuse our final offer, for the sake of one single world among infinite worlds? One Jean Grey among infinite Jean Greys?"

She moves carefully now, so carefully, coming to the realization even as she gives it voice. "If I could accept that a single world—or a single person—was worth sacrificing for the greater mission, then I accept that any world or any person is worth sacrificing. And if I could make a choice like that, how am I any better than Doom? How are *you*?"

The Watcher appointed her judge narrows his giant, illuminated eyes in a twitch of emotion. Not stone, then. "And how can you be sure, America Chavez, that your choice to sabotage our greater mission to change the outcome of one world is any less ill-fated than our own once was?"

"Maybe I'm not," America whispers, knowing they can hear her all the same. "Maybe I can't know for sure. But when was the last time you asked yourself whether inaction was right? When was the last time any Doom variant asked himself whether his actions were wrong? I've asked myself, and this is the best answer I've got. So I don't know, but . . . I hope." She wipes her wrist across her nose, focusing on the judge instead of her rumbling jury. "You all just keep sitting here behind your windows, refusing to lift a finger until you feel you know enough. But if you won't stop Doom, and if I'm not a Watcher, then you can't stop me, either. Take whatever you're gonna take away from me, then send me back."

Low protests and murmurings roil through the stands.

"So we shall, America Chavez. Your knowledge is your own, but further memories recorded by the Watchers belong only to the Watchers. We will send you back. However, if you seek to intercede again, be warned: You are already too late."

"How can I be?" She hears her voice rising again. "Time and space are nothing to you. You can send me back to any point in the timeline you like—you're Watchers!"

Her judge bows his formidable head. "But alas, America Chavez, you are not."

CHAPTER 40

JEAN

JULY 19, 1975

AS THE UNNATURAL FIRE SWALLOWS HER FRIENDS alive—*please, Lord, let them be alive*—Jean screams.

Not aloud; her fear is so great, so choking, that no sound comes out at all. It's a silent scream that erupts from inside Jean. A psychic energy infinitely more powerful than any she's conjured before.

A prayer.

As it does, the Doombots that crowd the room—with their pale imitations of their master's true powers—are dismantled in an instant by the psionic blast. They crumble into piles of bolts and circuitry and emptied titanium plates. Throughout the winding corridors of the subbasements, the classrooms, and the dormitories of the Xavier's School for Gifted Youngsters it carries, demolishing every bot in its path.

Out onto the mansion's grounds, then up. Above the quiet suburb of Westchester into a perfect, starry sky. Up and up and up, streaking across the solar system, the stars, the cosmos, where something perched at the end of the universe has heard her desperate prayer.

Something is stirring.

Something is coming for her.

If she had not collapsed to the floor and was not gathering the strength to crawl through the burning veil of Victor von Doom's magic to reach her friends, Jean would see him standing above her. She would see the makeshift psi-phon nestled on his head, and his gauntleted fists flexing. If she could read his thoughts, she would know they are hands that could crush diamonds. Hands that have been intimately acquainted with death countless times since his first kill, his childhood kill. He hesitated then, afraid of himself and his full strength, and of the path that the death of that Latverian soldier would set him upon.

Now he does not hesitate. This is what it's all been for, and there is no going back.

CRA

CRK!!!

CHAPTER 41

KITTY

JULY 19, 1975

"GO ON," SHE SHOUTS OVER HER SHOULDER AT BETSY AS SHE squares off to charge the line of advancing Doombots. "I'll—"

A scream like a blast wave washes over her, setting aflame every nerve in her unfortunately corporeal body. Kitty drops to her knees and grinds her palms into her temples as, through a red-tinged haze, she watches the Doombots in front of her halt, seize, and fall to pieces on the corridor floor. She wants to tell Betsy, but she can't even crawl she can't think she can't breathe she can't—

Then it passes, just as quickly as it came on. Her vision clears, and Kitty climbs shakily to her feet. "What *was* that?"

Already standing at the door of the Danger Room, Betsy doesn't answer. Her trembling hand is poised above the door panel to slide it open, but she can't seem to bring herself to enter.

Kitty doesn't want to wonder why. They have to keep moving.

They have to save Jean Grey.

She staggers down the hallway to link her arm through Betsy's. "Come on," she says hoarsely. "Together." Then, ignoring the panel, she phases them both inside.

Quickly, she takes in the scene: the missing X-Men piled together and unconscious against the far wall, electronic shackles on their wrists. Bloodied, certainly, but they appear otherwise unscathed. One lone Doombot that seems to have survived the robot massacre kneels in a ring of its fellow bots' crumpled parts and fallen cloaks. A small army demolished in an instant, but how? Then she notices the tremor in its gauntleted hands and knows him for Victor von Doom, hunched over a smudge of bright-red hair on the Danger Room floor.

Why is Jean just lying there on the cold steel floor?

Beside her, Betsy lets out her own scream.

And before Kitty sees that Jean's winged yellow mask has been ripped askew and discarded, so that her emerald eyes stare unobscured and unseeing at the ceiling above; before she sees the dried blood streaked down Jean's beautiful face, or the angle of her slender neck, or the stillness of her rib cage; before any of this, Kitty knows that Jean Grey is dead. She knows by the pain in Betsy's scream alone.

It's over, then.

"Betsy," she whispers, and her voice sounds impossibly far away to her own ears. "We have to . . . God, we have to . . . We need to . . ." Go? Where would they go?

Jean Grey is dead. America Chavez is gone. The world they wanted—the future that Kitty had let herself believe in so deeply that it seemed almost inevitable—is gone. There's nothing left to hope for and nowhere left to run.

Well then. There's nothing left to lose.

Her arm is still linked through Betsy's, and Kitty squeezes one last time before disentangling herself to step away. Then she points herself toward the monster who killed their friend and begins to run. He stands to meet her, arms spread wide as if to welcome Kitty to her own destruction.

She never reaches it.

Halfway there, the Danger Room floods with light so bright and pure and blinding, it feels to Kitty as though she's phased inside a star. Except there's nothing else here. No color, no smell, no temperature, no sensation of any kind. She's nowhere, adrift in an endless white void, but she isn't alone. Suddenly much closer than she was in the Danger Room, Betsy is here, too.

"The White Hot Room," she whispers reverently.

Kitty turns to her, and the movement is effortless, though there's no ground beneath them, and no apparent gravity. "The what?"

"I've been here before. Or . . . I will be in the future, or . . . I would have been. With Rachel." Then Betsy falls to her knees in the nothing and begins to sob.

"This place," says a voice like a knife slid between her ribs, and she whirls to find the man who's just murdered Jean adrift in the nothing as well. "I have heard of this place. Imagined it. Envisioned it. Studied it extensively in theory. Paid the toll in blood to gain entrance. But to experience the Above-place, the Heart of Creation . . . Know that you have stumbled clumsily into a place that you cannot possibly understand, and that you soil with your presence."

"*We* soil this place? You're a killer," Kitty growls.

Infuriatingly, Doom holds up a gauntleted hand to gesture for silence. "I did what was necessary to achieve my ends. Your X-Men are alive, are they not? Their deaths were unnecessary. Only the pretense of their imminent demise mattered. Now hold your tongue. Can't you sense it, child? It's here."

Then the nothing before them begins to shimmer. Light within light that somehow coalesces into the vague outline of a human, a form just beyond recognition. And when it speaks, it's in a voice that's inside and outside and everywhere all at once. **I have known Jean Grey since the moment of her conception, as I have known the universe. She cried out for aid. I heard. I came. But I, infinite and primal, life incarnate, am nevertheless too late.**

In the void before them, Jean appears as shifting versions of herself, like a prism of possibilities reflecting different light from different angles. Every aspect of Jean who was or would have been: A student. A mentor. A nexus. A hero. A daughter. A mother. A childhood sweetheart. A friend. An X-Men. An avatar. A person.

And then she's gone, and the shimmering, faceless specter remains in her place. **It seems there is a first time for everything.**

"Can't . . . can't you bring her back?" Betsy asks, still collapsed and tear-streaked and cradling herself. "If you're life incarnate, bring her back!"

Jean summoned me through a sacrifice, freely chosen, to save her friends.

"It was a trick," Kitty hisses, shocking herself by daring to speak in the presence of this entity. "Whatever he did to her, whatever he made her believe, it was a lie."

The silhouette quirks its head. **It was real to Jean. I would have offered her my bargain—to bond herself to me, to temper power beyond fathoming with humanity, with love—and had she accepted my price, I would have made her whole. More than whole. We would never have been parted, not truly. Not even by death.**

"Great, then bring—"

But no bargain was made.

"I would bargain with you," Doom announces, stepping forward through the nothing. "You've lost one vessel, Phoenix Force, but rejoice: I offer you another."

What can you offer me, Victor von Doom, while my perfect host lies at your feet?

"The worthiest host you could wish for. An indomitable will, an undefeatable form, and a clarity of purpose that no other being in the Multiverse possesses. Jean Grey would have been unconquerable because she was joined with you. But you will be unconquerable because you are joined with Doom. Once we're together, you will never need another."

Why didn't they see this coming? They were so focused on saving Jean, the warmhearted woman she was, that they never even guessed Doom could have designs beyond her death. And now Doom can claim the Phoenix Force for his own.

Another failure for Kitty's scorecard.

"Betsy, say something," she pleads in a whisper, crouching down beside her friend. "He can't have it, and you . . . You're strong. You can take it."

"I can't." She tilts her face toward Kitty's, and now her eyes are as dry as they are dulled with grief. "It should have been Rachel's. The Phoenix Force, it's her legacy. I can't."

"But . . . there's nobody else!"

The figure has turned in Doom's direction now, giving him its full attention. **And what do you know of sacrifice, Victor von Doom? What do you know of humanity?**

"I have sacrificed more than can be enumerated," he declares.

"That's a joke," Kitty sneers.

Doom turns his scathing gaze on her, those burning eyes the only human part of him, and she's not even sure about that. Then he turns back to the Phoenix Force. "Forget temperance. I would not temper you. I would serve your full glory through strength rather than watering you down with doubts and hesitation. Together we will create wonders worthy of you."

For an eternal moment as the silhouette appraises him, its shimmering humanoid form reshapes itself slowly, its outline growing broader, sharper, and somehow crueler. Wide shoulders and gauntleted arms outlined in blue and pink and yellow light, and the shape of heavy boots planted on nothingness.

This is happening, this will have always happened, and God, she can't stop it . . .

But who else can?

"Wait!" Kitty cries before she really knows what she's doing.

The Phoenix Force—or maybe just its avatar, because God knows how any of this really works—turns what would be its head in her direction.

"He's a monster, you can't—"

In two long strides and before she can think to phase, Doom is upon her, slamming a boot into her chest. And though there is no ground here, no anything, Kitty tumbles across the void, gasping for breath like a beached fish. Now Betsy stands, raising her palms to blast Doom backward with a vast wall of pink psionic energy.

ENOUGH

Like some kind of cosmic parent (it's enough to make Kitty laugh, if she had the air in her lungs to do it), the White Hot Room itself separates the three of them, hurling them into their own corners in the void. No farther from her than he'd be on the other side of a train track, Doom climbs to his feet to storm toward her again—

then jars to a stop as he seems to crash up against an invisible barrier. He hurls his great fists against it, but there is no impact, not even a sound. Standing back, he fires a blast from the weapon mounted to his gauntlet.

Nothing.

There's only his rage, obvious but ineffective.

Do not pay him mind, says the silhouette, now beside her, beginning to reshape itself again. It grows shorter, slighter, and—is that a fluff of hair, like her curly ponytail? **This is not his choice to make.**

Kitty tries to stagger to her feet. But between her hiccuping breath and the fresh pain in the side of her chest that suggests something broken, she falls again, coughing.

Then the silhouette is right in front of her, kneeling down, the familiar shape of her own face suggested in its luminescence. And suddenly she can breathe again, and speak. Of course: What's a broken rib to . . . how did America put it? Creation and destruction at the most primal level?

Be not afraid, it says.

"I'm not afraid," Kitty lies, and knows that it knows.

Who are you?

"I'm . . . Kitty Pryde?" she guesses.

Who is that?

"Well . . ." The urge to retreat from the question and make a joke—to make herself a joke—dances on her lips. And of course, the Phoenix Force must already hear the thought; she's fairly certain she never needed to speak aloud in the White Hot Room. She never needed to introduce herself to an entity that's known her from creation. But there's still a choice to be made. "I'm Jean Grey's friend. I'm an X-Men."

You believe this. It's a statement of fact that surprises Kitty as much as anybody. **But you are not a perfect vessel. You are not very strong, as mutants go. Not very strong, as creatures go.**

"No," she says, keenly aware of Doom as he pounds his gauntlets and kicks his boots and conjures blasts of purple magic to get to her, all blocked by the nothingness. "I am not."

I am a fire that burns as well as warms. Destroys as effortlessly as it heals and always, always consumes. Are you strong enough for me?

"I don't know," she admits.

But would you risk it for your friends? Risk your own unmaking to stop a man who would be a god?

Self-preservation is a useful quality in a knight. That's how Emma Frost—the woman who knew Kitty best, because she made Kitty what she was—once described her.

From her own corner of the void, Betsy watches them, palms pressed against air. Not trying to break through, Kitty doesn't think. She holds perfectly still and makes no attempt to speak. Tears still trace her cheeks, but the expression on her face . . . Kitty's seen it before, though not on Betsy. She remembers that could-have-been Emma Frost, in the other timeline that's always existed just beyond her reach. She'd looked at Kitty then the way Betsy's watching her now.

With pride.

And with love.

Whoever Kitty used to be, she isn't anymore. And she doesn't want to be.

"Yes," she says at last.

A worthy sacrifice. We will not truly be one, as Jean Grey and I would have been. But take my hands, child, and we will see what you are made of. The being of light with her shape reaches out for her, and Kitty reaches back.

CHAPTER 42

KITTY

JULY 19, 1975

KITTY PRYDE IS ON FIRE.

It isn't the kind of flame that consumes flesh. Not yet. But she can feel it everywhere at once, just the same. In fact, she can feel *everything*, from the birth of a star in some distant galaxy to the rapidly cooling dead body of Jean Grey at her feet. She feels the sufferings and the secrets and the hopes of each soul that ever was, or is, or might someday be. All of it is contained within the fragile, inadequate shell of her.

This fire will devour her.

Probably, she will deserve it.

The Phoenix Force was surely meant for a champion like Jean Grey to wield. Who else could possibly withstand it? It is *power*, raw and infinite, terrible and glorious. The power to eradicate a world, a dozen worlds, one thousand. To destroy and create and unmake. To collapse matter and defy time itself. Abilities like these would be an unfathomable burden on even the greatest of heroes.

And Betsy Braddock was right: Kitty was never a hero.

So what is she now, but frozen with fear even as she burns, every muscle in her useless, too-crowded body locked in panic? She can't phase free of it, can't save herself, can't save anybody. All she can do is d—

Kitty! A familiar voice inside her mind, though unplaceable through the pain.

She opens her burning eyes to find herself no longer in the White Hot Room, but the Danger Room. She is floating, writhing in midair. Her rib cage is a wood furnace, her heart, its kindling. Whoever she was in this world, Kitty will soon be nothing but a fistful of ash on the breeze, and she feels, she feels, she *feels* . . .

She feels arms wrap around her neck, pressing her close.

Through the flames, Betsy Braddock wraps her arms around her, telekinetic powers like a shimmering pink second skin that shields her body. It burns away in patches, then heals itself over and over; she hadn't known Betsy could wield her power like that, or control it.

"I can't hold it!" The words are caught between a whimper and a scream.

It's all right, Kitty. I've got you.

She clings to Kitty, and Kitty lets herself be clung to until she can raise her arms to hold Betsy in turn.

If she could pay attention to anything beyond the fire that wreathes them both, Kitty would see the X-Men beginning to stir. She would hear Cyclops's wordless, broken cry as he stumbles, still handcuffed, toward Jean's body. She would watch Doom climb to his feet, recovering from his own ejection from the White Hot Room. She would see the entrance to the Danger Room slide open to reveal this world's Victor von Doom, a menacing figure as broad as the doorway. And she would see a star-shaped portal crackling with brilliant light appear on the wall beside him, just before America Chavez leaps through, surveys the scene, and takes to the air, dodging a blast from Doom's gauntlet as she flies full speed toward the X-Men.

But Kitty is too busy burning.

Luckily and unfortunately, she isn't alone; the fire scorches through Betsy's psionic shield again and again, too quickly now, leaving wounds before she can summon the power to repair them. Even so, her friend smiles through tears that stream from her eyes only to dry on her cheeks in the unbearable heat. **Look at me. I know you can do this.**

"I'm not strong enough . . . I'm not . . . I need . . . help . . ."

Betsy reaches through the flame to cup her face in both hands. **I will. I can feel it inside you.** Even her telepathic voice is strained almost to breaking, but she doesn't let go. **I can feel you, too. I know why you're scared, but Kitty, don't be afraid of what comes next. Everything changes because everything must, right? Jean told us that.**

"We were supposed to fix things." Her own tears burn up even before they fall.

We tried. We wanted to stop all the bad things that happened, the pain that shaped us. But all we can do now is choose what comes next.

"I . . . I don't know how to . . . God, I can't!"

Betsy closes her eyes, and then they're back in the White Hot Room.

Distantly, Kitty knows she's still burning, but she can't feel it anymore. "Are we dying?"

"I suppose that depends on you," Betsy says with a hysterical little chuckle.

"Well, then we're epically screwed." Dropping her head into her hands, she sinks to her knees in the nothing. "According to America, the most powerful mutant on this planet could barely contain it. And I'm . . . not that. You should've taken it, Betsy."

"It wasn't mine to take. But you *can* hold it, Kitty."

"But I don't know what to do!"

"Sure you do," she insists. "You know it because I know it, and I'm in your head."

"A hint, maybe?"

Betsy kneels down in front of her, prying her hands away by the wrists so that Kitty's forced to meet her gaze. "Concentrate, Kitty. At the Massachusetts Academy, Emma Frost had a theory about how your powers worked. I know that you're on fire and all at present, but can you remember it?"

It was early days at school when Emma brought in some mutant specialist she had on retainer, a Dr. MacTaggart, to explain it to

WHAT IF... KITTY PRYDE STOLE THE PHOENIX FORCE?   277

her. "It's about atoms," she recites. She hadn't fully understood the science at the time, and yet just hearing an explanation and having the language to describe a truth about herself that had always seemed beyond logic had felt, for a moment, like peace. "When I phase, I shift the atoms in my body into the gaps between the atoms in other things," she recites. "Concrete, water, air, bone, anything."

"You make space for it inside you," Betsy confirms.

"Okay. And?"

"*And* everything is atoms, when you think about it, right? Concrete, water, air, bone, cosmic entities. You can make space for anything if you let yourself. So stop running from it, and stop waiting to become some other version of yourself. Just let yourself change."

Suddenly it isn't just her and Betsy in the void—or at least, Betsy's telepathic facsimile of the void. There are versions of herself stacked one after the other, standing shoulder-to-shoulder, stretching far and away. "Variants?" she asks, eyeing herself down the line.

"Not in a Multiversal sense. No, they're every version of you whom you ever wished to be. I can see it all."

Now Kitty can see it, too. There she is as a twenty-three-year-old, dressed to head to the bar with local friends on a Friday night, no mutation to consider, no secrets to cover up. There she is in running shoes and workout clothes, getting ready to jog to Millennium Park from her apartment in downtown Chicago. And there she is again, a professional ballet dancer in a black leotard, a glossy high bun, and, if she had to guess, a sparkling engagement ring placed on her finger by Mikhail Baryshnikov (that one's a little embarrassing). Possibility after possibility, all out of reach, and nothing can bring them back or make them real. She already knows this.

They're only cluttering her up. So, one by one, she lets them go until she's the only Kitty left. It has to be enough.

The White Hot Room fades away around them, and Kitty is flung back into her body in midair in the Danger Room. Betsy is on the floor, seeming to waver on the edge of consciousness. "Your uniform..." she slurs, injured and exhausted.

Kitty looks down with distant interest to find that her basic black-and-mustard-colored training uniform has transformed. The awkward triangular chest piece has been replaced by a representation of a bird as broad as her shoulders, winged and arrow-tailed. Her boots and gloves have sleekened and lengthened to points, her wide belt slimming to a narrow band that still displays the X, and all that was yellow now blazes like molten gold. "No roller skates," she considers aloud. "Disappointing."

Then she turns her attention toward the Dooms.

There's a pair of them now, and this world's Doom—she can tell by the mask that took a hit from Cyclops's optic blast—is being fended off from the still-chained X-Men by America. (When did she get here?) The other, Jean's murderer, is picking himself up from the floor not far from Betsy. With a sneer she can detect even through the mask, he raises an arm to point his fist toward Kitty, as well as what looks like a scaled-down missile launcher mounted to his gauntlet. With a concussive bang that seems disproportionate to its size, a slim missile as long as his forearm shoots toward her, only to pass harmlessly through her phased form. She watches with satisfaction as his eyes grow wide with fear.

He is right to be afraid.

The entity caged inside her could peel him apart and scatter him to the corners of this universe. She knows this, like she knows that the Phoenix Force could do the same to everyone in this mansion, in this city, on this planet, with as little effort as a single thought. That's the least of what it's capable of: creation and destruction and, ultimately, consumption. All she'd have to do is allow her atoms to collapse back into those of the cosmic entity inside, to let it have her. It's so much work, keeping herself separate. A constant, conscious effort to stay half phased. She's teetering on the edge of letting go when Betsy cries out in pain. Her friend tries to stand, falls, tries again, spent from physical and psychic contact with the Phoenix Force. "Kitty, the missile! I can't contain it..."

Spinning in midair, she sees the tunnel where it pierced the far wall of the Danger Room, burrowing through steel to lodge deep within the mansion's foundation.

Deep enough to bring the building down.

Turning back, she's just in time to watch Murderer Doom engage something within the panels and parts of his armor that splits the very air around him, purple light pouring out. He grabs his ally by the arm and runs toward the glowing gap in time and space.

She can stop them before they reach it, unravel them both with ease, no matter the cost to herself. But Jean is gone, and Cyclops is beyond reach, and America is sprinting to help Betsy, and none of the X-Men can free themselves from their shackles in the seconds before the missile detonates. She can't get to all of them in time to keep them from being buried under the rubble of the building's imminent collapse.

Or she couldn't have when she was only Kitty Pryde.

Sinking to the floor, she presses her palm to it just as the two Dooms disappear into the portal, space stitching up behind them.

The fire of the Phoenix Force roars forward, burning along her veins as though each is a wick leading to one of Betsy's psionic bombs. She phases along with everyone in the Danger Room, then everybody in the mansion, then the school itself as the missile detonates. It's a blast that should bring the building down on them all. Instead, and with no more effort than flicking on a light switch, Kitty shifts atoms beyond calculation to accommodate those of the explosion, fire and smoke and flying shell shrapnel passing through and settling again without impact.

And after the danger has passed, the Phoenix Force does what it was meant to do: It consumes.

CHAPTER 43

DOOM

ON THE OTHER SIDE OF THE PORTAL, DOOM LANDS along with his duplicate in a pocket dimension the size of a small parking lot. The ground beneath them and the air around them are like panes of glass, looking out onto endless, star-spackled space. Assembled by Doom himself (he can do that now; the nexus powers coupled with the unique awareness to use them can accomplish all kinds of fun new tricks), it's a sufficient rock to hide beneath, nearly as far off the map as he could take them.

Other-Doom is unimpressed.

In fact, he's furious, pacing the dimension's borders, slamming a gauntlet against its boundaries to test them. "Take us back at once," he demands, pounding a fist against unyielding nothing.

"To be obliterated by the Phoenix Force, in the body of a child? No, I think not. Besides which, I've plans for your timeline. You'd be better off finding another, believe me."

Other-Doom rounds on him. "What *plans* do you speak of?" he spits out. "This is *my* world. I have a country that needs me to rule it, and a people—"

"Unfortunate but necessary sacrifices on the altar of achievement." Having backed up to the edge of the dimension, he paces the border, keeping distance between them.

"What have you done?" There is rage evident in every line of his counterpart's armored body, though perhaps only because Doom knows himself so well.

"Without Jean Grey, your timeline will have changed already, torn down the center. Such was her impact upon reality. But without the nexus powers to anchor this new timeline, it has become ... malleable. Every reality without its nexus being will be raw, unstable material, ready to be molded by its new master into a brave new world."

"To what end?" Other-Doom demands.

"A contingency, of course. Had I acquired the Phoenix Force, as was my aim, then none could hope to stand against me, and my plan would be guaranteed. But I leave nothing to chance. I've studied every scenario observable to me across realities, calculated the odds as only Victor von Doom can. Even without the Phoenix, I will guarantee success by means of the Multiverse. Infinite copies of the timeline most precious, so that which is mine may never be taken from me again. But you ... well before you completed the work you are so desperate to return to, you will have become irrelevant to your own reality, and to the Multiverse itself. I can think of no worse fate for Victor von Doom. Truly, you should thank me for sparing you. But since you refuse ..." Doom raises a hand to blast his variant with a force bolt without further preamble.

Except that he doesn't.

Nothing happens.

Other-Doom laughs, or lets loose a vicious sound that might be mistaken for one. "Your betrayal was inevitable, and I factored it into my calculations. While we worked to repair your armor and to augment mine, I infused yours with the same nanotech as my Doombots. It will not work against its master. Its *true* master." From his belt, he pulls the stasis gun—the split-barreled, rifle-like device for which Doom provided him the plans—aims it at Doom, and fires.

Then it's he who's blasted back.

By the time the shifting golden energy shell that would paralyze him in place has spread to his chest plate, he's engaged his armor's defensive force field just in time to stop it from swallowing him whole. But his limbs are locked in place, rendering him immobile as Other-Doom takes his time strolling forward.

"I, too, leave nothing to chance," he says, a sneer in his words.

Doom doesn't bother struggling; he knows well enough how the shell works. Instead, he reasons. "Gifted with my perspective of the Multiverse, I'm sure you would have done the same."

"Doubtful. You claim we are equal in our genius, but you earn the title of madman with which inferior minds would brand me."

"What is the difference between us, then?"

"I seek to *save* my world. You seek to destroy it."

"You still believe this? Go ahead, then. Convince me, or try to, and perhaps you can convince yourself."

"I seek rulership of my reality because the only answer to a predatory species is a stronger predator. You said as much yourself in the laboratory. Once my planet is united under Doom—when I am both the law and the judge—only then will there be an end to war, an end to hunger, and an end to disease, including the disease of humanity's desire to destroy itself."

Doom sighs into his counterpart's face, inches from his own now. "Madman or not, you are *boring*. All of you, every variant I have observed or encountered across the Multiverse: utterly predictable, and little better than those you despise and disdain. Every world seems all-important to the people whom fate has placed upon its surface. But to those few who have mastered Multiversal travel—those like me—each world is only a grain of sand on a cosmic beach. It's regrettable that yours must end, but in the grand scheme of things insignificant. Only I possess the capacity and perspective to see things clearly." He bucks forward as far as he's able, which isn't far, but just enough so that Other-Doom rears back slightly, ceding ground. "Because we *are* different, Victor, if not in the way you've guessed."

"You're a fool," Other-Doom snarls. "You never would've gotten close to the nexus being without my help. I supplied our forces. I made my grand spectacle of an entrance so that you could slip in undetected while their psychics' attentions were trained on me. I held the line without killing, though now I see your lie; it wasn't to force Jean Grey to relinquish the nexus powers without a fight. You didn't want to risk her summoning the Phoenix Force prematurely, before you'd set your stage and occupied me elsewhere. Even so, I executed my part flawlessly while you lost your bid for godhood to little more than a teenager. You sought to betray me, even as you needed me."

As his counterpart rages, Doom is unable to twitch so much as a finger to stop him. Luckily, he does not require use of his weaponry, nor even his hands, to take control. He may not have the Phoenix Force, but upon Jean Grey's death, her telekenetic powers became his to command.

In an instant and without so much as blinking, he reaches out with his mind, finds the base elements that comprise the energy shell, and peels them apart. Once freed, he claps a hand to his chest plate, and the compartment built within where his old prize—the shard of the M'Kraan Crystal—is nested. He, too, made additions in the lab that he did not see fit to share with his then-ally.

"Doom needs no one," he reminds his lesser variant before engaging the magical charge which, working through the shard, turns his armor into a portal all its own.

The last thing he sees and hears before transporting out of the pocket dimension is the fury turning to fear in his variant's eyes.

Yet another unfortunate but necessary sacrifice.

At least there was no need to kill this Other-Doom, an admittedly difficult feat with his armor's unwelcome modifications. Still, the man knew too much of Doom's plans. Trapped in the pocket dimension, he'll be beyond reach of the girl who's managed to pursue him between realities: America Chavez. Somehow, despite all his work to remain hidden from even the omniscient eyes of the Multiverse, she saw him.

Having failed to acquire the Phoenix Force, Doom must keep moving. An unfortunate outcome, but one he was prepared for. While it would have been the ultimate safeguard against defeat, he has everything he needs to win regardless. With the nexus powers in hand, the Multiverse will finally bloom open before him.

Now to return to the one-among-infinite-worlds that he's been searching for, once glimpsed so briefly. Plenty of work lies ahead. Re-creating the psi-phon was one thing; re-creating the greatest of his lost inventions—the necrophone—will be quite another. And without the Phoenix powers, he'll need to find some other means of protecting and keeping hold of the one whom all this has been for. Because he may have misled Other-Doom, but he never lied to Jean Grey: Her sacrifice *was* for love.

Even if it wasn't her own.

CHAPTER 44

KITTY

JULY 22, 1975

THE STEADY *BEEP, BEEP, BEEP* **OF HEART MONITORS IN THE** medical bay—more than one—is the first thing Kitty becomes aware of when the fire withdraws.

The next is the smell of brimstone and, as she manages to peel her eyes open and blink away the lingering fog, a pair of sulfurous-yellow eyes peering down at her from above.

"Gott sei Dank," Kurt says, white fangs flashing with relief. "We've been worried about you, Katzchen. How do you feel?"

How *does* she feel?

In the same way she's phased instinctually at signs of danger, she shifted herself to accommodate the Phoenix Force upon consciousness, and it's no small effort to maintain. She can move; Kitty arches her back off the hospital bed, raises a hand to inspect her perfectly unburned skin. And she can breathe. She used to have to hold her breath to phase. Or used to think she had to hold her breath. Who knows? Maybe she didn't. Maybe she was only holding on to some younger, less capable version of herself that clung to control at her own expense. Now, in this half-phased state, she feels . . . everything and nothing. Like a receding tide, the fire inside her remains, but it no longer laps at her bones. The next swell could come at any moment, sweeping her out to sea. For the moment, though, she stands on damp sand, the Phoenix Force just a current tugging at her ankles. "Okay," she announces at last, the rust in her voice suggesting it's been some time since she last used it. "Right now, okay."

"That is good. Everyone will be glad to know it. We've all been worried, most especially her." He nods to Kitty's left, where Betsy Braddock lies in the hospital bed next to hers.

"Haven't left your side once," she croaks.

Relieved though Kitty is to hear her joking, Betsy does *not* look particularly okay. The shadows beneath her eyes are practically purple stamped against her pale skin, and white bandages twine around her left forearm, her right wrist, her neck. Wounds left behind where her psionic shield melted away over and over again while she clung to Kitty, stubbornly refusing to let go.

Kitty remembers that now.

"She will be all right," Kurt leans down to assure her quietly.

If I can hear your thoughts, I can certainly hear you whispering about me.

He clears his throat, then speaks too loudly. "The burns were not deep, and she heals quickly, your friend. Jean could do a better job of tending to you both, but I am our field medic for the moment." Kurt shifts his stance to stare intently at her monitor, though even she, who skipped every single health class at the Massachusetts Academy (*she* wasn't the Hellions' field medic), can tell her vital signs haven't changed.

Still, she's grateful for the excuse not to be looked at as every memory of every moment of Jean's death returns to her. "How long has it been since . . ."

"Three days."

"And no sign of Doom? Or . . . Dooms?"

Kurt shakes his head. "The professor has been searching, traveling to alert our allies and some of our, how would you say . . . more persuadable foes. He believes the end of the world is worth reaching across the aisle. At the moment, he is on Muir Island, visiting with an old friend and a very young enemy. But there has been no trace of either Victor von Doom. America suspects that the

Doom she's been chasing has likely moved on, now that he has what he wanted."

"America's still here?"

"Ja. She has been waiting to talk with you."

"I saw her," Kitty recalls. "She was fighting off the Dooms, wasn't she? Wherever she went, she came back."

"Only a bit late," Betsy says from her hospital bed, but without malice. Good. There's plenty of guilt to go around without piling it on America Chavez.

"And everyone else?" Kitty dares to ask.

"They are healthy." Kurt's tail swishes and flicks behind him, some kind of catlike emotional tell, she suspects. "We are grateful to be alive because of you two. You saved us, verstehst du?"

"Not all of you, though." Careful of the wires dangling off her, Kitty rolls to her side to turn away from him only to find herself facing Betsy.

But Betsy's gaze is pinned on the ceiling tiles above, so she only closes her eyes in a pretense at sleep that probably fools nobody, least of all a telepath.

There's a long silence except for the steady *beep, beep, beep.* Then, gently: "Rest, both of you. You tried. And Jean would not want any of us to blame ourselves. She was . . . a good person. Like you two." Then with a *bamf* and a billow of foul smoke, he vanishes, leaving them alone in the medical bay.

Another silence follows, long enough that she begins to think Betsy has actually fallen asleep on her. But no. "America tried to go back, you know," she says at last. "To before. But she isn't a Watcher anymore, whatever that means, and she couldn't get back in time with her own powers, though theoretically it should've been possible. She guessed this was when and where she was meant to be."

Kitty opens her eyes to gauge Betsy's reaction as she starts, "Maybe . . . maybe we can, though. Go back. We broke into Castle Doom once, right? We could do it again, especially if it's missing its dictator. We catch a ride to Latveria, sneak in, hijack the time platform. We could—"

"I'd say it's a bit too late for that, wouldn't you agree? You've the Phoenix Force inside you now. I doubt there's any undoing it. Not without Jean to take it on."

The words feel true. She may not be able to access a hundredth of the Phoenix's powers without destroying herself, flawed host that she is, but Kitty is the host that it has for now. And better her than Doom, after all, even if it undoes her in the end.

"Do you think . . . could you bring her back?" Betsy asks without looking at her.

She reaches tentatively toward the Phoenix Force inside her, shifts her atoms just slightly to approach, as she did in the Danger Room, and feels the flare of unbearable heat before quickly retreating. "I don't think so," she admits. "Not without burning myself up. It's just too big."

"Well. Jean wouldn't want that."

"Listen. Maybe the X-Men think we saved them, but it was *you*. You know that, right? Because you saved me. I didn't even know you could use your powers like that. I know we've been training nonstop, but how did you do it?"

"It was Rachel." The name doesn't seem to claw at Betsy the way she'd have guessed it would. Instead her friend is smiling fondly up at the ceiling. "The memories America gave me, of her, of us. Alone and then together. It hurt at the time, and it hurts now, but it's helped in a way, too."

"How so?"

Betsy shrugs, wincing at the tug of her bandages. "I suppose it's much harder to doubt myself, knowing that someone like Rachel believed in me so deeply. She was practically a goddess. How dare I question her?"

She ponders this for a while, because isn't that how she felt in Betsy's projection of her private White Hot Room? If someone like Betsy Braddock believed that Kitty was enough just as she was, then who was someone like Kitty to disagree? She draws in a breath. "Hey, Betsy?"

"Yes?"

"I saw her once, you know. Rachel? I mean, not *really*. Only from a distance, in a slip, and I never saw her face. It was the same night that you reached out. I saw you, too."

"You didn't think that was information worth sharing at the time?" Betsy asks dryly.

"I didn't know who she was, or what it meant. And by the time I did, we were trapped in a snowball of calamities rolling downhill. My point is . . . when America first showed you Rachel, you offered to show me. Do you think . . . when you're ready, do you think you still would? Any memory you saw. Not if it hurts too much, but—"

"It won't," Betsy says. "What America showed me . . . it wasn't just memories of us, though those came through clearest. There were others mixed in, and some, with you. Rachel belonged to you, too, after all. I think it might help, not to carry her all alone. She deserves to be remembered by everyone who loved her. Shall I?"

Kitty nods, and squeezes her eyes shut, and then . . .

She sees.

—

NIGHTTIME IN THE SCOTTISH HIGHLANDS.

Once they've cleaned up from the aftermath of today's battle with the Technet bounty hunters and the Warwolves, they sit in a clearing: Kitty, Kurt, Brian Braddock, Meggan, and Rachel. In the distance, the peaks of the Torridon Hills rise to pierce an astonishingly starry sky spread out before them, their crackling campfire the only competing light source for miles. Made up of some of the oldest rocks in this world, as Meggan informed them, the mountains seem a worthy backdrop as the five of them reminisce about their dead friends.

First up, Kitty tells the story of her first time in the Danger Room. "So Professor Xavier spends *weeks* programming the Danger Room for my trial session, and I walked through it untouched with my eyes closed." She can still taste the tang of adrenaline as she phased through whipping metal tentacles, flying buzz saws, and giant mechanical presses to emerge unscathed. Can still feel the rush of pride as her new teammates, her new family, cheered her on from the control room above. She was a thirteen-year-old kid at the start of an adventure that was grander and more terrifying than she could have imagined, and craved their approval so badly. She'd wanted nothing more than to belong, and in that moment, she'd finally and truly felt like an X-Men.

Most of them are gone now. Storm, Wolverine, Colossus, Longshot, Rogue, Dazzler, Psylocke, Havok, and even Madelyne Pryor, dead on Muir Island. Their souls sacrificed to fuel Forge's spell and seal away the Adversary while millions watched on their televisions, Kitty included. A devastated Scott has gone off to find his lost son with Jean, while Xavier has been off-planet for years, and who knows whether or when he'll return?

Either way, the X-Men are over, and all they have left of them is stories.

When it's Kurt's turn, he tells them about the time Wolverine challenged him to walk down the Main Street of Salem Center in his natural, furred blue form. Once upon a time, Kitty would've screamed and run to see him passing. She's not proud of it, and she's very glad she's grown up since; there are few people on this Earth better than Kurt Wagner.

Next they look to Rachel, levitating cross-legged just above the turf.

"Any memories of the X-Men you'd care to share?" Kitty asks.

But she shakes her head. "Not the kind you mean. Not the kind I can trust."

Patiently, Kitty waits for her to find the words to tell her own story.

"The facts in my head, they're so jumbled up," Rachel says at last. "I don't know anymore what's real and what isn't. What actually happened. What's a lie. But that doesn't matter. Because the clutter doesn't affect my emotional realities. Perhaps, in turn, because the Phoenix by nature relates and responds better to feelings than rationality. I know who I am, who I care for, who I don't. That's what matters. The rest, I can take or leave." There is fire in her bright-green eyes, but it isn't the reflection of their modest campfire. It's the light of the Phoenix Force; her mother's legacy.

As the stars overhead multiply, the fire burns down. Meggan and Brian rise to leave, promising to deal with the Warwolves, releasing the rest of them to go their separate ways and live their own lives.

"But how are we supposed to live them?" Rachel asks, giving voice to her own thoughts.

Brian pauses. "I don't understand what you mean."

"The *dream,* Captain. Charles Xavier's dream of a world where all Earth's children, mutant and otherwise, live together in peace and harmony. Where people are judged for who they are, not what they look like or how they're born. That's why he created the X-Men. To exemplify that dream. Are you saying that simply because the X-Men are dead, we're supposed to give that up?" Rachel turns to face them all in the glowing ember light. "I've run my whole life. I can't remember a time when I wasn't afraid. I let people tell me what to do—it's easier that way, you know? Saves you from having to take responsibility for anything. Well, I'm tired of running. I want to take a stand. Because if I don't, then maybe I better let the Warwolves carry me back to the make-believe Slaveworld where I belong."

While Meggan and Brian confer, Kurt turns to Kitty. "How about you?"

Kitty won't pretend to know what the past few months have been like for Rachel, kidnapped and tortured and enslaved by Mojo in the Wildways. When she finally escaped, she returned to a world without the only home or family she's known, even though her parting with the X-Men was . . . complicated (if that's what you'd call being stabbed through the heart by Wolverine to stop her from murdering the Black Queen, nearly psychically dismantling Wolverine in return, then running away only to be snatched up by Spiral and Mojo). And if Kitty's honest, things were bad before any of that, as Rachel teetered on the brink of succumbing to the same Phoenix-driven darkness that consumed her mother.

But Rachel is right. The past is the past. Miraculously, she's back now, and the few of them left have to find a way forward by caring for one another. What truly matters is that Rachel is her best friend in the whole world, and if nothing else, Kitty will always be certain of that.

The rest, she can take or leave.

"What the heck," she answers, looping her arm behind Kurt's back as a new team is forged, and a new story begins. "Count me in."

—

KITTY RESURFACES IN THE MEDICAL BAY, THE CRACKLE AND POP of the dying fire giving way to the steady bleat of her vitals monitor and the hitched breathing of her friend in the next bed over.

"Thanks, Betsy," she whispers, tears ponding on the pillowcase beneath her.

Betsy rolls to face her, and though the aisle between their beds is too wide to reach across, Kitty holds out her hand. A second later, she feels the butterfly tendrils of her friend's telekinetic power fluttering to land in her open palm.

"You're welcome, Kitty."

CHAPTER 45

KITTY

JULY 24, 1975

BY THE TIME BETSY IS PRONOUNCED READY TO LEAVE THE MED-ical bay five long days after the battle, Kitty is more than ready to be up and around. Honestly, she woke up ready, but neither of them really wanted to sleep alone. She's just surprised to find America Chavez waiting for them out in the courtyard when they surface. Kitty looks her up and down, from the soles of her red high-tops to the collar of her denim jacket to her black, summer-wild curls. She doesn't look any the worse for wear: Sadder, definitely, and angrier.

Plenty of that to go around.

Blinking against the sunlight and the powdery-blue brightness of the summer sky after their days underground—albeit beneath deeply unflattering fluorescents—Kitty greets her. "Figured you'd have moved on to the next world by now."

With a rueful attempt at a smile, America says, "Maybe I would have, if I knew which one to go to. But don't worry. Even if I have to search the Multiverse the old-fashioned way, Doom's gonna pay."

"Good," Betsy mutters.

America sinks down onto a wrought-iron bench in front of a cluster of shade trees bordering the courtyard, and Kitty joins her. Since she woke in the medical bay, every movement requires her attention, a deliberate effort to interact with the world around her while keeping the Phoenix Force caged between her own components. She feels the bench beneath her and forces her body to perch, the way she forces her lungs to invite air inside them. None of it's easy.

But all of it is possible.

Betsy sits just as stiffly on America's other side, but that's just because she's Betsy.

Together they face the front of the mansion. The deep trench Doom carved through the paving stones and the ground beneath leads to what once was the school's entrance. Now it looks like the aftermath of an avalanche. Piles of bricks, crumbled columns, crushed ivy among the rubble. Half of the second floor and attic have collapsed into the first. Really, it's a miracle that nobody was killed (nobody but the anchor of this world, anyway). Peter and Kurt buzz around the wreckage like worker bees, Peter hefting a chunk of debris like it's weightless, Kurt wrapping his three-fingered hands around a jumble of concrete to teleport it into a pile a few dozen yards away. At least Doom's strange aircraft no longer lies beside the ruined oak grove; Kurt mentioned that Ororo had called up Reed Richards, who'd arranged to have Doom's tech removed for quarantine and study. Maybe some good will come of it, though Kitty doesn't see how.

"Where are the others now?" she asks. "Kurt said the professor is someplace called . . . uh . . ."

"Muir Island," Betsy supplies for her and stands to pace in front of the bench.

America nods. "He's traveling with Banshee. The mutual enemy they're trying to recruit is being safeguarded by a friend. They'll be back tomorrow for the funeral."

Fire rises inside Kitty, magma percolating like a molten lake before erupting. Deliberately, she half phases beyond the grip of the Phoenix Force while gripping the iron bench seat beneath her until she feels as though her fingers might bend the iron. It's harder to keep herself separate from it whenever she feels . . . well, whenever she feels.

"And Scott?" Betsy asks, still pacing the courtyard.

"With Storm. She didn't want to leave him alone. Wolverine has gone off, and they figured it *was* best to leave him alone. Nobody's sure when he'll be back. He loved her, too, you know?"

It wasn't hard to work out. Poor Wolverine.

"What about Doom?" Kitty dares to ask. "Any idea where he's headed next?"

America slumps against the bench back. "I wish. He's got the nexus powers he wanted. But he wanted them for *something,* so I doubt he's planning his retirement cruise right now. At least he didn't get the Phoenix Force, too." Her gaze drifts sideways to inspect Kitty. "Wolverine said it was pretty wild, watching you go cosmic. How are you handling it?"

She shrugs. "To be determined." She's no Jean Grey, no perfect vessel. Just a cracked one trying to contain so much more than she was made to hold. "I'm sorry. I wish I could do more with it without, you know, spontaneously combusting."

"Are you kidding? Kitty, you stopped Doom from melding with the most powerful entity in all creation," America reminds her. "That's a pretty major win for Team Us. And *I'm* sorry. I'm sorry I was gone when you needed me."

"Geez, leave a little self-loathing for the rest of us, huh? That wasn't your choice, was it?"

"No." America stares down at her hands, curled into fists in her lap.

"Speaking of self-loathing . . ." Kitty takes a breath and asks a question that's been eating at her since she left the club headquarters. "In the future, in one of those slips, Emma Frost was there. She called me the Red Queen. It was strange, but I didn't think much about it at the time. Except now we know it was real, right? So how come, in the timeline where I'm Hero Kitty, I'm still in the Hellfire Club?"

America purses her lips. "I forgot about that."

"You knew about it?"

"Not everything. All the worlds out there that were and will be, they get jumbled up. But I know the Hellfire Club isn't always evil, same way power isn't always evil. It depends who wields it, and for what purpose, and how responsibly, yada yada. I mean, look at you. You stole the freaking Phoenix Force right out from under Doom. You *are* Hero Kitty. Come on, you have to know that by now, right?"

Betsy sighs from the other side of the bench. "We keep telling her."

If Kitty could speak, she'd say something perfectly withering, no doubt. Instead, she sits quietly with the shards of a feeling she doesn't know how to name sticking in her throat.

"Listen," America begins, saving her by returning to business. "You were right—the Watchers taking me wasn't my choice. But it wasn't for nothing, either. The Watchers made me an offer I couldn't accept, but now I know more about what I'm up against. It's Jean's death that split the timeline, yes, but it's Doom taking the nexus powers off-world that destabilized it. Removing this reality's anchor left the first timeline headed toward collapse, and the second, *this* timeline, toward some kind of corruption."

"What does that mean, exactly?" Betsy asks.

"I don't know. Neither do the Watchers, and I couldn't stick around long enough to find out. Still, we know Doom has plans for this reality, maybe for a whole lot of them."

"But if you get the nexus powers back and bring them here, then . . . we could still fix reality, couldn't we?" Kitty asks, something like hope starting to kindle inside her. "Un-destabilize it?"

"Restabilize," Betsy corrects automatically.

What a nerd.

"In theory," says America. "But it wouldn't spackle over the crack that's spreading from the point of Jean's death. The timelines would still split, and we'd still be stuck here in this one."

"Without Rachel," Betsy murmurs.

"Gosh," Kitty says with a painful attempt at cheer, "if only we knew someone playing host to the powers of creation and destruction."

America lifts an eyebrow. "You could do that?"

"No." Betsy stands now, whirling to stare down at her accusingly as she crosses her arms over the borrowed black-and-yellow chevron tracksuit she wore out of the medical bay. "You already said. You told me you couldn't resurrect Jean without burning yourself up. You can't just destroy yourself for me."

"It wouldn't just be for you," Kitty mumbles, her ears flushing. "It'd be for the world. Or the timeline, or whatever. Besides, I don't plan to destroy myself. We can find a way between now and then, can't we? And if it's moot without the nexus powers, guess that's item one on our agenda."

"*Our* agenda?" America asks.

Last night while her friend slept, Kitty—having no interest in closing her eyes and seeing the fiery afterimage of her dreams permanently burned behind the lids—stared up at the ceiling tiles and tried to decide what came next. She couldn't go back to the half-life she was living in the future, running errands for the Hellfire Club while trying to exist in the world as little as possible. And though she'd once wished to stay here in the past with the X-Men, how could she ever be more to them than a reminder of everything Jean Grey should have been? Now she shares the conclusion she came to by the time Betsy woke across the aisle from her at dawn. "I don't think there's a place in this reality for the version of me I am now. But . . . I don't know. Maybe I can mean something different in the next world. At least, I can try, if you don't mind the company."

America smiles, one cheek dimpling. "No. I've been alone for a really long time. I don't mind the company."

It's more than a relief. It's a purpose. One Kitty's been searching for her whole life, if she's honest with herself, and it's about time she was. With that settled, she turns to look up at Betsy. "You feel up for interdimensional travel yet, Bets?"

Her friend sighs, then crosses the courtyard to drop down onto the bench on Kitty's left, where there's just enough space for her to fit. "I can't go with you."

Again, the fire swells inside her, and it takes every bit of concentration to shift herself out of its heat. "But why not?" she asks, panting, once she can breathe again.

"There's no Rachel in any other world, is there, America? That's what she said in the memory you showed me—that there were a few past versions, no longer existent, but no variants."

"No," she answers softly. "She's unique."

"Well. It wouldn't have been the same, even if there was."

"So, what, you're going back to RCX?" Kitty snaps, harsher than she meant it to sound. Maybe even partially bonding with the Phoenix Force can't blunt the sword of rejection when you've spent your whole life afraid of it.

Betsy shakes her head. "I'm going to stay with the X-Men. I'm going to fight for this world with them, until you bring the nexus powers back. And when you do, I'll be waiting."

A different kind of terror grips her now. "But we know the future! We couldn't stop what happened to Jean. What if there's no stopping what happens to the X-Men, either? What if . . ."

"What if they're going to die, now that Jean's gone?" Betsy finishes the sentence that Kitty can't bring herself to speak aloud. "What if a solar flare wipes them all out, and me with them? I'm not sure. I'd say that you becoming the Phoenix may have been enough to disrupt our timeline once again. A boot on a butterfly, as it were."

"But you can't *know*."

"I suppose I can't. And I can't know whether the X-Men stand a better chance at surviving with me around. I'm no Jean Grey," Betsy says, echoing Kitty's own thoughts. "Still. We act in hope, right?"

Together the three of them look upon the Xavier's School for Gifted Youngsters.

"This seems unlivable," Kitty appraises the half-collapsed mansion, watching Kurt and Peter at their never-ending work.

"It's been destroyed before," says America. "Believe it or not, this won't be the last time. But it always gets built back up again."

ON A PATCH OF THE PROPERTY TUCKED AWAY BEHIND THE trees and beyond sight of the school, there stands a pocket-sized stone church. It overlooks a small cemetery bordered by shoulder-high shrub roses in full summertime bloom, red and white and pink petals sprinkling the neatly kept grass. A welcome breeze plucks off a handful of petals as it passes through. It tosses them against the two newest headstones, where they cling softly for a moment before they're swept away again.

Hanging back by the cemetery's gate, Kitty watches the mourners clustered close around the first headstone, which simply reads:

JEAN GREY
1956–1975

Was Jean really that young? Just a kid. There were Hellions no older than she was who had the bad luck to be managed by Emma's White Knight. Maybe without Kitty around in the future, they'll have a better squad leader to protect them from the White Queen.

At least, she hopes so.

Beside Jean's sits the second headstone, identical in shape:

RACHEL SUMMERS
FOREVER LOVED,
FOREVER MISSED.

"Scott's request," Betsy says as she joins Kitty. "The stone, I mean, once America and I told him about Rachel. Ororo came up with the inscription. She asked me, but I couldn't . . . it was better than anything I could offer."

"It's nice," Kitty says inadequately of her once-best-friend's epitaph.

"It's true enough."

"So, can I ask . . ." Kitty reaches up to tug gently on the tips of

Betsy's slicked-back ponytail, the naturally blond strands now a vibrant plum purple. It isn't a perfect match for the violet Kitty remembers from her slip, but of course, Betsy pulls it off beautifully. "I didn't know they had purple hair dye in the '70s."

Self-consciously, she smooths her hair down despite the absence of a single flyaway. "It was actually invented in the 1850s, though quite by accident. I dyed it once before when I was young. I just thought . . ." She palms the tears from her cheeks, eyes still locked on the headstone. "I suppose I wanted Rachel to recognize me, if we got her back."

"*When* we get her back," Kitty insists around the prickling in her throat. "We're going to get them both back."

"I believe you," Betsy says, and Kitty mostly believes that. "But in the meantime, it's important for them to mourn, don't you think? Whatever comes next, this will always have happened."

"Yes. I guess it will."

As promised, Professor Xavier and Sean returned this morning to join Scott, Kurt, Peter, and Ororo. Wolverine, too, has wandered back home for the funeral. They're joined by a man with salt-and-pepper hair and a black painter's brush mustache, and a slight blond woman partially hidden behind a veiled mourning hat—Jean's parents, Betsy told her—as well as a few assorted mourners Kitty can't place. Must be friends of the X-Men. It's good that they have each other.

Hunched in his black suit and collared black coat despite the punishing sun, Scott takes his turn by the priest to speak in a voice scraped raw. "All my life it seemed that, every time I turned around, I was losing people I loved: my folks, my brother Alex, the few friends I made at the orphanage. Each time, the loss hurt. But I always knew losing Jean would be the loss I couldn't take. That she was as necessary as air. And now, I'm standing over her grave. You . . ." He presses a fist to the bridge of his ruby glasses, clears his throat, and continues. "You all know our story. I wish there was more of it. I'll spend the rest of my life wishing that. I think . . . I'll reach for her hand on the day I die." Scott rests a palm atop each headstone, both hers and Rachel's, as if to hold himself up, until the professor rolls forward to lay his own hand on Scott's back. Then Scott clears his throat once more before finishing with, "It wasn't enough. And it was also everything."

Afterward, in a moment when Scott and the X-Men have been drawn into hushed conversation with Jean's parents, Kitty seizes the chance to pluck a stone out of the mulch beneath the roses and place it on top of Jean's headstone with her left hand in the Jewish custom. "May her memory be a blessing," she whispers to whomever may be listening.

For a moment, she slips and feels the Phoenix flames lick across her heart, seeking fuel to burn. She shuts her eyes and phases completely, holding very still until it recedes back into the spaces inside and between and around her.

Then she can breathe again.

"We should go," America murmurs beside her. And she's right. Not because they know where they're headed yet, or because it's a good time to leave, but because there will never be an easy one. They've already said their goodbyes to the rest of the X-Men; Jean Grey was the last goodbye left.

Well . . . and one more that she's been putting off.

Betsy walks with them both through the cemetery gate, but not for long. Just until they're out of earshot, where they won't disrupt the funeral and its mourners. Then they pause, turning to look at each other while America considerately strolls onward in the direction of the mansion, stopping by the cratered shore of the pond to gaze out across its sparkling surface.

"I suppose it's goodbye for now," Betsy starts.

The first real friend Kitty's had since she was thirteen looks different from the woman who was once an annoyance even more than she was an acquaintance. Her hair flows loose, shining purple under the blazing afternoon sun, and even under the fresh weight of grief, her spine is straighter, her delicately sculpted chin held higher.

Will you really have figured out how to survive the Phoenix powers by the time you come back?

"Absolutely," Kitty says aloud, unnecessarily. "I mean, if I live that long."

If *I* live that long.

"Fine. If we live that long, we save reality, ensure the birth of my best friend and the love of your life, then the three of us go to Mama's Maple Bacon and Eggs Diner for brinner. Deal?"

"Only if you pick up the check this time. I'm not on RCX's payroll any longer."

Kitty scoffs in protest. "How come I have to pay? You're the trust-fund kid. You have a private jet!"

"I *did* have," Betsy corrects her. "My jet is in future-Latveria, whatever that's like without a Doom to rule it, and my trust fund belongs to a rogue teenager and aspiring model who's presently living on Mug-o-Lunches in New York City. So I'm not quite sure how to explain my existence to my trustee. I might have to seek employment."

"If you live that long."

They laugh together, just a little.

Then it dies, and Betsy says, "In the medical bay, you mentioned seeing us all together in the present. Do you think I might see it? What the future looked like? What it *will* look like?"

"How would I show you?"

"The same way I showed Rachel to you. Just bring the memory to mind, and let me in."

Kitty shifts on her feet. "I don't know if I can. Emma could never read my thoughts when I was phased, and I'm halfway phased all the time now. I don't know if I can let you in while I'm keeping the Phoenix out."

"Of course. That makes sense. I shouldn't have—"

"But I'll try, okay?" she offers, meaning it. "I want to."

Betsy considers her carefully, then nods. "Only if you're sure."

She isn't, but if she trusts anybody inside her brain, it's Betsy Braddock. Closing her eyes, Kitty waits, keenly aware of the ever-present burning but, thus far, unscathed. Like standing close enough to a campfire that her skin flushes with the heat but doesn't burn. And when the shimmering pink butterflies of Betsy's telepathic powers reach toward her, Kitty welcomes them in.

She opens her eyes to find them standing together in that same strange room overlooking the ocean. A salt-scented wind ruffles the flowering vines that climb the walls and twine around the bedposts. Sunlight streams through a glass ceiling, gentler than it was a moment ago on the mansion's lawn.

The first time she stood here, Kitty simply held her breath and waited for what she was certain was proof of a faulty mind, a faulty person, to let her go. Now she knows that wasn't the case. There was an explanation just beyond her reach.

Whatever else Kitty was, she was never really broken.

"Love your view!" the voice calls from the balcony, this time familiar. This time, dear.

And it's the strangest thing. The Betsy beside her—Kitty's own Betsy—watches this timeline's Betsy, with her violet hair and red cape billowing in the sea breeze, join Rachel Summers at the railing. Kitty's Betsy grabs her hand, the pressure of their interlocked fingers slightly painful even in her mind, as her counterpart presses a kiss to the nape of Rachel's neck from behind.

Kitty swears she can hear Rachel's murmur of content from here.

Then other-Betsy turns and strolls toward them in the sunlit room, eyes on Kitty only. Of course, a memory can't sense an intruder. Other-Betsy grins broadly, with an easy confidence Kitty's just lately started to recognize in her own Betsy.

"I adore your . . . barrel full of swords," she quips.

Then the memory ends, as it had to, and Kitty opens her eyes again on the grounds of the Xavier's School for Gifted Youngsters. Betsy isn't holding her hand—she never really was—but holding herself, knuckles gone white as she grips her elbows.

"Thank you," she says shakily. "I wanted everything there was of her, you know? Of us. Everything I could have."

"I get it," Kitty answers, her voice just as unsteady, even though she doesn't. "So spill. What's it like to be loved like that?" It's meant as a joke, though somehow, sounds less funny than she'd planned.

But Betsy smiles anyway, surprising her. "Oh, you'll find out."

"Sure I will."

Her friend taps her temple. "Trust me. Telepath, remember?"

"That's not the same as a fortune teller," Kitty grumbles.

"Close enough." She looks to America in the distance by the pond, that annoying smile still hanging on her lips. "You two had better get going, hadn't you?"

Kitty nods. She wishes for a moment that Betsy were still inside her mind, so she wouldn't have to struggle to find the words for everything she wants to say. She tries anyway. "Betsy, I—"

But Betsy holds up a palm. "Do let's be a little British about this goodbye, or I'm never going to stop crying at this funeral."

"Okay." Kitty swallows down the ache. "Well then. See you at the diner?"

"I'll see you at the diner." Betsy leans in, presses a quick kiss to her cheek, then whirls around and strides with purpose through the cemetery gate without once looking back, her plum-colored ponytail whipping behind her.

After a long moment's wrestling with the fire inside her—it'll get easier with practice, she hopes—she turns away and joins America on the shore of the pond. "Hey . . . I know we need to start looking for Doom. But since we don't have a lead yet, could we make a quick stop? Just in case, if . . . well, just in case. There's someone in this world I need to meet before we go."

CHAPTER 46

KITTY

JULY 25, 1975

THE STAR-SHAPED PORTAL SPITS THEM OUT ON CENTRAL AVE-
nue in Deerfield, directly in front of Kitty Pryde's old home. Strange to think that it's newer and in better condition than when she last saw it. By the time her mom sold the house, summoning Kitty for a rare return trip from the Massachusetts Academy to sort through any childhood artifacts she wanted to keep, the egg-yolk-yellow paint on the door was chipped and peeling, raw wood peeking through, and the small lawn was somehow both overgrown and scrubby without her dad around to obsess over its care. This was years after he'd moved to his own apartment and their drawn-out divorce was finally official. All that remained was to finish cleaning up the wreckage of their marriage, which included digging through the boxed contents of Kitty's old bedroom. In the end, all she'd saved from the giant rent-a-dumpster parked in the driveway was her Baryshnikov poster. Everything else was a relic from a version of herself she could barely remember, even at sixteen. The Kitty Pryde who'd filled a dozen diaries with her complaints and fears and hopes and dreams in multicolored ink no longer existed.

But in 1975, the front door is still bright yellow, the grass and shrubbery neatly trimmed. Kitty's family is still intact, and her parents are still married, though not happily. She now knows that they were already putting up a front for her sake. Just like she now knows (or accepts, at least, because she always technically knew) that her mutation manifesting had nothing to do with their divorce, or with her being sent away from everyone and everything she could have clung to as she tried to figure out who she really was, and who she wanted to be. Her parents were always going to break up, and nothing she did or didn't do, nothing she was or wasn't, could have stopped it from happening.

Maybe the version of the family Kitty once believed in never existed at all.

So, like every version of herself in Betsy's White Hot Room, she lets it go. Then she turns away from her childhood home to walk down Central Avenue, America trailing silently after.

The ballet studio where eight-year-old Kitty should just be getting out of class on a Friday afternoon is only two blocks away. A small neighborhood place where she took lessons before her parents switched her to a bigger and more competitive studio, it's close and safe enough that she was already allowed to walk home alone. That's how, a block later, Kitty meets herself: four feet tall, wearing a one-piece leotard, her curly hair pinned back into a high bun, but with untamable frizz around her forehead.

Kitty breathes deeply to calm the fire that threatens to curl around her heart, as tender as it's ever felt, then kneels down on the sun-warmed sidewalk to look at herself. "Hello, you," she says, mustering a smile.

Vintage-Kitty blinks back at her. "Do you know my parents?"

"I do. But actually, I know you better. I've known you since you were born. We're family, Kitty."

"Really?"

"Yep. Though, like, still don't talk to strangers after this," she hurries to say. If (no, *when*) they save reality, she can't risk a world where she grows up totally naïve. "The point is . . . I'm about to go on a pretty long trip, so I won't see your family for a while, but there's something I needed to tell you first. Are you listening?"

"Yes," vintage-Kitty says dutifully.

"In a couple of years, you're going to change."

Vintage-Kitty's mouth screws into a frown. "I already know about periods."

Behind her, America snorts. So helpful.

"Great. I just need you to remember this, when it happens: Don't be afraid. Everything changes because everything must. But there's nothing wrong with you, no matter what the world tells you. You aren't perfect, because nobody is, but you aren't unlovable, either. So forget who you thought you were supposed to be, and when you meet the people who'll love you for who you are, just let them. Got it?"

Now vintage-Kitty's wide, formerly trusting brown eyes narrow. "How am I supposed to know when I meet them?"

"Um. Well, you know what it feels like now, when you're at school or at the ballet studio all day, and then finally, you get to go home and just be yourself?"

"Yes..."

"That's what it's gonna feel like."

After considering this for a moment, vintage-Kitty nods. "Are you coming over to my house now?"

"No, not right now. Just... remember this, okay?"

"Okay."

Then she stands and steps off the path so her younger self can march onward toward Central Avenue, throwing one last puzzled glance over her narrow shoulder.

Who knows whether the message will stick, or whether it'll count for anything. If they bring back the nexus powers, bring back Jean, and patch up reality, then perhaps she's saved herself some pain.

If she and America fail, and this timeline becomes corrupted while the other one shatters, then maybe nothing she does here matters.

Or maybe the attempt is the only thing that matters.

"Ready?" America asks.

"Yeah. I'm ready."

Drawing back a fist, America punches a portal into the steamy summer air. Then, together, they step into something new.

ACKNOWLEDGMENTS

When I first got The Email inviting me to write a Kitty Pryde story (and Betsy Braddock! And America Chavez!) I predictably spent the next twenty-four hours cycling between awe and impostor syndrome. I have loved the X-Men since I was a kid, and then a college student, who scraped together the dollars to pick up a new issue or two at the local comic shop every Wednesday, and used to loosely dream of drawing for Marvel. In particular, I have loved Kitty Pryde. So I wondered whether I could pull it off; whether I could do these incredible characters justice; whether I could even write a fight scene.

Then, of course, I said yes.

Thanks first and foremost to my agent, Kate Testerman, who kindly reassured me that The Email was not a mistake, and was, in fact, meant for me.

At Random House Worlds, thank you, thank you, thank you to Gabriella Munoz: for your encouragement, for your guidance, and for being ever-ready to hop on the phone and explain the nature of time travel and the Multiverse for the fifth time. Thank you to Tomi Tunrarebi for your incredibly valuable "explain it like I haven't memorized that one panel of one twenty-three-year-old issue of Uncanny X-Men" perspective. And at Marvel, extreme thanks also to Sarah Singer for your belief, your support, and your willingness to track down answers to the nerdiest of questions. This was truly a Dream Team.

Also at Marvel, thank you to Jeremy West, Jeff Youngquist,

and Sven Larsen, who patiently listened in our first meeting as I explained the plot of the Lego X-Men comic I drew, and then did not immediately cancel the project.

Speaking of which, thank you to Tamara McCool for driving to the comic shop in Santa Fe every Wednesday, and for staying up with me at the overnight lock-in to draw together, even though it meant you had to parallel park.

A giant existential thank you to Chris Claremont, who made these amazing and uncanny characters what they are, and whose '70s-era X-Men set the tone for this novel, hot pants included. And, while lots of comics across Marvel history are referenced in these pages, I'd like to especially thank Chris Claremont (again), Gerry Dugan, Kalinda Vazquez, Tini Howard, Bob Layton, Valerie D'Orazio, and Greg Pak, whose words all made their way into this book. It was an absolute privilege to reference legends.

Thank you once more to Books, whose encyclopedic knowledge and guidance gave me the confidence I needed to attempt this at all.

Thank you to Brennan Lee Mulligan, who doesn't know me, but whose work on *Worlds Beyond Number* taught me how to write a fight scene.

Thank you to Tom, who got up early so I could work late, and listened to one thousand "the really interesting thing about the gyroscopic aircraft is ..." lectures, and who always believes in me. And thank you to Asher and Anya, for inspiring me to act in hope instead of fear. I love you very much.

THE VASTNESS OF SPACE

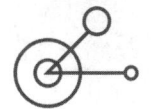

IT'S BEEN EXACTLY EIGHT THOUSAND AND FIFTY-TWO YEARS SINCE THE Watcher last detected something approximating surprise scratching at the edge of their consciousness. To be a Watcher was to become an observer, a stranger, not just to events but to emotions. *Surprised,* they think. *How odd.*

The unanticipated twist in their eternally predictable path occurred at the trial of the once-Watcher known as America Chavez. From their seat in the luminous Temple of Justice, they watched a girl in a denim jacket shout at her judge: "People died because I thought being a Watcher meant I was more important than any of them! Because I forgot who I really was."

It was then that the Watcher—who could see and know everything they turned their attention toward—remembered something new. Another life. Another self. Heat, and smell, and the prickle of wild grass underfoot, and the taste of . . . river, the memory drifts back to them. Water. They recalled, for a moment, what it meant to exist within a world. To feel. To care.

Though they have tried to perform their duties as before, to Watch, they haven't managed to forget it since. And so their gaze drifts, again and again, to America Chavez and her new companion as they search world by world with their plodding, mortal limitations. No different than any human in any reality.

Why, then, after eight thousand and fifty-two years, does the Watcher feel compelled to interfere?

They press a hand to the smooth, cold window of their cosmic chamber and step through the glass into a blizzard of a world. Driving snow, glittering white ground, and cold so sharp that it sinks its fangs into flesh in an instant of exposure. Or it would, were the Watcher who they once were, and not what they are now. With frost curling ineffectually across their unfeeling flesh, they peer between the constant snowflakes at two figures hunched against the cold.

Seeing them in turn, America throws an arm in front of Kitty (whether protecting her, or holding her back, even the Watcher can't be certain). She shouts through chattering teeth, "What do you want now? What else can you take away, cabrón?"

But they haven't come here to take.

Without needing to speak, they share with her a vision of a young man with short black hair and topaz-blue eyes, accompanied by a name.

"Franklin Richards." The words ghost through America's blue-tinged lips. "Are you saying he's next? That's where we'll find Doom?"

Their message delivered, the Watcher vanishes from this world without answering. But, as ever, they observe from their cosmic window. And so they see America stomp a star-shaped portal into the hard-packed snow, a destination in mind. She jumps through, and fearlessly, Kitty jumps in after her. It's all up to them now. It always has been.

Something is about to change.

OUR HEROES WILL RETURN FOR ONE LAST STAND.

MARVEL

WHAT IF...

ASSEMBLE. 2026.

ABOUT THE AUTHOR

Rebecca Podos is the Lambda Literary Award–winning author of YA and adult novels. *Homegrown Magic,* her adult fantasy debut co-written with Jamie Pacton, is their latest, with the sequel, *Homeward for a Spell,* to follow in 2026.

MARVEL

DISCOVER MORE MARVEL BOOKS BASED ON YOUR FAVORITE CHARACTERS!

© 2025 MARVEL

MARVEL COMICS

PRESENTS

The Marvel Premier Collection

9781302965983
6"x9"
$14.99

BY FRANK MILLER
AND DAVID
MAZZUCCHELLI

DAREDEVIL
BORN AGAIN
FRANK MILLER · DAVID MAZZUCCHELLI

9781302964856
6"x9"
$14.99

BY TA-NEHISI
COATES, BRIAN
STELFREEZE AND
CHRIS SPROUSE

BLACK PANTHER
A NATION UNDER OUR FEET
TA-NEHISI COATES · BRIAN STELFREEZE · CHRIS SPROUSE

9781302964863
6"x9"
$14.99

BY ED BRUBAKER
AND STEVE EPTING

CAPTAIN AMERICA
THE WINTER SOLDIER
ED BRUBAKER · STEVE EPTING

9781302964870
6"x9"
$14.99

BY JONATHAN
HICKMAN,
DALE EAGLESHAM,
NEIL EDWARDS
AND STEVE EPTING

FANTASTIC FOUR
SOLVE EVERYTHING
JONATHAN HICKMAN · DALE EAGLESHAM
NEIL EDWARDS · STEVE EPTING

PREMIER CHARACTERS. PREMIER CREATORS. PREMIER STORIES.
YOUR UNIVERSE STARTS HERE

© 2025 MARVEL   AVAILABLE WHEREVER BOOKS ARE SOLD